Joyce

Charlie

TWO PEARLS IDENTICAL – OR ONE?

C W Walker

UPFRONT PUBLISHING

LEICESTERSHIRE

TWO PEARLS IDENTICAL – OR ONE?
Copyright © C W Walker 2002

ISBN 1 84426 039 9

First Published 2002 by
MINERVA PRESS

Second Edition 2002 by
UPFRONT PUBLISHING
Leicestershire

TWO PEARLS IDENTICAL –
OR ONE?

This book is dedicated to
my wife, Mabel Walker,
for all the joy and happiness,
and a love that will go on forever.
Farewell, my one true love –
till we meet again.

Contents

At Last a Prayer is Answered

The light veil of misty dew, which had softly transformed into a knee-high feathery haze, had but a short time to live. As the east grew pale, and the wildlife began to stir, it was only a matter of time, now that the great pulsating ball of fire had wrested itself free from the edge of the earth, before it disappeared completely. Meanwhile, the white-hot sun, less than a third away from its zenith, looked down upon a paradise that was fresh, clean and very warm.

It is the first day of June 1914. The newborn countryside is in full bloom, thriving on its new-found glory, under a cloudless canopy of the purest sapphire blue.

Up and along the Ridge, the elegant chestnuts, each clustered as if with a thousand tiny candlelit Christmas trees, flanked here and there by their majestic friends, whose countless shades of green contrasts one against the other, yet blending only as nature can.

Vividly, and in all its splendour, stood the lone copper beech, giving the scene some russet relief, ever determined that its regal beauty should not be dimmed to the watchful eye of man. Far and near in the hedgerows the heavy-bloomed hawthorn deceived for a moment, appearing at first glance to wear a mantle of sprinkled snow. Now, silently and sweetly, the whole multitude of flowers gladly surrender their fragrant beauty, as the busy bee kisses each in turn on its search for the nectar of life; while mirth reigns on all sides, swelling each feathered breast as it throbs with its own special love song.

Listen! Here comes the mocking call of the cuckoo, bringing to reality a harsher side; perchance she is still searching for the lodge of her choice. While high up over those golden fields of buttercups, and the ones where man has already spread the scent of new-mown hay, the lark is heavenward bound, journeying like a bobbing cork on an empty ocean as it sings its almost endless and happy song.

This scene of breathtaking joy and beauty, which had gently smoothed itself o'er hill and dale, was one where the eloquence of nature had tipped far beyond the point of overflowing, to the point when man paused at his toil, and gazing heavenward, offered his Creator humble thanks for all the joy and beauty around him.

Could it be that an eye might rove over a scene so beautiful without surrendering to one drop of twinkling lustre? Could it be that an ear might vibrate to the sweet notes of the feathered flock, without creasing the cheek in the faintest smile? Could it be that the sweet-smelling perfume might fail to make those lofty senses swim in ecstasy or was it possible that a joy greater than these three divines, could suddenly descend, to bring unbounded joy and happiness, not only to this day, but to each and every day?

As Penny Stanton raced out of the farmhouse, up the drive and turned left on to the Ridge of the hill, quite unconsciously she gave the answer to these questions. The glitter in her laughing eyes, the rapture on her sweet young face, and the heady joy which drove her on, faster than she had ever run before, had nothing to do with all this joy and beauty around her. She was, to say the least, completely oblivious to it all. It was a joy greater than all else that was sending her on this happy mission, and in her heart she could hardly wait to spread the glad tidings.

Penny was nineteen; she had been working at Spring Farm for John and Madge Fraser since a few days after her fourteenth birthday. Now she was on her way to find Mr Fraser to let him know that all was well, with news to give him the greatest joy that was possible. She had gone about three hundred yards when she could faintly hear the sound of two or more mowing machines. Suddenly she saw them. They were just across the valley, just on the brow of the other hill; one had just stopped at the corner before getting the horses into line again. Getting off his seat was old Joe Smart, and standing there talking to him was Mr Fraser.

'Coo-ee, coo-ee!' she shouted, and the clearness of her beautiful voice reached over to the other side.

John and old Joe heard her instantly and had no difficulty in picking her out. With the sun behind them, and shining directly on to the opposite side, she stood out just as clear as her voice had sounded. She waved both arms and jumped up and down at the same time. Suddenly she stopped, and even at that distance, they saw her thrust both hands into the large pocket in the front of her apron, and in her haste and excitement, two pieces of cloth fell to the ground. From where they were, they could both see quite plainly that one piece was pink and the other blue. Quick as a flash, John wondered, which of those two she would pluck from the ground – and only Penny could think of anything quite like that. Hastily she bent down and picked up the blue one, waving it high in the air, jumping up and down once more, and dancing around and around.

John waved frantically back, hoping that Penny would see the great joy in each wave of his arms. Turning to old Joe, he said, 'Blue for a boy, Joe! That means that God has not only answered our prayers, but He has sent us an extra blessing by making it a son.' He must have shook old Joe's hand for a good half-minute.

'Yes,' answered old Joe, 'a farm without a son coming along ain't got a lot of future.'

'That's what I've been worried about,' replied John, but his eyes were all aglow now, and he couldn't get home soon enough.

'I must get back as quickly as possible, Joe, so if I haven't got time to come and see you again today, you'll know why.'

'All right, sir, I know how you feel, and tell Mrs Fraser how pleased I be.'

'Thank you, Joe,' called John he turned briefly, 'I'll tell her. Cheerio for now.'

'Cheerio, sir!' old Joe called back.

John's first thoughts were for his Madge. He hoped she had come through her ordeal without too much pain; then his thoughts turned to his newborn son. He wondered what he looked like, but try as he might, he just couldn't put a face to something which was his very own. He hoped he had inherited the beauty of his mother; that way, he would have fine features and grow up to be handsome. His Madge, God bless her, was thirty-one, and he was thirty-nine. Nine whole years they had been married, and three times during those years she had suffered during those early months towards motherhood, only for it to end in despair and disappointment. This time she had been in perfect health all the way through, and now the miracle had happened, and she had borne him a son – their son.

He wondered if the doctor was still there. He smiled to himself as he thought, how he and the nurse had practically driven him out of doors that morning; he could hear the doctor's words now. 'A man is better off out of the house at these times,' he had said, 'for he is no help to anyone – more a hindrance, if anything.'

He was nearing the house now and he could see the doctor's bicycle in the doorway of one of the outbuildings, where he himself had put it out of the sun. As he walked towards the door he could hear Doctor Banks talking to Penny.

'Ah, here is the proud father!' he exclaimed, as John crossed the threshold.

'You've got a fine healthy son, John, and Madge is in excellent condition.'

'Thank you, Doctor, I'm more than grateful to you for all your wonderful attention.'

'It is my job, John, just as yours is farming. Anyhow, I'll be going now, and I'll be in tomorrow morning to see that they are both doing fine. Cheerio, and thanks for the sandwiches and coffee, Penny.'

John looked at Penny; the delight on her face matched the joy on his. Penny, whom they had taken under their wing, and had looked upon more as a younger sister, was completely over the moon.

'I'm so pleased and delighted for you and Mrs Fraser, she said. 'It's going to be really wonderful having a baby to look after.'

'Thank you, Penny,' John answered. 'We were happy before, but it's going to be even more wonderful now.'

So saying, he started on his way upstairs, only for the nurse to meet him before he reached the door.

'Everything is perfect,' she said. 'I think your lovely son is fast asleep; you'll find Mrs Fraser is awake, but very sleepy. I'm sure she is hanging on to consciousness until you get here.'

He thanked her and went inside. Madge was as the nurse had said, and John knelt beside the bed, bent over and kissed her.

'How are you feeling, my love?' he whispered, thinking that he might wake their son.

'I'm quite all right really, darling, but so very tired,' she answered.

'I'm so proud and grateful for what you have given me, my love,' he said, kissing her tenderly.

'I knew you would be… it's really been worth waiting for, for he is so lovely,' she answered, with pride brimming from her sleepy eyes.

She watched as he tiptoed around to the cot on the other side for a peep of their wonderful son; she was still fighting hard to keep her eyes open, so as not to miss one tiny bit of the heavenly joy that covered his face.

The baby was a gem indeed, silver haired just like his mother, and the thoughts that went through John's mind were the most wonderful he had ever known. He was a father now, a helper in the most wonderful of all God's creations.

That was all he could stay for; her eyes were closed as he kissed her gently on the forehead. He slipped quietly out of the room, but looking back through the half-shut door, he took one more look at everything in life that he held dear to him. '*Thank you, Lord,*' he said, almost aloud, as he closed the door.

'He's a lovely boy and I'm so proud of him, Penny,' he said as he went into the kitchen.

'Oh, I should think he is! He's absolutely wonderful, and Mrs Fraser – I know she is in that heaven that only a mother can experience.' Then she asked, 'Shall I get the lunch as soon as possible, or would you rather wait till the usual time?'

'It's only half an hour to our usual lunch time, Penny, and I don't mind waiting,' he answered.

After lunch he crept upstairs, only to find mother and son both sound asleep; but before he left the house, he went into the kitchen to tell Penny that he would be working where she had seen him this morning.

Going over the Past

As he strolled along the Ridge, John was so deep in thought that he failed to notice all this fantastic beauty around him; yet the one thing he was always ready to tell others about was the glorious beauty of the southern Cotswolds. But now his mind was going back over the past, to the time when he had first met his Madge.

His father had died four years before that happy day, and his mother two years after him, and he had always looked back in horror when he thought of those years between his mother's death and Madge becoming his wife.

From the time he had been old enough, his father had sent him to as many exhibitions of farm implements as was possible, and it was a must that he should always attend the one in London.

'Things are beginning to move, John,' his father would say. 'We've got to keep up with the times, for if we fall behind we shall never catch up.'

Prophetic words, John had often thought since.

After his mother died, what with hardly having a minute to spare, he had only found time to have three days at the exhibition in London; and the next year, even those three days away from the farm were in doubt. But it was nothing short of a blessing that he had decided to go at the last moment. If he hadn't gone, he would never have met a London businessman's daughter, and within a year bring her to Spring Farm as his wife.

But his thoughts were jumping ahead, for only fate could have been responsible for the chain of events that brought them together. Sometimes now he could hardly believe it – how or why a girl so refined could fall in love with a man so near to the earth, a country farmer.

In his mind he went ten years back to that early October day, and step-by-step he traced the misery and the unexpected joy which followed.

Inside the exhibition hall the air had been so hot and stuffy that he had left early, but outside there seemed very little difference, for the day was heavy and sultry. To while away the time he walked wherever the fancy took him, and more than half the time he hadn't known or cared what street he was in. He knew the Old Brompton Road was over to the left, and that there was plenty of time for him to get back to his hotel at South Kensington by 7.30 p.m. He seemed to be the only one walking down the darkening street. He could hear the clip-clop of a cab coming up behind him, the steady trot of the horse showing that the very late Indian summer affected man and beast alike. It was almost abreast of him, when an almighty clap of thunder burst overhead, the horse reared and then bolted, and the inside wheel struck the curb on a corner some fifty yards ahead.

How the whole lot never turned over John would never know; how the cabbie stuck to his seat was only a miracle, and whoever was inside must have had an awful shaking up, for both doors burst open, and a black Gladstone bag was thrown almost to the other side of the road. By the time John reached the bag, the cab was out of sight, and as he bent down to pick it up, the second clap of thunder, even heavier than the first, burst once more above him.

He caught the name 'H F Bromsgrove' on the label of the bag, as the lightning turned a pitch-black sky into daytime, but that was as far as he had got, for the heavens opened up above him and the rain simply fell in bucketful's.

There was nowhere as far as he could see in the street for him to shelter. He caught sight of a shop sign down the side street, as the lightning once more lit up the whole area. He ran the sixty-odd yards as fast as he could, and was almost wet through when he reached the doorway. It was deep enough to keep the top half of him from getting any more soaked, but the bottom half was another matter, for the rain was so hard and heavy that anything a yard from the ground became saturated. That was how he had spent the next miserable hour and a half.

John smiled to himself as he left the Ridge and started on down the valley, but he could almost feel those wet trousers clinging to his legs now, and he remembered that the only distraction he had

had from his miserable plight was to hold up the bag and wait for the next flash of lightning so that he could read the rest of the label. It had taken him some time but he had managed it. It said, 'H F Bromsgrove, 18 Rosary Gardens, Kensington'. He knew where Rosary Gardens were, and he had decided that once the rain had stopped he would return the Gladstone bag first, for two reasons. Firstly, by the time he could get to his hotel and change, the dinner would have been over and finished long since; and secondly, as he had ran for the shelter of the doorway, he had heard money – a lot of money – shaking up and down inside the bag. He would have to return that first, to save the owner from any more unnecessary worry.

He smiled to himself again as he thought of those first few steps he had taken out of the doorway. If anyone had been behind him they would have thought that he had been born with the bandiest legs imaginable. He had been nearer to the Old Brompton Road than he had thought, and in a little under five minutes he was ringing the bell at number 18 Rosary Gardens. The door was opened by a butler.

'This is where Mr Bromsgrove lives, isn't it?' he had asked in his West Country accent; but before the butler could even reply, a voice in the hall behind asked crisply, 'Who's there, Brown?'

The butler swung the door wide open. 'This gentleman, sir,' he replied.

A young man of about his own age came towards John, who said, 'I picked this up, it must belong to you.' He held the Gladstone bag out for the young man to take.

The young man's eyes lit up as he answered, 'It's not mine, but it is my father's. Won't you come in, please? He'll be awfully grateful to you, he had given it up for lost an hour ago – with all that money in it.'

As he stepped inside the young man shouted, 'Father, a gentleman has brought your bag back!'

A grey-haired gentleman came out from what John thought must be the study.

He took the bag, opened it for an instant, and then said courteously, 'I must thank you very much. I thank you for your honesty – there's quite a lot of money inside – but it wasn't that

that I was most worried about; it was the papers, ones which I couldn't replace at any price.'

Then the old gentleman shook his hand warmly, while John himself expressed the hope that he was none the worse for such an awful experience.

'I've calmed a little now, but it must have been a mile before the cabbie could stop,' he replied.

That was as far as their conversation had got, for suddenly a lovely female voice said from the landing above, 'What's all the commotion about? Have you got your Gladstone bag back, Daddy?'

'Yes, my dear,' the old gentleman answered.

John remembered how they had all turned and watched her descend those stairs just as a princess would; he remembered how a greater part of his courage and confidence seemed to have deserted him, for he had never seen anyone as lovely. He remembered just as vividly, now, the moment when she had almost reached them, and the old gentleman had been about to introduce them, then suddenly realised that he didn't know the visitor's name.

'Mr...' he had said, looking enquiringly at John.

'I'm John Fraser,' he had replied, in a voice which didn't sound at all like his own.

'This is my daughter, Madge, and my son, Henry,' said the old gentleman with more than a little pride in sight and sound.

How John had torn his gaze away from the beauty before him, and let go of the warmth in her hand, he didn't know to this day, but it must have been while he was shaking Henry's hand that she noticed the condition he was in.

'Fancy both of you holding a sermon over the Gladstone bag, when the kind man who brought it back is wet through! Take Mr Fraser upstairs, Henry, and get him some dry clothes of yours to put on.'

John had tried to protest, but it was not the slightest bit of good; they just wouldn't hear of him being in those wet clothes a moment longer, least of all the young lady whose presence had put his mind in such a whirl.

Fifteen minutes later he had joined them again; Henry's

clothes had fitted him quite well. He remembered how much more confident he had felt, being clean, dry and comfortable.

'You're too late for your own dinner because of the bag, Mr Fraser, and we're late as well for the same reason, so you will dine with us, won't you?' Madge had said as she led them towards the dining room; then, almost in the same breath, she wanted to know where he was staying.

He gave her an answer to both her questions, but he was quite sure that it was only his answer of 'Delighted' to the first one that had really registered.

But that had only been the beginning. First they wanted to know what had happened to him out in all that rain; while he had been telling them, every time he looked in her direction, her eyes had been upon him – eyes which held more interest than just a casual glance. He remembered thinking what a fool he was to ever let the thought enter his head that he could possibly mean as much to her as she was already to him.

Then, secondly, they had wanted to know where he came from, and what he did, and about his family. Sadness clouded her face when she learned that he was alone, for she had lost her own mother nearly four years ago; but she wanted to know what life was like on a farm, to which he had replied, 'Very hard work, and long hours.'

'I love the country, but I'm afraid we don't see enough of it,' she replied, with half a sigh.

He still remembered how he could have kicked himself, for before he realised what he was saying the words just tumbled out. 'Any time you feel like a spell in the country, you are all welcome to Spring Farm.'

Surprisingly, it was her father who replied. 'We shall be very pleased to accept your kind offer, Mr Fraser, but it must be on two conditions. Firstly, that when you come to London again you will stay here; and secondly, that you will accept a reward from me for bringing my Gladstone bag back.'

He remembered word for word the answer he had given. 'I shall be more than honoured to accept the first, but I cannot say yes to the second. That is not our way in the country; just because I am the one to find your bag and bring it back to you, that doesn't mean to say that I am entitled to something which I haven't worked for. Your friendship and your hospitality has more than repaid me for any trifle which you think you are indebted to me.'

The old gentleman was silent for almost a minute before answering. 'Just as you wish, Mr Fraser, but I shall always feel indebted to you for your honesty.'

The food had been excellent, far better than he would have got at his hotel, and what with the drinks, he had felt well fortified against catching a cold after the soaking he had had. Cold or no cold hadn't worried him then. What did keep going through his mind was how often, and in what ways, she kept looking at him; and once or twice when he had held her gaze longer than he should have done, he was sure her cheeks changed to a beautiful shade of pink.

Time was getting on, and he had been almost on the point of enquiring about changing his clothes again, when her father came out with the most unexpected suggestion.

'You'll have to wear Henry's clothes tonight, Mr Fraser, then if you come here about eleven o'clock in the morning, Brown will have your own all ready to change into. Then if you have no other plans, why not take Madge for a walk in the park? Then you can lunch here, have a look round the shops in the afternoon, and I would like you to have dinner with us again tomorrow night.'

'I would love that, sir,' he had answered. 'That is, if Miss Bromsgrove is agreeable.'

'Yes, I'd be delighted,' she had replied, and the blush on her face grew a little deeper.

But that was not all. There had been one more bit of luck for him – or was it for the both of them? One more small thing happened which had meant so much in the preparation for the day to come. As he made ready to leave, and to wish them goodnight, she suddenly exclaimed, 'I'll see Mr Fraser out.'

So together they walked across the hall to the front door.

'Will eleven o'clock suit you all right?' he had asked.

'Yes, perfectly,' she had answered.

He opened the door, and took her hand in his to wish her goodnight, then gently whispered, 'I may not sleep very well tonight, thinking of you and tomorrow.' He hadn't dared to anticipate the answer, if any, which she gave him.

She replied, 'And neither may I, thinking of you and tonight.'

He smiled, as he slowly drew her hand up to his lips and sealed the first bond between them.

He remembered walking back to his hotel feeling as light as a feather. What had started out as an ordinary day had finished up far more wonderful than anything he had ever dreamed of. And the next day, after their walk in the park, and the lovely lunch, just for the two of them... the thrill of that moment came back so vividly just as he reached the floor of the valley. They had gone into the drawing room, where he had asked her if she had slept well the night before.

'Did you expect me to after all that had just happened?' she had replied, smiling.

He hadn't answered, for that would have broken the spell as their eyes met and held each other's. He had taken just one step forward, and took her in his arms. That first kiss had been no old-fashioned peck, but one which held all his desperate love for her; and in her shy way, her love for him had been just as overwhelming.

He remembered her first letter to him and the effect it had upon his heart. He remembered the first of their many visits to Spring Farm and how they loved his village of Beversbury, and the nearby town of Tetstone, two miles away; also their admiration for the fine old furniture which his parents had collected throughout the years.

He most vividly remembered the time when later on they came to the conclusion that they couldn't go on any longer being apart from each other, and when on his next visit to London, he had stood alone, shaking inside in front of her father, to ask for his daughter's hand in marriage. Even now he could hear her father's reply, as if it was only yesterday.

'Of course, I will give you both my blessing, John. I'm as happy about it as you are. It is a different life from what Madge has been brought up to, but I know the challenge of a new life will only serve to make her more determined to succeed, and I know I couldn't give my daughter into safer or better hands.'

What a wonderful wedding they had had, and the two weeks' honeymoon at Bournemouth had been absolutely divine! Right from the start her father's words had come true, for she took to her duties, not only as a housewife but as a farmer's wife, like a duck taking to water.

He then remembered their great disappointment, when after so long, there was still no patter of tiny feet; but even then, they had been in a world of their own. Only one black cloud marred all those years. That was when her father died, four years after they were married.

Henry had been left the business, and no doubt the bulk of his father's wealth. But even so, Madge was left so well off that she could have bought John out, farm, lock, stock and barrel several times over.

John felt he had lost a good friend, a true friend, an understanding friend; for how many men in his position would willingly give his only daughter to a country farmer?

He remembered over those last nine years how his precious wife had overcome whatever obstacles that had confronted her, apparently with ease. How she had improved the inside of the house, how she had taken a great interest in cooking, how she had taught their 'treasure', Penny, so much that in fact at nineteen Penny was as good as any of the cooks in the big houses for miles around. How when illness struck in the village, help in whatever shape or form was needed came knocking at the door. He remembered those nine years of bliss, when their love had blossomed; and now it was in full bloom. His Madge was the mother of a child, which she had yearned for, and he was the proud father of a son; their son.

War, and What it Leaves Behind

Two weeks later, the nurse had departed and Madge and Penny were left to dote over the new arrival; he was going to be called Phillip.

'If it's shortened it will sound better than a lot of names,' Madge had said, 'and besides, it's the only one in the two families, as far back as we can go.'

So, as week followed week, the overwhelming joy which young Phillip brought them almost dimmed their vision to the storm clouds which were gathering elsewhere, for on 4th August it was war.

To them it came as a complete shock. They had just brought a new life into the world, and someone somewhere was out to take life on a scale unheard of in the world before. They were in a paradise of their own. How hard it was to imagine a scene where man uses all his primitive skill to kill his own; how hard, when all around is touched by the hand of God.

It wouldn't affect John in a fighting sense; but as for Penny, she was courting young Ned Ashley, a carpenter, working for a local firm in Tetstone. Each day she became a little more unsure of the future, for Ned was twenty-two, and like a lot of young men, was keen to join the army and fight for his country.

Sure enough, on her next day off, when they were out walking arm in arm, by the old wicket gate Ned said to her, 'I shall have to go, Penny my love, sooner or a bit later, for I shan't be able to hold my head up much longer, knowing that I should be doing my duty by the side of so many others. I don't want to leave you, but inside I know I've got to.'

'Well, promise me to wait a little while longer, will you?' she asked pleadingly.

'I promise, my love, but I can't stay longer than the start of spring, which is five months time. So if it's not over by then, will you let me go, with your blessing?'

'Yes, my love,' she answered, hoping all the while that it would end long before then.

'Thank you, my love,' he replied. Then he went on, 'Will you marry me as soon as possible?'

That was the end of the dark cloud that had been with her for weeks.

'Of course I will, my love, with Dad's permission – there's nothing more I want than to be your wife!'

What a seventh heaven she was in! And that night, when she went back to Spring Farm and told them, and that her father had given his permission and that the wedding would be as soon as possible, it was like a tonic to them, seeing her once more as happy as she used to be. But next day the smile on her face grew just as great as the night before, for as she went into the breakfast room to clear the table Mr and Mrs Fraser were still there waiting for her.

'Oh, Penny,' said Madge, 'Mr Fraser and I have been talking, and we both agree that we want you to have a really nice wedding, so whatever you would like you shall have. We feel it is our right and duty, for you have always been as near to us as if you were our own daughter.'

Poor Penny hardly knew how to hold back those tears of joy and gratitude from trickling down her cheeks, as Madge went on, 'If it is all right with your mother, the three of us will go to Cheltenham on the train, and no matter what the cost of the wedding dress that you like best, it shall be yours, for Mr Fraser and I are determined that you shall be the loveliest bride to ever walk down the aisle at Beversbury.'

That was more than Penny could bear. They had always been so kind to her, now all this... She just buried her face in her hands and cried, 'Oh, Mrs Fraser, what would I do without you and Mr Fraser? For no one could have a better or happier home than I have here.'

But still that was not all, for as Madge put her arms around her to console her she said, 'We have decided to have your bedroom and sitting room redecorated, and any new furniture that you require you can have, so that Ned and you feel that you have a home of your own.'

Ten minutes later, Penny was like Mother Earth bathed in sunshine after a warm and tender shower. Her eyes shone, and her face was brimming over with happiness. So in a few days, all the plans were in operation to ensure that her day would be a great and glorious occasion.

So the great day arrived, and true to Madge and John's prediction, Penny was the most beautiful bride ever to walk down the aisle at Beversbury Church.

Even Henry came down for the wedding, and on top of the handsome cheque he presented to the happy couple, he gave himself another two weeks' holiday in Scotland, so that 18 Rosary Gardens would be at the disposal of the newly-weds, for their two weeks' honeymoon in London.

'We want you to have a wonderful time,' said John, as he and Madge wished the couple goodbye. 'It's only once in a lifetime, and the more wonderful memories you have to look back on, the better.'

So saying, he pressed an envelope into Ned's hand, and Madge did the same to Penny. There was more than enough in those two envelopes to make sure that they would have more good times than they could possibly cram into a fortnight.

Once the honeymoon was over, life at Spring Farm once more settled into its accustomed pattern. Ned in his spare time would pester John for any odd jobs which needed doing, and Penny's happiness knew no bounds; but even so, young Phil formed a very large slice of her daily life. Often in the weeks that followed John would say to Madge, 'What a blessing, dear, that youth doesn't worry about what might happen tomorrow, or the next day. I hope it goes on, but I am doubtful, for the war seems to be spreading instead of ending. What Penny will be like if Ned goes, only heaven can tell.'

So Christmas came and went, and the weeks stretched into months. The time when Ned's itching feet would set out for their goal came far too soon and painfully for Penny. She went as far as The Junction to see him off, and it was a downcast, tearful Penny who arrived back at Spring Farm, hours before she needed to. Madge was well on top of the job of consoling her; and then there was young Phil, that bubbling bundle of charm that meant so much to her. All this helped her over those first few weeks, which otherwise would have been dark and endless.

She never saw Ned again before he went to France, but in his letters to her, he was always brimming over with confidence and excitement. That was the one and only thing that soothed her peace of mind, the fact that he wanted to do what he was doing.

As summer passed, and each day young Phil became a bit more of her life, so did Penny inwardly prepare herself for whatever sorrow fate might lay before her; for already two from their village had been killed in action in the space of a couple of weeks, and the war was getting worse, not better.

As Christmas approached once more, all they could hope for, apart from his safety and well-being, was that Ned would get the parcels they had sent him, to bring a little homely cheer at a time when the whole world should be at peace.

In his next letter, two weeks after Christmas, Ned told them he had received the parcels safely, and sent his thanks and gratitude. He was still his buoyant self, with not a mention of the awful conditions which they had heard so much about.

Within a week, news once more buzzed around the village. Major Marchant, who lived at the Court some three hundred yards away on the opposite side of the road to Spring Farm, had been badly wounded; one leg had been amputated already.

So the weeks stretched into months once more, and all this time life went on for Penny as for a million others, getting a letter one day, then another long anxious wait until the next one arrived. It was the not knowing what might happen at any second in between that was the most unbearable aspect.

Almost five months after he had been wounded Major Marchant was allowed home. A week later, John paid him a visit. He looked well, and John marvelled at the way he was getting about with his artificial leg.

'It's terrible out there, John,' the major told him. 'At times you look upon the dead and count them as the lucky ones, and the worst part is that there seems no end to it.'

That was one thing he wouldn't breathe a word to Penny

about. Whatever picture Ned painted in her letters, that was the picture which he hoped she would visualise. But little did John know that as he wished the major good day and a speedy recovery, news – bad news – was already on its way, and would once again bring a lot more sorrow to their once happy village.

The next morning was another morning of dilemma for Alfie the postman. For almost thirty years, except for the odd day and two illnesses, he had travelled the same round. He had seen most of the people in Beversbury within days of being born, had watched them grow up, seen many get married and have families of their own, and always had a cheery word to and from all of them. Now he seemed to be the bearer of all their sorrows. What wouldn't he give to be able to pass on his unthankful task to someone else? For in his bag, in the bundle of letters for Beversbury, was one which would bring more sorrow to that once happy village. Poor Penny, there would be no cheery word, no happy smile, nor a steaming hot cup of tea for him this morning; for one thing, he knew he couldn't face her. There was only one way open to him, he would find Ned's father first, and if it was the worst, it would be much better for him to break the news as gently as he could to Penny.

So it was that at 8.30 a.m., Tom Ashley met John on his way to breakfast. Tom was unable to speak as he handed John that cold official document, and as he read 'Killed in Action', his hand went up over his face.

'What can I say, Tom, that will bring even a crumb of comfort to you and your wife, and my heart bleeds for Penny. Ned, your eldest son, your firstborn, Penny's first and only love – what can I say at a time like this, when words seem only meaningless?'

As they walked towards Spring Farm, only then did Tom find strength enough to talk.

'It's Penny that the wife and I are most worried about – the shock of it; she's so young for a blow like this, and they were so happy.'

Penny was coming out of the dining room as they stepped into the hall. In a flash she seemed to size up the situation. A curtain of anxiety instantly swept across her face, then her face went blank as she blurted out, 'Its Ned, isn't it – my Ned!'

John nodded, then said softly, 'I'm afraid it is, Penny,' as he went to comfort her, and then led her, sobbing uncontrollably, into the dining room to Madge.

Words and actions were almost useless at crises like these; only time, a lot of time, could partly cure a breaking heart.

So, in the days and weeks to follow, Madge and John devoted most of their time and understanding to help her get over the awful shock. But once again it was young Phil who gradually made her take an interest in life – a lesser one, but it was a start. She thought the world of him, and you couldn't stop a small boy from asking questions, and wanting answers. So as time went on, he not only became more and more of her world, he was her whole world.

A week after Phil's third birthday, Jane Marchant was born. There were great celebrations at the Court, and the major was dancing around on his wooden leg, so great was his joy at the birth of their only child. But at Northwood Hall, twelve miles from Oxford, the Marchants' friend, Colonel Shand, was in anything but a joyful mood. He had journeyed from Salisbury Plain, leaving his training camp as soon as he heard that Mary, his wife, was seriously ill. She too was expecting a baby, and although the two doctors had fought with all their skill to save her, it was to no avail. She had died in his arms within half an hour of the baby being born. He was in his study, pacing up and down, feeling shocked, helpless and so afraid. He heard someone coming down the stairs, and the next moment the older of the two doctors came into the study.

'I don't have to tell you how sorry I am for you, Colonel. My partner and I did everything that was humanly possible, but things seemed to be beyond our control right from the start, and we are both shocked over it. But there is one shining star in the dark sky over us, for you have a charming little daughter up there, as lovely a child as I have ever seen. Won't you come up and see her now?'

'Not now,' replied the colonel. 'If it had been a son, I might have found the strength. It's a terrible blow to lose my wife, but another female only makes it look as if my troubles are starting all over again.'

'What do you mean?' asked the doctor sympathetically.

Pulling himself together a little, the colonel answered, 'The awful truth is, Doctor, no female on my wife's side has lived to the age of thirty for about one hundred and twenty years, so you can't expect my mind to be exactly at ease for the future.'

'No,' responded the doctor, 'but all things have to end sometime, and I sincerely hope this is the end of your sorrow. Have you any idea what it was all about?'

'Only what my wife once told me. Apparently some gypsy woman had her caravan on their land, and she was picking up wood, when an ancestor of my wife's came across her. She ordered her off their land, and told her to put down the wood. That was bad enough, but she did the worst thing possible, she hit the gypsy woman several times with a stick; hence came the curse – a curse that seems to have run true to its words all these years. Whether that was all of it, I have no idea. My wife never did enlarge on it, but I wish now that I had pressed her for all the details, that is, if there are any more.'

'Very strange, and almost unbelievable,' said the doctor as he got up from his chair. Then he went on, 'I'm sure it would help you a lot if you would only come up and see this lovely daughter of yours. Have you decided on a name for her?'

'It was going to be Edward, after my father, if it had been a boy, and really I didn't have the heart to think that it would be any other; but my wife, being far more willing than me to face reality, always said, "If it's a girl, we'll call her Joanna." So that's what it's got to be.'

When the colonel reached the nursery, he knelt beside the cot and gazed down through tear-filled eyes at Joanna, his lovely daughter. Her skin was like silk and her hair like silver down. She really was far lovelier than he could have imagined. How proud Mary would have been of her, and how much like Mary she really was! But the most important thing on his mind was to ask God to help this little angel to overcome something which no one knew the answer to.

A week later, and with three more days to go before he returned to Salisbury Plain, the colonel was sitting in his study, still with a great sense of loss, sorrow and loneliness upon him. It was twelve noon on a beautiful day; the sun shone unimpeded through a cloudless sky, with not even the slightest haze to dim its downward path, and without even a breath of air strong enough to stir the leaves of the aspens which grew at the edge of the lawn. Suddenly the words of the doctor came back to him. 'All things have to end sometime.' Then he wondered if, among Mary's letters and papers, the key to this curse was lying hidden, and just waiting to be unravelled.

He went up to their room, and with the key unlocked the wall safe where she kept her jewel case. Next to it there was another case, slightly larger, and he placed both of them on the bed. He looked through the jewel case first; there were a few letters, but it took him less than ten minutes to realise that what he was looking for was not there.

He unlocked the other case, which must have contained almost a hundred letters. It was very hot and oppressive, even though all three windows were wide open, but he took no notice of the heat, not even bothering to draw back the fine net curtains which covered the windows. He picked up the first bundle and undid the narrow ribbon around them. Some were blue, some were white and some looked very old. He scanned through them one by one, putting the ones he had looked at in a scattered heap in the middle of the bed. He finished the first bundle, collected them and tied them up again. Then he started on the next. Several in this bundle looked yellow with age, but he didn't choose, he took them as they came. He had almost looked through half of them, and had already started on some of the old yellow ones, when the gong sounded for lunch. On the way down he took a quick peep at his lovely daughter, who was getting more like his Mary each day, and already he had lost his heart again, for their child was the only real visible likeness of the one he had loved with all his heart.

He was alone for lunch, but he took his usual time, for his appetite had almost returned to normal. Then he moved into his study, where he was served with coffee. He thought as he sipped this dark refreshing liquid. If only there was a breath of air, for the weather is almost as hot as the coffee itself... But as he put the cup to his lips for the fifth time, little did he dream that up in that room where he had spent almost an hour, something was about to happen; and had he seen it, he would have wondered what sort of trick fate was playing him now. For suddenly a gust of wind swept through the bottom half of the window nearest the bed, the curtains billowed out, almost touching the ceiling, and then, as if by some unseen hand, the letter on the top of the bundle, the one he would have looked at next, was lifted off and scattered among those already in the middle of the bed. Nothing else, not even the flimsy curtains at the other two windows, stirred.

It was 2.00 p.m., when he returned. Patiently he started on his search once more, but by 3.15 p.m., he had come to the end, and was no further on his tragic quest than before.

As he closed the door and made his way downstairs, totally unaware of what something he had always thought of as 'fate' had just performed, how could he even have dreamt that it had been ordained, over one hundred and twenty years before, that he should not find what he was looking for? For this wind that blew on a windless day was not fate, but a breath from a whisper of God, as straight as an arrow from heaven. The time hadn't come, the pieces of the jigsaw still had to be assembled; and as yet, not all His chosen ones had set foot on the earthly path, to be prepared.

Worry or sorrow touched almost every house in those times, and back at Spring Farm it was Madge's time for her share of worry. She had just heard from her brother, Henry; he and his friend George Parker were joining up.

It's now or never, he had written. *We wouldn't hear the last of it when the others came home after it's all over, if we hadn't gone.*

He also wanted John and Madge to go to London as soon as possible, implying that he would see enough countryside in the very near future. John could tell as soon as he came in from the fields that there was something amiss, and straight away after he had read the letter he said, 'We'll go today for as long as you want. Penny can have Sarah in to sleep here, and you know Phil will be in capable hands.'

When they stepped off the train at Paddington, no one

would have guessed that John was a country farmer. Madge, having moved in the upper part of society, had worked wonders with him in the years between, and he had been a most willing pupil. To say that she felt proud of him was a gross understatement.

For five whole days, life was one long whirl. Henry took them here, there and everywhere. But even during this hectic time, there were occasions when John noticed that Madge retired a little into herself, but he understood her silent agony at the grim prospect of what could happen to her only brother, her last relative. But there had been one more motive behind Henry's desire for them to go to London. Three times during those five days he had taken them to the office, and each time, Madge had been filled with wonder and admiration at the way he had expanded the business. However, it wasn't until their last visit that he had let them know what was really in his mind. He didn't know how to begin at first, but finally he spoke.

'In Newman and Gladwin, I have two of the finest men I could wish for; either of them are just as capable of running this business as well as I am.' He then looked at Madge as he added, 'But...' Then he paused before continuing, 'There must be a figurehead here sometimes; would it be possible for you and John to come up once a month? You are not exactly a novice in the running of this sort of business, besides if anything happens to me – which it could at any time, in the army or out of it – it's all yours, so you might as well know the "ins and outs" of as much as possible.'

John had put his arm around her for comfort, as she answered, 'Please don't talk like that, Henry. Of course John and I will come up once a month and do all we can until you come home again.'

At the station, the parting had gone off far better than John had hoped for. Except for a few tears, Madge had not let her feelings run away with her. Brother and sister had hugged and kissed each other, while he had bid the young man farewell and a safe return, as if Henry had been his one and only brother as well.

Month followed month, and during that time Madge received more letters from Henry in Flanders than she ever had when he had been at home; and meanwhile on their three-day monthly visits to London they learned more and more of the vast undertaking Henry had built up in a few short years.

So time passed, and once again the snowdrops and the daffodils had come and gone, and once again over a weary countryside there stirred the freshness of spring, young, sweet and fragrant. This was the season when man and all the creatures of this earth know the joy of living, when the start of each new day is a pleasure beyond words. But this was also the time when Madge was plunged into the depths of sorrow. Henry, the brother she had loved so much, had been killed in battle. Now it was Penny's turn, as well as John's, to pour their comfort and understanding on to those troubled waters. The shock, the numbness was what had to be broken through, before Madge could pick up the threads of life again. Then there was young Phil, almost four now, playing his part too; for the love the young son gave his mother also helped to dim the nightmare she was going through. But during that time, even in the depth of her own sorrow, she could fully understand what Penny had endured and was still suffering, and why she had often told her, that no one would ever take the place of Ned. She would never marry again, no matter what happened.

Twice John had made the trip to London by himself, but on the third occasion, Madge thought she was strong enough to face up to the business, the house and the legal affairs. The business would go on as usual, but the house and contents, except for the silver, glass, china and a few items of furniture which she wanted herself, would be sold. The servants would receive two years' wages, plus what Henry had left them, but she was quite unprepared for the shock she received over the legal affairs, namely Henry's will. He had left her over £70,000 in money and investments. She was now a very rich young woman.

When they were alone back at Rosary Gardens, almost the first thing she said was, 'With all that money, Henry should have been married to a nice girl and had a family.'

'I know,' John answered. 'He had plenty of chances, just counting the ones we know of, but there are quite a few these days who like their freedom better.'

'It's an awful lot of money, John, but we mustn't let it change our way of life, for I'm far too happy with the one you have given me.'

'All right, my love,' he answered, taking her in his arms. 'We'll still make our way in the world off the land; we've always managed so far.'

A Few Years in Between

The war had been over four months, and Colonel Shand knew he would not be out of the army for at least another six. He was on a few days' leave and at that moment was in his study at Northwood Hall, deep in thought. He was thinking of the time when Mary knew she was having a baby.

'Frank, my love,' she had said, 'if something should happen to me and the baby is all right, there is something I want you to promise me. I wouldn't want you to waste your life and not marry again, I'd want you to marry someone like Marie-Ann, someone who would be as near to a real mother as possible, someone who would give our child that vital mother love, and the feeling of stability that no nanny, no matter how good, could ever give.'

'Don't talk like that, my love. Everything is going to be all right, and I don't know what I would do without you, you know that,' he had answered. But he had noticed the tears in her eyes shining like dewdrops in the early morning sunlight, as she had thrown her arms around him and kissed him deeply.

Wondering about it now, he felt sure she had had some premonition of impending disaster from that curse. Since Mary had died he had seen Marie-Ann quite a few times, and they had been writing to each other twice a week. She had been Mary's dearest friend, and both had the same sweet nature.

If he had loved Mary with all his heart, for the time being he would like Marie-Ann to the same extent, and respect her. He could think of no one whom he could trust Joanna's future with more than with her; and so tomorrow they were being married quietly at the village church, and he knew Mary would smile upon his decision, especially now that Joanna was well into her second year, and would need a mother's love and care more every day.

So as time went on, this beautiful child, whose very existence had brought so much sorrow and deep foreboding, was now the very reason why family life at Northwood Hall contained a much deeper bond of love and happiness than Colonel Shand had ever hoped for or thought possible.

That was how life sailed beautifully along for the next two and a half years, not only at Northwood, but at the Court and Spring Farm as well. The only upheaval they had during that time was when Madge spared no expense on modernising the house; three bathrooms they now had, and all fitted up with the latest ideas, while her taste in decorating and matching everything up was that of an expert.

'I can't think where you get your ideas from, it's all so first class,' John had said as the work was in progress.

'This is our home, my love, and I want it as beautiful and homely as I can get it. And another thing, I know Penny appreciates all the new additions to her kitchen.'

'It's certainly lovely, and I'm more than grateful, for I could never have afforded all this myself,' he answered, kissing her lovingly.

Phil was now seven years old, and was one of the village boys down to the last letter; the only difference being, he had inherited his mother's refinement of speech, and the manners of a gentleman. He was just as polite to a certain knight of the road, who often called for a can of tea and a bite to eat, as he was to the major, when he called on one of his rare visits. That was what his mother and father wanted from him, the qualities that any man can face the world with. When he went on trips, or a school outing, he would bring Penny a present just as he sometimes brought his mother, and she loved him all the more for it. But while he was taking a lively interest in different games with the village boys, and with the workings of the farm, Jane over at the Court and Joanna at Northwood were still in the doll stage. Jane was dark and a real chatterbox; Joanna had silver-gold hair, and was more thoughtful. She was a lovely child. But it was just at this time that she started to suffer from nightmares – not the screaming type, but ones where she woke up in a bath of perspiration, with the feeling that it was blood that was soaking her; a horror that she always kept to herself, young as she was.

Who was She, and Where did She Come From?

It is Christmas Eve, 1921. The scene is a farmhouse set almost five hundred yards from the scattered village of Niendorff, thirty miles south-east of Hamburg, Germany.

Fritz Hanhart represented the third generation of his family to farm these lands, and except for his war service, he had spent very little time away from the place he loved. His wife Eva, whom he had married a year after the war, had been a teacher of English in one of the large universities in Hamburg, and over the last two years she had taught him to speak English quite fluently. They had both been in their early thirties when they had married, and as yet had not had the blessing of any children; and now there didn't seem much hope of any success, according to the last medical report they had received. Yet it remained their one burning desire. Fritz had only one eye; he had been badly wounded and taken prisoner in 1917. He had, he said, everything good to say of the British. Their treatment of him was beyond praise, and all knew in the village that he was sure he would have lost the sight of his other eye, if it had not been for the English doctor's expert skill and attention.

He was tired now, it had been a hard day. Snow had fallen steadily since noon and it had been much colder than usual, and now as he made his way towards the house, the sky was clear, with not a cloud in sight. The last curtain of evening shadows were falling quite quickly, and the stars gave every promise of showing their very best.

He thought of the little that Christmas had to offer to Eva, his dear one, and himself. It would be almost the same as any other day. They had by now received all their Christmas greetings, and the village children had made their final round of carol singing. He could see quite clearly the delight on Eva's face, also the touch of sadness, when two nights ago the three boys and three girls were in their big room singing his favourite and the loveliest of all carols, 'Silent Night'.

Fritz wanted a child more than anything, but it hurt him to know that his deep longing was only a fraction of the desperation that his dear one bore so bravely.

He unlaced his boots and stepped with stockinged feet into the kitchen. There just inside the door were his slippers, and the towel to dry Rex with. He slipped his feet into the slippers then bent down to give his faithful Rex – the third of that name – a good rub down. Man and dog welcomed the comfort and warmth after a day such as they had had. Rex licked his hand and Fritz accepted that he was the most loveable of the three Alsatians he had had so far. All had been called Rex, and so it would go on. Eva came into the kitchen to get the coffee, gave him a tender kiss, bringing a wry smile to his face as she said what most women would say, 'Are you cold, dear?'

'Just a little,' he replied, putting his stone-cold hand on hers.

'Oh, you're absolutely frozen!' she exclaimed. 'Make haste, I've got a lovely fire in the sitting room and some of your favourite teacakes.' Then she left him to have a quick wash and change.

He felt better already. The cold of the day that he had endured was only a memory now, and while he ate a good meal, they talked of some of the happier Christmases they had had, before their best friends had left the district; but both knew in their hearts that this one would be one of the quietest.

The warmth of the room made Fritz drowsy, and as Eva cleared the things he dozed off once or twice. He heard her, but only vaguely, about to close the shutters at the glass front door in the hall. Next moment she was by his side.

'Fritz, dear, she said, 'you must come and see this wonderful sight, it's a star brighter than I've ever seen before.'

He got up and followed her to the glass door. He too could hardly believe his eyes. To get a better view, he just had to brave the cold once more, by opening the door. There it was, straight in front of them, the brightest star he had ever seen; but what disturbed him most of all was how low it hung in the sky, and how near it looked.

'I don't know, my dear,' he declared, 'I've never seen anything quite like it before.'

And from the doorstep to a great distance, the star lit up the carpet of snow; a carpet that stretched from their feet as level as the beautiful lawn which it covered and then went on, as slight shadows appeared where the rougher ground took over – all untouched by bird, beast or man, still virgin white, and still precisely as the master had laid it.

'This is how it must have looked exactly nineteen hundred and twenty-one years ago around Bethlehem, only it was mostly barren land instead of snow,' he said.

Reluctantly, he closed the door because of the cold, but they both took another prolonged look before he finally closed the shutters.

The Christmas preparations had all been completed, so they read a little, but talked most of the time, and once or twice took another look at the star through the sitting-room window, nearer than before and still shining relentlessly bright. It was now eight o'clock; Fritz had just asked Eva if she would care for a drink, and was on the point of getting up to pour them, when Rex, who had been stretched out a safe distance from the fire, suddenly got up and went to the door.

Fritz rose and opened the door, giving his dog an affectionate pat, then made his way to the kitchen to let him out, but Rex wasn't following. Rex was standing firmly facing the shuttered glass door. Fritz knew better than to call him to come through the kitchen. He knew that when Rex did anything unusual, there was always a real reason. It might be a cat, or some other animal, but doubt soon crossed his mind, for Rex just stood there whining with not the slightest frenzy about him, and looking as gentle as a lamb.

'Come here a moment, dear, he's never asked to go out this way at night before,' he called, and Eva came into the hall.

'No, never,' she answered, as Rex started whining louder than before, making it quite clear that this was what he wanted.

Fritz moved to undo the shutters and Rex stood back with tail wagging. Then the door bolts were slid back, and with hand on the handle he slowly opened the door; but Rex made no attempt to rush out, or even to go out at all. The star was near, so very near and much lower in the sky, shining more brightly than ever before, shining on an object which lay right across the doorway, and in this brilliant light both Fritz and Eva instantly recognised what this object was.

It was a cradle so beautiful, so celestially white, that for a few moments their eyes were dazzled. Then Fritz lifted it gently off the ground and turned round into the hall. Even in that dim light, both of them beheld something which made their hearts jump for joy, for their eyes feasted upon the face of a beautiful baby, which was turned fully towards them. Two tiny eyelids, silky tinged, were closed in the depth of a peaceful sleep; two little cheeks, so pure, so fair, like twin petals of the pale pink rose; the soft downy hair that was gently shaped, not of jet, or of gold, but like the dancing rays of pure silver at the touch of the sun, casting a miniature white halo round a pure angelic face. A glowing rapture surged over them at what they beheld, at something they could hardly believe, but would always remember.

'How lovely, how wonderful!' Eva exclaimed. But who could leave a baby out on this, or any night? I wonder who it belongs to.'

Fritz looked up and caught that look of adoration, that look which could only mean deep mother love, one he had never as yet seen on her face before. He held the cradle towards her, for her taking – not just to let him close the door and shutters, but because he could hold her in suspense no longer. It wasn't merely the tenderness on her face, it was the movement of impatience in her arms, longing to hold, longing to fondle. She took her charge gently, and made her way into the sitting room, little realising that the life she had known was gone forever, and that out of this bitter cold clear night, the sunshine for the rest of her life had unexpectedly been dropped into her arms.

Fritz turned and once more gazed out upon that perfect carpet of snow. He looked for signs of the person who had placed that precious bundle of joy before their door, but the more he scrutinised the perfect carpet of snow, foot by foot, yard by yard, the more puzzled he became; not one blemish could he find to the right, left or in the centre. Everything was just as perfect as when they had first looked out at the star, only the oval shape where the cradle had stood was imprinted in the snow, with not a mark nor a footprint around it. He looked up for the second time; he knew this was surely beyond him, it couldn't be possible and yet he knew it must be. There was no other explanation. If so, then this could only be a miracle. As he thoughtfully walked into the sitting room, he found Eva on her knees bending over the cradle, which she had placed on the floor.

Love and pride almost dripped from her face as she said, 'I'm sure it's a sweet little girl, dear. She's so lovely, so beautiful and she looks just like a little angel.'

Fritz knelt down on the other side of the cradle, cupped one hand under the baby's chin and gently guided her face so that her eyes met his, and then solemnly said, 'I'm almost certain that this is what she is.'

Then he told Eva how his eyes had searched for signs in the snow which should have been there, and added, 'But the only mark is where the *cradle* stood, and nothing more. It is as though this little angel in this lovely cradle has literally descended from heaven.'

'That is the only place from which our prayers can be answered, my dear,' she replied, as tears rolled slowly down her cheeks. Fritz wiped her tears as she continued, 'I only hope and pray with all my heart that heaven means us to keep her.'

From that very moment, the pattern of their lives changed to the very foundations, and in no time Eva had all the necessary things together. They were mostly makeshift, but they would do until the morning. And later on when the couple gazed upon their little dream before getting into bed, she whispered to her husband, 'If she is going to be ours dear, can I call her Chrysta? For it is at Christmas time that she has come to us.'

He nodded, squeezing her tenderly to his side.

It was the happiest Christmas morning they had ever known. They were like two children, with one wonderful Christmas present between them.

No more snow had fallen in the night, Fritz knew, for the marks of the cradle were still there, and the untouched carpet of frost-crusted snow stretched out as before.

After breakfast, Fritz took the list Eva had made out and set forth on what he hoped would not be an unwelcome visit to the shop. The Schmidts were great friends of theirs, and after hearing his story were only too pleased and willing to get together all that Eva needed. Then he went on to another old friend, Carl, the village policeman, for they knew they would have to report the happenings of the night before.

Within half an hour of his return, old Carl arrived at the farm. He then asked to hear all the facts over again, noting down this and that, and went out to the glass door, where it was plain for all to see; but the plain facts only made Carl scratch his head. Even he had no answer as to how, where or why. Back in the sitting room, while they were having an early celebration drink, it wasn't only the face of the lovely baby that old Carl looked at; he didn't need his professional eye to see the volume of love and tenderness on the faces of these two friends of his, and he knew what a cruel blow it would be to them if they had to give up this lovely child.

'I can see that nothing would please you more than if you could keep her and bring her up as your own,' he said finally.

'Do you think we might be able to?' asked Fritz, his eyes shining.

Eva, with tear-filled eyes, could only look down at her heart's desire as old Carl put a comforting hand upon her shoulder.

'I'll see what I can do, so don't worry. I'll have to report it, but I know no child could have a better home.' He paused, 'Have a happy Christmas – and mind you don't worry,' he added, as Fritz let him out of the kitchen door.

During the weeks that followed, it became apparent that their greatest wish of all would be granted. No one went out of their way to take in an extra mouth to feed, not in Germany in those times; and so, a little later on this lovely child, who had come to them from out of the night, legally became Chrysta Hanhart, adopted daughter of Fritz and Eva Hanhart. Thus the love, joy and happiness that had started out of nowhere would know no bounds, as day followed day.

Growing Up

The year was 1930. Phil was sixteen, and two inches taller than his father, with fair tousled hair and eyes that were forever overflowing with the exuberance of youth. It was a certainty that he was the apple of his mother's and Penny's eye. He was on a long weekend from boarding school, and oh, how he loved to help on the farm at times like these and during his holidays.

'He's going to be over six foot tall,' his father said to his mother. 'It's wonderful how a bit of farm work develops the muscles. I was only looking at his strong arms and well-developed chest when he had his shirt off in the field today – he'll be much more of a giant than I ever hoped to be!'

However, it had been agreed between the three of them that Phil should continue at school until he was eighteen. Then he'd serve a year and a half on a farm in Norfolk, and another year and a half in Hampshire with farming friends of theirs.

'That should give you a good bit of practical experience,' his father had said. 'Then, by the time you have had two years at the Agricultural College, you should know a bit about farming.'

'That may be so,' Phil had answered, 'but don't forget, Dad, there's no one who knows the land better than the one that farms it. I know I shall often have to ask your advice. You're not just a part of it, you *are* Spring Farm, every acre of it.'

It was during this time that the farming industry was going through the worst times in living memory. Disillusion, and the hopeless task of trying to make a living, drove many farmers to sell up and get out, even though many of them received less than half of the real value. Two such farms were adjoining Spring Farm, and Madge, with her far-sighted business sense, said to John, 'Let's buy them, dear; you know I wouldn't miss the small amount that these two will go for.'

'I know that, dear,' he answered, 'but if you only knew the little we made ourselves last year, you might not think it wise to put your money into farm land.'

'I realise that, my love, but they are good farms, and it would put our acreage up to almost a thousand. You've got the car to get round them with, and I've got a feeling things will get a bit better later on. Besides, it's Phil's future we have to think of, for we may never have another chance to buy them after this one.'

'I suppose you are right, dear. Well, I know you are, so if you want them, buy them; it will only mean that I shall have to plan for three farms instead of one, and I have heard several times that there are some good workers on both places, and that is half the battle – when men know what to do, without being told every little thing. So it's "yes" – knowing that you have set your mind on them,' he answered, taking her in his arms.

In a couple of weeks, Madge had her wish fulfilled. Both farms were purchased in Phil's name, and the price she paid, because she was Madge, and felt sorry for the ones who could stand the strain no longer, was quite substantially over the asking price. She and Penny laughed among themselves to see John becoming daily more keen at the prospect of this big new adventure.

Depending on the season, whenever Phil came home for a weekend, he became an automatic choice either for the village football or cricket eleven. They all wished he could have been an ever present in both; in football, at centre forward, he was deadly; and only one person ever tried to change his approach to cricket, and that was the major.

'It's no good, Major, I couldn't alter my style of play to fancy strokes if you crowned me! It's runs that count, and that is what I'm after every time I walk to the wicket.'

They both laughed together, and the major admired him none the less for sticking to his guns.

This was more or less the pattern of Phil's life for two years, and he enjoyed every moment of it, but secretly he was looking forward to starting work in Norfolk. So, when at last that day came, he showed not the slightest sign of being downhearted, which surprised all three of them. After his first letter, telling them how much he was enjoying everything, they were really relieved.

'He's really grown up now, my dear,' said John.

'Yes, I know,' his wife answered quietly.

About this time, when Phil had been away for three months, at a young ladies' school a few miles from Spring Farm, fate had singled two people out of more than three hundred to be friends, very great friends. Jane, from the Court, and Joanna from Northwood, had been brought together at last. Both were fifteen, but there similarity ended. Jane was dark-haired, still as big a chatterbox as ever, and a tomboy. She was up to all the mischief that her wilful brain could think of. Joanna, on the other hand, was golden-haired, and was not only a lady by birth, but had been well in the forefront when Mother Nature had distributed all her richest qualities. Yet these two conflicting personalities not only got on well together, but were good for each other. One brought the other out just so far, and the other subdued the first, just enough. This was the start of a lifelong friendship, one that would be more expected of two sisters than total strangers.

During their holidays, Jane often went to stay with Joanna, or vice versa, and the older they got, the more firm became their friendship; yet in all the times Joanna visited the Court, never once did she and Phil set eyes upon each other. Jane often met him when he had occasion to see the major, and over the years, even during her most impressionable times, Phil always had that feeling that she never looked upon him as anything other than a country farmer, someone not quite her equal; though in fact he was far more grateful and proud of his station in life that she was of hers. But time would reveal that he was and would be far more of a real gentleman than the majority she would meet in her sphere of living.

So the time came when he had finished his year and a half in Norfolk, and although he had had a week's holiday every four months, it was a real bit of heaven to be home for a month in the middle of June; after that it was the time for Hampshire. He was always so full of fun and leg-pull that at Spring Farm the three of them wondered how they had existed without him. Penny came in for her share of the treatment, just the same as Madge. Only that morning she had caught him taking a couple of rock cakes that she had just made, and playfully she chased him out of the kitchen and into the yard.

When he had got a safe distance on his way to the Ridge, he turned around and, still laughing, he shouted back, 'The cakes are delicious, but not half as nice as you! Bye-bye, beautiful!'

She knew then what she would always know; it wasn't just her day he made, but her whole life.

That was how they all felt when he went to Hampshire. How they looked forward to his next homecoming! But the next year and a half simply flew by, probably due to the fact that he was not so far away, and had his own car now; and in addition he would be home for four months before starting at the Agricultural College.

Now twenty-one, and with energy to spare, Phil gave his father all the help he could, and John took the opportunity to show him all the know-how that his years of experience had stored away. Phil was so keen that he wrote everything down in a special book.

'I shall have this to compare with the college theory, for I don't suppose all their methods will suit our land, so I shall have the best of two worlds. Thank you, Dad.'

During the time that Phil was at college, Jane and Joanna had left the Cotswolds and were boarding at an exclusive ladies' finishing school on the outskirts of London. When their two years here were completed, it would be just in time for their coming-out. Looking ahead, Jane had no ambitions to do anything. Riding, tennis and parties was all she seemed to look forward to; while on the other hand, Joanna didn't like riding. She liked tennis, and was only partial to a party now and again. But she had a burning desire to do something. Actually she had set her mind on having a gown shop of her own, either in Oxford or London. They had a London house in Eaton Place, so there would be no problem about where she would stay, if she chose the city. At least she could always spend her weekends at Northwood.

This was how things went for most of those two years; Jane dreaming of the good times she would have, and Joanna thinking ever more seriously of what she had set her mind on.

The colonel had been quite agreeable to her suggestion of a gown shop in London, and he would help her find someone who had had previous experience to show her the ways of the trade.

Twilight over Spring Farm

Phil was now in his last week at college; his two years there had simply flown like the wind. What with work, sport, plenty of parties, and the opposite sex to distract him, he had been well initiated over the threshold of early manhood.

He had been home for the weekend as usual; his mother and father were going to London on the Monday, to pay their monthly visit to the business, which, after his uncle had been killed and the war finished, had gone from strength to strength.

It was the following Thursday afternoon, and a lovely day. Phil and the rest of his class were in the lecture room, all wishing that they were out in the sunshine instead of listening to the tutor for the last time. Suddenly the door opened, and in came the bursar. He spoke quietly to the tutor first, then his eyes went round the class until they rested on Phil.

'Oh, Phillip, I'd like to speak to you a moment in my office,' he said.

By the time Phil got to the door, the bursar was halfway down the corridor; he wondered what it was all about.

'Come in, Phillip, and sit down,' he said, standing aside for Phil to enter. He was a strict but kindly man, and Phil wondered which of those two attributes he was there for; but he didn't have long to wait to hear something which would drain all his strength, and numb his mind. During the few moments of silence which followed, he could sense that the bursar was under some sort of strain. Then suddenly he said, 'Phillip, four hours ago there was a serious railway accident on the London to Cheltenham line.'

Like a flash it hit him; this was the day his mother and father were returning home.

'Were my mother and father on that train?' he asked, somewhat hopelessly.

The bursar nodded his head, and with eyes downcast he went on, 'The Swindon police rang but a few minutes ago to tell me, and I am deeply sorry to have to tell you that your mother and father were two of the many victims.'

Phil was in a daze. It was so unthinkable that it just didn't seem to register. How could one lose all that one loved, by one stroke of fate? It was a question that surged through his mind time and time again.

'Can I get you a brandy or something?' asked the bursar, as he put a fatherly arm around Phil's shoulder. 'Or would you like me to get someone to run you home?'

'No thank you, sir, all I want is a few minutes in my room to pull myself together.'

'I'd much rather you stay here, Phillip, if you can manage it. It will be much better to talk than to be on your own, thinking.'

But during the next quarter of an hour, when the bursar did most of the talking, he could see what a great strain this nice young man was under. It was one thing to see a grief-stricken woman crying her heart out, but it was another thing altogether to see a strong man overcome by a tragedy such as this, fighting back the emotions which were overwhelming him.

Twenty minutes later, Phil was in his sports car, on his way home. How different he felt with the wind blowing through his hair, and cooling his face. Even so, the tears ran down his cheeks.

'Enough of that,' he said aloud to himself, for he knew he would have to steel himself to face Penny.

When he arrived, Doctor Brooks was with Penny.

'She's really overcome,' he told Phil when he asked how she was. 'And how are you, Phil?'

'Shocked and dazed beyond all measure, Doctor,' he replied.

'It seems so inadequate for me to say how terribly sorry I am, knowing what a close and happy family you were.'

'Thank you, Doctor,' Phil replied as bravely as he could, as they made their way into Penny's sitting room.

She seemed to pull herself together as he put his arm around her.

'My dear,' he said, 'somehow we've got to try to face the future together, you and I.'

She nodded, then looked up at him through tear-filled eyes. That little boy, who had unconsciously brought her through her own time of grief, needed all her comfort and understanding now. Those broad shoulders were already sagging under the strain of his great sorrow, and she knew that those were the bravest words he had spoken in his whole life.

So in the days that followed, when Phil had everything to see to, and worst of all make an identification of his parents, all her energies were directed in his direction. Mourn she did for the two she had loved; but he was alive, and had to be brought back into the world again. That was where her duty now lay, that was what his mother and father would wish her to do.

Four weeks later, when he was thinking of the time when he would have to go to review the business in London, he asked Penny if anyone slept at Spring Farm when she was on her own.

'Yes,' she answered, 'I always have Mrs White to keep me company. She does some of the housework, as you know, and being a widow she looks forward to the company as much as I do. She always has her supper and breakfast when she stays the night, that alone helps her along a bit. In fact she is always most grateful.'

'Do you think that is enough help, for this is quite a big house? Would you like your sister to come from Birmingham – that is, if she would?'

'No, there is no need for that, if I want extra help, I can always get plenty, that is if it is all right with you.'

'You're in charge here, so whatever is needed. I'll leave it to you to supply. There is no need for us to look at the pennies, or the pounds for that matter. Waste is one thing, but having what we need when we can afford it is the way that life should be lived. So I shall leave all that concerns the inside of the house in your hands.'

Preparation

To most people in Britain, the spring of 1938 was a carefree and happy time. Things were just getting into step again after the dark days of recession. To work and to enjoy oneself was the aim of most, and above all to live in peace. Was it the natural yearning for these things that was to blame for the nation's blindness to what was happening in Germany, or did people only believe what they wanted to? Some people in high places, and some in low, were guilty of this supreme folly.

But over in Germany, in the little village of Niendorff, Fritz and Eva Hanhart were more than aware of the inhuman treatment going on around them. To speak a wrong word, even in their tiny village, could mean your life, and the trouble was, the whole village knew how Fritz had praised the British for the way they had treated him when he was wounded and a prisoner. That alone left him as naked as the day he was born to questioning. If anyone let his feelings be known, he knew he'd get no mercy from the types who were looking for trouble. Fritz wasn't worried over his own skin, but there was Eva, and more especially the joy of both their lives, Chrysta. She was, at sixteen, beautiful beyond words in all things, an obvious target for some of those whom they had heard about. Talking it over with Eva, they decided it would be a good plan to have a hiding place, for they were determined that no harm should come to Chrysta, even if they had to die preventing it.

After a careful study of the house, and the farm buildings which adjoined, Fritz came to his decision. The outbuilding joined the kitchen wall where the big oak dresser stood. It was a fixture, and that made this the ideal step for what he had in mind. His plan was to build a false wall in the outbuilding six foot from the existing one. Then, if he whitewashed the whole inside of the shed, no one would know the new wall from the old, especially if he copied the old work as near as possible. That would be one side dealt with, but he knew he would have to summon all his skill to make a first class job of the entrance through the dresser. It would have to be some simple way, as the more complicated it was, the greater the chance of things going wrong if there ever came a time of crisis. The lower half of the dresser had an open compartment at each end; the centre section had a door, but it didn't take him long to decide that the best place was the open end, which was hidden when the kitchen door was open. The hardest and trickiest part was cutting the back of the dresser out; this had to be done perfectly, for when it was replaced the joint had to be as nearly invisible as possible. Then he had to make the hole in the wall. Once that was done, he was able by the light of a lantern to re-fix the back of the dresser as a door which opened into the hideaway. Then he shuttered and made good the wall.

All this took him weeks, but he hadn't finished yet; the hideaway wasn't safe enough as it was. So out in the yard he made a box the exact size of the wall opening, and with some old gate hinges, he was going to cast a concrete door, which he would make in the hideaway on the spot. Three weeks later he had finished, and was more than a little proud of his handiwork, but what pleased him as much as anything was when he tapped the entrance of the hideaway from the kitchen, it gave the same solid sound as the rest of the dresser. In the hideaway itself, the concrete door worked perfectly, and the iron bar which swivelled across it like a giant bolt slid into position between cloth-covered jaws as silent as the night. The three spyholes he made, one through the carving on the dresser, and two looking out into the yard, not only provided tiny shafts of light, but also kept the air moving; only a tiny touch of stain was needed to cover up his handiwork on the face of the dresser.

Everything needed in an emergency was ready inside the hideaway, and they soon became experts in the art of disappearing, with not the slightest thing showing amiss from the outside. But still they heard of things which made them shudder and feel uneasy; so much so, that they both impressed upon Chrysta that if she ever heard either of them call out 'King Charles' in English, she was to hide as quickly as possible. They had decided on that call sign, for he was the king who had hidden in an oak tree. And although they talked a lot in English, it was only when they knew no one would overhear them, so if they used English, it would alert Chrysta more quickly. That was all they could do, and at least they felt a little more at ease now that their plans were made.

Back at Spring Farm, Phil was in a different kind of preparation, getting ready for a future that he had been trained for, but one which had come all too soon for his liking. He just threw himself into the running of the farms to help ease the great loss which he had suffered, but often the men would see him just walking aimlessly across the fields, when his grief suddenly became too much for him to bear in front of anyone else. But he was wise enough to have his relaxation. He loved sport, which was one good thing, and the two or three days at the business in London were a blessing in disguise. Whereas over the years he had been known as a 'good honest flirt', he still took out different girls now; but the competition seemed to be getting keener, and 'wedding bells' were the farthest thing from his mind.

'An exceptionally good catch', was the phrase Penny had heard, and she repeated it to him when she chided him over all his girlfriends.

'There's not one out of the whole number that I would want to marry, nice as they are,' he replied.

'That may be so,' she answered, 'but I shall be glad when you are happily married to some nice girl, I shan't worry so much on my days off, or when I go on holiday.'

'There's not the slightest need for you to worry over me, Penny. You know I can do a bit of cooking at a push, and when you go on holiday in three weeks' time, Mrs White can get my breakfast. I can go to town for lunch if I haven't got time to get my own, and I'm sure I can manage the rest myself.'

As the time drew nearer for her holiday, the busier Penny became. She was going to make sure that there were enough of all sorts of her cooking to last Phil as long as possible, but deep inside she knew he wouldn't go hungry.

The First Sight of Heaven

It had been cloudy and wet for almost a week, but two days before Penny was due to go on holiday the sky cleared, and better weather seemed to be a certainty for this early June. Now, on the morning of her departure and a few minutes before eleven, Phil was putting her two suitcases in the seat of his two-seater sports. He was taking her to The Junction seven miles from Tetstone, to catch her train to Birmingham, where her sister would meet her by car. They had just gone through the village with the beautiful countryside opening up before them, the smell of new-mown hay hung heavy in the air, and the whole world seemed alive with the joy of living. They were just relishing this to the full when round the second bend and only half a mile from home they saw Major Marchant's car. It was at a standstill, with two of the occupants half hidden under the bonnet.

Phil pulled up and asked, 'Is there much wrong?'

'I'm sure it's engine trouble, Phil,' replied the major.

'Well, I'm awfully sorry, I can't give you a hand, as I've only got enough time to get Penny to The Junction to catch her train to Birmingham, but if you like I'll pop into the garage and ask them to send someone up.'

'If you've got time, Phil, I'd be very grateful, for I think that is the best plan,' answered the major.

He was just on the point of moving off, when Jane Marchant, who was in the back of the car, suddenly said, 'As you're going to The Junction, I wonder if you would collect my friend Miss Shand and give her a lift back, for it doesn't look as though this car will get there today, or tomorrow!'

'Certainly,' Phil shouted as he put the car into gear.

'She's golden-haired,' Jane called, leaning out of the window.

Phil signalled his understanding by putting his hand up. At the same time he felt quite relieved to think that it was impossible to offer her a lift, as his car was full up already, and the less he had to put up with Jane Marchant's spoilt snobbish attitude, the better.

It took him only half a minute to deliver the message at the garage, then it was open country once more. They arrived at The Junction before the express got in, and Phil carried Penny's cases to the far end of the platform, as she always liked to travel in the front of the train.

However, they had only a three or four-minute wait before the train arrived. Luckily he found her a compartment with only two more ladies in, so she was sure of a corner seat.

'You'll be quite comfortable,' he said as he stood on the platform.

'Yes, it couldn't be better, thank you,' Penny answered.

The whistle blew. Phil kissed her, wishing her a happy holiday, and pressed an envelope in her hand, at the same time saying, 'A bit of spending money.'

It was too late for her to protest, as the train had started on its way. All she could do was to wave back at him, until the line curved in the distance and they lost each other.

He was thinking that he just couldn't imagine what he would do without her. He could manage quite well while she was on holiday, but Penny had always been a blessing to Spring Farm, and now she was the mainstay as well. He turned to walk down the platform and there, waiting at the far end, a little beyond the exit, stood a lone figure.

She had her back to him, but as he drew closer he could see the sun reflecting from the loveliest golden hair he had ever seen, and he took note of the figure. She was beautifully attired in a lovely pale blue costume, one which moulded itself to each rare curve with delicate perfection. Swiftly his approving eyes moved once more from head to foot, and instantly he became sure of two things. Firstly, if her facial beauty matched what he had already beheld, then this lovely creation must be a goddess, for only a goddess could look so divine; and secondly, that while his eyes glided admiringly over this sight, his instincts told him that the sheer natural elegance which shone out like a bright glowing light was something that was always there, no matter how the figure was adorned.

'Far better than Venus,' he almost said aloud, and with each step taking him nearer, he became aware of a tumultuous feeling, like a man who has searched long and is now on the threshold of making his great discovery.

'Excuse me, are you Miss Shand?' he asked, as he reached her side.

Joanna turned, a little startled. 'Yes,' she answered, and as their eyes met for the first time, his gaze dwelt upon loveliness of such rare perfection, that he had never thought it possible to exist.

For quite some time, being confronted by such unbelievable beauty, his whole world stood still, as fleeting thoughts of wonder and admiration raced across his mind. For those few moments he was lost, lost, but in a sunnier and happier dream world than he had known before. Then, with the return of his normal friendly personality, he introduced himself.

'I'm Phil Fraser,' he said. Then, stretching out his hand, which she took a little nervously, he explained 'the major's car has broken down half a mile from the Court, and seeing I was on my way here, Jane Marchant asked me if I would give you a lift back.'

'Thank you very much, it is very kind of you,' she answered.

Being him, he just couldn't resist a chance like this. Picking up her large suitcase with the right hand, he tucked the smaller one under the same arm, then with his left hand holding her arm, as though he had every right in the world to, he led her out to the red sports car.

Well-mannered as always, he hurriedly put the cases on the dicky seat, then went round to her side to open and shut the door once she was settled in. On leaving The Junction, he enquired to how long she was staying.

'For three weeks,' she answered. 'But I have often stayed for a fortnight in the past, as a matter of fact. I love this part of the country.' Then almost in the same breath she asked, 'Do you live in Beversbury?'

'Oh yes,' he answered, 'I was born there, I'm farming over on the other side of the Court. Perhaps that is why I have never had the pleasure of meeting you before, its only the major that I go to see occasionally – not Jane.'

She laughed with him at that one. Then the conversation turned to how lovely the weather had been during last few days, and as they talked on, so could he sense a more friendly atmosphere between them. Then, when he stopped so that they could watch an aircraft land at the aerodrome, one second his eyes were on the aircraft, and the other on that wonderful profile of hers, and once again he realised she was much more than he had seen before, much more than he had ever dreamed of.

Suddenly his eyes were glued on her hands, as almost unconsciously she slipped off her fine white gloves. No, there was no ring on the finger that mattered; as a matter of fact, no ring of any sort on either hand. It was beyond his comprehension that someone so lovely and enchanting as this should be unattached.

'I'm sorry I kept you waiting at the station,' he said, but I had to see my housekeeper off on her holidays.'

'That's quite all right,' Joanna answered. 'But I was beginning to wonder what had happened until you came along.'

Her smile came more readily now, and he was in a dream world, a world which he had never known before, with all the other girls he had been out with. After a few more minutes of watching another aircraft take off, and a little more conversation, they started on their way once more.

'Well, there's one thing, if you do get bored with nothing to do, you can always be my housekeeper, till Penny comes back! Three pounds ten a week – not as much as you would get in London, but think of the fresh air for nothing!'

She laughed aloud at this, and more so when he added, 'I should have asked if you can cook, before offering that big wage.'

'I can, but only a little,' she managed to get out.

The rest of the journey went far too quickly for him. He wondered, was she enjoying it as much as he was, or would she be glad when they reached the Court?

'The major's car has gone,' he told her as they passed the spot, and within minutes they were going up the drive to the Court. He got out, quickly opened the door, and was helping her out when the major, Mrs Marchant and Jane arrived on the scene to greet her. Phil greeted them all as usual, then proceeded to get the luggage out of the dicky.

'Come in and have a drink, Phil,' suggested the major.

'Thank you, Major, I'd appreciate one very much. It's rather thirsty weather.' Phil followed them in; they turned left and went down to the far end of the big hall, the bare oak floor shining like a mirror in the sunlight, to the drawing room. Mrs Marchant and Jane had sherry, but Joanna refused, saying, 'I'd much rather have a glass of orange juice, if I may, I'm feeling more like a long drink after the journey.' The major and Phil had a small beer each.

'Thanks for calling at the garage Phil,' said the major. 'They were out and towed us back in no time.'

'You know, Major,' replied Phil, with his face beaming, 'I've told you before that those foreign cars aren't reliable, you'll have to get a good English one!'

'I'm beginning to think you're right, Phil, this is the third time it has let us down in a matter of weeks,' observed Mrs Marchant.

'Well, let's get off that sore point,' said the major, 'and talk about cricket. We haven't got a match for three weeks, but we are at home for the next one. And by the way, Phil, don't forget it's the cricket dance a week on Friday... we should make a good profit if there are as many as last year.'

'I won't forget, Major. For one thing, I've heard it's a much better dance band than last year. But there is one thing I meant to mention before, do you think it would be a good idea if we went a little further with the refreshments – more fancy things and suchlike?'

'Yes, I think it's a good idea, Phil,' Mrs Marchant agreed. 'Most people appreciate the more delicate things when they are out for the evening enjoying themselves.'

'That's the weekend when Gerald is coming,' said Jane, looking at Joanna. 'I've been expecting to hear of the engagement at any time,' replied Joanna, smiling back at her.

The major coughed a trifle unnaturally before he said, 'It's about time! It's three years since he first came here. Some of the young ones these days want a bomb under them... and by the way, Phil, isn't it time you looked out a nice girl and settled down?'

It was Mrs Marchant who answered him. '*You* married when you wanted to, or should I say when I decided to say "yes", so it's up to everyone to do the same!'

The major laughed with everyone else, even though it was at

his own expense.

Whenever it had been possible, and often when it was not, Phil had found his eyes drawn towards that beautiful face almost opposite him; but it wasn't only her dazzling beauty which almost took command of him, it was those fleeting moments when their eyes met. Whatever message those beautiful pools of mystery held could only be guesswork, and he was left wondering.

'Well, I must be going,' he said, drinking the last of his beer and getting up. He wished the three ladies good day, and was just thanking the major for the beer, when Joanna said to Jane, 'I'll change before lunch.'

So saying, she picked up her handbag, but those fine white gloves were nowhere to be found. Turning to Phil, she said, 'I must have dropped my gloves in your car. Can I get them?'

'I will,' he answered. He crossed the glass-like front hall in a few seconds and out to the car. The gloves were down the side of the seat and still spotless; he had just got back to the front door as Joanna reached the inner one, which meant their meeting place just had to be in the porch.

'Lost and found, on the floor and not a speck of dust on them,' he said smiling.

'Thank you very much,' she replied returning his smile.

Phil held out his hand to wish her goodbye, saying as he did so, 'I hope the weather will continue to be really gorgeous for you, so that you will have a most enjoyable time, and I would be telling a lie if I said I wasn't looking forward very much to meeting you again.'

All this time his eyes had once more been flitting over this face of angelic beauty, only to halt as they became united in a bond of unspoken love with hers. Her loveliness, her magnetism, the pureness of her personality, drew him like a moth to the flame. As far as he was concerned, the first of the barriers were banished between them. The next thing he did was something he would most surely have done in one of his devil-may-care moods, but what made him do it at this early moment and with this almost unknown girl who seemed so reserved he would never know. Quite gently, he put his hands on the top of her arms, drew her towards him and kissed her. His lips held hers for a little longer than ten seconds. She made no attempt to deny him; her eyes were closed as he looked down at her, and once more his gaze was transfixed on this face of breathtaking beauty, which now held a look of deep contentment.

'Perfectly divine, the most delicious lips and intoxicating perfume,' he whispered, smiling as he released her.

Then he made his way out to the car, got in and switched on. But before he started the engine, he looked back at the doorway. Joanna was still standing there, still lost for words, and looking somewhat dazed. With all the humour that was possible beaming on his face, he said, 'If you do happen to consider my offer, it's worth at least seven pounds a week now!'

Waving to her, he started the engine and was soon away down the drive.

So Much in Love

As Joanna made her way upstairs, her mind was in a whirl at the sudden change in her life; had she been taken so unaware that she had failed to realise what this almost unknown young man had accomplished, when no one else had dared? She went into her room; the maid had unpacked and departed. Why was her heart beating so fast? It wasn't just walking up the stairs; she knew she was quite capable of running up them without all the tumult that was going on inside her at the moment. Was she on the verge of falling in love, or had she already fallen? She looked at her watch, it was just an hour ago that she had been standing at the station. She suddenly remembered how she could hardly tear her eyes from his, at that first moment of impact, how those first few words somehow had to be forced out, and how her legs had seemed to turn to jelly.

Now in her heart she realised what had happened to her in so short a time. He hadn't swept away her defences with sheer strength. They had just melted, from the friendly way he had talked to her, the naturalness of his manner – and, she somehow knew, the honest sincerity of his feelings. This was something that had always been there, and always would be; she knew those qualities were what she would have looked for, but up till now that had been the furthest thing from her mind.

He was also very handsome, and every inch a man. She had taken a long time changing and now she was gazing out of the window, lost in all thoughts, except the thrill of his kiss. How long would it be before she would meet him again? It could be that they might never meet again; their paths hadn't crossed until today.

'Oh no,' she whispered aloud to herself. Surely life could never be so cruel as that? Could it really be that she had been in his company for so short a time, yet was willing to spend the rest of her life with him? She had no way of seeing him. She might, with luck, if the major took them to the cricket dance, but that was a week on Friday and this was only Tuesday. She must not let Jane even dream what had happened to her, so she would have to take that faraway thoughtful look from her face before going downstairs. During lunch, try as she might, she couldn't completely stamp out those tormenting thoughts from coming back, and she almost missed out on the conversation twice. She knew she would have to take more control of herself and only let her dreams come back when she was alone for any length of time!

Every morning she went into Tetstone with Jane to do some shopping, but so far she had not caught sight of Phil. Now this was the third time and it was Friday. Would she be lucky enough to see him today? She hoped and prayed so! Meanwhile, the last three days had been an endless time of frustration for Phil. Not one excuse could be found to go to the Court; no cricket match this week, no village meeting, not anything that would give him the chance to see the most wonderful girl he had ever set eyes on – the one who made his heart miss a beat every time he thought of her, much less the sweetness of her lips. However, he always went to Tetstone on Fridays to draw the men's wages. He had already been to the bank and was on his way to the post office; hope had almost gone, for he had looked in every shop which he thought Jane was likely to visit. Was it fate or lady luck that smiled on him? For as he went round the corner he almost bumped into the two girls.

After the usual greetings he said to Joanna, 'So you are seeing the sight of our big city?'

'Yes,' she replied smiling, 'and we've not been lost once!'

Jane, a little more amiable than usual, chimed in, 'Well, if we did get lost, we could always depend on you to come and find us, just as you helped out on Tuesday.'

'Frankly I couldn't think of anything better then if you'd both come and have coffee or a sherry with me now.'

'We'd love to,' Jane replied, much to his surprise, and judging by the look on Joanna's face, he couldn't have suggested anything more wonderful. All through this brief conversation his eyes had delved into that beautiful face as often and as long as it was safe to do with Jane present. Her loveliness charmed him each time his uncontrollable eyes strayed in her direction.

He ushered them into the coffee room at a nearby hotel, and much to his delight, Jane chose to go to the far end, away from the half-dozen or so people who were already there. He ordered coffee for them, and the conversation went mostly about the new car that the major had ordered. Then Jane switched to the subject of riding, and how she wished Joanna would go with her. Just then the coffee arrived.

'That reminds me,' she went on, 'I wonder if you would excuse me if I popped out to the saddlers to see if a bit of harness is ready. I've overlooked it all the week and I can manage that while the coffee is cooling.'

'Certainly,' said Phil, standing up and thinking, *this must be my lucky day*!

Jane had hardly disappeared out of the doorway before the heartaches of the last three days started to become a thing of the past. Joanna had one hand on the table, and reaching forward, he took it in his, asking, 'Am I forgiven, or have I got to apologise?'

Not only looking, but feeling far happier that she had ever felt before, Joanna replied, 'There's no need to apologise, but you don't exactly let the grass grow under your feet, as the saying goes...'

Both of them had to restrain themselves from bursting out laughing. The ice was really broken now, and they were completely at ease in each other's company. However, a sorrowful look came over his face as he said, 'I don't know if I have any right to say this, but these last three days have been absolute torment to me, the thought of not knowing when I should see you again, or if at all, and the worst part, being so desperately in love with you and not knowing if you gave me even a second thought.'

With a look full of understanding and tenderness on her beautiful face, she replied, 'If I told you that it has been the same for me, would that make your anxiety any better?'

'Do you really mean that, my love?' he asked pleadingly.

'Yes, my darling, every word is from the bottom of my heart,' she answered, lowering her eyes to look at his big strong hand holding hers.

'You're an angel – my angel,' he said quietly and sincerely, as he leaned a bit further across the table. Then he continued, 'Until now I have never thought much about "love at first sight", but I know I was half in love with you as I walked down the platform towards you. Then, as you turned around when our eyes met for the first time, suddenly the world I had known vanished and a far more wonderful one took its place. I knew I was completely and utterly yours, willing to be your slave for the rest of my life.'

'My darling,' she answered, 'whatever touched your head and your heart touched mine as well, but that is how it can happen, though it's not often. Far too many people marry and yet never know what true love really is, and yet two strangers can come face to face and just for a second their eyes meet… and there is more true love and understanding recognised in that brief moment than a lot of people are capable of finding together in a lifetime. The eyes are the windows of the soul, the deeper you see the truer the love, so if that is the love that I have for you, and you have for me, then darling, we are really blessed among many.'

Life at that moment seemed a little cruel to them. All they could do was to watch a true and desperate love for each other eating their hearts out. Only as she put her other hand on the top of his in a tender caress, did the longing for each other's arms cease.

'There is so much I must ask you before Jane comes back,' he said, half pleadingly. 'Do you come into town every morning?'

'Yes, so far we have,' she replied.

'Only, if we can't get a few moments like this on our own, how can I get in touch with you once you have gone back?' he asked.

'I know your name,' she answered, 'and I have in a roundabout way found out the name of your farm… also that you are known as the biggest flirt for miles around!'

They both laughed as he answered, 'Not any more! It could be that I was searching for you, my love, and I must say that I certainly found you when I least expected it. Now, before Jane comes back, I must tell you that I love you with all my heart and I'm just longing to really hold you in my arms and to give you a much better kiss than the last one.'

'Is that possible?' she asked.

'Definitely, my darling,' he answered, as Jane came through the door.

'Well, I must say you both look pleased with life,' she said, smiling quite radiantly herself.

'Yes,' Phil answered, 'we've been talking about the weather; a lovely sunny morning and a smile on the face go well together.'

'Tell me another,' Jane replied amid laughter. 'Besides, you've hardly touched your coffee.'

'We thought it good manners to wait until you returned,' he answered, amid more laughter.

When they were ready to leave, Jane did what Phil hoped she would do; she led the way, and he then held Joanna's hand, caressing it gently, and once more he was reassured that her love for him was as deep as his own was for her, reassured by the way she returned his caress and the loving smile on her face as she looked at him. All this sealed that kiss of three days ago and the future, which now looked endless before them.

Outside both girls thanked him.

'The pleasure's all mine,' he replied, 'I've really enjoyed it. Without you two young ladies, I wouldn't appreciate going in for a cup of coffee, and I don't make a habit of daytime drinking, so I hope we meet again soon.'

As they said goodbye, the look in Joanna's eyes told him that she hoped it would be soon, very soon.

The next morning he was out of luck; they were nowhere to be found in any of the shops. He was disappointed, as his next hope would be at church tomorrow morning, and that seemed an endless time away. He felt loath to go anywhere where there were a lot of people; seeing other fellows with their girlfriends would only make matters worse, so he roamed the fields getting lost in the Creator's handiwork as much as possible, marvelling at the hills and dales and all things that sprung from the good earth.

Sunday morning arrived, and how the minutes dragged from the time he was ready until it was time to go! How he felt as he walked up the lane he couldn't have explained to anyone; there was nothing definite in front of him. Would she be in church was the first burning question? If so, would she see him – and oh, if he could only speak to her! That would be another time when his eyes would pour out the yearnings of his heart, and his lips would only be able to say 'good morning'.

His first prayer was answered. The major's pew was occupied; next to the major was Mrs Marchant, then Jane and then Joanna. Phil sat on the opposite side and behind a little. He knelt down, paid his homage to God and as he sat up he glanced over to the other side, as he did so, Jane looked round and across to him. The vicar was leaning over talking to the major. Phil saw Jane turn and speak to Joanna, and instantly that beautiful face turned in his direction. He bowed his head in acknowledgement, but only so far, lest the vision of all he held dear be cut off for even a second. The smile she gave him made a mockery of all the suffering that was his; there was her greeting, the longing for his arms, and her undying love all rolled into one.

He wondered why Jane had told Joanna he was there, and all through the service, try as he might, he just couldn't stop his eyes from straying towards that lovely golden hair, which was gleaming in the sunlight. When the service was over he lingered as long as possible, and was glad when old Mrs Jones stopped and asked him if Penny was on holiday. By the time he was free, quite a few people were gathered outside talking. The major and Mrs Marchant were well occupied, and he was surprised when Jane and Joanna made a beeline straight in his direction. They exchanged greetings in the usual way, then quickly Joanna said, 'Darling, I've told Jane about us.'

'That is only partly true,' Jane interrupted. 'I had a strong feeling on Tuesday and again on Friday that you two meant a little more to each other than just casual acquaintances; you don't know a person as long as I've known Joanna without noticing each little change, so I just couldn't miss something as big as this, could I? Well, I asked her, or I don't think she would have told me.' Looking straight at Phil she continued, 'I'll do all I can for the both of you, but Phil, you must promise me to take the greatest care of her.'

'You know I will,' he answered, 'and you can rest assured on this I am in love for the first time in my life – and with someone far more precious to me than anything else in the whole world.'

'Then it's coffee tomorrow – same place, eleven o'clock!' said Jane briskly.

'I can only thank you with all my heart, I didn't expect anything nearly as wonderful as this,' Phil answered.

With Jane covering them from the major's view as much as possible, and with the happiness on their faces a joy to each other, this desperate love of theirs was beginning to see light. It might be only a chink, but it was a start.

Holding Joanna's hand, Phil said, 'What wouldn't I give for the rest of the day to be ours? I shall be counting the minutes, the hours, knowing all the while that I have to exist until tomorrow, knowing that my next ray of sunshine can only come when you are standing before me again, my love.'

'I shall be longing for tomorrow just as desperately, my darling,' Joanna answered.

'Till then, my love,' he said, as the major started to look around.

'And may it come quickly, my darling,' Joanna replied.

Phil was up early the next morning, getting as much of his work done as quickly as possible. Whatever happened, nothing must make him late to meet the light of his life. By 10.50 a.m., he was outside the hotel sitting in his car, but he was only there a few minutes before they drew up behind him. Quickly he got out and went to meet them.

After the usual greetings, Jane said, 'I was just thinking, if you two go and order the coffee while I go to the shop, it will give my coffee a chance to cool a little and for you two love-birds to have a cosy chat.'

Smiling, they both thanked her. They chose the same table as before, and they were alone. The same waitress approached and Joanna ordered the coffee, and Phil held her hand as soon as the waitress had disappeared.

'Have you missed me very much, my love?' he asked.

'You know I have, my darling, it has seemed like a lifetime from yesterday, but we are together now and life is so wonderful,' she answered, caressing his hand with both of hers.

'I know, my love,' he answered, 'but life can be so cruel when you think about it. If we have a few moments like this on our own each morning, I doubt if there's another two people who will have poured more of their hearts out to each other, or been more desperately in love than us, and with only one small kiss to show for it.'

'That's probably the best way in the end, my love,' she said, as the coffee arrived. As soon as they were on their own again, she placed her hand over his once more and said, 'I don't think I can accept your offer, my love, of looking after you while Penny is away. But if the major and Mrs Marchant go out long enough one day, Jane is going to work out how I can come over to see Spring Farm – that is, if you can find the time at short notice.'

'That's the best bit of news you could give me,' he answered, 'and as regards finding the time, all the time belongs to you my love, you know that!'

They were still full of laughter and love when Jane came in, and they were so thankful now that they didn't have to pretend in front of her. She was the most vital part in their secret, the part that would bring their first real kiss closer than anything.

So the days went by, Jane had given them their few minutes of heaven each morning and now it was Friday, the day of the cricket dance, and once again she had laid all their plans.

'Gerald is coming this afternoon, so tonight at the dance if we talk as a foursome, Daddy is not likely to suspect anything.'

To Phil, the difference in Jane was so surprising; she was so helpful and so understanding that he had already altered his opinion of her considerably. As the rest of the day progressed, so was he looking forward more and more to whatever joys the evening would hold; but at six o'clock his stockman rang to say that one of their finest Jersey cows was in difficulty having her calf.

'I'll ring the vet at once,' Phil answered, 'and I'll be with you as soon as possible.'

It took the three of them, with all their experience and knowledge, to save both the cow and the calf, and it was gone nine o'clock by the time Phil reached home to bath and change. Being late, he drove down, and just as he pulled up, he could hear the band coming to the end of a foxtrot. He went in through the side door. The hall was crowded, a group of people were standing in front of him and for a while he was quite content to be almost hidden as he gazed around the room looking for his first and only love. He could just see the major's party, which included most of their local friends, but he noticed that Joanna was however looking towards the main doors at the other end of the hall.

The band struck up a dreamy waltz and the floor began to fill. The major's party were already on the floor as Phil made his way around the side; only Joanna still sat there, still with her eyes fixed towards the main doors. He reached her side just as she turned in his direction. Her eyes held the fullness of relief as she rose and whispered, 'My darling.'

'My love,' he answered, and then added, 'May I have the pleasure?' – which seemed a bit unnecessary, for they were already in each other's arms.

'I'm so glad you are here, my love,' she whispered in his ear, as they drifted round the edge of the room.

'We've had a spot of trouble on the farm, but I'm pleased to say that mother and daughter were doing fine when the three of us left.'

'Good,' she answered, and for the first time she felt the thrill of his strong arms around her, as he guided her expertly around the outside of the crowded floor.

'If we stay on the outside, I can prevent you from getting kicked, and we can talk much better without being heard,' he said. Then he went on, 'This is the second time I've kept you waiting, my love. Did you think I wasn't going to turn up?'

'I was much more worried this time than the last, my love, I knew it was you that I was waiting for this time, but the joy of this moment has banished all the fears I had,' she whispered.

He held her closer, fully realising just how much of heaven he held in his arms, and whispered, 'You're my angel.'

'So are you my angel too,' she replied and he felt her arm tighten around his shoulder.

'This may not be the finest dance we shall go to, but it will always be the most wonderful, the fact of being in each other's arms for the first time will make it one of our most sacred memories,' he said, as he held her close once more, and the waltz came to an end.

Jane came threading her way through the crowd, bringing Gerald, whom she introduced to Phil.

'You were late tonight, Phil, did the car break down?' she asked laughing.

'No,' answered Joanna, 'domestic trouble on the farm, but it's all right now.'

'Anyway,' said Jane, 'there's a big enough crowd here tonight for you to almost get lost in.'

'I don't think we'll try that, for I'm sure the major has seen us together already, and he might start wondering if we disappeared,' said Phil, as the next dance started.

Occasionally they had a rest and talked. That was one good thing, the refreshments were a good excuse to be a little more on their own, but the night slipped away all too quickly for them. Soon the last waltz had been given out, and the lights were always dimmed for this one. Each time round, at one darker corner than the rest, their lips met; each time he held her close and each time she showed her love for him, with the pressure of her arm over his shoulder.

'I shall always remember this night, my love,' she said at the end. 'I shall always treasure the joy of our first few hours together.'

'All I hope,' he answered, 'is that the next bit of heaven comes very soon.' Then he added, 'I'd love to be able to see you home, my darling, but I know that is out of the question... so it's eleven o'clock in the morning as usual, but I'm staying with you now as long as possible.'

So they held hands outside, talking to Jane and Gerald until the major and Mrs Marchant appeared.

'Hell's bells!' said the major. 'I've hardly seen you all night, Phil, in that crowd – a great success, I should say.'

They all agreed that it was, and the farewells came soon after.

The next morning, Phil was in his usual place waiting for them, and as before almost on the dot they pulled up behind him. Gerald seemed a little more friendly as they greeted each other this morning.

'Do you mind if we can't give you a few minutes on your own this morning,' said Jane, 'only we haven't a lot of time and I've got something to tell you.'

'Certainly not,' answered Phil. 'I'm more than grateful for what you have done already.'

They went into the coffee room and ordered. While the waitress was present they talked about the dance, but as soon as she had gone Jane said, 'Now, Phil, Daddy has had a phone message this morning that his brother has had an accident, so the position is this; Mummy and Daddy are going to London tonight, leaving about seven; if Uncle isn't very ill they will be back to be met at The Junction tomorrow at 9.30 p.m. We can't do much about this evening, but the three of us have talked it over and decided that we all go to church in the morning as usual, then Gerald will take me out to lunch and so forth, and you can take Joanna wherever you decide. But there are two musts; one, we will bring Joanna to the entrance of your drive, where you will be waiting in your car; and secondly, a greater must, don't be later than 9.30 p.m., at that same place, so that we can pick Joanna up.'

'I really don't know how to thank you,' Phil answered, beaming at them all each in turn, and giving Joanna's hand, which he had been holding all the time, an extra squeeze, while both their faces were alight with happiness as they looked at each other.

Sunday dawned, and it was a beautiful day. Phil felt on top of the world as he got his breakfast. He didn't think he had left anything undone; he had booked lunch at his favourite hotel, The Calling Seagull. There, from the dining room, the River Severn glistened like a silver ribbon in the distance. Then if Joanna wanted, they could have tea somewhere nearer home, or if she would rather come back to Spring Farm he had prepared a dish of fruit salad and a jug of the finest cream; the chicken now cooking would be cold for supper, and with all the other tasty things that went to make up a delicious meal. He was well satisfied, and more than glad that his mother and Penny had showed him the right way to look after himself.

Everything was ready, and by 10.50 a.m., he had locked up and was in his car on his way to church. The three of them were already there, and just as before she turned and looked across at him, there was no mistaking it, there was a lot more extra joy and happiness on her beautiful face this morning. After the service, there was not much time for words when they met outside, but the joy of the next few hours together alone at last was overwhelming.

'We'll be there in five minutes,' said Jane.

Off he went, and in no time had reversed just inside the drive of Spring Farm. He got out to wait for them, and when they arrived he opened the door and took Joanna by the hand for a graceful exit. Then they both thanked Jane and hoped they would have a lovely time.

'The same to you,' came the joint reply as they moved off.

Their eyes sparkled as they walked arm in arm to his car.

'I can hardly believe it, my love,' he said. 'Nine whole hours together after all that loneliness…'

'Nine whole hours of heaven, my darling,' she replied, as he sat beside her. Cramped though it was, love soon found a way for their aching arms to encircle each other, and for hungry lips to find a bit of heaven in a long and tender kiss. As they moved off, he told her where they were going for lunch, then he asked her if she would rather have tea out or come back to Spring Farm, where they could either have a short walk before tea or a longer one between tea and supper.

'I'd much rather go back to Spring Farm, if it's all right with you, my love, for I'm dying to see the place that must be you,' she answered.

'Well, it's your day, my darling. Whatever you choose, I'll try to make it the happiest day of your life,' he said giving her a loving smile.

She fell in love with the hotel the moment she saw it.

THE CALLING SEAGULL, she read out, as she saw the large gold letters that took up two-thirds of the length of the building. Then she continued, 'I feel a bit like a seagull myself, darling, so high up, and with a view such as this.'

'You're much more wonderful than any seagull,' he answered, smiling and catching hold of her arm. 'And the view from the dining room is even better.'

The lunch turned out to be as fantastic as the surroundings, and he could tell that, like himself, she savoured each precious moment as something special and heavenly. Later, during coffee, as they gazed out of the window to the strip of water which shimmered in the sunlight, he knew her desperation for a shared embrace was as great as his.

'You know, darling, I've never seen it look as beautiful as this before today,' he said. 'But then, I've never been in love before... it must be that your beauty brings out the best in everything in my eyes.'

She blushed a little at his compliment, and so they talked on, but it was inevitable that sooner or later their families would have to come into the conversation. Jane had told her about the tragic way he had lost his mother and father.

'I know what half of your grief is like, my love, and that is bad enough,' Joanna said. 'I have a stepmother; my own died when I was born, and every day I miss her just as much, and try to conjure up in my mind what she would look like at the present time... That reminds me, there is one thing I must tell you, my love, it wouldn't be fair to you if I didn't. You see, there is a curse or hoodoo, or whatever you like to call it, on my mother's side of the family. No female has ever reached the age of thirty for generations, so I couldn't have you risking your happiness unless you are prepared to face whatever might come.'

'It could be coincidence, my love; you'll probably live to be a hundred now that you've got my strong arms to take care of you.'

'So you'll still risk the rest of your future with me, darling, in spite of what has happened in the past?'

'Couldn't think of changing my mind for the whole world, my precious one,' he answered, smiling.

Reassured, she smiled lovingly back at him.

Once outside, they walked around the grounds, still taking in the wonderful view. He had his arm through hers while he pointed out the various places to her with the other. But it was not long before he turned to her and asked, 'Are you ready to go, my love?'

'Whenever you are, my darling,' she answered almost

subconsciously.

On the way back he asked her if she liked working in London.

'Not really,' she answered. 'Most weekends I go down to Northwood, rather than stay in London, but I'm wondering if you think you will be able to come up sometimes if I stay more often?'

'I always have two or three days in London once a month, but if you promise to meet me and give me a kiss on the station, I'll definitely manage one day a week. I'm so much in love with you, my darling, that I just couldn't wait to find another porch, before taking you in my arms.'

'You know I will, my love,' she answered, and briefly a lovely smile was exchanged between them.

They were now on the last few yards of their journey.

'Here we are, home at last,' he said, switching off and getting out.

He hurried round to open the door and help her out. Her eyes lit up as she saw how spick and span everything was.

'It's lovely, darling, really lovely!' she exclaimed.

'I hope you will like the rest of it as much,' he replied, leading her towards the door.

'May I carry the bride over the threshold?' he asked playfully.

'Not for a little while, my darling,' she answered, holding his arm more tightly to her.

'Only a little while?' he asked playfully.

'Yes, my love,' she answered.

'A year?' he asked again, as they walked with arms around each other into the front hall.

All her emotions seemed to rush to the surface as she replied, 'There is nothing more I want, my darling, than to be your bride before the end of this year. The love I have for means I cannot bear for us to be parted a moment longer than is necessary.'

The kiss that followed seemed to her as wonderful as it was inevitable, and as he still held her he whispered, 'Do you really think that you could give up working in London, and two wonderful homes, my love, all for my sake and the quietness of a country farm?'

'Wherever you are, my darling, that is not only where I want to be, but where I must be,' she answered, closing her eyes as his lips touched hers, this time in a slightly deeper kiss.

Her eyes lit up as he showed her over the house. 'It's all so lovely! Three beautiful bathrooms, and the rest so tastefully furnished to look like a real home, and all so cosy,' she exclaimed.

'I'm glad you like it,' he answered.

'I've fallen in love with it already,' she replied, as he bent down and kissed her.

'Now for the garden,' he said, opening the French windows.

There it was, a beautiful big walled garden, with a blaze of flowers and shrubs some eight feet in depth around the most perfect lawn she had ever seen. The only thing which towered from its lush perfection was the large bird bath, carved by some head and hand whose skill was clearly unsurpassed and to whom time was a mere nothing.

'I've never seen anything so beautiful, my love, it's really fantastic,' Joanna exclaimed, as he led her up one side, across the top and down the other side.

'Shall we have tea out here, then go for a walk after?' he asked.

'Wonderful, my darling,' she answered. 'It's so peaceful out here with only the birds singing.'

'There is one important thing which we haven't discussed yet, my love, and that is, what do you think your papa will say about us? For there aren't many country squires who would want their only daughter to mix with a common farmer – much less marry one?'

She turned and faced him, saying, 'In the first place my love, I don't like the word "common" applied to decent people, rich or poor; in the second, I am just twenty-one; and thirdly, I know Daddy. Whoever I fall in love with, he will be happy because I am. I shall tell them both as soon as I get home, but you need not worry, my darling, I'm not going to lose you for anything. I'd die without you, now I know you are the only one that I was meant for. You are my past, my present and my future, darling.'

One hour later they were strolling up over the Ridge, arm in arm, and both were in seventh heaven. It was under the old chestnut tree that he took her in his arms. True, shrouded under its leafy folds, the intimacy of a kiss was almost shut out from the world outside. Over stiles and through kissing gates, through the spinney, where the trees were only about twice their height, this was the way he took her to the foot of the High Ridge, the place which had the finest view for miles around.

'We can't go the way of the bower today, my love, it's a bit too muddy after the rain a couple of nights ago, but I'll take you to the top that way as soon as possible. You'll like it, it's really fantastic.'

Once on the top, he pointed out the various landmarks. The furthest were the rolling hills of Wiltshire, almost fifty miles away, while the nearest was his own farm, neat and well tended, and beautiful in its naturalness.

'It really is wonderful, Phil,' she exclaimed as she turned a full circle, not once, but three times. Then she asked, 'In what direction is the house, my love?'

'Straight over the top of that hill, and a little to the right of those chestnuts,' he answered.

For a few moments she seemed deep in thought, then she said, 'Do you know what comes to my mind up here, my love?'

'No, darling,' he answered.

'It's the hymn, "Could we but climb where Moses stood, and view the Promised Land." What else does it look like but that, my love?'

'It's going to be our Promised Land, yours and mine, and that is my promise to you, Joanna,' he answered, holding her a little tighter as they stood side by side.

On the way home, several times the flash of the sun danced from her golden hair and dazzled him, and for a while he was lost in wonderment at its beauty.

'What are you thinking, my love?' she asked.

'If you want the honest truth, it was how lovely you are, and how lucky I am to have your love. I never dreamed that morning that I was going to meet someone who would alter my whole life, someone who would make the sun shine for me always.'

She turned to him just as they reached the shade of the old

chestnut.

'I know one thing,' she said. 'Our love is so true, so strong, that it will last forever, and I often wonder how did I manage to live my life before we met, a life that amounted to nothing more than an empty existence; but I would gladly go through all those years of emptiness for one day of heaven with you, my—'

She didn't get the word 'darling' out before he kissed her and whispered in her ear, 'My angel.'

'My own true love,' was her reply between the first kiss and those that followed.

As they neared the house, he turned to her and said, 'I hope the walk has given you a good appetite, my love, for I was up at six o'clock this morning getting everything ready. So it's cold chicken and all the things I could think of to go with it, and I'm sure that an occasion as great as this must be toasted with the best champagne.'

'Wonderful, my darling,' she answered. 'Then in the future whenever we have champagne, it will always be a celebration of our first meal together in the place we both love.'

'I won't be sorry when Penny comes home on Tuesday. Cooking is all right, but there's not a lot of spare time for that and running three farms as well... and I do hope you will be able to meet her before you return, my love. You'll like her very much, she's really sweet.'

'I shall be very glad when she is back, not only to meet another person who is a part of Spring Farm, but I shall know that you are being properly cared for, my darling.'

Within minutes of reaching home, they both busied themselves laying the table and bringing the food in, and although it was still light, he just couldn't resist lighting the candles on the table.

'How's that?' he asked.

'Fantastic!' she answered.

At last all was ready, and with Joanna seated, he poured the champagne and, still standing, he raised his glass, saying, 'To you, my angel, and to our future together!'

'Thank you, my own true love, and the same to you,' she answered.

That first meal in Spring Farm was as near to heaven as they had ever known. His cooking had been excellent, but the joy of togetherness and their pure love for each other was the greatest thrill of their lives and couldn't be measured by any ordinary means. This time she insisted on doing the washing-up, while he dried, and already she knew she would hate leaving this beautiful cosy house with its dream garden. While she was pouring the coffee, he saw to the liqueurs.

'Can we take them out on the lawn, darling?' she asked.

'After you have given me a kiss – it might be only a minute since the last one, but it seems ages to me,' he said.

'Me too, my love,' she answered, smiling and looking more beautiful than ever.

Blackbirds and thrushes were singing their evening love song and high above they could hear the last joyous song of a lark – a creature who, like themselves, didn't seem to want this wonderful day to end. Then, as if from nowhere, two beautiful jays flew over the garden wall and perched on the bird bath; neither of them took a drink or looked for food, all they did was to keep fixed eyes on the young couple who were sitting on the seat a few yards away. Then just as suddenly, both took off, giving a rasping call and showing their plumage in the last ray of the setting sun, as they disappeared over the garden wall.

'Do you know my love, that is the first time I have ever seen a jay in this garden; and another thing, that is the nearest I've ever been to one. It's a well-known fact that you can never get close to one, and that they are one of the hardest birds to know,' Phil said, looking somewhat puzzled.

'Perhaps they don't trust man as much as some of the other birds, dear,' she answered.

'It's almost time to go, my angel,' he whispered as he kissed her again.

'Oh my love, you are far more wonderful than I ever imagined. How could I have dreamt that with one perfect kiss you would have made me completely unaware of this world – a world that nevertheless grows more exciting and beautiful each day?'

His answer was another kiss. Then, holding her tightly to his side, they made their way out to the car. They stopped at the place appointed, and had just had their first kiss when Jane and Gerald arrived. Time was short, but they had had a lovely time too.

'Goodnight!' they called.

'Goodnight!' Phil answered, still holding Joanna's hand as the car drew away; and as it gently slipped from his, he knew the wondering and the desperate longing would start all over again.

An Unexpected Invitation

Joanna sat on her bed, not bothering to undress, still in a whirl over the perfect love and kisses Phil had showered upon her. She felt sure of one thing, he must have been born to love, born to master the finer arts of loving, for had he not beyond all doubt proved to be one of the masters, with his pure love and subdued strength? He had swept her along on an irresistible tide, almost up to that ultimate barrier of love, a barrier where reality reigns on one side and paradise on the other, one which she knew they would never cross until they had been joined together before the eyes of God.

She loved him deeply and desperately, and as she undressed and got into bed, she knew that her whole life before her would be worthless without him, far worse than it had been before they had met.

She woke to see the grey clouds hurrying across a leaden sky, the sun shut out, as if with a blanket of despair. Joanna took little notice – she would see her love this morning, and that alone made it a beautiful day. At breakfast the conversation was mostly about the major's brother. He was still very ill, and most likely they would be going to see him again on Friday and staying in London until Monday. She was very sorry over the major's brother, but privately she realised that it would give Jane and herself a whole free weekend. Over coffee that morning she told Phil the news.

'If they do go it will mean that we shall have a nice long time together and also that you will be able to meet Penny, my love,' he said, and then went on, 'and by the way, I shall be here tomorrow as usual, then I have to go to Cheltenham on business.' He thought for a moment, then added. 'If I had thought to let Penny know, I could have met her there, but it's too late now. However, I expect I shall have enough time to get back and meet her at The Junction.'

'I wish I could come with you my love,' said Joanna, 'but I know that's impossible. All the same I am more than grateful for the precious hours we have had together already.'

He didn't dare tell her what he was going to Cheltenham for. This would be the last chance he would have to go there without anyone knowing that he was going for something special; he just had to buy his love something really good in the jewellery line, something that would forever remind them of their first wonderful days together.

'Did you sleep well, my love?' he asked.

'Wonderful, my darling,' she answered. Then, after a moment's thought, she went on, 'It's funny, really, that is another thing I should have told you about myself. Far too often I have the most awful nightmares, and yet since I have met you, my darling, I've not even had a suspicion of one.'

'Good – and wonderful,' he said. 'Now I know that my strong arms are really taking care of you, my darling.'

'That's what I'm beginning to think, my love,' she answered, pressing her hand over his.

The next morning they had their usual few minutes together.

'How I wish, my love, that I could give you just one small kiss,' he said as they were leaving the table. Her look and her smile held in abundance the understanding and sympathy she had for him, yet her longing for even one small kiss was as great and as desperate as his was.

Jane was at the hairdresser's, so they strolled in that direction down the street together. For a little while they talked outside before Joanna went inside to wait for Jane. Phil held her hand as he said, 'Till tomorrow, my love.'

'It can't come too soon, my darling,' she answered.

She watched and waved to him until he turned the corner, and once more those dark clouds of loneliness blotted out the light of togetherness from before their eyes.

At Cheltenham, Phil had a quick look round the shops first, then he had lunch. He had a good idea which was the best shop – he had to get Joanna something really good, for she was worth the entire world to him. He looked around carefully, and finally decided that the double row of pearls was what took his eye most. The young lady assistant was most helpful to him, even taking the pearls out of the case to show him that their lustre was just as beautiful as it was against the dark green velvet background of the case itself. The price didn't concern him one bit; nothing was too good for his first and only love. Phil was so pleased that when the assistant had packed them up and was about to hand them to him, making sure there was no one within earshot he asked 'Is it your birthday today, miss?'

'No, sir,' she answered.

'Well, here is a pound to buy yourself a box of chocolates when it is – and thank you very much for your wonderful help.'

'Thank you very much, sir,' she said, as he wished her goodbye and set off on his way to The Junction.

He had ten minutes to wait before the train arrived. When it did, he was already on the spot where he expected Penny's coach to stop. He was as near to right as could be, and in no time at all he had her cases out on the platform. He kissed her, and enquired if she had had a good holiday.

'Wonderful, thank you,' Penny answered, and she looked as though the change had done her the world of good. 'I hope you have been looking after yourself all right, and having your meals at the proper time.'

'I've managed quite well; you can see how fit I look,' Phil answered, laughing, and then continued, 'I don't know, you females seem to think that we men are helpless without you!'

'Well, you are really, and you know it,' she said, with her face beaming.

'I suppose we are, but we're not going to admit it,' he answered with the boyish smile on his face that she knew only too well.

It was 4.30 p.m., at the time they reached home. Phil carried her cases up to her room, leaving Penny at the door.

'Don't be long,' he said, 'I'll put the kettle on, for I'm sure you can do with a nice cup of tea.'

'Won't be more than a few minutes,' she answered.

Together they had tea in the kitchen. She had bought him a lovely pleated shirt for wearing in the evening.

He thanked her, then added, 'But you shouldn't...'

'Why not?' she replied. 'When you were a little boy you used to look for me to bring you a present, and to me you are still that same little boy – and always well be.'

She had just sat down when he said, 'I've got a wonderful surprise for you.'

'What's that?' she asked, all alert.

'Well, you know that perfect girl that you are always so anxious for me to meet – I've found her at last. She's a real angel, and worth waiting every second for.'

'Wonderful,' Penny replied. 'Can I ask who she is, or can't you see I'm just dying to know?'

'Well,' he said again, 'whatever it was that got into the major's car the morning you went on holiday was definitely on my side!'

'If it's Miss Shand, the one they asked you to give a lift to, then all my prayers are answered,' she said with her eyes shining.

'Right first time,' he answered.

'I haven't seen her for three years, and she was a lovely sweet girl then. In fact, I've never seen any girl to touch her,' Penny remarked looking thoughtful.

He then told her about the major's brother, and the proposed visit again this weekend. Looking starry-eyed, he said, 'So if they do go, you will have the pleasure of meeting Joanna; she's looking forward to meeting you very much and I'm sure you will love her.'

'I'm sure I shall, for I could hardly keep my eyes off her, the last time I saw her,' Penny answered.

'There is only one snag,' he said, looking a little serious. 'I've no idea how her father will act, seeing as I'm only a country farmer. He could say "no", and what would we do then?'

'He could, but why should he? You're both very much in love, and you are not exactly poor. Personally I wouldn't worry over it, that is one bridge we shall have to cross when we get to it. However, I shall pray for you both!'

It was coffee together for Phil and the girls on the next two mornings. However, on the Friday he looked everywhere but there was no sign of them. He thought it might have had something to do with the major going away. After lunch Phil made his usual visit to the farms to pay the men, that alone took him most of the afternoon.

Meanwhile, Jane and Joanna had been unable to go to town, for the reason that the same old car was unusable. It hadn't broken down this time, but it had run out of petrol, so the major had to use Jane's for his needs before they finally left to catch the 3.30 p.m. train at The Junction.

Jane had it all planned. She would drive her mother and father to The Junction, then go on to pick up Gerald. Then Joanna could go over to Spring Farm as soon as they had left, and if she wasn't coming back to dinner she could phone them.

The car was hardly out of the drive before the call of Spring Farm was in full cry. To Joanna, it was like going home. She got to the door, rang the bell and almost immediately came face to face with Penny.

Before Joanna could utter a word, Penny said, 'Come in, miss, I've been expecting you, and although I haven't seen you for three years, I could have picked you out of a million by the description I've had – and believe me, it doesn't do you justice!'

'No wonder my ears have been burning,' replied Joanna, and they laughed heartily while Penny put a friendly arm around her. They were off to a wonderful start, and their liking increased as the afternoon wore on.

She told Joanna what a good, sweet couple Phil's mother and father had been, and how all their goodness had been inherited by Phil.

'He is exactly the same as they were. In the winter when there is always more illness in the village, I often do far more cooking for the sick and needy than we have in the house. That's the way it has always been, and I hope it always will, for I love doing it.'

Joanna liked this outspoken Penny; she was like a breath of fresh air every minute you were in her presence, but with all the talk going on, it was only by chance that they heard Phil's car coming down the drive. Penny, always out for a bit of fun, told Joanna to hide behind the door! Straight into the kitchen he came.

'Any luck?' he asked.

Penny, pretending that she didn't know what he meant, answered, 'What do you mean, any luck?'

'I mean, any phone call from the Court?' he said, looking a little worried.

'No,' she replied.

Just then Joanna touched his arm from behind the door and he turned quickly.

'My love,' he said, as he took her in his arms and kissed her. 'Fancy causing me even one unnecessary moment of suspense. I can see I shall have to be more wary of you two in the future!'

Penny needed only half an eye to see that this was the real thing, that these two were hopelessly in love, and above all, that they seemed to have been made for each other.

'Tea for three out on the lawn – I'll help you carry it out as soon as I've washed and changed,' said Phil, his face all smiles now. By the time he was ready, they had the table laid and the tea made.

'Is it too much to hope that you can stay to dinner, or have you got to go back, my love?' he asked.

'No, darling,' she answered, 'I can stay for as long as you want me to, as long as I phone and tell them.'

'That would be for always, if I had my way,' he replied.

Tea took a much longer time than usual. There was so much to say between the three of them, and it was a long, long time since Penny could remember an afternoon so happy.

Joanna had phoned the Court, and now they were walking over the fields while Penny prepared the dinner. It was a whole weekend of joy and happiness, the sort that Spring Farm was meant for, and Penny was just as sorry to see it come to an end as were the two lovers.

'The most ideal couple in the world,' she said to herself, as she watched Phil drive Joanna back to the Court, after coming to lunch on the Monday.

The major and Mrs Marchant arrived back at three in the afternoon, so Phil knew the next time he would see his beloved would be at The Junction at ten o'clock in the morning. That night he wrote his first love letter, putting more than a little of his heart into words, which seemed only a glimmer of the burning love he had for her. Then he undid the wrapping round the present he had bought her, slipped the letter on top of the case and repacked it.

He was up early the next morning and was already at The Junction when they arrived. He got her cases out of the car and was on the point of carrying them in when Jane said, 'I won't spoil your last few minutes together, and I do want to see Gerald as soon as possible.' Looking at Phil, she continued, 'I know Joanna is in capable hands – you proved that when she arrived three weeks ago!'

The laugh that followed was more than welcome on his part. It would help to get his angel over the agony of parting.

'Seriously,' he said, 'I want to thank you for all that you have done for us. Because of your understanding and help we have both had the most wonderful time together, and I know Joanna appreciates it as much as I do.'

'She is not only my best friend, Phil, but as near to a sister that I shall ever have,' Jane replied, as she kissed Joanna and wished her goodbye and a safe journey.

He held the cases, just as he did the day they had met, only now his other arm held hers with the confidence that she now belonged to him.

'I'll ring you at six o'clock tonight, my darling,' Joanna said as he put the cases down. Then she confessed, 'I won't be able to wait twenty-four hours before ringing you again, so you must expect a call at any time, my love.'

'I know I shall be waiting every minute of the day, my darling, but it won't be long before we can meet in London; and if we can only speak to each other once or twice a day on the phone, it will help the parting to be a little more bearable,' he replied as their eyes searched each other's faces, determined to hold this vision of each other until they would meet again.

Hearts sank a little further, as the sound of the express was heard and grew louder as it sped towards them. When it stopped he had difficulty in finding an empty compartment.

'I won't put your cases on the rack, my love, then you won't have to struggle to get them down,' he said smiling.

'Thank you my darling,' she answered, with a little more evidence of tears in her eyes by this time. There was no one near as he took her in his arms and gave her quite a bit more than half of the wonderful kiss that would be her passport to heaven.

'Do you think that will last you until we meet again, my angel?' he asked.

She nodded, but held her lips up for one more kiss, lips which were trembling, a trembling that was only stifled as the strength of his took command. With her arms still around him, and with those watery eyes looking into his, she said, 'My own true love, you are my whole world, my wonderful world, and I shall miss you far more than I know how.'

He simply replied, 'I shall be lost without you, my angel.'

The train was almost ready to go, so he got out and fastened the door. Then he took the parcel out of his pocket, saying, 'I just couldn't resist giving my love something that she can look at, and remember our first few days of heaven together. Don't open it until you get home, and also when you are alone, my love.'

'Thank you, my darling, very much,' she answered, almost completely overcome.

The whistle blew and he held her hand saying, 'I love you more than words can tell, my darling.'

'And I do you, my love,' she answered.

They just had time for one swift kiss as the train started on its way. He stood and waved her out of sight, knowing that heartaches and loneliness would be theirs until they would meet again.

She arrived at Northwood a little after twelve. Her father and Marie-Ann had met her at the station, and by the time they had reached home they had learned – and more especially could see – that she had had a most wonderful and enjoyable holiday.

'I won't be any longer than possible because there's something I want to tell you both before lunch,' she said as she was going upstairs. She washed and changed quickly, then sat on her bed and undid Phil's present. She read the letter first, and all her emotions took control as she read these lines for the second time:

> *...The love I have for you, which burns deep within me, is not like the urge, the inspiration or the desire of the man who plays a haunting melody, paints a beautiful picture, or serenades with a true love song. But, like the tremor of an earthquake that vibrates the heart of Mother Earth, it sweeps up and surges over me and I am engulfed in the splendour of your enchantment and beauty. I am wholly yours, my love...*

She dried her tears and made sure there were little or no signs of them before she went downstairs. Then she opened the case and the sparkle returned to her eyes as she beheld the beauty before her. How sweet of him, and what wonderful taste! They were beautiful, in fact the most beautiful pearls she had ever seen; she just had to find time to try them on.

'Perfect in every way... thank you, my darling,' she said aloud, putting them safely back into the case. Then, making sure once again that her eyes looked all right, satisfied, she went downstairs.

Her father and Marie-Ann were in the drawing room talking as Joanna entered. Looking up at her, he said, 'Well, I must say you look a million pounds' worth! I've never seen you look so well and happy before, no matter where you have gone on holiday. And by the way, what have you got to tell us? Is ten minutes long enough?'

'Yes, I expect so, Daddy,' she answered. Then, looking at him eye to eye, she said, 'Straight from the shoulder, Daddy.'

'Yes, my dear, as always,' he replied, with an extra smile upon his face.

'I have fallen in love – very, very deeply in love,' she said.

'Well, that's what I've hoped you would do – and before now, as a matter of fact,' he answered. Then he added, 'Is he in the army?'

'No, Daddy,' she replied, 'he farms at Beversbury on the other side of the Court.'

There was a silence, and Marie-Ann looked more than a little apprehensive as it lengthened but both women were relieved when the colonel said, 'A farmer... Well, it could be a change to have an honest worker in the family after all these years.' More seconds ticked away before he went on, 'When have you arranged to meet him again?'

'Next week in London, Daddy,' Joanna replied.

This time he seemed deep in thought for a whole two minutes. Then, glancing at his watch, he said, 'Well, my dear, you've just got time to ring him before lunch to invite him here for the weekend, and if you would like, for him to get here for lunch on Friday.'

'Oh, Daddy, you're wonderful! But I knew you would understand,' she cried, rushing over and smothering him with kisses, and a few tears as well. And Marie-Ann came in for her share too, for she had already mopped a tear or two away.

'He will want two or three days to get his work planned, so I hope you can get through now,' said her father, as she hurried into the hall to telephone.

They heard her ask for the number, then after just over a minute say, 'Is that you, Penny? This is Joanna, how are you?' Then a pause, then, 'Hello, my darling.' Another pause, then, 'Yes, thank you, my love.' Then, 'Mummy and Daddy would like you to come for the weekend, to be here for lunch on Friday. Can you manage that, my love?' A pause, then, 'Lovely, darling.' Another short pause, then, 'I'm absolutely thrilled with your lovely present and the letter, my love. I'll ring you again at six, for I'm missing you terribly already.' A pause, then, 'Bye-bye, my darling.'

While the conversation had been going on, the colonel had cast several cheeky glances at Marie-Ann, and as Joanna came back into the room he said, 'Straight from the shoulder, my dear.'

'Yes, Daddy,' she answered.

'Well!' he said with a saucy smile upon his face, 'I'm dying to have a look at that lovely present!'

'You would, and you shall!' she said, running upstairs to get it.

On coming down, she sat between them on the sofa and opened the case on her lap.

'Beautiful, they are really superb, please try them on for me to see,' said Marie-Ann, all in one breath, while her father took a good long look before saying, 'Lovely, my dear, and very elegant. That must have cost him something.'

'His independence, I hope!' Joanna replied, looking her radiant best.

For the next two days the phone between Northwood and Spring Farm rang, as often as possible, and on the morning of the big day, she was up extra early to catch him at breakfast and again before he started on his journey. He expected to arrive about 11.30 a.m.

The colonel had more than one laugh with Marie-Ann over the way Joanna was cutting flowers and arranging them, a thing she had never done before.

'Busy as a bee this morning,' he remarked.

'That's quite natural, it's her first love, and I expect I was the same myself before your visits,' she replied.

By 11.15 a.m., Joanna had changed and was all ready for the sound of Phil's car coming up the drive.

'You're not going to be late to greet him?' said her father, playfully putting his arm around her.

'Not likely, Daddy!' she answered, laughing. 'I won't even keep him waiting on our wedding day.'

'Steady on,' he said, returning her laugh. 'I haven't even met him yet!'

'You won't have long to wait,' said Marie-Ann. 'I can hear a car coming up the drive now.'

Joanna was at the door before Phil pulled up. He laughed and waved as she came down the steps to greet him.

'It's just wonderful to be with you again my darling,' he said as he kissed her.

'Nothing short of heaven, my love,' she answered.

Taking his arm, she led him up through the doorway, saying as she did so, 'You drove carefully, didn't you darling?'

'Of course, my love. All I wanted was to see you as soon as possible, so don't ever worry, my angel.'

The colonel and Marie-Ann were both standing as they entered the drawing room. Joanna introduced Phil to Marie-Ann first, then to her father, who at that moment was thinking to himself, *I don't know what I expected, but my girl has certainly made a wonderful choice.*

'We are very glad you could come at such short notice,' he said as he shook Phil's hand warmly, 'for I expect you are very busy at this time of the year.'

'Thank you very much for asking me,' Phil answered. 'We are busy, but I can always leave the work in capable hands.'

After a wash and a drink, Joanna took him for a walk round the garden. While she was saying to him that their garden, although nice, didn't look anywhere near as nice as his, the colonel and Marie-Ann were watching them walking arm in arm, then looking in the summer house, and even from a distance they could see that here were two young people very much in love.

'You had a surprise, Frank,' said Marie-Ann, chiding her husband.

'I know; at times like these, one doesn't know what to expect; but it's funny, whatever fears I had, they have all disappeared,' he answered. Then he went on, 'And by the way, what does your womanly instinct say?'

'Makes me wish I was young again!' she answered, with a laugh. Then, being serious for a few moments, she continued, 'Joanna certainly deserves a nice young man. Knowing that she wouldn't fall in love with anyone, and seeing how desperately in love she is at the moment... I realise it is only a first impression, and not much of that so far, but if you want my honest opinion, plus a little bit of womanly intuition, I'd say that Joanna has not only got a nice young man, but as good as you could find anywhere.'

In the years to come, the colonel would often think of her words, and the only question he would ever ask himself was, *Were those words an understatement?*

It was clear, even before lunch was finished, that a more joyous atmosphere had descended on Northwood. Happy as they had been before, the fact of having two young people in love, laughing and full of life, didn't leave much time for straight talk or thinking; and not in the least was the colonel enjoying himself.

'What have you decided to do this afternoon?' he asked, looking at Joanna.

'I thought about showing Phil some of the beauty spots, not that there are nearly as many as in the Cotswolds, but there's one or two, and not too far away either.'

'That's right, my dear, but don't go too far, for Phil has driven quite a distance already. We've got people for dinner tonight, and we're out to the Manor tomorrow night, and he will be tired if he gets a lot of extra driving.'

'All right, Daddy,' she replied. 'We'll just have a quiet drive to the nearest place of any interest.'

So they set off in Phil's two-seater, but after a short while he pulled in to the side of the road and turned towards Joanna.

'I'm terribly in need of a kiss now, after two whole days without one,' he said.

She bent closer and closer until their lips met, and they made up a little of what they had lost in that lonely time.

'You're more wonderful than ever, my darling,' she whispered, pressing her lips on his in a flurry of ecstasy.

'Darling,' he said, 'what a lot seems to have happened since we met. Less than a month, and here I am with you, and I've met your family as well.' She bent down and kissed him lightly on the lips as he continued, 'I wonder what would have happened if I hadn't been a little cheeky, or perhaps man enough to have given you that first kiss.'

'It was a cheek, really,' she answered, smiling sweetly down to him. 'I might have had a boyfriend, or been engaged.'

'Oh no, I knew you weren't engaged,' he said. 'That was the first thing I looked for, when you took your gloves off in the car.'

'Do you mean to tell me that you had those sorts of designs on me even then?' she asked.

'Right from the start, my angel. I told you the other day that I was more than half in love with you as I walked down the platform towards you, but I had to be sure and diplomatic at the same time.'

'Diplomatic and scheming, you mean,' she said, giving him another light kiss on the lips.

'You were almost out of my reach, my angel. If I hadn't schemed and followed a daring impulse, we would almost certainly have been lost to each other,' he replied.

Joanna, still looking down at him, became serious for the first time as she said, 'I knew, my love, the very first moment our eyes met, that the world around me had suddenly become so beautiful and wonderful, and I would have got Jane to arrange for us to meet again if things hadn't worked out the way they did. I suppose I could have had many boyfriends and been probably kissed a thousand times, but that day, my lips to you were as pure as my body is now, so you can tell what a big slice of my heart you captured in that very first moment.'

The colonel seemed relieved when they got back. Whether he thought they would drive too far or whether he had missed their company, they couldn't tell.

'Did you have a nice afternoon?' he asked.

'We've had a lovely stroll along the river bank,' answered Phil.

'It's very pleasant there,' said the colonel, 'and some very good fishing too. Oh, by the way Phil, it's dinner jacket tonight and tails tomorrow, have you brought both?'

'Yes Colonel,' he answered. 'Penny always makes sure that I am prepared for any eventuality.'

'She spoils him, really,' said Joanna, laughing. Then she continued, 'I was telling Mummy and Daddy the day before yesterday what a sweet person Penny is.'

'You're very fortunate to have someone like that, Phil,' replied Marie-Ann.

For almost an hour they played clock golf on the lawn, then it was upstairs to get ready for dinner. Phil was glad of a refreshing bath after a very hot day, but even though he took his time, he was still downstairs just before the colonel. They stood outside talking and looking over the lawn and gardens, but no matter what interest the topic of conversation held, the colonel couldn't help thinking each time he glanced in Phil's direction just how immaculate this young man of Joanna's was.

It was Marie-Ann who joined them first. She looked very chic in her beautiful red dress, but Phil held his breath as he caught the first sight of his loved one; her dark green silk dress only seemed to serve as a background for a loveliness and beauty whose intensity seemed to grow second by second. Her fair hair looked like pure molten gold in the late sunlight, while the pearls which hung from her slender neck, the ones he had given her, not only blended with all around, but were as a symbol to the one they adorned, a symbol of loveliness and purity. She came straight towards him, holding out her arms.

'I must give you another kiss for the nicest present you could possibly have given me, darling,' she said.

'You look really wonderful, my love,' he replied, holding her tenderly while their lips met. The colonel and Marie-Ann looked on, thinking how pure and unashamed was their love.

The dinner was in full swing. On one side of Phil was Mrs Stapleton and on the other Janet Turner, but he wouldn't have minded who was next to him, as long as Joanna was opposite, for whenever their eyes met, which was very often, a message of love was flashed to each other, and when the time came for the ladies to leave for the drawing room, the look which she gave him was a look that could only have spelt one thing – 'I hope you won't be long, my darling.'

However, it was an hour before he was by her side again, but he had quite enjoyed himself listening to the different topics of conversation. The last one had been the likelihood of a coming war, which most of them thought impossible, and it was only when Brigadier Smythe looked across at him and asked, 'And what do you think, young man?' that he was forced to take one side or the other.

Without considering for a second, he replied, 'I think war is inevitable. Hitler has said in his book and openly in his speeches what his aims are. He'll get what he can with bluff, no doubt, but once that fails it will be war – in fact I'd say in eighteen months to two years, so I think we shall be very foolish if we don't prepare ourselves as quickly as possible.'

The colonel gave him a very approving look, as the brigadier said, 'He'd never dare.'

'We shall see,' Phil replied, as they prepared to go to the drawing room.

Later, after all the guests had departed, it was Marie-Ann who asked, 'Is there time for us to have a few minutes' chat, and perhaps another drink?'

'Ample time, my dear,' replied the colonel. 'It's only a quarter to twelve, quite early for a change.'

So they enjoyed another drink and a bit of local gossip. Then Marie-Ann, with a smile upon her face, said to Phil, 'You must have frozen Clare Smythe with the first look, she was really subdued tonight.'

'I never disobey orders,' he answered, laughing and putting his arm around Joanna.

'I was glad,' said the colonel, 'when the brigadier asked you outright what you thought, and I was more than pleased with your answer. I bet that was the most straightforward bit of good sense he has tried to evade in years.'

He then told Marie-Ann and Joanna what had been said in their absence.

'And do you really think that's what is going to happen, darling?' Joanna asked Phil.

'I hope I'm wrong for all our sakes, but I honestly think that nothing short of a miracle will stop it, my love,' he replied.

The next morning, Phil was down first and was already looking round the garden when she came to him. They greeted and kissed each other and then walked arm in arm around the rest of the garden.

'Did you have a good night, my love?' she asked.

'Slept like a log,' he answered. Then he asked, 'Did you, darling?'

'Yes, my love,' she replied. 'Knowing that you love me has made a world of difference to me in all things. Do you know, darling, that I have had only one nightmare since we've met, and that was my first night here, when inwardly I must have thought that I was alone again. But last night I absolutely had to have a wonderful night, for it was our first night under the same roof, and it was all so wonderful to know, my love, that you are so near, and that my dreams don't have to fly very far.'

Looking round into that beautiful face, Phil could see how blissfully happy she really was. At breakfast, the colonel couldn't hide the fact that he felt on top of the world. His own happiness was so great because he knew Joanna was happier than he had ever known her before. It would have been an awful situation if she had fallen in love with someone whom he could never take to, or someone who was not worthy of her. Although it was less than twenty-four hours since he had met Phil, so far he had liked everything about him; and with the fact that Joanna had kept all men out of her life until by chance she had met him, and the way she loved him, there didn't seem any cause to worry over whether he was worthy of her.

'We're going to Oxford for something special, my love,' said Joanna. 'So I want you to start thinking, for I'm going to buy you a present. Just as my pearls reminds me of all the joy we had at Spring Farm, so too must I buy you something that you will look at often and remind you of your first stay at Northwood. Have you any ideas, darling?'

'It's a wonderful thought, my love, but really I have no idea,' he answered.

'Well, I've just got to buy you something... How about a wristwatch, one that you can wear just for evenings? Then you'll never be late to take me in your arms!' Smiling at him, she continued, 'Is that all right, my love?'

'Wonderful, my darling,' he answered, 'I'll be awfully proud of it, you know that, and you know that every second away from you, my love, is a disaster to me and always will be.'

They both fell in love with the same watch in the first shop they went to.

'All that for a watch,' he whispered to her as it was being packed up; but once outside, she turned and said to him, as the most serene and beautiful look came over her face, 'What is money, my love, when you are worth more than all the world to me?' And he felt each of those words emphasised by the pressure of her arm against his.

'I should think it is quite enough for me to give my angel the best part of "half a special" for my lovely present.'

The stars were really in her eyes when they started off again. She snuggled a little closer to him, thinking how grateful she was to God for bringing them together.

When they arrived home, Phil lost no time in showing the colonel and Marie-Ann his beautiful watch.

'I shall have to wear it while I'm here on holiday,' he said looking very thrilled. Then he turned to Joanna and kissed her, saying, 'Thank you very much again, my love.'

Lunch time was another happy occasion, and afterwards as they all sat outside Joanna said, 'We're going for a quiet stroll around the park this afternoon, why don't you and Mummy come too?'

'We would love to, as long as you two young things don't mind the intrusion.'

Phil laughed and said, 'You can show us all the whys and wherefores. I'm always out to learn something.'

'I don't expect I could teach you anything about the land,' answered the colonel with a hearty laugh.

So off the four of them went. Joanna arm in arm with her loved one, happy and as radiant as ever, as the colonel talked and showed Phil this or that, with Marie-Ann adding a little here and there; but only one half of Joanna listened. The other half was in her new-found world, a world where her contentment was complete, just by having hold of his arm and walking by his side. Who or what had put her foot onto this first step, towards a love and happiness that she had never dreamt existed? And who or what in the first place had brought him into her life? The one man, the only one who could make her his very own; he was her whole life, and even after so short a time she knew the depth of their love could only be measured by heaven itself.

They had a most enjoyable afternoon, and after tea they all seemed quite content to sit and talk, for they had walked a few miles that afternoon. Joanna held Phil's hand and her gaze hardly left that side of his face as the two men did most of the talking. She knew her love was really enjoying himself and she knew, beyond all doubt, that from the way her father talked to Phil and his manner toward him, he really liked him. Not only did the intensity of her new-found heaven shine more and more brightly before her, but its size was growing daily, and soon she would be enveloped in a paradise where all was well, where not one tiny thing could possibly mar the joy of their daily life, as they walked forward together.

The next day, as before, Phil was first down. He had only been outside the door a minute or so when she joined him. Quickly her arms glided over his shoulders while those beautiful lips were held up for his taking.

'I'll have to be careful not to smudge your lipstick, my love,' he whispered.

'It's all for you, my darling,' she answered, drawing him down for a much longer kiss than he had intended. Then she continued, 'I wish we weren't going out tonight, my love. I would much rather have stayed here than go where there are a lot of people. I feel I am losing so much of you that way, Phil.'

'We can't do much about it, my darling,' he answered, 'Besides, the time will soon go as long as I am by your side every moment I possibly can, and you know you can count on that.'

'I know you will, my darling,' she said, and just then the colonel and Marie-Ann came down and said they were ready to go.

When they got to the Manor, Phil was introduced to everyone; but true to his word and the feelings of his heart, he never left Joanna's side except when he was bound to. During dinner, their eyes almost clung to each other's across the table. He knew she disliked as much as he did that tedious long hour or so when the ladies left for the drawing room. However, that lonely hour slipped away, and just as he got to the drawing room, someone suggested a walk along the terrace and around the gardens.

'What a wonderful suggestion,' Joanna whispered, as she put her arm through Phil's and squeezed his hand, while the look he gave her showed with his eyes his deep and tender love for her.

On their return to Northwood, there was a few minutes' chat as usual.

'We won't be late, for it's church in the morning,' said the colonel. Then, turning to Phil, he continued, 'Do you go to church very often Phil?'

'I hardly ever miss a Sunday morning, Colonel,' he replied. 'I've had a lot to be thankful for, and now I have much more that I had five weeks ago, so mine is not only thanks now but gratitude as well.'

It was at breakfast the next morning that Joanna asked Marie-Ann, 'Are we having a quiet day, Mummy?'

'There's only four extra for lunch, dear, otherwise we shall be on our own.'

'Good,' replied Joanna. 'Perhaps we can have another nice long walk after they have gone.'

'I hope so, I really enjoyed myself yesterday,' added the colonel.

They walked to church, and as they entered, Phil thought to himself, *it's nice, but not quite as beautiful as ours at Beversbury.* The service was good, with some of his favourite hymns, and then came the time for them to receive the Holy Sacrament. Phil walked behind Joanna to the altar, they received the bread and while they were waiting for the wine to reach them, he stole a glance at her. On her face was a look he had not seen before. If she had been beautiful beyond words before, she had at least looked earthly. Now the only word he could use to describe this heavenly aura was *angelic.* He knew she was pure in mind and body, but he had never seen the purity of the soul show on a face before. He had the feeling that he was in the presence of something greater than he understood, something that made the depth of his love seem so inadequate, yet he loved her more than his own life.

Once more back at Northwood, while the colonel and Marie-Ann sat outside, the two young lovers strolled around the garden making a visit to the summer house their last port of call.

'I like the design of this immensely,' said Phil.

'Yes, it's quite pretty really, darling,' she answered.

Lunch went by, and they were able to have another enjoyable walk through the parkland. He knew how much Joanna was looking forward to a quiet evening together, just the four of them. He was at the bottom of the stairs when she came down. He held his arms out for her and she came readily to him.

Sunday night supper was a heavenly and happy time. Joanna had all the freedom she had wanted to look and to talk to the one she loved, and it was while they were having dessert that the colonel said, 'What time do you propose leaving tomorrow, Phil?'

'I shall have to leave about eleven, Colonel, that will give me just enough time to be home before lunch.'

Then, turning to Joanna, her father asked, 'What have you decided to do next weekend, my dear?'

'Phil is going to meet me in London on Friday. He has got some business to see to on Monday, so we shall have a nice long time together.' Looking at Phil, she continued, 'You're not leaving me until Tuesday, are you darling?'

'Definitely not, my love,' he answered, then turning to Marie-Ann and then to the colonel, he went on, 'I very much appreciate you asking me here for this lovely weekend. As you have just heard I shall be in London next week, but I wonder if you would accept my invitation to come to Spring Farm the weekend after, and you can stay as long as it suits you.' He looked at Joanna. 'You can manage that, can't you, my darling?'

The look of joy and relief on her face spoke a hundred times more words than the ones she said with her lips.

'Nothing will stand in the way of that, my love,' she replied.

Marie-Ann and the colonel both looked very pleased, and without a moment's hesitation he replied, 'We'd both be delighted to accept. I'm sure the Smythes' can do without us for one dinner at least.'

'Thank you very much, Phil,' added Marie-Ann.

Phil was delighted too, especially when Joanna got up and ran round and kissed him.

'I can't help being over the moon, with all that to look forward to, my love,' she exclaimed.

Then, turning to the colonel and Marie-Ann once more, Phil said, 'You have both made me happier that I can say. Spring Farm isn't as big or as grand as this lovely house, but I think we can make you comfortable.'

'I'm sure we will be,' they both agreed.

'I'm convinced you will love it as much as I do,' added Joanna.

At breakfast the next morning, the colonel's watchful eye could see that quite a few of the stars had faded from Joanna's eyes, and after when the two lovers were walking round the lawn, he turned to Marie-Ann saying, 'Do you know, my dear, I've enjoyed this weekend more than any for years and years.'

'I know you have, and so have I too, dear,' she answered.

Phil drove his car round to the front door just before eleven. Now all was ready and his luggage already stowed in the dicky.

'Would you like a drink before you go, Phil?' asked the

colonel.

'No thank you, Colonel, I'm not at all thirsty at the moment,' he answered.

They went to the door to see him off, and shaking his hand warmly the colonel said, 'It's been a great pleasure to have you, Phil, and we're certainly looking forward to our first visit to Spring Farm.'

They watched as Joanna kissed him, half with passion and half with emotion. Looking up into his eyes, she said, 'Take great care of yourself, my darling, and drive carefully, won't you?'

'Yes, my love, and God bless you too,' he answered.

Then as they walked with arms around each other down to the car, he tried to keep her spirits up by saying, 'Would seven pounds a week be enough for you now, my love?'

She smiled half wistfully and told him, 'right now, I would walk a hundred miles to take that job for nothing, my darling.'

'Better still, when you take it for love and love alone, my angel,' he replied.

Another lot of kisses before he got in, and after he had started the engine, he waved to the colonel and Marie-Ann. Then Joanna leaned down for one final kiss. She watched as he went down the drive waving and disappeared from view.

Her father looked on as she walked slowly round the garden. It wasn't the flowers nor the trees, nor the beautiful sunshine, nor the fresh morning air which she sought to comfort her, it was solitude, and he knew why. So much in love, and too upset to face or talk to anyone, when she did appear she looked a little more composed. She walked straight up to him and found the comfort of his arms before asking him, 'Well, Daddy, were all my years of waiting worthwhile?'

'Straight from the shoulder, my dear?' he asked.

'Yes, Daddy,' she answered.

'Well,' he said, 'if the Lord had blessed me with a son and he had been like Phil, I should have been the proudest father in the world. However, I'll be more pleased to settle for him as a son-in-law one day. Can I pay him any greater compliment, my dear?'

'No, Daddy – and thank you,' she answered a little tearfully.

Then she kissed him several times, and Marie-Ann came next, a Marie-Ann who showed her agreement with an extra loving embrace.

For the next few days, the phone link between Northwood and Spring Farm came into operation at all times, and before Phil started for London on the Friday, he rang Joanna before she started for the same destination by car.

'It's wonderful to think that we shall be together in just a few hours, my love,' he said.

'I can hardly wait to be in your arms, my darling,' she replied.

Together Once More

Phil left the car at the garage just outside the station. He managed to get a corner seat, for he wanted to have a good view of the farm land as he went along, but his mind wouldn't stay on those sort of things for very long. Always the vision of her beautiful face came back to him, and before the train pulled into Paddington, he could hardly hold back his excitement at the thought of holding her in his arms once more.

He was all ready and standing in the corridor before the platform came into view. He looked out and almost immediately his eyes picked out all that was heaven to him, he knew he could have picked that lovely golden head out of a million. The train stopped just before he got to her, but she had seen him and was in his arms for a short kiss almost before he could put his case down.

'My angel,' he whispered.

'My love,' came her soft reply, 'I've missed you terribly, my darling.'

'And I've had a very hard time keeping my mind on my work, my love,' he answered, smiling.

She held tightly on to his arm as they walked towards the taxi rank.

'I'll check in at my hotel first and leave my case, and while you are waiting in the taxi outside you can choose wherever you would like me to take you for lunch, my love,' he said.

'That has been taken care of, my darling,' she answered. 'Daddy has given me strict instructions that we are to have as many meals at our house in Eaton Place as we want to, so after you have been to your hotel, it's lunch for two at Eaton Place.'

'That's not only very kind of him, but I suspect a bit canny as well,' Phil answered, laughing.

'That's what I thought too, my love,' she answered.

She had ten minutes to wait in the taxi, and as she saw him coming out of the hotel and watching his every step, she thought to herself, *how lucky I am – if I had to describe the sort of partner that I was looking for, I could never have made up such a wonderful picture that I have got in reality, with all the fine qualities he is so richly endowed with.*

It took them only a short time to reach Eaton Place. She went quickly up the steps and had unlocked the door by the time he had paid the taxi. She led the way upstairs to the cosy morning room.

'It's a beautiful house, darling, from what I've seen,' Phil said as he went into the room.

She closed the door, and was in his arms before another word could be spoken. All the pent-up longing and loneliness of the last three days had been more than a little too much for her, and he felt her tears wet his cheeks.

'I'm sorry, Phil,' she cried softly, 'I'm on top of the world when we are together, but when we are apart, it is as if my whole world is in pieces – far, far worse than the life I had before we met.'

'Well, I'm with you now, my angel,' he answered reassuringly.

'I know, my darling, but it's not only the daytime, it's the night-time as well,' she said.

'Have you had any more nightmares?' he asked.

She nodded. 'One,' she replied, still a little tearful.

There was only one way to bring the smiles back to her face, and he took it. His lips sought hers in the power of a special kiss, and gradually the agony of those three days apart drifted into the background.

After lunch, they walked to Hyde Park Corner. They caught a number 74 bus for the top of Baker Street, where they alighted only a short distance from the entrance to Regent's Park. Hand in hand, or arm in arm, they were enjoying to the full the beauty of everything, not least their closeness to each other.

'Shall we go for a row on the lake?' Phil asked.

'I'd really love it, darling, the last one I had here was when Daddy took me years ago,' she answered.

He rowed down the lake towards the island, and once again he thought, how beautiful she looked. As her eyes rarely left his face, the love and devotion which burned out of them would have put any lesser man than him off the job of rowing!

'Could I please ask what you are thinking, my sweet one?' he asked, smiling.

'Just how happy I am, how wonderful you are and how much I love you, my darling,' she answered.

'Well, remind me when it's a little safer to move around to show you that it's not exactly a one-sided love affair!' he replied, watching her eyes shine and her face light up.

He took her to a nice cosy yet select restaurant, one which he often used when he was in London. They had a corner table, so they could hold hands at odd times and talk quite freely.

'Only five weeks since we met, my love, and I would marry you tomorrow if I had the chance,' he said.

'You've always had the chance, my darling,' she answered. Then she continued, 'Who knows, perhaps in another five weeks the day when we shall really belong to each other will not be too far in the future. Five weeks isn't very long, I know, but these last five weeks have eclipsed the whole of my life before.'

'There is one thing I meant to ask you yesterday, do you know if Jane is in London?' he asked.

'Yes, she is, she is staying with Gerald's parents at St John's Wood. Why, my love?' she answered.

'I was wondering,' he said, 'if you would like them to make a foursome for dinner tonight? I feel it's the least I can do after all she did for us, when we were desperate to snatch those few precious moments together.'

'Of course, my darling, I'd be delighted. Jane will be so pleased to think that we are in our heaven and haven't forgotten her. I'll ring her in a few minutes,' Joanna replied.

'It's funny,' he went on, 'Jane was one person who I never cared very much for, and yet after she knew about us, she seemed to go out of her way to do all she could for us. She proved to be far more human than I ever thought she could be.'

Back at Eaton Place, Joanna rang Jane. 'Yes,' said her friend, she and Gerald would be delighted to dine with them at the Dorchester.

'No mention of an engagement ring?' Phil enquired.

'She didn't say, but I may hear something this evening,' she answered.

The shopping had gone well; both had got the few small things they wanted. They had had a good lunch, and Kensington Gardens had been beautiful. In fact they had enjoyed every minute to the full, and now Phil was already dressed for dinner and waiting in the drawing room for Joanna to come down.

He rose to greet her when he heard her coming, and as she entered the room, the sight of her almost took his breath away. It was a long white gown of elegant design which adorned her, one which brought her innocent beauty to its peak.

'You look more wonderful than ever, my darling,' he said as he kissed her.

'Thank you, my love, but don't forget that to me you are *always* wonderful,' she answered, tightening her arms around his neck for their lips to meet once more.

They had arranged to pick Jane and Gerald up in her father's Rolls. How pleased they all were to see each other. The evening looked like being a great success, with plenty of light-hearted chit-chat. They had hardly sat down at the table when Jane looked at Phil and said, 'I see the stars in someone's eyes are even brighter than the last time I saw them.'

Joanna, radiant with joy, put her hand on Phil's arm, saying, 'Thank you, my darling, for making me so wonderfully happy... and I'm not blushing one bit, either.'

They had a few dances, and during one when Phil was dancing with Jane she said to him, 'I never thought that a man living in Beversbury would capture Joanna like you have.'

'Do you think I have?' he asked, looking as unconcerned as possible.

'You know very well you have,' she said, 'you've annihilated her!' She went on, 'Seriously, Phil, knowing Joanna as I do, I can see that she is deeply and desperately in love. Well as a matter of fact, both of you are, and I wouldn't be surprised if she doesn't hear her wedding bells before I hear mine!'

'We're not even engaged yet,' he replied.

'I know, and neither are we,' Jane answered.

Walking across the floor after the dance, Phil said to her, 'I'll have to ply Gerald with some champagne, then he may pop the question!'

'Yes, you do that, Phil,' she answered, looking a little more confident.

True to his word, Phil made sure that Gerald's glass was kept topped up.

'Steady, Phil,' he said, 'Many more and I shan't know what I'm doing!'

'That's all right, Phil replied, 'it's a good thing to let your hair down sometimes,' he said, giving Jane a cute glance.

Joanna was glad to be back in Phil's arms for the next dance. He told her what had been said while he was dancing with Jane. Putting her lips as close to his ear as possible, she whispered, 'I realise more every day, my darling, what a lot I've got to be thankful for. What you are, and what you mean to me, casts only happiness and sunshine over me. I just couldn't stand the thought of being dangled on a string.'

His response was to hold her a little closer, and as they looked into each other's eyes, both could read the same message – that this great love of theirs was only at the beginning, that they were at the entrance to the valley of perpetual sunshine and fruitfulness, where only a deep, pure love as theirs could blossom to its rich fulfilment.

It was past midnight when they left the Dorchester. Jane insisted on taking a taxi to save them going out of their way, but before they parted Gerald asked if they would come to lunch on Sunday. Quickly, Joanna answered, 'I'm awfully sorry, but we are booked up for lunch and supper tomorrow.'

'Well, how about tea?' asked Gerald.

'Yes, we could manage that. Thank you very much,' she answered.

A few minutes later they were back at Eaton Place. Phil had just poured himself a brandy and soda when Joanna came from upstairs.

'A drink, darling?' he asked.

'Just a small one, my love,' she answered.

'Are we going anywhere special for lunch and supper

tomorrow, darling? Only I wondered why you declined Gerald's invitation.'

'On no, my sweet,' she answered. 'It's just that I want you as much to myself as possible. I can't bear to have to look at you across someone else's table. We'll have our meals here, if it's all right with you, my love.'

'I can't think of anything more wonderful, darling,' he replied.

Gently, she took the drinks from the table and, with his arms still around her, they talked for the last ten minutes before he rang for a taxi.

The next morning, she was already down and waiting for him, even though he was on time. After the first kiss she said, 'I had a wonderful sleep, but once I awoke, I couldn't get down here quick enough to have your arms around me again, my love.'

He half sighed as he answered, 'That's the trouble, my darling, the more we are in love, the worse it is when we have to part. I only wish that it was at least six months ago that we had met, then I might have a reasonable excuse to knock at your father's study door. I couldn't expect much joy after only five weeks, could I, my love?'

Tightening her arms around his neck, she answered, 'I know my love, that time is not exactly on our side, but I can't help feeling that something will turn up to solve our problem very soon.'

After lunch, just for a moment or two, Phil looked a little downcast.

'Fancy, we are already halfway through this bit of heaven of ours; but one good thing, it will only be Wednesday and Thursday when I won't be able to hold you in my arms, my darling,' he said.

'Our only hope is to live in the dream of these wonderful happy days, my love, so that it will carry us over that loneliness, but Friday won't come a moment too soon for me,' Joanna answered.

Putting his arms around her he asked, 'Are you coming up to the office with me in the morning, darling? Only I would like you to. I may have to leave you for a few minutes, but not a moment longer than I am bound to.'

'To be with you, my darling, just going and coming back is a few more minutes of heaven for me,' she answered.

Tea with Jane and Gerald was pleasant and enjoyable, but they were back in Eaton Place just after 6 p.m. Up the stairs she led him to the cosy morning room, and once the door was closed she flew into his arms, saying, 'There's no need for you to go all that way to change tonight, my love. You can bath here, for I don't want you out of my sight a moment longer that need be.'

'All right, darling, if you don't mind seeing me in the same suit all day. I won't mind either, for it will give us another half an hour together, even more if you really make haste,' he answered covering her in a flurry of kisses.

So the rest of the evening they spent, as they wanted to, quiet and alone, where the presence of each other was the greatest joy on earth. The next morning, after breakfast and an hour of togetherness, they set off on their way to the office. All the time she sat in the reception room, not for one moment did she dream that this hive of activity belonged to her loved one.

John Randell, who was in charge of this great undertaking, and also those under him, had been brought up to realise that the success of the firm was their success also, and to their benefit; consequently both had prospered. Property had been bought and branches set up in eight other cities, while the turnover and profits rose steadily each year. After a quarter of an hour, Phil appeared, bringing John Randell, whom he introduced to Joanna.

There were a few more moments of talk, at the end of which Phil said, 'I'll probably see you in two weeks' time, John.'

'Very good, Mr Fraser, and I'll see to the things you mentioned,' he answered, as they shook hands and said goodbye.

When they got outside, it was Joanna who asked the first question as she put her arm tightly through his.

'Would you like to come and see my gown shop now, darling, as there are one or two items which need my attention.'

'Well, my love,' Phil said, not showing the slightest sign on his face of what was in his mind, 'there's one more thing which I must do, so say I take you to your shop, then do my own errand, then come back and you can show me the business you have built up.'

'That would be lovely, Phil, as long as you are not away from me more than half an hour,' she said.

'I'll be back just as soon as I can, my sweetheart,' he answered, squeezing her hand tenderly.

The moment he left her, Phil took a taxi to the finest jewellers he knew, looked over some of the most gorgeous diamond necklaces in the whole of London, finally chose the one he liked most and knew it would be her choice also, and had his cheque cleared for £2,500. He was just fifteen minutes late getting back to her shop.

'I'm awfully sorry, my darling,' he said, 'but it didn't work out quite as quickly as I thought.'

'I'll forgive you this time, my love,' she answered, closing the door of her private office, and throwing her arms around him.

Then, one by one as the opportunity arose, she introduced him to the other young lady assistants, and he could see by the business going on around him, how hard she must have worked to build it up, and he congratulated her on it.

'That was before you came into my life, my love, when all I thought about was building this up. Now I have something much more real to occupy my thoughts,' she answered, with one of those irresistible smiles upon her face.

Back at Eaton Place for lunch, and the first long kiss for hours, Joanna was still in his arms when he suddenly said, 'I've bought you a little present, my love. Would you like to see it now or wait until after lunch? On second thoughts,' he went on, 'I think you had better wait.' He indicated the small parcel he had left on a side table.

'You shouldn't, my darling, you've bought me enough already,' she answered giving him a kiss. Then she continued, 'But may I, my love?'

'It's all yours my darling,' he said, knowing that she didn't have the faintest idea what was inside.

She undid the wrapping, and a look of wonderment spread over her face as she opened the case before her, while her eyes shone more than the diamonds themselves. But then came a sudden change as she quickly realised the wealth that was on her lap.

'Darling!' she exclaimed. 'This is far too much… I daren't ask how much it cost!'

'Does it matter what it cost, my love?' he answered.

'Yes, it does! You can't afford to give me this sort of present. Tell me what it cost. I want to know, my darling,' she insisted.

'Only £2,500,' he answered, laughing.

The look of amazement on her face only made him laugh more and more. Then he said, 'Let me tell you a little story, my angel. My grandfather – that is, my mother's father – had this business. When he died it went to my uncle, but he was killed in the war, so it all went to my mother. Those offices I took you to this morning is that business; not only that, but there are branches in eight other cities. I don't know much about it, other than it's making a lot of money. But to John Randell, the man you met this morning, and all those under him, I am the boss. It is all mine – lock, stock and barrel. I know some of the profits are put into stocks and shares, but if you crowned me, I couldn't tell you how much money I am worth at that end. But – and this is a big but – if I had to choose between losing that business, or a hundred acres of my farm, I'd keep my hundred acres. For I, like my father before me, am a farmer, and just like him, I base my prosperity on my own efforts and the good earth.'

The diamond necklace was pushed to one side on the sofa as Joanna flew into his arms. His wealth was forgotten; it was his wonderful nature that brought the tears running down her cheeks, the definite preference he had for the things nearer to God than all the money in the world. For a whole minute she clung to him, and once again he felt those tears wet his cheek.

'What is it, my love, tell me what is the matter?' he asked.

'Nothing, my darling, only that I love you so much, more and more every day if that is possible,' she answered.

'Are you quite satisfied that I am able to afford it now, my love?' he asked.

'Oh yes, my darling, and thank you a million times for it, for I am overjoyed and thrilled beyond words…'

It was one more of his special kisses that finally brought all the stars back to her eyes. How she loved him, and how each day she seemed to learn a little more of him – things which made him ever dearer to her blissful heart. There was just enough time for her to try the necklace on before lunch. She looked fantastic; not that the diamonds added a scrap to her beauty. To Phil, it seemed the other way round.

'I think I chose the right one,' he said smiling.

'I'm sure you did, my darling, it's absolutely wonderful,' she answered, kissing him as deep as her innocence would allow. Then she continued, 'But my love, I shall always treasure my pearls a little bit more than anything else. To me, they are the symbol of the moment we met, of a stolen kiss and a love which went on from there and will never end.' She paused a moment before adding, 'Often, when we're apart, I look at them and try them on, just to reassure myself that I am not having just a beautiful and wonderful dream.'

What else could he do but to hold her tight, and with his lips lead her once more along that sunlit path?

In the afternoon, they looked around St Paul's Cathedral. When there was no one close enough to hear he half whispered to her, 'Whenever I am in church, I always long for the day to come when I shall be waiting there for you, my angel, waiting to see my princess coming slowly up the aisle to join me, bringing the whole of my future with her.'

Joanna turned towards him, and with a divine smile upon her face she answered, 'Never fear, my love, I will take the greatest care of that future, but if by chance we are ever parted I promise it shall only be for a little while. If anyone had told me two months ago that I should have been so desperately and hopelessly in love these last five weeks, I would have laughed at them; yet here I am, my darling, with one thought in all my waking and sleeping hours – you and only you, my own true love.'

'Two months ago,' Phil replied. I was just as much in the dark as you, my angel. But for five whole weeks, my love for you has been just as deep and as desperate too.' He gave her hand an extra squeeze, then, raising two eyes to that beautiful golden halo around her head, and searching the pure depth of her tender violet eyes, then on down to the utter perfection of her smiling lips, he went on, 'But I often ask myself why I am blessed with the complete love of the sweetest and most beautiful girl in the world.'

Phil was already downstairs and waiting for her on this, his last morning in London. To him it was all too visible that too many stars had already vanished from her eyes, and even after a morning of going round the shops and a lovely lunch at Eaton Place, she was nowhere near back to her normal self.

Up in the morning room, after they had finished coffee, he took her in his arms saying, 'Please don't fret, my angel! Three days will soon go by, and this time my arms will be waiting to hold you, right from the very start. You won't be left waiting on the platform this time, and now you know the wonderful reception that will be waiting for you, my darling.'

'I know, my love,' she answered, 'but even that doesn't stop my desperate yearning to be with you always, a yearning that will be with me for every second until I feel the comfort of your arms at Spring Farm.' Her eyes lit up a little as she went on, 'I know it will be so much more wonderful for us this time, but even now I can hardly believe everything that happened the last time. How I was coming to Jane's for three weeks' quiet holiday, how my heart missed beat after beat when our eyes met, how you carried my two cases on the right side and held my arm with your left hand! If you had only known, my darling, the joy and anticipation that you had opened up before me. I, who had never given any other man a first thought, was suddenly confronted with so much more than my heart could desire. Then that stolen kiss, which changed the rhythm of my blissful heart to a frightening pace; then the awful thoughts, knowing that my future could have melted back to what it was before, a life of little purpose; then over that first cup of coffee, when we dispelled each other's fears, and the joy of all heaven was opened up for our taking! That is the future which I want to grasp with both hands and hold on to forever, when that heaven is ours each day and night, my darling.'

Only a special kiss could answer that, and help banish the thought of those three days of loneliness for a little bit longer. Afterwards with their cheeks still pressed together Phil said, 'Try to think of those wonderful three weeks over the next three days and please remember, my darling, that for something which didn't seem to have much chance at the start, this wonderful love of ours has travelled further along that heavenly road than you and I dared to imagine a few weeks ago. All we can hope and pray for now is that the future will carry us towards our great day at the same pace, my darling.'

'Dear Phil! I'll remember, and I'll try very hard; but as you know, it is the night-time when I am most helpless,' she answered, looking not very confident.

They had an early tea in the drawing room. She had ordered the Rolls to take them to Paddington to catch the train just after five o'clock, but those last few minutes at Eaton Place were spent in the quietness of the morning room. Her eyes were watery, rimmed with the suspicion of a liquid diamond in each corner. It hurt him to see the inner torment which shook the rhythm of her heart. She was like a flower, one which had just opened up its delicate beauty for the first time and was suddenly being deprived of life-giving sunshine. It was her trembling lips which worried him most, for not even the power of a special kiss could hold them firm for very long.

'What time will you go to bed, my love?' he asked.

'Somewhere around ten, my darling,' she answered.

He held her tightly to him, pressing his cheek reassuringly against hers as he said, 'I'll ring you as soon as I arrive at Spring Farm. Then when I ring you again at ten o'clock we'll have a long, comforting talk before you go to sleep.'

'Thank you, my love,' she answered. 'I know you will do everything in the world to bring a little sunshine into my life when we can be together, and I love you so much for it.'

On the way to the station, they stopped at his hotel to pick up his cases. At Paddington, once he had made sure of his seat and put his cases on the rack he stood outside on the platform. He was doing all he could to keep her spirits up, but their time together was almost at an end now.

'How can I thank you, my darling, for all the heaven you have given me, and for my beautiful necklace,' she said.

'By being you, my darling. That's all the thanks I shall ever need,' he answered as the whistle blew. Quickly they touched lips, but once he was aboard he leaned out to give her the farewell kiss.

'My angel,' he whispered.

'My own true love,' she replied, while all the unsaid last messages of love were transferred between them and the train started on its way.

'See you on Friday for lunch, my love,' he just had time to say, and at the same time he read her lips as they said, 'Bye-bye, my darling.'

He leaned out, waving to her until she disappeared from view.

The First Big Step

When he arrived at Spring Farm, Phil rang Joanna immediately, telling her that the journey had gone quickly. He daren't say too much about missing her terribly; that would only make the time of parting seem longer, and harder for her to bear. Penny came and spoke to her, asking if she had had a lovely time, and said among other things that she was longing to see her on Friday.

When Phil took over the phone again, Joanna said, 'There must be something special in the air at Spring Farm! There are only two people I know there, and they are both the sweetest in the whole world; you, my precious future, my darling; and Penny, not only the perfect housekeeper, but the most wonderful friend as well.'

'If that is the case, my love, then I know the only one who was born to make the perfect third,' he replied.

For a few more minutes they talked of Jane and other things, but ended declaring their undying love for each other, in the knowledge that they would hear each other's voices at ten o'clock as planned.

The kitchen was Phil's first port of call. Penny wanted to know what Eaton Place was really like, and so forth. He told her that it was a lovely house and beautifully furnished, also where they had been for their different meals and the places they had seen; but Penny couldn't fail to see that half of him was missing, and that the other half was a hundred miles away with the loved one he had left behind.

'It won't be long before Friday is here,' she said.

'I know,' he answered, 'but it's the waiting in between that is the hardest. It's bad enough for me, but it's a hundred times worse for Joanna.'

He seemed deep in thought for a few moments, then suddenly he said. 'Penny, 'I know I haven't a worry over the food question while Joanna, her father and Marie-Ann are here, but I'm always worrying whether you have enough help. So I'm going to impress upon you not to do so much, I don't expect you to; you need more help, even if it is only at odd times, or when we have parties or visitors. You know I can well afford to pay for all the extra help that you need.'

'All right,' Penny answered, 'I suppose we often try to get in more work than we can. Anyhow, I think I know just the person we need, and she's reliable, so I'll see her later.'

'About time too,' Phil replied, putting a friendly arm around her.

For two days the weather had been a little unsettled, but as Friday dawned, it seemed those few warm showers had given the countryside an extra freshness. As he looked out of his bedroom window at the hour of 5.30 a.m., smelling the sweet fragrance and cleanliness of everything, Phil couldn't help thinking, *I'll bet the colonel will love it here, especially if the weather stays kind.*

He did all he could before breakfast, then he rang Joanna at Northwood. She, like him, could hardly wait for these last few hours to go by, and the conversation finished on the phrase, 'See you around 11.30 a.m., my darling.'

As Phil walked across the drive towards his car to go to Tetstone to draw the wages, Penny couldn't miss that extra bit of zip in each step he took, and she knew beyond all doubt that the empty loneliness of these partings couldn't last very long. Very soon – perhaps in only a matter of months – there would be a new mistress at Spring Farm, and one that she loved dearly.

By eleven o'clock he had returned. He washed and changed quickly, then made his way to the kitchen, all ready for what he thought as one of the most important day of his life.

'Do I look all right Penny?' he asked.

'Perfect, and every inch a gentleman,' she answered. 'I'll be frank,' she continued, 'I'm more than thankful that you didn't choose a girl who was marrying you for your money. I know with Joanna it wouldn't have mattered whether you had had money or not. Besides her great love for you, she adores you for what you are, and that is an excellent foundation on which to build a perfect marriage.'

She had hardly finished before the sound of a car could be heard on the gravel. He was up in an instant and got to the door just at the Rolls pulled up.

Joanna was out and in his arms in a flash, but before their lips met she whispered, 'My darling, my own true love,' to which he replied, 'My love, my angel.'

These phrases were to them the ultimate spoken words, which signified all that their pure and undying love meant to them.

He noticed that her eyes looked a little moist, but it wasn't the thought of parting, this time. This was the strain of emotional joy, which touched the strings of the heart a little too heavily; this was the case when the depth of love ran at too great a volume.

It was a happy meeting all round, with the colonel well in the forefront.

'Do you know, Phil,' he said as he placed his hand on Phil's shoulder, 'I've been looking forward very much to coming here, and I like what I've seen already.' For quite a while he stood there admiring the smartness of everything and all the flowers in the oval patches of garden and stone troughs.

'This is only the back of the house, Daddy. Wait till you see the front!' said Joanna quite excitedly.

She led the way into the lounge, but while Phil was seeing to the drinks she disappeared towards the kitchen. Within a matter of seconds she was back again, bringing Penny, whom she introduced to her father and Marie-Ann.

'This is our Penny,' she said, 'the finest cook for miles and miles, and a very great friend of mine.'

'Quite right,' answered Phil, 'she's the mainstay of Spring Farm, and I don't know what I would have done without her.'

Joanna, who had already asked Penny what she would like to drink, soon put a large glass of sherry before her, and in very little time, the colonel and Marie-Ann could sense how well these two got on together, and that here was a case of perfect harmony. After a while they had a tour of the house, and like Joanna both were amazed at how beautiful and comfortable it all was. All this time Joanna had her arm through Phil's, and it was only on rare occasions that her eyes strayed in any other direction than his.

'Now for the garden,' she said, leading the way.

Once outside, the colonel and Marie-Ann came to a halt; they were both completely spellbound.

'It's so beautiful, Phil, it's really like something you only dream about,' said Marie-Ann.

'My dreams have never got this far!' said the colonel, laughing, 'It's too fantastic for words, so beautiful and so secluded.'

Joanna turned towards the table and chairs and said, 'Daddy, this is where Phil and I were sitting the other Sunday evening.' Looking round into Phil's eyes, she went on, 'Just you and I, my love, listening to the birds singing, but worrying and wondering how long it would be before we should be here again together.'

'Yes, my love,' he answered, 'and little did we dream that time would arrive much sooner than we thought possible.'

They strolled on up, right around the beautiful lawn, looking at the loveliest of flowers, shrubs and trees you could wish to imagine, and came to the wonderfully carved bird bath.

'It's the biggest I've seen. I don't suppose you want to sell it, do you?' said the colonel, laughing.

'Oh no,' said Phil, looking at Joanna. 'In any case I don't think I would be allowed to even if I wanted to.'

'It's got too many pleasant memories for me already to let you sell it, my love,' she said, looking at him as lovingly as ever. Then she continued, 'Besides, that is where my blue birds came to look at us.' She then proceeded to tell her father and Marie-Ann all about the two jays.

It was while they were having their coffee outside that the colonel and Marie-Ann both remarked on the wonderful lunch they had just had.

'Wonderful, as usual,' added Joanna.

That was when Phil turned to her saying, 'Now, darling, there is one thing I have got to do this afternoon. I shall have to take the men's wages round. Would you like to come, or shall I go as quickly as I can alone?'

She looked at him with understanding as she answered, 'I don't mind you going without me now, my love. I'm quite all right as long as I know I can see you within a few hours; so why don't you take Daddy, then perhaps Mummy and I will have a walk over to the Court to see Jane and her mother and father.'

'I'd really love that, Phil, if you don't mind my coming,' said the colonel.

'Only too pleased, Colonel, it's quite a change for me to have company,' he answered.

They were ready to leave at 2.30 p.m.; Phil had already kissed Joanna goodbye while they had all been in the lounge, but as he and the colonel were in the hall, after he had got the wages from his study, Joanna came running out of the lounge.

'I must have one more kiss before you go, my love,' she said, as her father walked slowly out of the door; it was a little more than half a special he gave her.

'After almost three whole days without you, it is only one of your wonderful kisses that puts me back into that heaven which only you and I can share, my darling,' she whispered.

'And what a wonderful heaven too my love,' he answered, giving her one last kiss and caress.

She stood by the door and waved them off, and once out on the road the colonel turned to him, saying. 'You think a lot of Joanna, don't you, Phil?'

For a split second Phil turned and looked the colonel in the eye. He said, 'I love Joanna more deeply that I thought it was possible to love anyone, and when we are apart I go through the same torment that I know she suffers, and I have never stopped telling myself how blessed I am to have met her.'

'I know she thinks the same about you, Phil. You are her first boyfriend, serious or otherwise, and when she told us how deeply she was in love with you, I knew then that it would have to be someone really special.'

As the colonel finished his sentence, Phil pulled up for the first payout, they both got out, and almost straight away he was introducing the colonel to two of his men. These would be the only two he would meet that afternoon. What Phil hadn't counted for was the great interest that the colonel took in everything; it was almost like a conducted tour, and that is how it went on, so that by five o'clock Phil had just paid the men on the third farm.

'Can we have a look round this one, Phil? I'm not at all hungry, are you?' he asked.

'No,' answered Phil, 'but I'd better ring the house to say we'll be late, or they may start wondering.'

He was back in less than five minutes and then proceeded to show the colonel most of the farm from different vantage points, but it was a quarter to six o'clock before they left. To save time he took the shortest way home.

'How big is all this, Phil?' asked the colonel.

'Nine hundred and eighty acres,' Phil answered, smiling.

'By Jove!' replied the colonel, 'You're not exactly destitute, are you?' He was clearly having a good laugh.

'Not quite,' replied Phil, joining in the joke.

It was past six o'clock when they arrived home. Joanna and Marie-Ann had already had tea, but as the car drew up Penny was making a fresh brew for the late arrivals. There was a look of relief, which soon gave way to joy in Joanna's eyes as they kissed.

'Have you missed me much, my love?' she asked.

'Just as much as I always do, and just as much as I always shall, my darling,' he answered, kissing her again.

The colonel was so busy telling them about all he had seen that they had finished tea before Joanna or Marie-Ann could mention their visit to the Court. Joanna was sitting on the lawn, facing Phil and almost at his feet.

'You'll never guess the news we had at Court this afternoon, darling,' she said.

'Not an engagement?' he asked.

'Yes,' she answered, 'it's happened at last. Gerald has popped the question and they are getting married at the end of March.'

'Fancy,' he replied, 'Gerald has plucked up courage at last! I'm glad for Jane, and I bet the major's pleased.'

'That is one wedding we shall all be going to,' said Marie-Ann, 'We've had our spoken invitation this afternoon.'

As further discussion on the forthcoming wedding went on, only the colonel refrained from making any comment, but suddenly he turned to Marie-Ann, saying, 'I've been thinking... I shall have to have a new outfit for that wedding. Neither of my tailcoats and trousers are quite good enough, so you'll have to remind me, dear, when we get back to Northwood, to make a note of it, so that I can arrange a visit to my tailors after Christmas.'

Joanna looked up from the daisy she was twirling in her fingers and straight towards her father, and even before Marie-Ann could reply, she said, 'You'll want one before then, Daddy.'

Silence reigned for quite a while longer than was normal, before her father answered. 'Why, what do you mean, my dear?'

Joanna, with a slight touch of emotion showing already, but still looking straight at her father, said, 'Daddy, I have two wants, one concerns you and the other Phil. Yours, the first and most important, is that I want to be Phil's bride before the end of this year – I'd like the end of September, if we could get everything arranged by then; and the second one is, I don't care where Phil takes me on our honeymoon, but I want to spend my wedding night here, in this house, our future home.'

The silence lasted a little longer this time. There was only one person who could answer that statement, the colonel; and true to his understanding nature, and knowing how desperately in love these two were, he said, 'If that is what you so desperately want, my dear, you had better come and give me a kiss and let me congratulate you.'

Joanna was off the ground in a flash, saying as she hugged and kissed him, 'Oh, thank you, Daddy! You're the most wonderful father in the whole world, and I love you so.'

Marie-Ann came next, and while they were having a big hug too, the colonel held out his hand to Phil and said, 'Congratulations, Phil! It was so sudden that I was almost lost for words, but believe me I'm very pleased about it.'

'Thank you very much, Colonel,' he answered, brimming over with happiness, for was not a wonderful future already opening up before them?

Then Joanna came to her beloved. There, kneeling on the ground and sliding her arms around his neck, she whispered, 'My own true love,' as that heavenly presence built up around her.

'My angel,' he whispered back, as their lips met, sealing their undying love on this, the first step towards finality.

'We must go and tell Penny the wonderful news,' she said, and with their arms around each other they made their way to the kitchen.

Penny was ecstatic. 'I'm so happy for you both. It is what I have prayed for, and I am not in the least bit surprised that it has come so sudden, for I felt sure the other day that neither of you could go on being parted for much longer.'

They both kissed her, and as they were going out of the door, Phil turned around, saying, 'It's champagne tonight, Penny and you're to have as much as you want, and I'll bring you a bottle of brandy, knowing that it's your favourite nightcap, for I want you as much as anyone to give us a good start off, bless you.'

Once out on the lawn again, Phil turned to the colonel and Marie-Ann, saying, 'I know it's a little early, but I feel we ought to have a drink. It won't be a proper celebration, we'll have to wait for dinner and the champagne for that.'

'A good idea,' they both replied.

So into the dining room the two lovers went; once inside, of course the thought of drinks came second. What else could take place over all but a special kiss? What else could set the seal on their love, a love that could now see the light of day?

'It won't be long now, my darling, before we shall really belong to each other, and there'll be no more partings,' Joanna whispered, searching the depths of his eyes.

'Much sooner than I dared to dream of this time last week, my love,' he answered, kissing her on each of her beautiful eyelids.

When the drinks were ready, Joanna took two into the kitchen for Penny and the dependable Mrs White, while Phil carried the tray of bottles and glasses to the table outside. It was a time of happiness and excitement for all, while on the face of the bride-to-be was a radiance in full bloom. This was the moment she had longed for, prayed for, after all those empty years.

'I'll be a good wife to you, my darling,' she said playfully.

'I know you will, my love,' he answered, and asked 'when would you like to go to London to choose your ring?'

'As soon as possible, darling,' she answered.

'Then it's Monday,' he said.

'I can hardly wait until then, my darling,' she answered, leaning sideways and kissing him.

Marie-Ann, the colonel and Phil were already dressed for dinner and having a cocktail in the drawing room, before Joanna came down. The colonel was sitting in the chair opposite the door, which gave him the first sight of his daughter as she entered the room.

'My goodness, what beauty we have here!' he exclaimed, as Phil and Marie-Ann turned and beheld the loveliest sight the eye could wish to see.

Sheathed in a beautiful pale blue gown, the diamond necklace flashing a thousand stars, Joanna's natural beauty cascaded like a gentle waterfall, while triumphant bliss shone from her face like the rays of the morning sun. With arms outstretched, she glided towards her beloved, and before kissing him she said, 'Thank you once again, my darling, for my beautiful present.'

'Just a moment,' said the colonel. 'Let us two see what that present is.'

'A beautiful diamond necklace that my future husband bought me last Monday,' she answered, looking thrilled beyond words.

By now the colonel and Marie-Ann were standing up and giving the necklace an admiring examination.

'You're spoiling her, Phil, you've spent more on her in two or three months than I have in years!'

'She's worth every penny, and more,' replied Phil, holding Joanna tightly to his side, adding, 'Aren't you, my love?'

'Yes, my darling, and there are a lot of pennies in £2,500,' she answered, turning round and kissing him once more.

The colonel's face dropped as he said to Joanna, 'You really shouldn't let Phil spend that kind of money, my dear.'

'It's quite all right Colonel,' Phil interrupted. 'There's no danger. I get quite a good living from the farms, but the money I bought the necklace with came from my business in London.'

He then proceeded to tell them all about it and, as he went on, so the cloud gradually lifted from the colonel's face. As he finished, the colonel had a good hearty laugh, saying, 'And to think that when Joanna told us you were a farmer, I was actually totting up how much I would have to allow her to help you both along!'

This caused an even greater laugh all round.

Joanna then disappeared, but Phil knew where she had gone; she was like him and his family where Penny was concerned. Penny had to be brought into all the happenings, big or small, at

Spring Farm, and now she and Mrs White were no doubt admiring his beautiful gift – and the beauty and sweetness of the gift he himself had received direct from heaven.

As dinner started, the colonel asked Joanna, 'Would you like me to give you a toast tonight, my dear, or wait until Monday when you have your ring?'

'Both, Daddy,' she answered, 'I know the magic of this day will be with us for ever, for tonight, Daddy, you consented for Phil to take my hand in marriage. But on Monday I shall have the outward visible sign to realising my heart's desire, and I don't want to miss one beautiful moment or gesture after all the emptiness and waiting before we met.'

Accordingly, the colonel rose, saying, 'I give this toast to the dearest and nicest young couple that anyone could be blessed with. I know that they will be attended by the greatest happiness and that their love for each other will have no bounds. So, as we lift our glasses to them, we can only drink to a long and fruitful life together. To you, my dears, you who are precious to us all, we drink to you and your future, wishing you the very best of everything to Joanna and Phil.'

Penny and Mrs White both raised their glasses of champagne with the colonel and Marie-Ann, as Joanna and Phil held hands across the table, looking into each other's eyes with all the devotion that betokened a real true love.

Now it was Phil's turn to speak. He got up and said quietly, 'I know I am speaking for Joanna as well as myself when I say we both thank you all from the bottom of our hearts.'

The next morning, he had already made a quick journey out to see how some of the farm was getting on and, quite satisfied, he returned home and was now walking round the garden, waiting for the call for breakfast. Joanna, knowing that this was his usual practice, had got up early so that she could join him. He was right at the far end when he saw her coming, and retraced his steps to meet her. They both held arms out ready to enfold each other, their lips ever yearning for a deep loving kiss.

'And did my love sleep well on her first night at Spring Farm?' he asked.

'Oh, wonderful, my darling, although we were late going to

bed, I don't think I could have stirred all night! Yet I still feel so wonderfully refreshed,' she answered.

'Do you really think you will be able to get all the arrangements fulfilled for the end of September, my love?' he asked.

Still looking into his eyes, she answered, 'You watch me, darling! In a week's time I shall have the most important things running to schedule. I don't intend to be parted from you a moment longer than possible.' She paused and went on, 'Fancy, my love, we have waited for this moment all our lives, and you know my darling my love for you is so great that I wish our wedding day was tomorrow.'

'So do I, my love,' he answered, 'but things have moved far quicker than either of us dared dream of a few weeks ago. I often want to kick myself to make sure that this is really happening to me, and then, as now, when I hold you in my arms, when I see the innocent longing in your eyes and when the responding warmth of your sweet lips enfolds me, I know that this is not only an earthly love but a heavenly one as well, one which must rise and fall, rise to its all-consuming power when we are together, and fall to the depth of despair when we are parted; but don't worry, my love, I'll see that we are together as much as possible in the few weeks ahead.'

They had almost finished breakfast when the phone rang, and Phil answered it.

'It's Jane, darling, she said she would like a few words with you.'

Joanna then took over and from the dining room they heard her say, 'I'm sure we would all love to, thank you very much.' Pause. 'And are you going into town this morning? Only I've got something wonderful to tell you.' Pause, 'We'll meet you at the usual place, thanks once again, dear, bye-bye.'

'Jane has invited us all for dinner tonight, and they'll meet us in Tetstone, darling,' she said as she entered.

'What a pity,' said the colonel. 'I shan't look forward to it one bit, for I don't expect the cooking is half as good as Penny's.'

'You'll enjoy it once the major and you get together,' said Marie-Ann.

'Are you coming into Tetstone with us?' asked Phil.

'Not this morning, thank you, Phil,' answered the colonel. 'Last night I promised Marie-Ann a nice walk up over the fields, and besides, you young things will have so much to talk over when you meet in town.'

Jane and Gerald were already waiting when their friends pulled up at the usual place. They were all very pleased to see each other, and almost the first words Phil spoke was to congratulate them on their engagement. That was the reason why, as they entered the hotel, he said, 'I think we had better have something a bit stronger than coffee this morning.'

So in they went to the lounge bar, where they picked the quietest spot. Drinks were ordered and brought as the usual pleasantries went on. Then Jane, leaning towards Joanna, said, 'I'm dying to know what that something is that is so wonderful.'

'See if you can guess,' answered Joanna, her eyes twinkling like a million stars, and her hand caressing Phil's.

'You're not trying to tell us that you are going to beat us to the altar, are you?' asked Jane, looking almost as excited.

'Right first time! Daddy consented and gave us his blessing last night, so it's the end of September,' answered Joanna, more radiant than ever. Then she continued, 'You will be my bridesmaid and I shall be your matron of honour.'

'That is what we always promised each other, if and when; but when we did I know you never dreamt that you would be married before me.'

'No,' replied Joanna, 'to me marriage was something in a far-off land, but then I didn't know that your father's car would break down and alter my whole life at the same time.' She turned to Phil and said, 'Darling, I wonder if you would mind me asking you a favour.'

'Certainly not, my love,' he answered. 'You know I'll do anything you ask.'

'Well,' she said, 'when I buy your ring on Monday, I would like to have "P" for Phillip engraved on it, also "J" for Joanna intertwined, so that I am sure I shall always be with you, my darling.'

'It's a lovely thought, my love, and you know there is nothing I would like better,' he answered, looking into her eyes for a moment and thinking, was there no end to her sweetness? Was there no end to all the little ways in which she expressed her great love for him?

The colonel and Marie-Ann were still out on their walk when they got back to Spring Farm.

'Shall we go and meet them darling?' Joanna asked.

'Yes, my love, it will do us good to have a walk before lunch,' he answered.

They had almost reached the old chestnut tree when they saw the colonel and Marie-Ann coming towards them.

'Did you think we were lost?' shouted the colonel, when they were still some way off.

'Not likely,' Phil answered, 'knowing that you come from the country, I reckoned you could find your way around.'

'It's all so lovely, Phil,' said Marie-Ann when they finally met, 'I had no idea that the countryside could look so beautiful, but then you seem to have everything here to make it so.'

'Yes,' he answered, 'we really are lucky to live in such a beautiful spot.'

'Did you get as far as High Ridge?' asked Joanna.

'Yes, but only to the foot of it,' her father answered.

'We'll have to take you to the top one day, it's like being on the edge of the world, Daddy,' she said, quite excitedly.

'That is a must before we go back,' he replied.

As they approached Spring Farm, Penny was just putting the tray with a jug of ice cool orangeade and glasses on the oak chest in the hall, and they were all grateful for a refreshing drink, for the temperature was in the seventies already.

After his first drink, the colonel went to the kitchen door and, holding up his glass, said, 'Home-made, Penny?'

'Yes, sir,' she answered.

'I thought so… Besides saving my life, it's the best glass of orange I've tasted. No wonder Joanna is so eager to stay here! I think you look after them too well,' he said, smiling his friendliest.

In the afternoon, Phil drove them round to see more beauty

125

spots, making sure that he would arrive at The Calling Seagull for tea. This again was one more pleasant memory for the lovers, but back at Spring Farm it was Marie-Ann who said, 'Thank you, Phil, you've given us a most wonderful afternoon, and I've enjoyed it immensely,' to which the colonel fully agreed.

Jane and Gerald must have been watching for the Rolls to come nosing its way up the drive, for before the car had even stopped they were at the door and ready to greet them. This was always a great occasion, for the colonel and the major only met once in a while, but this time it was somewhat over-shadowed as the major and Phil came face to face.

'You haven't been up to see me for a long time, Phil, not even for me to congratulate you,' he said. Then, with a whimsical smile on his face he continued, 'When you were here last, I said it was time you found a nice girl and settled down, but I didn't necessarily mean the one that was sitting opposite you at the time! However, I am glad you took my advice so soon.'

It wasn't because they were all having such a good laugh that Phil didn't answer. It was Joanna, looking her usual radiant self and with her arm through his, who spoke.

'You were a little late even then, Major, for the die had already been cast. I know it was too soon for either of us to talk of how we felt towards each other, but it was at The Junction – the first time our eyes met – that told us there couldn't possibly be anyone else in the whole world.'

'And do you mean to tell me,' said the major with the broadest of smiles upon his face, 'that you sat on that sofa listening to what I was saying and knowing all the time that Phil was everything in the world to you?'

'Yes,' Joanna answered, with her eyes shining like stars and nestling closer to the one she loved.

'You're shot down once more,' said Mrs Marchant, as she led another round of mirth.

It was later on that evening that Jane took Joanna up to her room, and naturally the plans for both weddings were discussed in some detail; and naturally too that topic would have been the only one, but it was Jane who suddenly said, 'It will be wonderful to have you living so near, and you're quite sure Phil won't mind me coming over as often as I want to?'

'Of course not, you will be more than welcome at any time. He would be very put out if you didn't come when you wanted to,' replied Joanna.

'I can see your love for him grows deeper each time we meet,' said Jane.

'Yes, if that is possible.' Then, holding Jane's hand, she continued, 'Life for me couldn't be more wonderful, so much so that I know I would die without him now.'

Monday morning dawned as beautiful as one could wish. The colonel and Marie-Ann were up early to see Joanna and Phil off at 8.20 a.m.

'Have a good day, and we hope you will find what you are both looking for.

Remember, it is one of the greatest days of your lives. We'll see you around 6.30 p.m.,' said the colonel, just as the car started to move.

The feeling couldn't be described; the joy and happiness that was theirs could not be measured in any way. As they went along the road towards The Junction, all around them looked a million times more beautiful that ever before, for was not this their first step on to the threshold, where their two lives and the yearning passion of their hearts would soon be one? Phil let go of the steering wheel with his left hand, and took Joanna's right hand, passing it over his heart in a gesture that could only have come from that selfsame spot.

'My angel,' he said, looking into those lovely eyes for just a moment.

'My own true love,' she answered, moving a little closer to him.

The express was on time, and, except for one lady standing in the corridor saying her last farewells, their compartment was empty. As the train moved slowly out of the station, Joanna, looking the peak of happiness, whispered, 'I'm thankful that you are here with me now, my darling, not like the last time, me here and you back on the platform, and our next meeting seeming like years instead of days away. But even in my despair, I still realised, and was thankful to God, that the wonderful love and kisses we had truly shared gave me far more than a glimpse of the heavenly future that lies in store for us.'

'I shall never forget that loneliness, my love...' He got no further, as the lady came in and sat down.

After that, the conversation was mostly about the things which came into view as they sped along, but farther up the line, the lady once more got up and went out into the corridor. It was then that Joanna said, 'Darling, once we've chosen our rings, do you think you could spare me a little time to go to my shop? I have phoned them two or three times, but it's much better for me to see to things on the spot and get that part of my plans moving as I want them.'

'Certainly, my love. It's your day, and I'm sure I would be only in the way with you having so much to do, and so much to think about. In the meantime I'll pop over to my tailors, as quickly as I can, I'll be back to take you somewhere nice for lunch.'

That was how the sequence of events turned out, except for one thing. So thrilled and fascinated were they both – he with his broad gold signet ring with "P" and "J" intertwined around each other, she with her one large beautiful diamond with two smaller ones on each side, set in platinum. It was almost the last word to a beautiful girl of twenty-one, desperately in love with the young man who had made all this heaven possible. If she had finished all that she had set out to do, no one knew, for at 12.45 a.m., when he arrived at the gown shop, she was just inside the door waiting for him. Almost eagerly, she ushered him into her room beyond and, hardly before he had time to close the door, her arms were over his shoulders. One long beautiful kiss followed, one which held all there was in a pure and requited love.

'I'm so completely thrilled with my beautiful ring, my darling! How I stopped myself from kissing you at the jewellers' I just don't know, but I just couldn't wait until we got back to Spring Farm to thank you. Words, ordinary words would have been inadequate, only by my heart telling you how much I love you, my own true love, can I give thanks enough.'

'It's all the world to me, my angel, to know you are so thrilled with it, and I'm thrilled beyond words with my beautiful ring also,' he answered, giving her one more special kiss. But, unknown to these two in love, these two who were blissfully blinded by the slightest touch or glance one from the other, dreaming and yearning only for the time when those symbols of unity were to be exchanged, plans were afoot. For they had arranged that their pledge of love should take place before dinner, just an ordinary dinner, with champagne and just the family. But if only they could have seen Spring Farm at that moment!

The colonel had started it when he asked Penny if she wanted anything special from Tetstone for dinner. He saw her face light up and a sudden thought came to him.

'Good heavens!' he said. 'Shall we invite the four from the Court and give them a surprise party? Can you manage that at such short notice?'

'Certainly, sir, it's what I've been hoping you would say. I can get all the help I need and, if you will get all the necessary in Tetstone, we'll give them the party they deserve.'

So as the day progressed, dishes of all sorts, shapes and colours gradually took shape, and the colonel and Marie-Ann were completely fascinated at Penny's skilled handiwork.

Back in London, Phil had taken Joanna to Harrods for lunch.

'Are there any other shops you want to visit, or anything else you would like me to buy you, darling?' he asked.

'No, my sweet, everything is going along nicely, and I must leave one or two things for you to get for me after we are married, or you won't know you have got a wife,' she answered, giving him the loveliest of smiles with those love-filled eyes.

'Your love and your sweetness will never let that escape me, my darling, for my eyes have beheld a beauty that is pictured forever before me.'

It was a little after 6.30 p.m., when they arrived back at Spring Farm.

'Well, was it a lucky day for the both of you?' enquired the colonel; but the look on Joanna's face should have told him that.

'Oh yes, Daddy, and when you see the beautiful ring that Phil has bought me, you'll know that I am not only the happiest girl in the world, but also the luckiest,' she said excitedly, as she walked arm in arm with her father into the house.

It wasn't long before they found out about having visitors for dinner. Joanna had noticed the table laid for eight o'clock when she had gone into the dining room to get Phil a drink. That lovely gesture really put the seal on the most wonderful day of their lives so far, and it meant a host of heartfelt thanks for the colonel, Marie-Ann and Penny.

It was just after seven o'clock when the colonel and Marie-Ann went upstairs to dress for dinner, and it was no more than a minute later when Phil led his future bride over to the privacy of his cosy study. Between the first and second special kiss he whispered, 'My darling,' only to hear the loveliest voice in the world whisper back, 'My precious love.'

It ran into minutes before the haze had cleared from the ecstasy of that second kiss. That was when he took the dark blue velvet box from his pocket, while she took the beautiful leather one from her handbag. She watched as he opened the box, taking this glorious symbol of their love from its elegant surroundings. Tenderly he took her left hand on his, then blessed her ring with a kiss, before gently slipping this sparkling array of diamonds onto her third finger, saying as he did so, 'With all my love, with all my life, from the very first moment my eyes were privileged to behold you, till right through eternity, my angel.'

She then took his left hand in hers, then holding the other ring to her lips, she blessed it with a kiss, then she slipped that symbol, that broad gold band, onto his third finger, and, looking up into his eyes, she said, 'I thank God more than a thousand times a day, my darling, for your wonderful love, your true devotion and, above all, for you, my own true love.'

It was a quarter to eight o'clock when he stood in the same spot again and called out, 'Are you ready, my love?'

'Yes, my darling,' she answered, and a few minutes later she came out and melted into his arms.

She had a magnificent gown on, white, and from each fold there flashed a tinge of a beautiful shade of mauve. The glittering diamonds on her finger, and also those that graced the beauty of her neck, were dimmed only by the joy and happiness which sparkled out of her eyes.

'You look absolutely divine, my love,' he said as he kissed her.

'You mean the world to me, my darling, and I'm desperately proud of you,' she answered as he escorted her down the stairs.

The colonel and Marie-Ann were already in the drawing room. They could hardly wait to see the symbols of all this joy, and naturally it was the diamond ring which held most attention.

'It's beautiful, it's really fantastic,' said Marie-Ann as she kissed Joanna, and held her in a tender embrace.

'Looking at this beautiful ring, my dear, I should say you are the luckiest girl in the world, and bless you both,' said her father, as he kissed her quite emotionally. Then he shook Phil warmly by the hand and, still with that touch of emotion upon him, said, 'There is so much I want to say, Phil, but no words can express the happiness I have known since you first came to Northwood; for I know yours is a real love match and, where kindness and care is concerned, I know I have not the slightest worry over Joanna.'

'Thank you, Colonel, you do me a great honour,' Phil answered. 'And you know that Joanna is everything in the world to me, and her future and happiness is mine also.'

While Marie-Ann was congratulating Phil, first with a kiss and then saying, 'We are desperately happy over it, Phil, you're the nearest to an ideal pair that I have known,' the colonel asked, 'What was that engraved on your ring, Phil?'

'It's "P" for Phillip, and "J" for Joanna – that's what Joanna wanted, and I think it's the loveliest thought that could be,' he answered.

'What an idea,' said the colonel, turning to Joanna.

'I'm always with him now, Daddy, not only in thought, but when the pangs of parting hurt most, I shall have my beautiful ring to comfort me a little, and with my initial engraved on Phil's, I shall know that it is not only me he will think of, but my undying love which has sealed our bond forever.'

Penny was alone in the kitchen when they went to see her; Mrs White and Mrs Dodds, the new help, were in the room beyond. After Joanna had kissed her, and the sparkling array having received the most admiring examination, Penny said, 'It's lovely, it's the most beautiful ring I have ever seen, and I'm just as excited as you two are.'

Then came Phil's turn. He kissed her first, then told her about the "P" and "J" engraved on his ring.

'What a lovely thought! And it's really beautiful too – there's one thing, you've both got the same wonderful taste.' Then, looking up into Phil's eyes, she went on, 'You've not only got the most beautiful and sweetest girl in the world, but you've both got the same tender nature, which will make this the happiest marriage in the world too.'

From her face they both knew that their happiness was her happiness, and that now her life would be dedicated just as much to Joanna as it had been to him almost from the time he was born. After they had thanked her for the efforts she had put in to make their great day a wonderful success, she called Mrs White and Mrs Dodds so that they could see the beautiful rings and, not least of all, the radiant bride-to-be – and someone who to her would always be her handsome little boy, her Phil.

Just then the guests arrived, and naturally the admiration of the symbols of love took up at least ten minutes before dinner.

It had been arranged by the colonel that the champagne should be served almost at the start, so that it would give Penny and also Mrs White and Mrs Dodds a better chance to join them when he gave the toast. He knew that this great moment concerned the two Penny loved most dearly, and it was to her during the peak of their great occasion that the eyes of Joanna and Phil wandered most, eyes which were full of love, joy and gratitude. So, for the next hour, the fantastic creations of Penny appeared and were highly appreciated by all, the champagne flowed at will and a wonderful time was the keynote of all. But for those two who were truly and desperately in love, every time their eyes met heart their souls opened wide, giving each other a new glimpse of that wonderful happy future beyond. Later on, and just after the gentlemen had joined the ladies in the drawing room, the two lovers slipped out to see Penny, and on the way Phil got a bottle of brandy from the dining room.   .

'That was the most superb dinner that ever could be,' said Joanna, giving Penny and big hug and kiss.

'Really out of this world,' added Phil, 'and have you had enough champagne? You know you are to have what you want; anyhow, I've brought you a bottle of your favourite.'

'Thank you very much, but I'm really only halfway down the last bottle. It's only a small glass that I have most nights, but if I do have an extra one tonight it will be because my happiness for you both has only two more steps before it's complete.'

'Yes?' enquired Phil.

'Yes,' she answered, with her eyes twinkling. 'One is to see you married, and two, well, you're a bit too old to run in here and ask for a slice of cake, a biscuit, or a glass of orange.'

'So you want to spoil someone else, like you used to spoil me,' he said, while Joanna laughed and snuggled closer into his arm.

'Well, that's what I'm expecting of you two, and I hope I won't have to wait very long.'

'One step at a time,' he said, all smiles, and then continued, 'Well, thanks a million for everything... now I suppose we must get back to our visitors.'

Once again they kissed her.

'Bless you, and thank you once again for that wonderful dinner,' said Joanna as they turned to make their way back to the drawing room.

But in the study, on the way, they realised that impatient arms had been empty too long already, and lips with a passion to conquer pressed those with a yearning and surrender. It was exactly sixty seconds from the time they entered the study until they were on their way to the drawing room, but in those sixty seconds an old world had been shut out and a new one had descended to envelop them, one where the whole being drifts as if on air, just as if in the wonder of sleep, as it gently edges one over into the unknown. This was love; pure, true love, a blessing from God for only the pure in heart and mind; this was paradise, the place where one walks with one's loved one through lush green fields and in perpetual sunshine, where even the touch of a little finger results in the highest ecstasy.

'Have you been to see Penny?' asked Marie-Ann when they returned.

'Yes,' answered Joanna, 'and we thanked her for the wonderful dinner.'

'Wonderful… I should think it was,' added Mrs Marchant, and continued, 'you must tell her how much we all appreciated it.' Then, smiling, she said 'And tell her if she ever wants a change, she knows where to come.'

'Not Penny,' replied Joanna. 'You would want all the horses for miles around to drag Penny away from Spring Farm; besides, she's one of the family.'

'I can well imagine that,' said the major, 'but you know, Phil, you are really lucky to have one in the top bracket and so loyal these days.'

'It's a little more than luck, Major, it's a blessing,' replied Phil.

So the night drifted on, but not for one moment did the light in Joanna's eyes dim, or her radiance falter, and more than once when Phil looked at her he thought to himself, *What special thing have I done to be blessed with someone so wonderful?*

Then his mind wandered to the tender crush of those lovely arms when they enfolded him; to her luscious lips that yielded, ever willing to respond, if only so far, and would not lie dormant; to her pure, deep true love, reserved for him alone.

Although he was aware of it, the seed of her perfect true love for him had been sown years before they had ever met. It had been born as an ideal, an ideal that took shape when her girlish figure changed and assumed the curves of womanhood.

But, above all, it was an ideal that could only blossom into perfect love, when all her womanly instincts gave the signal.

That first moment of heaven would be locked in her treasure chest of memories for all times, when her eyes were magnetised to his, held by that compelling beam of love at first sight.

The quickening of the heartbeat, which catches the breath and dims the mind. And then she felt that tremor surging, bringing an uncontrollable trembling. Not in the light of excitement; nor in the darkness of fear, but in the silent glory of awe.

It was love where there could be no second best, a love with no real beginning and no end.

All this was his alone; her wonderful sweet nature joined hands with his in perfect harmony; her figure, that of a goddess, so rare, so very rare; and her beauty, fashioned and administered by the hand of angels, which dazzled, yet poured a peaceful serenity over him. And he asked himself inside, could any man have God's blessing greater than he had? To which his answer was, as the thousand times before, a definite 'no'.

It was an hour past midnight when the visitors departed.

'The usual nightcap?' asked Phil.

'As usual, and the family five minutes,' the colonel replied, and, while Marie-Ann was pouring out what each of them wanted, he went on speaking, as he put one arm through Joanna's and the other through Phil's.

'It's been a wonderful day, for two absolutely wonderful people, and I'm as happy as any father could be.'

Just then, Joanna swivelled round in front of him, and, as her arm glided over Phil's shoulder. Before their lips met, she said, 'Thank you, Daddy, for thinking of the lovely party.'

Then she kissed her father next, and Phil thanked him too. But to Joanna, her joy was not only for the lovely party that had been arranged for them, nor for what her father had just said, but for the thought that soon, very soon, and with her father's dearest blessing, she would take hold of this same fatherly arm, walking slowly and serenely and with her heart full of desire towards the love of her life, dressed as his heavenly bride; and for his eyes alone, laying her life before him, her undying love, her purity of mind and body, all for him to share and hold in his safe keeping.

It was a quarter of an hour before they made their way upstairs together, and on the landing, after they had wished her father and Marie-Ann goodnight, they were once more in each other's arms, and, as the ecstasy of this very special goodnight kiss stole over Joanna, her fleeting thoughts were only aware of pure contentment, perfect happiness and a love where there could be no end.

But though she was now suddenly kindled with the fire of abandonment, whose fiery flame reached for the unknown beyond her melting thoughts, her subconscious mind was at ease – at ease in the awareness that even if most of her consciousness had now slipped away, due to the ecstasy from the power of his passion that engulfed her, she knew that the arms she was in would not only love and caress her and carry her into those misty realms, but would hold her up from the darkness and keep her safe in the light of purity.

Being both young, perfectly healthy and deeply and desperately in love, they, like most, had witnessed during these last few days together fleeting glimpses of the pitfalls of being just human. But to them, their love for each other was a gift from heaven, and all too sacred. Not for them would the shifting sands of petty affection dim that light before them; they were on that straight and firm path of a true and lasting love, the path that was a vow to them, where the perfect start of their married bliss, on and after the day they would become one before the eyes of God, was their most cherished dream in the immediate future.

Getting Ready for the Big Day

Sadly in one sense, the colonel and Marie-Ann knew their visit to Spring Farm would have to be cut much shorter than they would have liked. They had only seen a small portion of the beautiful countryside around, and both had experienced a feeling of well-being in the cosiness of this lovely house, and utter joy in the beauty of its garden. But on the other hand, no one could ignore the air of excitement which seemed to grow in volume day by day, for almost everything touched on the preparations for that great day, not too far ahead. Their visit had lasted exactly a week, but they still remained all together, for Phil had driven Joanna back to Northwood, so that they would have one more weekend together before the three of them set themselves up for at least a fortnight at Eaton Place, during which time Phil would go up for weekends or any other times he could spare. But no matter whether it was Spring Farm, Eaton Place or Northwood, as time proved, not only did the young lovers' sun shine perpetually, but for the colonel, Marie-Ann and Penny, life became that much more exciting, as each moment brought a happy smile or a tender thought.

It was some time during Sunday afternoon that Marie-Ann said to Phil, 'If we can keep all the arrangements going to schedule, would you mind if we came down to Spring Farm before the wedding, if only for a weekend?'

'I'm only too delighted that you suggested it. You know Spring Farm is yours at any time, and for as long as you wish, and if the weather is fine, Joanna and I will take you to the top of High Ridge this time.'

The next morning, and just half an hour before he was due to start for home, they were strolling arm in arm around the garden. Phil knew Joanna's emotions were balancing on the point of a needle; he could feel her pain, so close were they. With tears glistening in her eyes, and an uncontrollable tremor in her voice, she softly said, 'I'm sorry, my darling, for shedding tears, especially when I know we shall only be apart for a few days; but as soon as we are separated I have that awful feeling of being lost, and all the sunshine disappears from everything.'

'If that is the only sort of tears that will dim the lustre of your lovely eyes, then we are more than assured of a future full of happiness, my darling,' he answered, holding her close to him.

She had recovered somewhat by the time he had to leave, and the response she gave him in their last kiss, while he was in the car and ready to move off, only made him more sure that her love for him was far deeper than any ordinary love; it could only be an infinite one, and one that was only prepared by heaven itself.

He arrived home for lunch, and by six o'clock he had checked on most of the work on two of the farms. He had just finished his tea when Joanna rang from London, once again setting the pattern for the next few days. Five times each day the telephone rang at Spring Farm, sending out its welcome call to the ever-willing receiver. Even with all the shopping and the fittings, which took up most of her time, she still missed him desperately. And so it was with Phil; with all his work to organise and the paperwork as well, he could never for one moment get away from that feeling that one half of him was missing, that without her now, life for him could not exist again. She was the very heart and soul of him; she was the key which drove him relentlessly on at one moment and gave him perfect tranquillity the next. That, and all else, was pledged to give a purpose in life; her life and his were bound up in all things that were most sacred to them, where not even death would bring an end.

At last Friday arrived. Phil was whistling as he came downstairs. He had already phoned a few last minute instructions to the farms, and was now ready for his journey to London, after a quick breakfast.

Joanna rang on the dot of eight, saying towards the end of their conversation, 'Give my love to Penny, darling, and I'll be waiting in the same place for you at Paddington, but it won't be patiently, for I don't know how to occupy my thoughts until I catch the first glimpse of you, my darling.'

No wonder his heart beat wildly at the thought that the most beautiful and sweetest girl that there possibly could be should feel like that about him. He went into the kitchen, where Penny had waited to have her breakfast with him.

'Excited?' she asked.

'Just a little,' he answered, laughing, and then continued, 'There's one thing for sure, Joanna and I are a real pair; three days apart and we're both like a couple of lost sheep!'

'It won't be long now, and I dearly hope that they will be able to come down for at least a week before the wedding,' she said.

'I hope so too,' he answered.

Ten minutes later he was ready to go.

'Give Joanna all my love,' said Penny.

'I will if there is any room left, but I can't promise,' he answered, laughing as he kissed her.

She waved him off, offering up a silent prayer for blessing him with this great joy and happiness. Then she felt a moment's sadness, as she thought of the son she might have had, and all the other joys that had passed her by; but there was no bitterness in her heart. Since then, this had been her life, the looking after the one light in her life and the running of Spring Farm. And now, she hoped it would always continue, only with two lights instead of one.

Phil was all ready and standing in the corridor just after the train got to the outskirts of Paddington. He could see Joanna as soon as the platform came into view, and it was only a moment after the train came to a halt that they felt the swift touch of each other's lips. In her joy and desperate relief, her beautiful eyes were watery rimmed.

'My own true love,' she whispered.

'My angel,' he replied, and, as they started to walk up the platform, arm in arm and with hands in a loving clasp; only then did the joy of living come flooding back to both of them.

They went on to Eaton Place in the Rolls where, on their arrival, the colonel and Marie-Ann had only a few moments to greet him before they were off once more on another of their many appointments.

'Going on at this rate, Phil, I shall need at least a week in the peace of Spring Farm to get over this,' said the colonel, laughing.

'We're all ready for you, Colonel, and judging by the way Penny was talking this morning, she's definitely looking forward to it, and hopes it will be longer.'

The Rolls moved silently away, and the two lovers, with arms around each other, made their way to the cosiness of the morning room.

'Oh my darling, how I've missed you!' she said, as he closed the door.

It was a special kiss that had to come first, but even after that he could tell that all was not as it should be.

'What is it, darling?' he asked, 'Is it another bad dream?'

She nodded, then whispered, 'Yes, my love – two. One last night and one the night before.' She paused for a moment, then continued, 'You are not only the whole world to me, my darling, but you are all that is good, so much so that you are the barrier between that which torments and frightens me, for only when I am close to you are my sleeping hours safe, untroubled and heavenly.'

He didn't answer. Words would have had no effect on trembling lips, nor on a dark cloud within; only the power of his love and the depth of his kiss could hope to bring the sunshine back to her. Time after time his lips sought hers in the sweetness of a pure love, one where the tenderness of each caress, the ecstasy of each lingering kiss, is measured only by the volume of joy that overflows from each brimful heart. That was how he subdued her fears, brought the stars back to her eyes and poured the golden rays of the setting sun all over her.

'Can you stay until Tuesday, darling?' she asked.

'Of course I will, my love. Penny can always ring if there is anything urgent,' he replied, then continued, 'oh, that reminds me, she sends her best love to you.'

'Dear Penny, our Penny,' she answered. Then, almost out of the blue, she announced, 'I've got a little present for you, my love. I'll run up to my room and get it, and I hope you will like it.' She gave him a big hug before she hurried upstairs.

'Don't be more than a minute, darling,' he called, as she disappeared.

She wasn't even a minute, and as she closed the door and came towards him her eyes were shining as bright as ever as she handed him a flat parcel.

'I have just had these done for you, my darling, and for you alone.'

He opened it, and his gaze fell upon two beautiful photographs of her, one each side in a twin leather holder. In both images she was as beautiful as she was in reality; one was from the side, and the other full face, so that her eyes could tell him just how much of her world he really was.

'You look so wonderful, my darling, so lovely, and I'm more thrilled than I can say,' he said.

'I'm glad you like them, my love,' she said, as she unwrapped something out of tissue paper, 'And here's something special,' she added, handing him a beautiful tan leather wallet, in whose protection on one side was the photograph where she showed her beauty to the full. This was just under postcard size, specially made to fit the wallet. He thought for the hundredth time how beautiful she was, and how her loveliness made his double row of pearls look even priceless.

'I want you to carry this wallet always, darling, so that whenever we are apart, I know you will often open it to look at me, and that way alone will your comfort and love be transmitted to give me strength to bear my loneliness. You can tell from the supreme joy on my face that it was you, my darling, who I could see in my imagination; and not the cold reality of a camera with my eyes; for I knew no such look of joy and happiness until you gave me life through the magic of your first – albeit stolen – kiss.'

The look on his face revealed all that someone so truly in love should show, and, putting down the photographs, Phil gathered her tenderly into his arms, saying as he did so, 'You know I will carry it always, my darling, and only with a special kiss can I hope to express my thanks and joy for something so lovely, and you can be sure that I'll be forever looking at the likeness of my love every opportunity I get, so that in thought I shall always be with you, holding you in my arms as I am now. And, with our love so true, I know you will feel my nearness, and the pressure of my lips to comfort you.'

For the next few days their happiness knew no bounds. Sometimes it was shopping, or a lunch or a dinner out, and a generally good time in between. But it made no difference whether they were dining out at some elegant place, or just walking arm in arm across one of the parks; she was in heaven, and during those few days he became more seriously aware just how heart-rending their partings were to her, and how truly deep was her love and her need of him. For she had only to think of two days apart and tears of despair would drown the lustre of those lovely eyes, and take most of the meaning out of life. He had always acknowledged that a woman's love was much deeper that a man's, but what he had come to realise these last few days was that so too were her agonies.

So it came as no surprise to him while they were having dinner on the Monday to see a change in her already, and by the way she toyed with her food, he realised just how much torment she was going through. Dinner was almost at is end, and he wished with all his heart that Penny would ring soon with the latest farm report. He had one ear on the conversation and the other listening for the faint sound of the telephone. Suddenly he thought he heard it, and a moment later was called to the phone. It was Penny; everything was going splendidly, according to the reports she had had from the farms, the weather was perfect and all the usual extra help had turned up.

'Well,' Phil said, 'as long as everything is all right and you're quite happy having Mrs White for company, I would love to stay another week with Joanna, and then if it suits the colonel and Marie-Ann, we could all come down a week tomorrow.'

'Lovely – that will please Joanna,' Penny answered. 'Besides, it's a pity if we can't manage so that you can have another week with the girl you love. I know her whole world comes to an end every time you leave her; I can feel for her, and she has my sympathy. You stay, Phil, and I'll redirect the letters that I think are important. Whatever you do, don't let Joanna have even one moment of sadness, if it can be avoided; she's not only your special girl, but mine also.'

After a few more minutes of chit-chat he said, 'I'll ring you tomorrow. Bye-bye, and bless you.'

The first thing Joanna asked when he entered the dining room was, 'Was that Penny, darling?'

'Yes, my love.'

'Did you give her my love?'

'Of course, and blew a kiss as well for the news she gave me. According to her report the work is going perfectly, the weather is gorgeous, so if you would like me to stay, there is no need for me to go back until we all go together.'

Formality went completely overboard. She was out of her chair and into his arms in an instant. Tears of joy were showing already as she said, 'I have prayed all day that something wonderful like that would happen, without daring to hope for one moment that I would be blessed so perfectly.'

'It's the finest thing that could happen,' said the colonel.

'Couldn't be better,' added Marie-Ann; for they had seen what Phil could never see, just how painfully she pined for him when they were parted.

The fact that they had seen how little she had eaten at dinner prompted her father to say, 'I'll get a table somewhere so that we can have a night out; even if we don't eat very much, at least we can drink and dance.'

So, less than an hour later, and with the lights once more shining brightly in her eyes, the two lovers were in each other's arms, gliding smoothly to the strains of a dreamy waltz. As Joanna's lips caressed his cheek for the fourth time, she asked in a loud whisper, 'Whose wonderful idea was it for you to stay another week, my love?'

He told her all that had been said on the phone and, at the end, he felt the extra tightness of her arm around his neck as she replied, 'I might have guessed that if there was the slightest chance of you, my darling, being able to stay with me, Penny wouldn't need any help in trying to persuade you, for only a woman who has given her love as deeply as mine is for you can hope to understand what happens to me inside when you have to leave me, and I am sure that her one object in life is to ensure that our happiness is the most important thing of all.'

'I know, and I understand what you say,' he answered. 'But if we can all be at Spring Farm next week and for as long as I am hoping, then there will only be a few days when we won't be together, darling. And by then our wonderful day will be so near that I am quite sure the joy and excitement will crowd out all the troubles and the emptiness away from you, my love.'

They danced closely for the rest of the waltz, and just before it finished he whispered softly in her ear, 'My darling.'

As she whispered back, 'My love,' she suddenly looked up into his eyes, and her searching gaze travelled quickly over his face, just as though she had forgotten what he looked like, or that she was looking at him for the very first time, or still couldn't believe that all this joy and happiness was really hers for always.

He understood, or thought he did; he could sense her thoughts and thought, he knew the answer. Whereas before they had met he had flirted here and there, she had kept the opposite sex not just at arm's length, but as far out of sight as possible. Then all of a sudden he had walked into her life; she was far more than anyone he had ever hoped of being loved by, and he knew he held the same sacred place in her heart also. That is what made their partings so painful for her. She had lost her heart completely, right from their very first meeting. It had been too much all too quickly; it had been one extreme to the other in the twinkling of an eye, so that each time they parted, her whole world came to a sudden halt. He felt sure that that was what it was. But was it? Was there something else which left her with this hopeless feeling of helplessness when he wasn't by her side? Was the unconscious fear within her only concerned with losing her love for just two or three days, or was there a tiny seed of doubt that their parting might be for always? Could it be that curse – the one that had taken all her female forebears when they were still in the bloom of youth? Was it gradually sprinkling her mind with something out of the unknown? Could that something be the first grain of uncertainty, an attitude of mind, where only the future could reveal the climax of a grim prophecy? Had fate, through that age-old curse, started on its cruel mission once more?

But as they walked arm in arm back to the table, their faces showed not the slightest suspicion of any dark cloud, conscious or unconscious. For weren't they in heart and mind as one? Weren't they together, with a love touched only by the grace of heaven? For she was his 'angel' and he, 'her own true love' – to each the supreme in all things from the beginning to the end.

So the scene was set for another whole wonderful week together, and during that time Joanna made certain that all possible was done to ensure that her wedding gown was as near completion as could be, so that later, she would only have to come back for the final fitting; but even then she would make sure that he was in London with her. For him, this week was a real bit of extra heaven, but to Joanna, it was completely out of this world. Her joy and happiness was at its peak, especially knowing that they would all be travelling down to Spring Farm together. She prayed for their stay to be as long as possible, for the beautiful setting was nothing short of paradise to her – one which, unknown to her, had been partly redecorated, and generally smartened up; so that when he did carry his lovely bride over the threshold of their own home, it would not only be more beautiful, but more fitting as a love nest, one where the fiery flame of each other's yearning would only be quenched in the demanding yet tender comfort of each other's arms.

It was a happy journey down to Spring Farm, and a quick one too; like a hungry giant the Rolls ate up mile after mile, and in such elegant comfort the skies over home came into view in no time. All were looking forward to the beauty and peace of the countryside, and the feeling of homeliness at their journey's end.

Penny was at the door to greet them almost as soon as the Rolls had stopped, and it did Phil's heart a power of good to see the genuine friendliness between Joanna and Penny.

'I didn't know that there had been some decorating going on,' said Joanna, looking quite excited.

'You weren't supposed to, my love,' Phil answered.

'Oh yes,' said Penny, 'we had eight men here for the first week, and ten for the second, so that it would all be finished for us to get it straight before you arrived.'

'Expect you were glad to get rid of that lot, Penny,' said the colonel.

'Well, it's lovely now it's tidy, but I must say they were very clean and helpful, and we had less extra work to do than I

145

imagined,' she answered.

It was shortly after this, while they were having a good look around at all that had been done, and all expressing their praise and approval at the fine workmanship so far, that they found themselves in Phil's room – their room to be. Here, Phil felt her arm squeeze his in a still deeper loving caress, and as he looked at her, her face bore the perfect picture of joy and happiness. Was it the new soft yellow figured wallpaper that brought her happiness to such heights, or was it the thought that it would be in this room, this little niche of heaven, where once they had breathed the same sweet air in sleep together, there would be no more partings?

During the next four days, which were full to the brim, Phil was up at the crack of dawn and working through most of the day. The harvesting was going perfectly, and as long as the weather stayed fine, he would have no worry over the crops. Joanna helped him all she could with the paperwork, but even with almost every minute having to be accounted for, they still managed to have a dinner at the Court, and a return at Spring Farm, and take in a lunch at The Calling Seagull. But while the colonel always accompanied him around the farms in the morning, Joanna hardly left Phil's side from that time onwards, going wherever the need of his supervision took him. His nearness captivated her, and often when they were driving along he would turn just for a second towards her, and she would be feasting her gaze upon him, a gaze that could only be described as 'spellbound'. She seemed charmed almost out of this world by all that he stood for, and for his perfect love, which gave her life; and in that second her eyes would surrender her all to him, yet still capturing the admiration and love that his sent out to her.

'A penny for them,' he would say, and she would snuggle closer to him and answer, 'It's just that I love you so much, my darling, and at times I still can't believe that you are absolutely all mine, and that this perfect love and happiness is really all ours. It's all so wonderful that in my moments of daydreams it is quite beyond me.'

Sometimes when it was quiet on the road, Phil would stop the car and give her a quick half-special kiss; otherwise he would keep driving, but would squeeze her hand tenderly, and, from the joy that fanned through her whole being, she would know that all his love was pressed into that tiny caress, and her whole world would become a beautiful reality.

Early on Saturday afternoon, he was making his last check round the farms for the weekend. They had left the car in the gateway to one of the fields, and arm in arm were crunching their way across the unploughed golden stubble.

'You're quite sure, darling, that you are perfectly happy over the arrangements for our honeymoon?' he asked.

For they had decided that after spending their wedding night at Spring Farm, they would have a touring honeymoon in Cornwall. They'd stay at one place as long as they wished, then move on when they wanted a change.

'Of course I am, my darling,' she answered. 'To me, it just couldn't be more wonderful, and if the weather is fine, it may still be warm enough for us to swim, or do some sunbathing; but if it rains, or the wind blows a gale, we can have our storm clothes on, go strolling over the cliffs or make our tracks along deserted sands, bending forward in the face of its fury, but still enjoying its salty freshness.'

By now they had reached the clump of sycamores in the corner of the field, and gently she pulled him to a stop and turned towards him. Her overflowing love-filled eyes shone more brightly still, as the love from his mingled eagerly with hers, then, as her arms glided over his shoulders, she continued, 'It won't worry or concern me, my darling, if the sun shines each and every day, or if the wind is heavy with rain; for I know I shall have my love with me, my darling husband, the one that only God alone could have blessed me with.' She paused only for a moment or so before continuing, 'You see, my love, only God knows the depths of my thanks and gratitude for that blessing, for these past two months or so the tide in my heart has overflowed with it, and yet with all its power, it still seems so inadequate, knowing as I do that in return I have you and your true love, my darling, and that is more to me than there is in the whole world.'

No words could be spoken at that moment, only the ecstasy of a really special kiss could hope to answer this declaration of a love so true, so deep – a love where in each moment of joy, each caress, each kiss, saw only a path of sunshine.

'My angel,' he whispered, as his lips caressed her cheek, then glided down to a passionate halt on the beauty of her neck.

'My own true love,' she whispered softly, as desperate lips sought the mystic unity which carried them into a world of permanent beauty, a kiss which unlocked the invisible entrance to the heart, sprinkling each moment with stardust, as they drifted from one joyous dream to another... then on, as it forged their burning love to an ecstasy, giving them a peep into the future, a peep into their own paradise, while loving arms yielding to tender spasms of strength guided them into the deepest spell of a glorious kiss, a kiss that is the wonder of all wonders, the key to nature's greatest emotion.

A minute or so later, with her head resting lightly against the trunk of the tree, while his fingers fondled her lovely golden hair, his lips touched her love-closed eyes as gently as a summer shower. At the same time, he marvelled at all this beauty, which would always leave him spellbound.

Then, as she opened her eyes, but still holding him tight, she said, in just above a whisper, 'You're so wonderful, my darling, so much so that there just aren't words great enough to express the joy of my fleeting thoughts and the heaven which enfolds me; for when I am in the comfort and sanctuary of your arms I am floating on a cloud, and when the supple strength upon your lips guides the tenderness on mine through the valley of sunshine, the world and all its beauty fades completely in the distance. Whether I am conscious or unconscious I can't tell, for I am left with only one thought – one consuming thought, which is more heavenly than all else – that you, my darling, are my life, my all, my own true love.'

Lips once more answered what the hearts demanded, where words couldn't be found to express the desire of two such blissful spirits. Already their two daily lives were as one, where a joy to one was an even greater joy to the other; but likewise, if the slightest shadow fell on one it would mean a painful heartache to the other. So with their arms still around each other, they made their way out from under the trees. Even so, it wasn't entirely out into the world that belonged to other people. The invisible power which guided them, the one that moulded their two lives together in heart and soul and soon to be in holy matrimony, had long since ordained that with a love such as theirs, whether they were in the comfort of each other's arms or far apart, they would journey on as one, a heaven-blessed union, one which could only be broken if and when time or events made inevitable its dissolution.

Was their love so perfect that it blinded them to any dark cloud which might lie upon the horizon, after all that had happened to her female ancestors before? Did neither of them pause for one moment in their perfect happiness and feel their heart miss a beat in anguish, so happy and carefree were they that never for one moment did the slightest thought of disaster cross their minds? Or was it ordained and erased by the power that guided them, erased so that they would enjoy their beautiful love and happiness to the full? Were they being spared the agony of those tragic thoughts, which, if it were meant to be and came to pass, would mean her losing all, and him being condemned to a life of utter desolation? It was in that carefree, perfect happiness that they kissed each other goodnight, and were to welcome each other at breakfast time the next morning. Life was wonderful, and walking to church in the beautiful sunshine only just put an extra gloss on a radiance and happiness that was so much a part of loving and being loved.

Once in church, however, all worldly things seemed to float away from Joanna. The angelic look, the presence, descended upon her as always, so that in spirit Phil felt alone. But this morning it was for him also to know, to feel something very much deeper than he had before thought possible. It happened while they were kneeling before the altar; he lifted his eyes to the cross before him, and everything on and about that altar gave off an aura of mystic purity, a purity that definitely was not earthly. He had the feeling that he was being held under water by an invisible hand, without any gasping for breath or busting of lungs; for the whole space around him was filled with an unseen pressure, something which was determined to make known its presence to him. And so, for the first time in his life, he thought deeply of mankind in the light of the world and its darkness, its leisure and its toil, its joy and its suffering, its love and its hate. Were these things but a small part of man's ability to know? He was sure he understood now; there was far more to this life than just living and taking things for granted, there was something all-powerful, something which you could feel, and yet not see – but above all, something which was everlasting.

So a little later on, as they walked out of the church into the beautiful sunshine, Phil was still happy and carefree and still his normal self; but underneath he was a far deeper thinking man than he had been when he had walked in. On the way home, the four of them strolled slowly down the narrow back lane, where they passed the ruins of the castle. The colonel and Marie-Ann stopped and were admiring some of the stone carvings, still in a good condition from an age so long past.

Meanwhile, the two lovers had got some way in front and it was then that Joanna said to Phil, 'You know, darling, there is only one thing I would like altered concerning our wedding. I know it wouldn't have been proper, but I can't help wishing that we could have been married in your church, the one we have just left; for when I am there inside, I have the feeling that everything is so perfect, the world seems such a wonderful place, with no suffering and no sadness. It is there, and only there, that I find a peace where there is not the slightest room for another thought.'

'That is because you're a real angel, my darling,' he answered, smiling and caressing her tenderly. Then he continued, 'Perhaps one day, when we are there alone, I'll hold your hand and let you imagine that it is our happiest day all over again.'

'That will be wonderful, and heavenly too, my darling,' she answered, looking into his eyes with a look which held so much love that, had they been entirely alone, he would have swept her into his arms, there and then.

Later, during lunch, the colonel suddenly said, 'If you two young things could manage it, us two older ones would like to be taken up to the place that Joanna calls "the edge of the world".'

'You'll both love it, it's fantastic,' replied Joanna, as Phil added, 'I nearly suggested it on our way to church, but I thought it might be a little too hot, as it's a very hard pull right to the top.'

'I think I'm just about fit enough to manage it,' said the colonel, laughing.

'Well, we've got all the afternoon, so we can take our time,' said Marie-Ann.

'In any case,' said Phil, 'I'll take you the way which has most shade, so it shouldn't be too exhausting.'

As they left the dining room, on their way out to the lawn to have coffee, Phil slipped into the kitchen to tell Penny their plans for the afternoon, and not to worry if they were late for tea. So, twenty minutes later, just as they were ready to start their journey, Penny produced a sling bag with a large bottle of orangeade and four beakers, saying as she put the strap over Phil's shoulder, 'I think you will need this when you get to the top.'

'Thanks a lot,' he answered.

'And for the thought,' added Joanna, as she kissed Penny goodbye.

Along the Ridge, they made frequent stops to admire so much beauty. Joanna, as usual, had her arm through Phil's, and whether they were just walking, or showing the colonel and Marie-Ann the most beautiful views, now and again he would feel her arm tightly caress his, always in the mood of unconscious adoration. But as they passed under the shade of the old chestnut, he returned her caress and looked into her eyes, and in that tender moment, both of them read the same message; in that twin caress was all the longing for a wonderful kiss, and the willingness to capture the soothing ecstasy that abounded in each other's arms and surely had they been alone, only the overpowering magic of a special kiss would have quenched their deep longing for each other's pure love. But as desperate as this longing was, this was no time to let it take precedence over the task of showing her father and Marie-Ann the best of everything. They knew they would have to wait for a few precious moments together, then she would once again feel the strength of his loving arms, and the unconscious feeling as his lips charmed most of her senses away. Oh, how she loved him! More than her own precious life – and didn't she have absolute proof by his every thought that his love for her was equally as strong and true, and that it would be hers for all time?

On they went, leaving the old chestnut behind, but as they looked back to admire the beginning of the autumn tints, the broad spread of the old tree suddenly gave way to am impression of height, but only because their path was leading them gently downwards. Perhaps Mother Nature, in a moment of thoughtful humour, decided to pity man in his weakness. Did she purposely give him this downhill respite, so to rest his tiring legs and to retrieve his quickening breath, before he became fully committed to the long and weary struggle to the peak of this majestic crown?

Still arm in arm, the two young ones led the way, on through the cool shade of the little spinney. Then they broke free to cross the still rich green, absolutely flat expanse which encircled the whole of High Ridge so that it seemed viewed from above, like a rare jewel in an emerald green setting. Then, bearing right, Phil led them towards the beginning of the hedge, the one which clung to the side of High Ridge, its spidery arms clawing its desperate way to the top, there soothing its bleeding hands in the moisture of the friendly clouds which hurried by, before disappearing over the crest, and finally coming to an abrupt halt almost in front of the largest oak, either in a gesture of silent respect, or a sign of utter fatigue.

Joanna, her father and Marie-Ann just stood there amazed as they viewed the entrance – for it was a perfect entrance; the fury of the prevailing wind, sweeping around High Ridge day after day, year after year, had incessantly buffeted it, deforming it into something much more than a canopy. It was nothing short of a continuous bower with two openings – the lower one, which they were closely admiring and about to enter; and the other over the summit and out of sight, and a long exhilarating climb away.

'It's perfectly wonderful,' said the colonel and Marie-Ann.

'It's really fantastic,' said Joanna, adding, 'I shouldn't think there is anything quite like it anywhere else in the world.'

'There's almost perfect shade from here to the other end, and it fascinates everyone who sees it for the first time,' added Phil. Then in the next breath he asked, 'Would anyone like a drink before we start?'

They all declined, thinking they would be in greater need on reaching the top. So, slowly but surely, and with a short stop for a breather now and then, they gradually pushed their way up and up, winding round here and there, and with them all enjoying every moment of it. Then suddenly they were on level ground, and, glowing in the distance like the open mouth of a furnace, was the end, as the glare of the sun reflected back at them, giving them a warning of what to expect once they had stepped out into the open. Even at this height, there was only the remotest breath to fan the cheeks, and hardly a leaf stirred, either wilting in the oppressive heat, or succumbing to its afternoon siesta.

'It's too wonderful for words, Phil,' said Marie-Ann, taking a quick look all the way round.

'No wonder you call this the edge of the world,' said the colonel, turning to Joanna. Then he went on, 'What a wonderful spot for a house – if only it was easier to get to, Phil.'

'Yes, it would be, but it's rather rough in winter,' replied Phil. Then, with Joanna's help, he proceeded to show them all the views and places, near and far.

They saw the final fling of all the flowers spelling out their message of regret that they had missed the splendour of the gala when spring and summertime were here; they heard the happy song of all the birds who loved this beauty as their haven, proclaiming this is how all life should be, natural, warm and cheerfully free. All this, as the sweet scent of the yellow gorse, scattered by the beating wings of ten thousand bees, drifted slowly round on the still air.

'I would love to see all this in each season of the year, darling,' said Joanna.

'You'll have to bring us up here in the springtime Phil,' Marie-Ann said, half pleading.

'You shall both have your wish granted,' he answered, smiling. He watched their eyes feast upon the changing beauty away on the hills beyond, then far down and just beyond the green belt was his large flock of sheep, spread out like small knots of cream-coloured cotton on a bedspread of changing colours. On the trunk of a fallen tree they sat and quenched their thirst. Then on down the bower they went, but as they reached the old chestnut this time, Joanna said, 'This is the place where we always have a kiss, Daddy. We missed on the way up, but I'm not waiting for one any longer.'

'If that's the custom,' said her father, turning to Marie-Ann, 'then we must join you.'

What a sport, thought Phil, as he gave his love quite half a special.

Back at Spring Farm, it was time for a quick change and freshens up after the roasting they had had. Phil was in his study, making some papers tidy, when he heard Joanna coming downstairs, As if by instinct, she made her way not out on to the lawn where Penny had laid the tea, but straight to his study. She entered, half closing the door.

'This is where I belong my darling, either in your arms or by your side,' she whispered.

'Well, from now on, there will only be two more days before our wedding when we won't be together, my love,' he replied.

Deeply she looked into his eyes as she said, 'Does that mean, darling, that you are going to be with me all next week, and right up to those two last days?'

'Yes, my angel,' he answered. 'Whatever work is left undone by Friday will have to wait; I won't on any account take the chance of you being lonely, or upset, if I can help it. You and your happiness, my darling, is more to me than anything else in the whole world.'

'You're sure you can manage all that time away, darling?' she asked.

'Definitely, my love,' he answered.

'Oh, thank you, my darling! It's as if a large dark cloud has disappeared from before me,' she whispered, squeezing him as tight as those lovely arms would allow, and crushing his lips in her desperate relief.

For most brides-to-be, time would have dragged when there was only the matter of days separating them from the greatest day of their lives, but Joanna clung to each moment, living each as vividly as was possible. Yet time marched on, as it must, first taking them to Northwood, then to London and finally back to

Northwood. Everything went according to schedule, even the big marquee was already erected on the lawn, and there was an air of excitement everywhere. But now it is three o'clock and Phil is due to start for home in a few minutes' time, and as usual they are having their last few minutes together, walking around the garden, arm in arm.

'You're quite sure you'll be all right, my love? You've only got to say and I'll stay, or I'll come back tomorrow if you need me, even if it is only for a few hours.'

'No, my darling, I shall be all right,' she answered quite confidently, though he could see those little wisps of doubt cross her face. But she continued, 'Besides, my love, you have been so thoughtful and wonderful to me, and I know you have given me much more time than you could really afford, but in forty-eight hours from now I shall be the happiest bride that could be, knowing that you, my darling, the one that I was born for, will be all mine and by my side for always. That wonderful thought should keep my mind at rest for so short a time – together with making myself as beautiful as I can, so that I shall be worthy of you, my darling, in all things.'

'That is the greatest understatement that could be, my angel,' he replied, caressing her tenderly. 'However, my darling, I'll phone as often as possible, except on the morning itself; then Penny will, for on that day I want to reserve not only your beauty, but also the sound of your voice, my love, until the hours of my waiting are over. Then my heart shall rejoice as never before, seeing you walking slowly up the aisle towards me, and my eyes will be dazzled with all your beauty. And then, I will take your hand in mine, pledging all my love and devotion with my eyes, and hear your whispered reply, "my own true love", when I greet you each night; and you, my love, shall find the peace you seek in the comfort of my arms. No more downcast eyes, no more partings, and no more tears to stain those lovely cheeks.'

'I will be brave, really, my love, so please don't worry,' she answered, pulling him round for one quick kiss.

Ten minutes later, the real farewells were already over, and the colonel and Marie-Ann were standing on top of the steps waiting to give Phil a last wave as he moved off; while Joanna, who was by the side of the car, leant down and said to him, 'Drive carefully, my darling, won't you.'

'Yes, my love,' he answered, 'and don't forget, if you want me to come back tomorrow, promise you'll say so.'

'I will, my love, but really, I'm sure I'll be all right,' she replied.

One more deep long kiss, then as he looked into her eyes which already appeared a little moist, he said, 'Take great care of yourself, my love, my life, my angel.'

'I will; never fear, my darling,' she whispered.

One more wave for the colonel and Marie-Ann, and one last quick kiss as he gave her hand a reassuring squeeze, and then he started on his way home.

His First Real Warning

How happy and thrilled Phil was, motoring along in the beautiful sunshine; yet that one small shadow among all this joy crossed his mind quite frequently, and he hoped and prayed with all his heart that those watery rings around those lovely eyes wouldn't give way to real tears. How lucky he was, how blessed he felt, and, for the sake of his lovely bride-to-be, he desperately wanted those clear skies to continue. As the only setting for her beauty and radiance that was worthy of her. This would definitely be the most wonderful day of his life; but, even with all his consideration, love and tenderness towards her, he would never quite realise the innermost feelings of a young girl on her wedding day, for it was something much deeper than nature had made him, or any man, capable of knowing or understanding. For this great day would surrender itself and belong to her alone; the day of her life when she would be adorned as never before, and, with her eyes and heart as always, only for him.

This would be the day when she would take his name and pledge her desire for his lifelong comfort and love. This day would be the key which would open the door to all her unknown dreams. This would be the day when, in her deepest love for him, she would place her hand in his and step upon the path which led them as one into an unknown future. This would be the day when the pureness of her infinite love would yield all; when their yearning passion for each other, breaking loose at last, would out-glorify all imaginations, overwhelming them in a heavenly turmoil of united ecstasy, whose elusive climax, teasingly dancing just out of reach, yet surging ever more urgently towards the grasp until it burst like a multicoloured bubble, blinding the whole being to the last shred of all that is earthbound, tenderly sprinkling its soothing spray of the purest love and ecstasy over mind and body. Only such a perfect love, only such a perfect unity, could release such power in the surging, to such depth in the giving, blending both in a heaven most sacred and beautiful.

Yet in the beginning it was only a spark, fanned into a flame of explosive emotion, born to erupt in the all-powerful kiss, cradled and nursed through rapturous joy, then soaring so quickly to the realms of sheer bliss, whose glory and wonder cannot be compared as it overwhelms each of the senses. Yes, in the beginning, it was only a spark; and arms which felt lost are lost no more, holding, caressing, possessive but tender, guiding them on through paradise, the passionate probe in each loving embrace sketching a picture as each dream appears, staying a second before flitting on, but leaving its memory, all glorified. This would be theirs in two days' time, when a touch would be heaven itself, when a kiss and caress would bring a new dawn and the call for the whole being to awake.

On reaching home, and after seeing Penny, Phil phoned Northwood. Joanna must have been waiting near the phone, for she answered almost immediately; she missed him terribly.

'But don't worry, my darling, if you are around the farms,' she said. Penny is the next best thing to help me over my loneliness, if I happen to ring in between our agreed times; for I do realise how busy you will have to be, before I catch the next wonderful sight of you, my love.'

'It won't be long now, my darling, and you can bet that I shall ring you every chance I have,' he answered.

'Even if I can't be in your arms, my love, it's wonderful to hear your voice and to know that at the other end of these wires is the one who is my whole life,' she replied.

After a few more minutes he called Penny to have a little chat. Then he gave Joanna a few more words of endearment and encouragement before he rang off.

Being a woman, Penny wanted to know as many of the details as possible. So, while they were having tea, Phil told her all he knew, but he felt sure he hadn't satisfied her curiosity.

'That reminds me,' he went on, 'Vicar Brown has offered Bob and me rooms for changing when we get to Northwood. Jane is staying with Joanna tomorrow night, so the Hall will be pretty full up, with all the others as well.'

'I'm glad you chose Bob for best man; I always liked him

when he used to come with you from college,' she said.

'One of the best,' he replied. 'It will be nice to see him, after over six months. However, I must get to work, I think I'll have a quick look round Spring Farm now, then the other two tomorrow. I can always ring Joanna from either if I can't get back here in time.'

Twenty minutes later, he was walking around that same field that he and Joanna had walked across. It was stubble then, but now the plough had done its work, and from the top corner he was able to survey quite a lot of the progress that had been made while he had been away.

Yes, he thought to himself, *the lads have really got on with things, and all up to the standard that is their pride.* He knew he was really fortunate, but he wished with all his heart that fate hadn't robbed him of his mother and father, when the fruits of all their planning and hard work were beginning to be realised. He kept down the lump in his throat as he thought of all the joy they would have known, if only they had met Joanna; how proud and happy they would have been, if only they could be here now, when in two days' time she would become his bride. But he knew that whenever they looked down upon all that was near and dear to them, his Joanna would receive the same measures of their blessing and love as he would himself.

Still he remained deep in thought, still in that heaven where all the wonders of the past few months flitted backwards and forwards. But here he was, twenty-four and with three farms to run, all providing quite a good living, as well as the business in London. He had always been deeply thankful for the fact that he had never wanted for anything. Life had given him all the material things he needed. Life had been so good that way – so good, in fact that it had seemed to him that the whole world lay at his feet. But as he walked slowly around the field, he took stock of how much his outlook on life had changed these past few months. For, from the moment he had met Joanna, when in that second their eyes had flashed a thousand questions and just as quickly received most of the answers, when his whole life before had disappeared under an avalanche of wonder and speculation, when the only thought that was uppermost in his mind was if only he could feel the joy of holding her in his arms, and he hoped the look in her eyes was really a message, telling him that she was as hopelessly in love with him as he was with her; and when, after that first stolen kiss, as he had looked into that beautiful face, it wasn't only the beauty he had seen, but a tranquil peacefulness, a peacefulness which had he but known even then might have revealed that in this her first moment of bliss, she had become his already.

But afterwards, he had felt the first sign of panic, and of what it was like to be alone; for the world, his world, suddenly seemed out of touch with life, and oh, so empty. All the wealth he had, all the land he owned, meant absolutely nothing compared with his desperate longing for this sweet beautiful girl to return his love. Only when their lips were united again and he could feel a tender welcome in her arms, only then would his world revert to what it had been before, and he would also be overwhelmed with a sense of well-being and joy, as yet unknown to him. How that desperate helplessness had made his lonely heart ache with the pain of not knowing what the future held! But there was one thing he had been sure of; if it had been ordained that they should meet again and be really meant for each other, to love, to cherish, and to possess, from that moment onwards, all the material things he owned would count as nought; for the joy and happiness of sharing his life with her would not only be the most precious thing in the world, but the whole world itself.

So, as Phil slowly made his way towards the clump of sycamores, he was still deeply conscious of the joy that had been theirs under those trees, and he still marvelled at how much more perfect everything had turned out than at first he had ever thought possible. Joanna was not only the loveliest girl he had ever seen, but also the sweetest and dearest, and their love for each other was totally unstinting, so what more could any man ask of life? Was it just common luck that had brought them together, was it earthly fate, or was it something which was heavenly and infinite? He was not meant to know yet; he could only surmise, but after this coming night, he was to know that even though they were miles apart, there was an endless invisible beam joining them together, one where her subconscious anxieties travelled a troubled road, to seek the comfort and safety that only his great love could give. But at this moment, he was only aware of the fact that from now on, all his efforts and work and the many hours of running the farms and the business would be for her alone; all his thoughts and actions would be directed to bring her the greatest happiness; nothing else mattered, nothing else could bring to him that sense of purpose that would make his life worth living; and deep inside he knew that after their marriage, theirs would not be a love which would gradually fall from its pedestal. He could never bear that, for he knew it would erode the light and love of her life too.

Theirs would be a love that would always demand perfection, from the moment their eyes opened to greet a new dawn until they sleepily surrendered to the joy of peaceful togetherness. In between, their whole waking hours would be hours full of affection, whether it was in the ecstasy of a 'special' kiss when time was on his hands, or as he dashed out to see to the unexpected, gathering her in his arms for a quick 'cheerio'. Every kiss and caress would always have the same tender urgency, and their eyes would send out the same silent message to each other, saying, 'My eyes are full of joy, my heart is full of love, and from the very source which is deep inside, I am privileged to belong to you, my love.' This was how he wanted life, this was what he expected of marriage, for this was how he was made – and, oh, how grateful he was, knowing that his partner for life had been moulded the same.

Slowly his mind turned to the job he was there for, and for the next half-hour he took mental notes of the work to be done while he was on honeymoon. Then he turned and he retraced his steps to the car. But love, their wonderful love, would not be denied its place over all, for not once, but many times, did he glance towards that clump of sycamores, and each time his heart raced faster. Strange, he thought, a month or two ago, he would have felt quite calm; but now, as each hour dragged away, bringing him closer to that great and wonderful moment, so too did his impatience grow. A month or two he could have taken in his stride; but the hours, the slowly diminishing hours, seemed almost unbearable. Outwardly he looked quite calm, but inwardly all was astir. Only when he knew that she was walking up the aisle towards him would these unaccustomed signs of panic leave him. Were these just pre-wedding nerves, or was it something deep down inside, something that he was not even aware of? Could it be an unconscious fear which brought about this uneasiness, a fear that something final could or would happen, with no indication of when?

There was no more surveying of work on the way home, and, just as he pulled up at the door, the phone rang. Penny had got there first.

'It's Bob on the line,' she told him.

Phil then told him that he was about to telephone him to tell him about the changing arrangements, also that they would be lunching at the vicarage, but there were other things as well which could be better explained when Bob arrived. A few minutes of leg-pull followed, then they rang off. Next he rang Joanna. Confidence he gave her a plenty, yet knowing all the while that it was only his presence that could dispel her inward fears. For had he not himself these last few hours felt a little of what she must be going through? But he dared not let her even dream that with all his strength and willpower, he had faltered a little, and even that little was too much for him. So heaven only knew how she bore the torment which shook the very foundation of her sense of well-being without him. She would ring again at ten, and reminded him that he must have an early night, with such a busy day ahead of him and his stag party in the evening. He promised, saying that he would go to bed as soon as they had finished their last goodnight.

That was how things turned out, for by the time she rang, except for undressing, he was ready for bed. He had steeled himself, so as not to say the slightest thing which would make her miss him more than she already was, but to give her as much confidence as possible. Those ten minutes of heaven glided by all too quickly; each blew the other a kiss to seal their undying love, but it was still a few more minutes before they rang off, for both seemed reluctant to say goodnight, until she whispered finally, 'Goodnight, my own true love, sleep well and God bless you.'

'I will, my angel, and the same to you my darling. Bye-bye.'

Actually, he was really tired, and as he opened his bedroom

door, his left hand went up instinctively to switch on the light, but it never completed the full motion that was intended. For his room was not in the darkness he had somehow expected; the scene before his eyes was so out of this world that for a moment he was completely spellbound. For the beauty of a full harvest moon, which had almost cleared the distant hills, gave out its mellow glow from a clear night sky, flooding his bedroom with a soft crimson hue, to beautify whatever it touched, softening all in its misty tone. As Phil slowly made his way towards the side window, he realised that he was actually on tiptoe. He felt a stranger in his own room, a trespasser in fairyland.

If only she were here in his arms now... the joy that they had known so far was bound to be a little more wonderful in an atmosphere such as this.

But the scene outside was even more wonderful. Walls and most of the hedgerows had disappeared under a sea of crimson mist. Most of the trees looked trunkless, as their leafy fingertips dipped into that colourful veil – a motionless veil, as it clung to the curves of Mother Earth, presenting him with a picture of dreamland, and a landscape that he hardly recognised. Dare he hope for the same dreamland on their wedding night? Could it be possible for that large red-orange ball to look just as fantastic on their first night together, even though it would be two hours later? He hoped again, realising that in all his years he had never seen a sight like this before, and especially knowing how deeply Joanna felt over these wonders and the beauty of nature. For only the heavens could send out a light tinted so delicately, and only the red harvest moon could send out such a restful glow.

Phil undressed in the subdued light and got into bed, and, in a little over ten minutes, during which time he offered up his humble thanks for all his blessings, the glow of the unknown crept over him, lulling him gently into a sound and peaceful sleep. Slowly but surely, the big hand on his bedside clock wound its merry way, round and round, round and round and round, while outside, what had been a large red-orange ball five hours ago, had now changed to a smaller brilliant disc, which was now not far from the peak of its nightly celestial run. No longer did it give the merest peep through the side window; both the two windows in the front trapped its steely stare, magnifying its light on to the white-painted window sills inside, there to reflect into the whole room, bringing day into night-time. The bright light brought to the depths of his sleep the first signs of a tortuous dream, a dream from which his only release would be on awakening. He dreamt he could see Joanna, though some way off, floating in the air. With her arms outstretched, she was calling his name, as though pleading with him to rescue her. He ran towards her, uphill and downhill, never seeming to get much nearer, until suddenly he seemed to catch up with her in one stride. She called to him, and the painful look of anxiety on her face spurred him on to one last effort. He jumped to catch her, only to see her rise further out of his reach and disappear. He awoke with a start, perspiration oozing from every pore of his body, and with the sound of her voice still ringing in his ears. Instinctively, his thoughts were first to pray that she was all right and, secondly, to find out what time it was, only 3.30 a.m. If only he had overslept and it had been eight, so that he could ring her at once to find out that all was well, and put his mind at rest; but no, for the next two and a half hours he was doomed to a fitful sleep, and the following two were two hours of increasing impatience, a time when his thoughts could not be forced to dwell on anything, great or small, for more than a minute, before the vision of her face and the sound of her voice flooded back to blot out all else.

Not for a million pounds would he have ventured far from the house, but if he had had a million, he would have gladly have given it, just to know that she was not being tormented by the anxiety over which she had no control whenever they were apart. But the chance to ring her did not fall to him, for at exactly 7.50 a.m., the phone rang. He raced to answer it, and instantly suspense gave way to welcome relief as he heard the sound of her voice. Naturally, in the way of all true lovers, it was their undying love for each other which came first, poured out along a frail, thin wire, which made a mockery of the strength of the loving words that flowed along it. For love, their wonderful love, was fashioned and held together by a bond far greater than the strongest steel, something which was absolutely indestructible, something which was totally infinite.

But the time came when he asked her if she had slept well. She hesitated a while, then replied, 'Well, no, darling, I didn't.' She then related word for word the exact dream he had had himself. 'In fact, my love,' she continued, 'it was calling to you aloud that woke me up, and that was the end of any sound sleep; but now I am feeling on top of the world, knowing that it was only a dream, and that you love me so much, my darling.'

He had long since made up his mind not to tell her of his dream, not unless she asked a question which would mean him telling a lie, just in case she might worry a little deeper. He cheered her up as much as possible, asking her if she would like him to come and see her.

'Oh no, my darling, as much as I would love to see you, it wouldn't be fair, with you so busy; and I know I shall be all right by the time I go to bed tonight, for I shall be able to stretch out my hand and almost span the gap of time which separates us. And don't forget, my darling, I must look my very best for your eyes alone tomorrow, so that alone will make me sleep soundly tonight; and lastly, my darling, I must thank you again a million times for my lovely dressing case, it's really beautiful.'

More loving words followed, with the approximate times he would ring her from the other farms, and finally came the ultimate spoken words of their undying love. But as Phil put the phone down, the look of joy on his face turned to one of thoughtfulness. How was it possible for two people, miles apart, to have the same vivid dream and its consequences at the same time? For in his mind they were just two ordinary people; but, like all others, they were completely in the dark about how deep the hand of destiny controlled their daily lives; an unseen hand which dictated the volume of their haves or have-nots; one which decided upon their earthly measures of good or ill; one which, in all its spiritual mystery, could flash a vision, whisper a name, or make a presence felt, anywhere, or at any hour of the day or night. This was the never-ending invisible beam, a guiding force, a guiding hand, one which had watched over them since the day they were born; yea, even uncountable years before, and one which had unflinchingly planned the rest of their lives upon this world, a power, a force, a mystery – no one on this world would ever know for sure; but, whichever it was, it had been sanctified in the beginning, touched by the hand of God, and so it would go on, on and on, right through eternity.

Later on that morning, when Phil had almost finished summing up the work to be done on the farthest farm, and was making his way back to phone his love again, the thought suddenly came to him of that strange feeling he had had in church that Sunday morning. Now there was the dream; both were unexplainable, and both a mystery.

Then, as quickly as it came into his head, so it vanished, for other than his work, his whole thoughts that morning were, *As long as she is all right, nothing else matters, for it is only a matter of hours now, before we will be together for always.* Anything deeper than that never crossed his mind for even a second, for, unknown to him, that unseen hand was now in the position where those who looked on saw most of the game, and little did he dream that he had been chosen as one of its chief participants. However, this was no ordinary game. This was something that would involve life and death, where the joy and happiness thereafter was solely dependent on the blessing of God's hand. So the day wore on, and he had almost finished his round of inspection of the second farm. Remembering what he had already seen, and what perfection he was looking at now, the words of his father rang true in his ears.

'You can't teach the men that work on these farms much about farming.'

In most cases, they had been born and bred and had worked on their particular farm, going back as many as four generations, knowing it not yard by yard, but inch by inch. That was why whatever he said to them, it was always given as a suggestion, and not an order. They thought the world of him for it, and also for the fact that he made their conditions something for others to envy. That was why they all worked with a will, and sense of ownership, realising that the yield of their work was partly theirs. Only this way could he have run such a vast acreage; only this way could he have left them to their tasks, without the slightest worry or concern.

But now as he started on his way home, Phil was feeling much happier than he had been on the outward journey. He had phoned his love three times, and each time she seemed more at ease, and with all the confidence in the world. He laughed to himself as he thought of Penny's orders this morning, telling him that he would have to sleep in another room tonight, as the bridal suite would be out of bounds. She had also found out that Joanna's favourite shade was gold, so he had with her help chosen the new gold curtains and a most beautiful eiderdown and bedspread. How well it all blended with the pale green carpet which had been fitted less than a week ago! Meanwhile Penny and her helpers had been busy for the last four days, making sure that everything possible was done, so that when he did carry his lovely bride into the home she loved, everything would be looking at its best, and fitting for their love nest.

Nevertheless, it wasn't until they had finished tea that Penny said to him, 'I'd like you to come upstairs and have a little peep at your room, now that everything is finished.'

What he saw as he opened the door made him gasp. He had never seen such a transformation before, and especially in so short a time.

'It's absolutely fantastic! Joanna will be thrilled beyond words with it,' he said, putting his arm around her.

'It was nice before, but now it's perfectly lovely, and it really looks a little more worthy of all the joy and happiness that I know you and Joanna will find here,' she replied.

'Thanks again for making it look a real bridal suite,' he said, while his happiest smile took supreme control of his handsome face.

Bob arrived half an hour later and, judging by his state of excitement, one would have thought that it was his great day on the morrow. After a little time, while the three of them were having a drink, Phil explained, with Penny's help, the plans he had spoken of on the phone, The three of them would drive to Northwood in Phil's car, but, after the wedding, would Bob drive Penny back here an hour before Joanna and he set off?

'She's determined,' Phil went on smiling towards Penny, 'that Joanna and I will have a really wonderful dinner, and in fact, between ourselves, Jane has invited you to dinner and to stay the night at the Court; but you must say, Bob, if the arrangements don't suit you.'

'Suit me?' said Bob gleefully, 'I'm looking forward to it already! Don't forget, it was through Jane that you met Joanna, and if there happens to be just one lovely, lonely female there tomorrow night, and if I'm only half as lucky as you, then I won't have the slightest grumble.'

'You could be lucky,' replied Penny. 'From what I've heard, there's going to be quite a party there tomorrow night.'

'Couldn't be better,' responded Bob, as Phil gave him a friendly pat on the shoulder.

Bob had always been known for his carefree outlook on life, but later on that night, after the dinner at the Green Dragon, a few of those at the stag party who were staying at the hotel, and were already quite merry, wanted Phil to stay now that the party was in full swing.

'No, fellows,' Bob replied quite firmly. 'The rest of you can, and it's all laid on for you to have a good time, but whether Phil wants to stay or not makes no difference, when I say we are going home, we're going. The job I am privileged to perform tomorrow makes me responsible for him tonight. Besides, Joanna would never forgive me if when they meet before the altar tomorrow, he is so washed out and bleary eyed that she'd hardly recognise him. I should do the same for any one of you, so you know what to expect if you have me as your best man.' Then laughing happily, he made his way in Phil's direction.

'Well, chaps,' said Phil, amid three hearty cheers, 'first I've got to thank you all for turning up tonight and giving me one of those rare nights in anyone's life; and, secondly, it's all been arranged that no matter what time Bob and I leave, the party can still go on for as long as you wish. Now, it's one more drink for us two, and the rest is up to you boys. So here's wishing you all the best of health, and I hope you get to Northwood quite safely, and in time for the wedding.'

With This Ring

But now the still night wearies, and a bright new day is born, the skies grow pale – but oh, not ill, for the signs around call to rejoice, with not a thing to mourn. For soon the sun, from a cloudless sky, would beat down its September best, lighting the couple's future path with happiness, to live, to love, and to be blessed.

Before eight o'clock, this was already the theme inside Spring Farm. Expectant joy and happiness filled the whole house, with snatches of melodies ringing upstairs and down. Penny had literally worked wonders, even to having his cases packed as far as possible for the honeymoon on the following day.

'Nervous?' Bob asked the bridegroom, while they were at breakfast.

'Not a bit,' Phil replied.

'No, I didn't think you were! You look as fit as a fiddle, and on top of the world, considering our night out.'

Phil smiled, answering, 'I took good care last night that everyone had plenty to drink. It didn't matter if they got drunk, as none of them had any driving to do, but I made doubly sure that I had under my usual; I just couldn't risk having any after-effects, or the chance of an accident on the way home, for there was too much at stake. To me, and I suppose to most bridegrooms, this is a landmark in our lives; but to a bride, it is the one big day of her life, and as far as I could help it, there wasn't anything that I was going to do to spoil it in any shape or form for my bride, Joanna.'

Penny had rung Joanna, sending her all his love, and receiving hers for him in return. It was one whirl of excitement at Northwood, she had told Penny; also that she could hardly wait for the next few hours to pass.

At 10.30 a.m., all was ready for their journey to Northwood and, as could be expected, all were in the best of spirits as they motored along the road for this great occasion. Whilst in the countryside around, it was only the changing tints of the trees which told the age of the year; for the clear blue skies, and the warmth of the sun so early in the day, gave more of a hint of spring rather than that summer had just departed.

Passing the Green Dragon, they all looked to see if there were any signs of the late-night revellers outside for a breath of fresh air, but not one of them was glimpsed outside the inn.

'Perhaps they're not even up yet,' said Bob jokingly.

'More likely they didn't even get to bed,' added Phil, amid laughter at the very probability.

However, they motored on, having a very pleasant but uneventful journey, arriving at the vicarage a little before the time that Phil had estimated. It was lunch first, then changing afterwards for the groom and best man, but Penny had been taken over to the Hall to help with the bride's dressing, as this had been a special request from Joanna herself. But was it Penny's help she wanted, or the nearness of the one who was so closely connected with the welfare of her one and only love. So it was to her that he had entrusted his extra gift for his bride. He had bought it secretly and, as yet, not even Phil had seen it, but it was one which he knew his love would cherish always. For this beautiful diamond cross, with lustrous pearls completely forming the whole of its outline, had held his fascination the moment he had seen it, and now, in less than a quarter of an hour, how right the instinct of his choosing would be proved. For as Joanna, his bride-to-be, first gazed with shining eyes upon this beautiful gift, she exclaimed, 'Oh look, Penny! It's perfectly wonderful... It's just as though my love knew I was wearing the family diamond and pearl tiara, for no other two pieces of jewellery could match more perfectly! One could easily have been made for the other, except that one is very old, and the other a new symbol of our everlasting love.'

'It's not only wonderful,' answered Penny, as she took the cross in her hand, 'but it's an absolute reflection of the love and devotion that I know he could only bestow on you. The day that I learned that you, my dear, had come into his life, was one of the few real happy ones in mine. For I have prayed for this very day a thousand times, just for him to meet a really nice girl, to marry her and settle down. But then, as I thought, the worry would start. Who was there, who had the sweet personality, the desire to be his alone for always, someone who would love him as he deserved, and should be loved, all rolled into one? I have seen him grow from a baby, watched his character mould itself, where anything else but goodness was unknown, but I was sure the very moment I opened the door that afternoon, and met you really for the first time, that it was you, only you, who had all the goodness and love that could make his happiness complete in all things. You are the other vital half, as if you were made solely to share your lives together, and I know that is one thing you will never regret.'

For over a minute there were no more words, only a scene which any stranger would have interpreted as the love between a mother and daughter, for each took comfort from the other, and what trace of tears there were, were only the emotional signs of love, joy and thankfulness; a scene that would make absolute the already perfect understanding between these two so perfect, in fact, that it could never be surpassed. For one, the older woman, fate had only touched her lips with married bliss, but had also decreed that a child – albeit not her own – should cushion the shock and the numbness of her senses, and made her find life again, and willingly dedicate her life to that child, who was now a man. That child, and later man, through all these years in her imagination, and to her innermost self, was as her own; and now, as a bridegroom on this day, he was bringing into her life the young woman she held in her arms at this moment, someone who, in a very short time, would be the other half of her broken dreams.

Now the younger woman, for whom life appears to be only at its beginning, is in heavenly thoughts and earthly form, barely an hour away from the altar of everlasting unity. Radiant, beautiful, with an inborn tenderness which borders on the angelic, hers is a life that had, or could have had, most of the things which money could buy; but not until these last few months had she even known or yearned for anything beyond the fringes of her normal everyday existence. Had she been taking life as it came for granted, or was it a kind of fatalism, the total acceptance of an empty life, which in the twinkling of an eye became utterly shattered the moment she had met her first and only love? 'Heaven' was the only word that could express the depth of her feelings since she had known Phil, and now, at this moment, with Penny displaying the finer arts of being her maid, making sure that nothing about this bride would be amiss, she caught the reflection of Penny's face in the mirror, as she was holding up the veil in admiration. On that face was something far more wonderful that she had ever seen before. Penny was caught unawares and absolutely intent as her gentle fingers now attended to the merest detail of the gown. Moreover, she was so completely oblivious that her face, her thoughts and her actions spoke not one small message, but registered her complete joy, telling in volumes the story of her life, and 'of dreams which might have been'.

The role she was now in was that of a real mother performing her duty to her own daughter on her wedding day.

But this depth of thought and feeling was not only on her side, for Joanna, who would have been the first to admit that Marie-Ann had always been good and kind to her, and had always shown a great amount of tenderness towards her, as she looked at the reflection of Penny, found there was something much deeper, and there had been ever since they had known each other – something which had been gaining force, especially now on this all-important day, in the last hour of her single life, when the pangs of being alone, with no one to turn to like her own mother, would have given her remorse. The sudden realisation came to her that this was no ordinary love, admiration, and pride which radiated from Penny; it was the sort which every bride felt a desperate need of, just before she took the walk of her choice to the altar. This was true mother love, with all the depth of understanding and confidence that went with it. A link as close as blood itself had formed between them, covering them with a sense of tender thoughts, calm and serene, a comfort in her hour of need when trembling hands, or quivering lips would easily mar an occasion as great as this. This was what she had been denied for so long, a love she had unconsciously craved for, and not known the wonder of until this moment; this was the last possible thing from out of the past which would make her happiness complete, as it in a seventh heaven. It lifted her up, giving her that extra guiding light into a future which seemed already assured.

The bells rang out their message of joy, calling Phil on as each peal ended, only to begin again. It seemed to quicken their footsteps, as Bob and he took the winding narrow path from the vicarage to the church.

With his head held high, and eyes shining with quiet confidence, Phil felt at ease with the whole world. Walking up the church path, they passed groups of people already gathering for what he knew was the first glimpse of his lovely bride. The two men greeted each group with 'good afternoon' as they passed. Many of the onlookers had already seen this smart, handsome young man during the times he had stayed at Northwood, but he had now captured a niche in the hearts of all with his friendly smile and greeting, and many a female heart fluttered as he and Bob disappeared into the church.

Standing at the foot of the chancel steps, they waited patiently, holding a whispered but intermittent conversation, with an occasional glance around the church, as it quickly filled to capacity. Then as if from nowhere, the Reverend Brown appeared, looking resplendent, as he always did for these solemn but happy occasions.

So Phil now knew that his love, his bride, could only be a minute or so away, and he remembered what Penny had said. 'Don't watch the bride as she walks up the aisle, only one quick glance if you must. Some say it's bad luck, but I think that's nonsense; it's more likely that even the calmest of brides would feel nervous if her intended partner watched her all the way up the aisle.'

And so he remembered, and so he was ready, ready and waiting, calm; yet keyed up for this greatest of all moments in his life.

Then, through this church, gaily dressed with lovely flowers, where autumn sunshine filtered through the stained glass windows to dab one shapeless patch of colour here, another there, and so on, there came the opening strains of the *Bridal March*.

Phil knew she had entered the church, even if the organ hadn't announced her arrival, for somehow he could feel her presence, while his heart beat a little faster, knowing that she was on her way to be with him for always. Dare he steal that one quick glance before she reached him? He turned his head and there, a little more than halfway up the aisle, was the most wonderful sight he had ever seen; his love, his bride, was gliding gracefully towards him. And he remembered his first thoughts of her, as he had walked down the platform to meet her for the first time… Only a goddess could look so divine; and 'divine' was the only word great enough to try to describe this creation of beauty who would soon join hands with him.

Desperately he tried to tear his gaze away, and only succeeded at the second attempt. It wasn't the lovely crinoline gown, sparkling with a thousand diamantine jewels, nor the brilliance of the tiara, nor his cross, now resting on her breast, that held him spellbound; it was the look upon her beautiful face which transfixed him – or to be precise, the light of relief which shone out of her eyes, telling him of her love, devotion and desire, that at last she was released from that inner torment which took all the beauty out of life whenever they had been parted. No more darkness now; only his strong arms to reach out and guide her, and only his love to carry her into a heaven on earth.

The swish of silk sounded very near when he turned for the second time and, lovingly, he took her hand, as their eyes flashed to each other the ultimate words of their undying love. If they had been alone, the sight of her would still have held him speechless, for what rare beauty, what radiance, what tenderness, and what perfect pure love she was placing in his hands, for him to cherish! All this rolled into one, and adorned far beyond his imagination, was bound to take his breath away. But since his love for her was greater than his own life, he soon collected himself completely, and all through the service, whenever there was half a chance, he would caress her hand or arm with so much depth of feeling, not only to comfort her at that moment, but to reassure her that she was his whole life, and that he would guard her against all.

Today, however, there was no sign of emotion about his bride; she spoke her vows as plainly and firmly as he did. This was no time to falter, for wasn't he a gift from heaven, someone who would be her one and only love? Then the time came when the vicar pronounced them man and wife; and then Phil took charge of his lovely bride, attending to her as he thought he should. A queen she looked, and as a queen he treated her, for this was her day when all the glory that abounds was rightfully hers. But to them both, the most solemn part was yet to come, when they knelt before the altar, just the two of them, and received the Holy Sacrament. Then the joyfulness of the day was put aside for a few minutes, and they were overawed by the invisible presence of their God, to whom they solemnly offered up their heartfelt thanks for His wonderful blessing in bringing them together, and into this union of holy matrimony.

Hardly were they in the vestry before the colonel, brimming over with the joy of this happy occasion, kissed his daughter and shook his son-in-law warmly by the hand, giving him a good friendly pat on the shoulder to go with it. For on this day he had not lost a daughter, but had gained a son, one he looked upon as closely as his very own. However, the most important thing to him was that this was a real love match, not the sort where two people gradually get to know each other, and fall into each other's ways. This was one of those rare happenings, where they were literally born for each other, where even by a slightest miscalculation they had married someone else would have meant two lives only half happy, and, at the worst, utterly miserable. But together as now, and as far as the span of their lives kept them on earth, their horizon was as a true and lasting love demanded. A love that would never fade, a love which from this day onwards would control the mind and extract from the heart thoughts and feelings so wonderful, so deep, that no sound expression could ever tell of them. Even as he escorted his lovely bride down the aisle, oh, what joy he felt! Though her arm to all those present, appeared to be only lightly through his, he could feel the affectionate grip of her hand, and the impatient tension of her arm, now that those last two days apart were over. She was at the peak of her happiness, as radiant and sparkling as a diamond, yet with the quiet charm and lustre of a pearl. Out they went into that still warm sunshine, where cameras clicked in a metallic rhythm, capturing as much of the splendour of this regal pair that time would allow. Out into the world, to take their first few steps together as one, while their joy and happiness infected all who watched, as they made their way down the church path for their journey back to Northwood Hall.

There, to continue this unforgettable day, they enjoyed a wedding breakfast where champagne flowed, and with the most delicious food in abundance, where the party spirit of the occasion poured over all to its limit. But later on, as they moved amongst their guests, when the strain of a long and exciting day might begin to show its signs, she was still in her seventh heaven – her eyes told him so. This was the day she had been born for, and this was the blueprint for the rest of their lives together.

Happiness, gratitude; and enthusiasm flowed from the faces of the colonel and Marie-Ann, and of course Penny, who was literally overjoyed. This was the day that the colonel and Penny had secretly longed and prayed for, for so long, and now the prides of their hearts were together, joined together as husband and wife. No wonder their eyes seldom strayed from the happy pair; she, who had known this handsome bridegroom since the joyful day of his birth; and he, who had hardly taken notice on that tragic day that this lovely bride had entered into this world. But it was onto these two, the elder two, that the thought descended at the same time. What wonder had brought the light of their lives together, what chain of circumstances had made it a 'must', so that events should turn out so perfectly, even to the point where their own happiness had found a new life, and also dimming the tragedy they had both suffered in days gone by?

'Happy?' the colonel asked, as he watched her drag her feasting gaze from the happy pair.

'Wonderfully, in fact it is one of the three most happiest days of my life,' Penny answered, and continued, 'I was so lost in their world of happiness, that I almost forgot that it is time for me to start back and for Joanna and Phil to change. It's not the changing part that will take the time, but the getting away afterwards – an hour soon goes by.'

'I'll try and give her a sign,' he said.

'No, Colonel don't bother, I will if I can get near enough,'

Penny answered, giving him a most pleasant smile.

'Safe journey, then, and we'll see you as soon as it's convenient, that is if you want us,' he said, returning the same quality of smile that he had received.

'More than welcome,' were her parting words, as she made her way through the crowd.

It could only have been a minute or so later when he saw Joanna and Penny going out of the marquee, but he could see Phil still surrounded and quite unable to get away; anyway, he could do nothing about it, as he was completely occupied himself with some of his old friends. But a few minutes later he was relieved to see Penny and Phil on their way out, but there was no way of him knowing that Joanna had especially sent Penny for her bridegroom, or why. Yet Penny knew, for she waited on top of the stairs while Phil went along the corridor and into his bride's room. She was standing facing the door as he entered, holding out her arms ready for his to enfold her.

'My angel,' was his ultimate and tender greeting as he hurried towards her.

'My own true love,' she replied, with all the emotion of her pure desire coming to the surface of her lovely eyes for the first time, as – also for the first time – their lips met to surrender and conquer in what was the most wonderful, passionate kiss for them so far. But before, even though she had loved him with all her heart, and had always had complete trust in him, there must have been an awful lot missing on her part. For now in the ecstasy of this kiss, when so many little endearments could happen at once, each giving a glimpse of heaven on earth, for the first time he could feel her hand stealing across his shoulder, gliding slowly up his neck, then opening wide to clasp the back of his head, firmly holding it with a possessiveness that continued down from her responsive lips to the tiptoes of her feet. Except for the merest vestige, her shyness had gone from her, and in the back of her mind, the full force of her whole being cried out, that in the eyes of heaven they were now as one, and it would only be a little while before they would know complete fulfilment.

But a kiss must come to an end sometime, and the body must relax. Then, looking into his eyes, Joanna said, 'It wasn't only that

I was yearning so desperately for that wonderful kiss after those two lonely days apart that made me ask Penny to bring you to me, my darling. I just couldn't bear the thought of being dressed as your bride without knowing the wonder of your arms, and the heaven upon your lips, when it is for you and you alone, my darling, that I am a bride this day – or ever a bride!'

Holding her close once more, Phil answered, 'It must have been at least a thousand times during this afternoon that I have longed to sweep you into my arms my darling, but the joy of it now has made all that waiting more than worthwhile, and no word in the world could describe the heaven that is mine, knowing that we belong to each other, and will be together for always.'

One more deep loving kiss, then almost breathlessly she said, 'Thank you, my darling, for the beautiful cross; it was almost as if you knew, for look how perfectly it matches the tiara.'

'Just couldn't resist buying it for you, my love. But to me, nothing in this world will be good enough for my bride, my angel.'

A minute later, Penny wished them goodbye for the time being. Then Phil made his way along the corridor to change. But in the room he had just left, it wasn't just the changing that concerned Joanna. There was one special case that would travel with her to her new home, something which was being packed with gentle fingers and loving care, something which was most sacred to her; her wedding gown. This in the future she would often caress and fondle, not to remind herself of happier times, for that would be impossible, but to satisfy her grateful thanks for the answer to all her inward prayers, prayers that were rewarded far beyond all her imaginations. For as each day would dawn more wonderful than the one before, she would know what a heavenly blessing really was.

Twenty minutes later Phil was still in his room; he guessed there was no need for him to hurry, for his bride would surely take much longer that he had. Whether he realised it or not, in his tailcoat and striped trousers he had looked the last word. But now, in a dark green single-breasted suit with its faint red stripe, and a tie of a beautiful shade of red, contrasting with his bronzed tan and his fair hair, he looked every woman's dream of what a man should be. He looked out of the window watching some of the guests strolling round the outside of the marquee. It was still warm, even though the sun was gradually sinking down towards the horizon. He left his room, and from the top of the stairs he could hear voices coming from Joanna's room. One was Marie-Ann's, and the other Jane's. Should he go and knock? No, he thought, he would wait for his bride in the hall. But he didn't have long to while away the time, for he had hardly looked at one of the beautiful paintings before he heard her door open and the voices were almost at the top of the stairs.

Joanna saw him just as he reached the bottom of the stairs. He looked up with an expression on his face, as though he could see the inside of heaven and was beholding an angel for the first time. She looked as divine as ever, wearing a costume in a lovely shade of tan, with a pale yellow blouse that blended perfectly, while her golden hair crowned her as a queen. She was as near to Mother Nature as could be, as she unconsciously displayed the beauty and grandeur of the autumn tints. But on her face and in her heart was the first puff of spring, a time of joy that had only just begun, a carpet of joy that was spread out way ahead before them, where, side by side, even in the depth of thought, they would know the unspoken meaning of a touch, or a look, and, in the joy of an embrace, their hearts would reach out to each other, to give and to mingle, for so close were they.

'Have I kept you waiting long, my darling?' she asked, stepping quickly down the stairs.

'That tiny half-hour has seemed almost as long as all those years that I was without you, my love,' he answered, smiling as he embraced her, while she drew his head down to taste the sweetness of his lips once more.

'That's only the start, Phil. I expect you'll have much longer to wait than that in the future,' teased Jane.

'I expect you'll get used to it, Phil, for it's a woman's privilege to be late,' added Marie-Ann.

'That won't apply to me, my love,' replied Joanna, her eyes burning with love and admiration for him. 'For I promise, darling, that not one more moment than possible shall I ever dream of letting you out of my sight,' she added, kissing him once more.

'I believe she means it,' said Jane.

'I'm sure she does,' Phil answered, as he escorted her out to the marquee to say farewell to their guests.

It was a good thing they hadn't been any longer changing, for there were times when both of them thought they would never come to the end of the handshakes, and the few words exchanged almost everywhere. Yet among that crowd, there was one poor soul who would have given anything for a few words alone with them – her father; but, as things turned out, his luck was yet to come. For suddenly, they seemed to come to the end of the greetings, and with such a good time being had by all, they were able to almost disappear before the majority of the guests realised.

'Have a wonderful time, my children,' the colonel said, 'we shall be thinking and talking about you for most of the time, and praying that this lovely weather lasts for another two weeks... but you'll be sure to phone sometimes, won't you?'

'Of course we will,' answered Phil. 'We'll phone every evening, just before eight.'

'We'll look forward to that,' said Marie-Ann. 'It will give us two here and Penny at Spring Farm a good appetite for dinner to hear your voices and to know where you are and where you plan to go next.'

'Oh, Phil,' said the colonel, just before the nearest part of the crowd came within earshot, 'would it be possible for us to come and stay at Spring Farm the day after you get back?'

'Phil, giving the colonel a quick wink, said, 'You know you are more than welcome at any time as far as I'm concerned, but I'm not the one in charge of the house now.'

'Oh, is that so?' answered the colonel, putting on a look that suggested that he didn't quite understand.

Joanna knew she just had to answer that, and, at the peak of her happiness, she said, 'I don't believe there has been one in charge at Spring Farm ever; it's far too happy a place for anyone to set rules or anything like that.' Then, turning to her husband and sliding her arm lovingly through his, she continued, 'And I don't think Daddy can see that vacancy being filled in our time! Already he thinks you are spoiling me, my love; but who but you and I, my darling, will ever know the perfect harmony and the heaven we are in when we are together?' Turning to her father and Marie-Ann, she went on, 'You know it will be wonderful to have you, and we shall be expecting you there, waiting when we return.'

She then kissed them both, just as the crowd caught up with them.

At the bottom of the steps the gleaming Rolls stood ready for the departure, while cheering and shouts of good wishes rang through the air. The happy pair waved to everyone and said their goodbyes to her father and Marie-Ann. All was ready except for shutting the door, but, before that happened, her father leant into the car and, taking them both by the hand, said quite emotionally, 'God bless you both, and have a wonderful honeymoon, my children.'

So saying, he closed the door hardly before they could thank him properly, and the next moment they were off and waving frantically through the back window. They were intent on watching her father, who stood in the middle of the drive waving back to them right up to the very last as they disappeared round the bend. A solitary figure, perhaps at that moment feeling very lonely; and yet it was to him one of the greatest and happiest moments of his life, for he had given his daughter's hand this day into the charge of someone who, deep in his heart, he thought of as his own son. He had no fear for her future, for as far as was humanly possible, she would be perfectly safe and ideally happy in his tender and loving care, while that wonderful great love of theirs would be with them always, on and on. For all things wither and decay, and man must pay his price and die, but a true and faithful love is absolute, and must bloom forever.

When Pure Desire Becomes Reality

They were now homeward bound, with every mile taking them nearer, and still totally overwhelmed with happiness, as they talked over most of the happenings of their wonderful day, a day which was not a dream world, but a day of perfect reality; one where they clung to each precious moment for memory's sake, to live, and relive, as time took them slowly down the broad walks of life.

'It's been a long and busy day for you my love,' Phil said, 'but there's one thing, as soon as we get to Spring Farm, if you are feeling at all weary, a glass of champagne will revive you.'

'Funny, with all the hustle and bustle, I still feel as fresh as any other day, my darling. It's just that my cup of happiness is brimming over, knowing that soon I shall be in your arms, and with no more partings,' she answered, squeezing his hand tightly and snuggling closer to him.

'It's wonderful what a pair of lost gloves can do, and so quickly,' he said, smiling.

'Yes, it really is, darling,' she answered, looking round into that smiling face. 'And do you know my love,' she went on, 'I haven't worn them since that day; they are the first of my treasures, now they are labelled and put away safely.'

'What's on the label – "exhibit one"?' he enquired.

'No,' she answered, '"lost", on the one hand, and "found the whole world" on the other. I wrote the labels that very same evening, when I was even as sure of your love then as I am now, my darling.'

His eyes told her how sweet and pure she was, and how thankful he was to be blessed with her love, but with his lips he said, 'Looking back from this wonderful day, those three awful days of torment were all so unnecessary.'

'I know, my love,' she answered, 'but that is how it was meant to be, for the amount of pain we suffer when we are parted is the amount of true love we give when we are together.'

'You were my "angel" right from that very first moment,' he whispered as he slid his arm around her waist, and drew her gently closer.

'And you were "my own true love",' she replied, as the lids of her love-filled eyes drooped with the ecstasy of the moment, and both of them wished at that instant that they were alone in the car.

With no special kiss to satisfy the lips, there was only the longing in each other's eyes to tell of the hunger in the depth of their souls. She was divinely happy; her starry eyes were a blush of pink as she watched the dying rays of the setting sun, probing its spindly fingers across the changing blue, seemingly stretching, but ever retreating, each second by second. They watched all these wonders gently fade, giving up their place to something new, while here and there a beauty rare stayed only as long as the flash of an eye. All would give way and soon be gone all would sleep through to the dawn, nursed in the lap of this autumn twilight, the lull before the whole heavens awoke.

She snuggled up closer to him as the shadows began to fall, and the darkened glass, which separated them from the chauffeur, Henry, formed the impression that they were heading already into the night. She tilted her head upwards and backwards, parting her lips in a seductive yet innocent welcome, a welcome which he had not the slightest hope of resisting, even if he had wanted to; for theirs was a love of equal desperation, not a love of demanding, but one whose whole delight was in giving. With his arm still around her, he held her close, so very close, while bowing his head until their lips met, gently at first, until the nearness of each other, and the thought of the divine togetherness that would soon be theirs, threatened to overwhelm them in a flood of passion.

'My own true love,' she whispered, as her hand caressed his cheek.

'My angel,' he replied, still holding her firmly but tenderly to him. Then, as the ecstasy of those few moments cleared from his mind, he realised that he had little idea of what the impact of married bliss would have upon them, the delight of it, the wonder of it; yet here they were, only at its beginning. For in that kiss, there in the car, which made it almost like a stolen one, she would not even dream of showing a tiny part of her willingness to surrender herself in any degree. She had, with all the innocent magic and mystery of her femininity, stirred the very depth of him. It was as though the other half of her magnetism had been held captive inside, a willing prisoner, one who had suddenly cut all bonds asunder, and whose only object now was to envelop him in its fire of ecstasy, to consume all that was hers and his, and to refashion it into something far greater and more wonderful. It was a mystery potion, which could only be mixed by the hand of God, to ensure that they were as near to one, and only one, and as divine an entity as could be expected to come out from all that is human.

'It won't be long before we are home, my love,' he said, as the glare from the landing lights at the aerodrome lit up a dusky sky.

'Remember, darling?' she asked.

'How could I ever forget, my love, the most wonderful day in my life, until this one,' he answered, kissing her tenderly on the forehead.

Looking up into that handsome face, she said, 'It was not only a wonderful day, my darling. Except for those agonising three days, it was three whole wonderful weeks. For no matter where we were together, or the precious times you held me in your arms, when with all the love I had for you, which almost took control of my senses, when you my darling, guided me safely over that overwhelming joy, from one special kiss to another. Each moment brought a new world, a new life to me, and now each of those moments is as pure and fresh in my memory as the day it happened, and I know it will always be. For wherever we strolled during those three weeks of heaven is sacred to me, while the joy upon your lips, and the whisper from your heart – "my own true love" – is locked in my heart forever.'

He half turned towards her, drawing her round with his other arm, while his lips met hers and savoured the joy that she willingly bestowed upon them. It was almost as though they were completely on their own, for the still night had gathered in around them, shrouding them with its blanket of secrecy, and shutting them into a world of their own.

'You're so wonderful, my darling, and I love you more than I know how to say,' she whispered, somewhat breathlessly.

'And I love you more than I shall ever know too, my darling,' he whispered, kissing her once more.

They had hardly noticed Tetstone as they passed through, and now it was a bare two hundred yards before they would turn into the drive of Spring Farm, their beloved home. The thick high hedge which flanked the road blotted out the surprise welcome that awaited them, and before the Rolls had nosed its way along barely a quarter of the drive, the hill, which curved from the left of the Ridge, drew their attention. But it wasn't until they had almost reached the house, and were properly in the line of sight that they could see clearly the message which was for them and them alone. For there were literally dozens of storm lanterns hanging in the trees, spelling out the words WELCOME HOME, perfectly arranged, and reflecting the glowing warmth from the true and joyful hearts that were responsible.

'What a wonderful surprise, and how thoughtful of them, darling,' Joanna said emotionally.

'It really is, and it looks absolutely perfect,' he answered, as the Rolls came to a halt.

Penny and Bob were standing in the doorway ready to greet them.

'There's plenty of room to carry your lovely bride over the threshold, Phil,' said Bob.

'That's one thing I did make sure of,' answered Phil, laughing. 'If there hadn't been, I should have had the doorway made larger.' And so saying, he picked up his lovely bride, so lovingly and tenderly. Then, kissing her quickly on the lips, he carried her through the doorway of their future home, there to set her gently down in the centre of the hall. But ere her two feet touched the ground, her other arm automatically went round his neck, and their lips opened another page of their new life together.

'It's wonderful to be home, my darling,' she said, and her eyes shone like stars.

'It's wonderful now that you are here, my love, bless you,' he answered, kissing her once more.

185

'Did you have any trouble getting away?' Penny asked Joanna, as Phil and Bob went out to call Henry in for a drink.

'Yes, that little chat with almost everyone took longer than we thought, but however, we are here now, and you've got it all looking so beautiful, dear,' she answered, as they walked into the lounge arm in arm. They were quite content to talk about the wedding, and how wonderfully everything had turned out.

'Even the weather couldn't have been more splendid,' said Penny, as the three men came in.

Looking at Penny, Phil said as he entered, 'I didn't think we had enough storm lanterns to spell out WELCOME HOME as large as that, and so perfectly!'

'We haven't,' Penny answered. 'The lads all scouted around among the other farmers and borrowed them, last Saturday afternoon when you were away. They were up there until dark, measuring and tying on bits of cloth, so that all they had to do this evening was to substitute the lanterns for the cloth.'

'It's really fantastic,' said Joanna. 'We must have another look or two later on, and, apart from being cleverly done, it's a wonderful thought on their part.'

'They must think a great deal of you, Phil, or they would never bother with anything so elaborate,' said Bob.

'They do,' answered Penny, 'and there isn't a single one among the whole lot who doesn't appreciate what Phil does for them.'

'Yes,' said Phil, 'it doesn't matter how long I am away, I am always certain that the work goes on the same. Only the other day, when I went around asking them about the harvest supper, they were all adamant that it should be put off until we returned from our honeymoon. 'It wouldn't be the same without you,' they said. He went on, 'They're a fantastic bunch, without any doubt,' as he got up and poured the second round of drinks. Once again their future was toasted on its happy way.

'You'll be late getting back to Northwood, Henry,' said Bob.

'I'm not going back to Northwood tonight, sir, I'm staying at the Court. In fact my orders were to take you there when you were ready.'

'Of course – you didn't know, Bob,' said Joanna, 'Henry is

courting Vivienne, she's lady's maid to Mrs Marchant and Jane, and a very nice girl indeed. They met when she came to Northwood with Jane, over a year ago, and I expect it was Jane who gave Daddy the idea for you to stay tonight, wasn't it?'

'Yes, ma'am,' replied Henry, looking not the least bit bashful.

'Soon be wedding bells?' asked Phil.

'I hope so, sir,' replied Henry.

'Well, don't forget we shall want an invitation,' said Phil.

'I shall be only too happy to return the compliment, sir,' replied Henry happily.

'That will make it tit for tat,' said Joanna, laughing, 'one girl stolen from Northwood, so Northwood steals one back.'

'More like the other way round,' replied Bob, amid laughter.

A few minutes later they were ready to leave, but it was Henry who showed the most urgency, and, while they were having another look at the lights, Phil could tell that he was thinking more about those precious moments slipping away than anything else.

'Well, on your way,' he said, 'or Vivienne will think you are not coming.' Then, turning to Bob, he continued, 'Besides, I think the dark-haired bridesmaid I saw you talking to more than once this afternoon is staying there tonight.'

'Well, why didn't you say so before?' said Bob, pretending to be in a hurry, 'I wouldn't have had that second drink had I known that!'

Penny said her goodbyes before they got into the car, then disappeared towards the kitchen.

Thanks and gratitude were expressed all round, and the happy pair were once more wished every joy for the future, and a wonderful time on their honeymoon. Then away they went, shouting, 'Goodbye and all the best!' as they went up the drive, only to leave the newlyweds in silence, gazing towards those lights, with arms around each other, and in a heaven of their own.

Turning round so that Phil's other arm held her as well, Joanna said, 'How can I thank you, my darling, for all the joys of this day? And the wonder of it, knowing that we belong to each other and will be together for always.' She paused for a moment, then continued, 'I hope, my love, you didn't mind my not wanting to spend our wedding night anywhere else but here, in our home, our happy home, for I just couldn't bear the thought of this sacred night belonging to any other place but here.'

'Of course not, my love, I'm as happy about it as you are; and little did you know that it was my wish also, for anything as great as our wonderful love should always have its birth in homely surroundings, and if it is possible to love you more for being so sentimental, then I do, my angel,' he answered, as he kissed her very deeply, then lovingly guided her through the doorway.

'How much time have we got before dinner is ready?' she asked Penny, as they went into the kitchen.

'About twenty minutes, my two precious ones, that is if you can hurry,' Penny answered, looking delighted.

'We'll make it,' said Phil, as they both gave her a kiss of gratitude before hurrying upstairs.

But once inside the bedroom, time disappeared from their thoughts in the sort of kiss that he had promised her always, once they were married. A glowing sensation swept through her whole being, leaving her with no alternative but one compelling desire to cling to him with all her womanly might. For with his passion, he was sweeping her along on an irresistible tide and, holding her deep in the sanctuary of his arms, shaking the very foundation of her vestal innocence, which now rocked from side to side on its pedestal of white. He could feel the loving desperation of her hands and arms over his shoulders, and for the first time, he could sense the willingness of her body to know him more. This was as all true love should be; for only a short time, but the right time, now stood between them and what they had been created for. Then, as lips parted and cheeks were pressed together in silent adoration, she could feel his hands moving over her, from her tingling shoulders to the new-found suppleness of her slender waist, driving on that overpowering surge of yearning, which seemed to sap the last bit of her normal strength.

She was saturated by the magic from his lips, but from the caress of his hands, there came a feeling of an overwhelming but clear transformation, a feeling that she was being lifted up, and that each tiny part of her was glorified whenever he touched, glorified to that utmost degree; and if it was right for him to worship someone other than his own Creator, then he worshipped her with all he had, blessing the very ground on which she walked, and taking loving care of the air she breathed.

'My wonderful husband, my own true love,' she whispered.

'My precious bride, my angel,' he replied, as he looked into the depth of her love-filled eyes.

'Now we must hurry, my love,' he said. 'You're to use our bathroom, and I use the pink one, and see who is ready first.'

'I'll beat you by a whole minute,' she said, going on tiptoe to kiss him once more.

The sound of rushing water didn't quite drown his cheerful voice, as he switched from one gay tune to another, and, just under a quarter of an hour later he was back in their room, and all ready except for putting on his tie and coat.

'I said I would beat you, darling,' she said as he entered, while a look of surprise came over his face as he saw her not only sitting at the dressing table, but actually putting the final touches to her lovely golden hair.

'However did you manage that, darling? I hurried as fast as I could, and I'm still behind you.'

'Ah,' she answered whimsically, 'all I had to do was to step straight into the bath, for our wonderful Penny had made everything ready for me.'

'She's spoiling you again,' he said, as he sat on the seat by her side and kissed her.

'So are you, my darling,' she answered. 'A new world, and a new life all in so short a time – what more could any one person give to another.'

'You're a new world and a new life to me, my darling, and that is what we shall always be to each other,' he replied, sealing their love once more with a kiss, then standing up and fastening the diamond necklace for her.

'All secure, my love,' he said. 'Now let me see once again how beautiful you are.'

She rose and turned towards him. Her gorgeous pale blue gown was in the Grecian style, adding elegance where there was already an abundance of elegance. She was a perfect dream, with the diamond necklace flashing like a thousand stars; yet with all its brilliance, there was not the slightest chance that it could dim the radiance of her natural beauty. For fine clothes and sparkling jewels were only minute decorations around the most perfect gem of all.

Taking one long enchanted look at the heaven that stood before him, he said, 'This is the second time today that I have looked at you, my angel, and wondered if I dare to hold you in my arms… the second time when you have looked so beautiful that the slightest touch or caress might mar some of your perfection; and yet my arms cry out to hold you, for only there are I assured that you are real, and all mine.'

Her response was to close what distance there was between them and to slide her arms around his neck, using her utmost strength to make him match her and hold her tight. But if he had intended that this should only be a short embrace, then he was mistaken. For once his arms were around her and his hands came in contact with a bareness which yielded at his touch, and so much more than he had so far explored, the intriguing soft velvet nakedness of her skin wiped all thoughts of what he might crush completely from him. For this turned into a kiss engendering more passion than any he had given her, one whose gush of ecstasy almost took their last breath away.

'Don't ever worry, my love,' she whispered softly and breathlessly, 'whether my hair is absolutely "just so", or if I am dressed in my finest gown. Promise, my darling, to take me in your arms whenever you will, for nothing must be a barrier between this wonderful love that we have been blessed with, my own true love.'

'I will gladly, my angel, always,' he whispered, as their lips met once more in a kiss. But one that was to last them out of their room, down the stairs and until the champagne had been served at dinner. That was when he lifted his glass to her, and she to him, and, when their eyes met and were gladly held by their burning love for each other, revealing the innermost part of their souls; eyes which steadfastly peered over each rim of pure cut crystal, never flinching for one moment, even as the sparkling bubbles of wine burst a few in all directions. The excitement of this great occasion was still all theirs, and nothing could break the spell which was drawing them ever closer together. He leaned across the corner of the table, holding her by the top of the arm to steady her, so that his lips could find and hold the position of hers in which they revelled. One point of joyful contact only, one point where all the vibrating life of two so desperately in love was funnelled and exchanged in a force more powerful that a bolt from the blue.

But this time, most of the sparkle had receded from her eyes, having been overpowered and pushed into the background in the misty veil of surrender. For love, his wonderful love, had at last swept one more barrier aside. She had always been his completely in heart and soul, but now, in the closing hours of her virgin whiteness, she had given one more physical sign of her readiness for his ultimate nearness. For those misty eyes were heavy and half closed by the ecstasy of the moment, and from that fire within there came a mighty glow, filtering up to touch her cheek, like the bloom of the red rose, to burn there uncontrollably. But even with only one hand holding her, and with his eyes now marvelling at the even greater softness of her facial beauty, he could sense her womanly warmth radiating around him, and in her innocence unconsciously inviting him.

'My angel,' he whispered.

'My own true love,' she replied softly, leaning towards him for one more kiss, a kiss that would put its seal on this wonderful moment forever.

So for the rest of this unforgettable celebration dinner, which Penny had prepared especially for them, they talked and laughed most of the time, as newlyweds will do, of the past, of this, their greatest day, and of a future which glistened before their eyes. What possible fear was there, that could cast its shadow across such a vision before them, even to spoil one small part of their happiness? For weren't they both in the bloom of youth, and with a love that was almost at its breathtaking climax, a love that would recognise no bounds in its efforts to give, and to give all. For only when two give all do they become one in all things.

It was almost ten o'clock when they adjourned to the drawing room and, within a minute or so, Penny appeared with the coffee and liqueurs.

'Only two cups!' said Joanna, 'Aren't you going to have your coffee in here with us?'

'No, my dear,' Penny replied. 'I've heard you both laughing and talking during dinner, and it has made me happy also, and I'm sure you two will never be at a loss for words now that you are together. Besides, this is your wedding night, when most of the things you say to each other will be remembered always.'

'Well, that doesn't mean you shouldn't have your coffee and a few minutes' talk with us,' said Phil.

'No, really,' she answered, smiling, 'I should only feel like a intruder, and besides, Mrs White and I haven't quite finished work; and, what with the champagne I had this afternoon, I don't know how many times we have toasted your future in the kitchen. I can tell you, I won't want any rocking tonight!'

'You know best, but you're more than welcome,' Phil said, and then went on, 'but before you go, there's a little proposition that we discussed during dinner. Why don't you have ten days' holiday while we are on honeymoon? The house is in perfect condition, and Mrs White can keep her eye on things. It will be a bit back for all you have done for us, and for how well you organised everything.'

'What you give me when I go on holiday more than covers any extra I do for you, so I don't think you owe me anything,' she answered with emphasis.

Smiling his happiest smile, he said, 'You worked hard and organised just the same then, and look how I was repaid for what I gave you last time! Look what was waiting for me at the other end of the platform, after I had waved you goodbye. For one thing, you must have had a lot to put up with when it was only us two, and I know I changed a lot after losing so much all at once – not that I didn't go on the same way as before, because I did. But whether it was football or cricket, having a drink with the lads or taking a girl out, nothing seemed to have any importance. It was only when I was at work on the farms that I was able to find any contentment, so I couldn't have been anywhere near my usual self in the house, nor much fun – and I expect nowhere as easy to live with.'

'You weren't as bad as all that,' she answered. 'Probably not as much fun, but I never expected you to be, after such a shock. All I could do was pray for you to meet a nice girl, for I knew it would only be the sharing of another life that would make you return to what you were before. And now, see how my prayers were answered, more fully than I ever thought possible.'

'I couldn't agree more over the last part,' he said, putting his arm around his lovely bride. Then, as he looked into her eyes, he continued, 'You're the answer to our prayers, my darling, and the reality of my wildest dreams, for no one else but you, my love, could ever have brought the sunshine and happiness back to Spring Farm.'

Closing up to him, and giving him just one tender kiss, she replied, 'You know that as far as is in my power, sunshine and happiness will always be here, my darling.'

'I must be off,' said Penny, 'or Mrs White will have finished the work.'

'So the holiday is on?' said Phil.

'If you insist,' she answered, smiling.

'We definitely do,' replied Joanna. 'Then you and I will have that much more to talk about while my husband is getting back in his stride on the farms.'

'Thank you very much, but I really must go… so goodnight, and God bless you both,' she said, as she disappeared round the door. Then in a flash she was back and, with a saucy look all over her face, she said, 'Don't either of you fall out of bed tonight, will you!'

'That's not likely!' they both replied, laughing as Penny disappeared for good to their shouts of 'Goodnight and thanks for everything.'

Once more alone, with the spell of this night steadily closing in upon them, Phil and Joanna were in a wonderland, where every time their eyes met, a lifetime of sunshine paved the way before them, where the clasp of a hand carried them on as in a dream, into a world of beauty, there to be dazzled with this tiny touch of unity. Then, as their lips found the magic of each other, and their priceless spoken vows were even more glorified, there came through the mist that shrouded them a thought, a feeling, a certainty that they were being borne far above all earthly things, and that soon, very soon, the whole heavens would open up and, stretching forth its arms, would hold them close as one. But for a while, the desire of their burning love would fly no further, even though they were both unwilling to let this feeling of heaven fall from their grasp for even a second. Just as a thousand times before, his eyes wandered over this face of tranquil beauty, a face which now seemed to be slumbering peacefully in the crook of his arm; and this time, like the other thousand, he saw one new mystery, one more touch of beauty to wonder and marvel at. Here was one more little miracle, an outward sign to all the perfect goodness that she really was. Angelic – yes, his eyes told him so; but in his heart he knew she had been made angelic within.

'My darling,' he whispered, as he gently ran his fingers through those golden threads of silk.

'My wonderful love,' she replied, opening her eyes, but showing considerable effort in the process.

For, deep inside, she had been striving hard to keep herself above the surface of that pool of heavenly half-consciousness, but all the while, in the back of her mind, she had been filled with peace and tranquillity, knowing that soon the wonder of his love would gently steal over her and completely submerge her in a heaven she had not known before.

'One last drink before we retire, darling?' he asked.

'Yes, just a little one, my love,' she answered. Then she continued, 'But what I would like to do first is to put on a coat, and for you to take me outside to see what our lovely garden looks like in starlight.'

'Anything you wish, my love, is granted,' he replied, getting her coat and helping her on with it.

Outside it was one of those nights that are all too rare. From all points on the horizon, the whole heavens were determined to do themselves justice, and to show their awesome splendour at its most revealing. Not the slightest cloud blotted their view of the inky depth of space – a jet-black void brought back to life by the twinkling gaiety of a thousand gems. For the furthest star, like the nearest star, revelled in their unique array, all happy and carefree, all seemed to be dangling just out of reach, by the brightness of their twinkling light. Only away in the east was the clearness of this happy throng put to any peril, for the dull pink glow of the still invisible moon was already searching upwards and outwards and slowly diminishing those heavenly wonders in its path. Soon, even before the moon would take its first inquisitive peep over the edge of the earth, this, their wonderful earth, now coy at the thought, and knowing that she was at the mercy of this staring intruder who laid her bare, became determined that she would hold the purity of her hills, and the sweetness of her valleys close to her breast. To guard her nakedness, she would use the cover of her breath to filter down this all-revealing light, into a soft, sleepy, pink glow.

'It's the most wonderful night I have ever seen, my love, and, even if I can't see much of the garden, I can sense its loveliness and its welcome,' Joanna said, holding Phil's arm even tighter.

'Spring Farm means a lot to you, doesn't it, my love?' he asked.

'Yes, my sweet – everything in the world, really, for this is the only place where I feel at home. But on the other hand, wherever you are, my love, and as long as I am with you, any place would be absolute heaven to me. But here is the place which was meant for us, a place which will always be blue skies and sunshine, throughout our lives and in our memories.'

He held her close as he told her of that wonderful sight he had seen two nights ago, how he had prayed that it would be just as wonderful on this, their first night together. For even he had never seen anything quite like it before, and he would dearly love for them to be able to share such a phenomenon together. It was a rarity, one which was way past the point of fascination, one where so many wonders have timed their perfection together, so that for a mere hour or so, those who had not laid down their heads in slumber were privileged with a sight which only happens once or thrice in a whole lifetime.

'It's going to be just as wonderful tonight, my love; I know, for the mist is holding steady at three to four feet high, and soon only parts of the hedges will show above a placid pink sea. Even the trees will look different – marooned they'll be, but never more majestic. It'll be a fairyland, and all for you, my darling – all, so that nothing within the sight of our home will ever let us forget that this is our night which has been sanctified for us, and the heavenly blessing which has made this wonderful day and our future possible.'

Turning round to him, she said, 'I know, my love, that this moment will be with us for ever and, just as I now feel that I have been standing here with you for all of my life, there's no obstacle before you, my darling, and the wonderful love and happiness which you have given me.'

His answer was revealed in the loving tenderness of his arms and in the depth of his kiss, and, as they stood there, lost in the spell of each other, the wonders and beauty of all around them silently acknowledged them. While above on high, those twinkling eyes beheld and blessed them with a smile of joy and understanding.

Less than half an hour later, when the end of their wonderful day was but ten minutes from its conclusion, they were arm in arm on top of the stairs, and about to enter their room – the room where their heavenly dreams and a future unknown would unfold around them, a future which could mean the finest day of spring, or the most dreaded day of winter.

But now, as he opened the door, that soft pink glow of the harvest moon greeted them, just as it had to him alone two nights ago, when his thoughts had been. If only she was here with me... and now he was holding reality in his arms. She too had never seen a sight so wonderful, and so fascinated was she that in the space of minutes the spell of it drew her once more to the window. It was a moment or two before he was ready to share one last look with her. She stood there, and his admiring gaze became transfixed at the dream before his eyes. The outline of her form was clearly visible through the flimsy silk that adorned it, and that soft pink light from a long way off glorified her virtue.

Then, before he could bring himself to tear his gaze away, the soft pink glow which had been spread so evenly over all suddenly thickened a hundredfold around her. It was as if this boiling mist was rising her up and setting her apart from everything he had known or dreamt of before. She seemed out of this world, and more like a goddess of the sun than a virgin bride in moonlight. But as he walked towards her, it wasn't the excitement of this great moment that caused him to tremble, it was the doubt and the uncertainty whether he was worthy of all that she really was. Yet before he reached her side, those tremors and the fear of not knowing were dispelled in an instant. She turned, and her arms went around his neck all in the same motion, her lips, those lips of silk which brushed across his cheek, were as firm as a luscious nectarine at its peak; hungry and responsive lips, which would only find the heaven they sought in their unity with his. And so they stood there, locked in each other's arms, seared by that burning fire of ecstasy which each had set aflame in the other. Then, with cheeks pressed together, they took that one last lookout upon a dream world.

'A night whose rare beauty is dedicated especially for you, my love,' he whispered.

'And it's all thanks to you, my darling,' she answered, tightening her arms around him.

'My angel,' he whispered.

'My own true love,' she replied.

Those words, those ultimate words of love and belonging, came from the depths within her, for at last the time had come when in all things, they would belong to each other, a unity that would be absolute and for all time.

So, with their arms around each other, and with this fairyland night-time still at its mystic best, they walked away from the window.

A Honeymoon that Would Go On Until...

Was it the sun shining on his face that brought him back to this world the next morning, or was it a noise from downstairs, as Penny busied herself with the usual chores? All Phil knew for sure was that it was 8.15 a.m., and that he hadn't slept as soundly, and until so late an hour, for years. But as he turned his head, he realised what a wonderful excuse he had, if only to himself. For there she lay, and on that beautiful face was the last word in contentment, while her breathing rose and fell in the rhythm of a deep and peaceful sleep. What chance did his waking thoughts have of staying on the surface, with all the tranquillity of her loveliness at its most peaceful? It mesmerised him completely.

Gently, he raised himself on one elbow, so that his adoring eyes could feast more closely on this face of loveliness, a loveliness that showed the sweetness of her nature and all its tenderness. All this raised his fierce desire to taste the sweetness of her lips, and to once more tell her that she was his whole life; tempted he was, but he wouldn't wake her for the world. He was completely carried away by all before him, for even each strand of golden hair which glistened in the rays of the morning sun added its share to the message that his was a blessing far above anything he had ever dreamed of, even though he had already told himself so ten thousand times or more. So for the next few minutes he watched, keeping as still as possible, watching over her as a guardian angel would, and up before him as always came the same question, and at the end never knowing the answer. Why, why should so many tiny sunbeams of beauty be set on one face alone? Why should those now sleeping eyes light up at the very sight of him, and why should those gently closed lips tell him of her undying love and then lead him on into a heavenly orbit? It wasn't just love at first sight, for their love had grown stronger and deeper each second since they had met. There was only one answer; they had been born for each other, or most likely created, or joined even before that first little spark had given life. They were like two pebbles that had been cast up out of the sea of time, chosen out of all others to lie on the sunny beach of love and life together. Come wind or rain, storm or gale, nothing could possibly part them, he knew, not even when the tide of age crept over them and committed them to the deep once more. They would still be together holding hands, and he would look upon her then with all his love and tenderness, just as he did in these few minutes – minutes that were sacred to him, and to his thankful heart.

He felt he could go on watching her forever, but slowly and reluctantly, he started to slide out of bed, having decided to go downstairs to get the morning tea. But before that, he went to the bathroom to freshen up, so that he could face Penny at this late hour.

'Down already?' said Penny, smiling as he entered the kitchen. 'I didn't expect to see or hear you for at least another hour.'

'Well, it's like this,' Phil answered, putting his arm around her shoulder, 'Surely you didn't think I could go on sleeping after being used to getting up so early for years? And besides, I'm as dry as a piece of straw – it must have been all that champagne, or more likely the spirits.'

'Is she awake?' she asked.

'No,' he replied. 'Sleeping as peacefully as a lamb, and looking more beautiful than ever.'

'Bless her,' Penny said, then continued, 'I've got your tray ready, except for making the tea, but really I wasn't going to bring it up for another hour or so.'

'Well, the point is, I'm hoping we shall be ready to start at 10.30 a.m., but I won't wake her.'

'Well, it will only be your two selves to get ready. I can pack the few small things that you'll need – and, by the way,' she went on, as he stood there with the tray in his hands, 'you look really handsome in your new dressing gown! Blue suits you, you know.'

'Go on,' he answered, 'you'll have me blushing in a moment, and anyone would think it was the first time you've seen me in a dressing gown.'

'It is the first time that I have seen you about to take the tea up to the loveliest girl in the world, and it's surprising what love will bring out in anyone. You look younger and happier already, and I know that the world of happiness that you finally entered yesterday will never disappear from before your eyes.'

'It had better not! I shouldn't be worth knowing if that ever happened. All I want is for this house to hold happiness supreme for the three of us.'

'Four or more!' she called out to him, as he started on his way upstairs.

'Stop trying to rush things,' he answered quietly, with more than a hint of merriment in his voice, while his eyes shone with the thought of all the joy that the future could hold.

Opening the door as silently as he could, his first thoughts were that his lovely bride was still sleeping soundly, but before he had even started to cross the room, her loving voice, the sound of all that was near and dear to him, broke the magical silence.

'Good morning, my darling,' she said, at the same time raising her head up off the pillow, and giving him a wonderful smile.

'And a wonderful good morning to you, my love; but really I thought you were still asleep,' he answered, looking somewhat surprised.

'It must be that even in my deepest dreams, I can sense the moment that you leave me, for when I woke I knew you hadn't left me long, for the place where you had lain beside me was oh so warm and comforting to the touch. It was so wonderful my darling, that as I moved my hand over the sheet, the nearness of you and your heavenly love swept over me, and had I closed my eyes, I would almost have known the reality of your arms.'

'You shall too my, love,' he answered, as he put the tray on the bedside table, then, sitting on the bed, he bent over and took her in his arms for a full five minutes.

Then came the very first talk of an intimate nature, as he looked into those beautiful eyes, saying, 'My love, are you quite sure you are fit enough to face that long journey today? If not, we can stay at an hotel, whenever you find you've had enough travelling, whether it is halfway or two-thirds.'

She could see the perturbed look that puckered his brow, and she was deeply moved by his thought and consideration for her.

'Really, my darling, there's no need to worry. Actually I'm feeling more wonderful than before,' she answered, caressing his face in her hands, and putting a lock of his hair back into position. Then she continued, 'Already I have surrendered to the fact that most of the pain that a woman suffers is the price she pays for all the joy and happiness which is the light of her life. For no words could describe the paradise that was mine as you carried me into the unknown. For suddenly, I thought, I heard the sound of strange, but beautiful music. So sweet was it, that it might even have been the love song of a thousand birds. But no, my darling, it was neither, it could only have been the voices of angels; for with my eyes closed, I saw the glories of heaven as its gates opened up before me, and from inside a soothing light shone over me. Yet one was more brilliant that the noonday sun, and all I knew, my love, was that I was being borne in the tenderness of your arms, and engulfed in the wonder of your love. Pain, or even the thought of it, was a long way off, for around me you had woven a silky gown of ecstasy, and my whole being rejoiced at the nearness of you, my own true love.'

'It was only natural for me to worry and wonder, my angel,' he replied.

'I know, my love, and thank you,' she said, smiling, and went on, 'now please take that look of concern from your handsome face, it doesn't suit you one bit, my darling.' So saying, she pulled him down to her for one long heavenly kiss, a kiss that would start their first whole day of married bliss, and continue on, as the night just past had made them one.

Once downstairs, their first call was to see Penny, then five minutes out in the lovely garden. Happiness and dreams of the future in and around their lovely home crowded in upon them from all sides as they walked back down the lawn towards the house.

Penny, appearing at the doorway, said as they reached her, 'You just couldn't have a better day for a long journey, and all I hope is that you are as lucky for most or all of your honeymoon.'

'You'll have to pray for us that little bit extra,' he answered, at the peak of his happiness.

'I shall,' she answered, 'and I shall also long for you to come home, for I can hardly wait for this house to come properly to life all the time.' Then, turning to Joanna, she went on, 'You'll love it here in springtime, my dear, when all the flowers and shrubs smell at their sweetest.'

'I know I shall love it here at any time of the year, and I can well imagine the springtime fragrance of all that is in this little paradise, especially my favourite of all, the beautiful syringa.'

'That's my favourite too,' Phil remarked, 'and I should think it is one of the finest for miles around. It holds its blooms for a very long time, and is always smothered. You can smell that and the honeysuckle all night if you like to stay awake; only here my love, we never call it syringa – from way back it's been known as orange blossom to the locals.'

'Then it's orange blossom to me, my darling,' Joanna answered, holding her face up for a kiss, which was gladly given.

During breakfast, whenever Penny came into the room, either to bring something, or to know if there was anything else that needed packing, Phil could see with half an eye that his days of claiming one hundred per cent of her attention were gone. *It was much less than fifty now*, he thought to himself.

How she fussed and doted over his bride, who in his eyes also seemed to welcome this loving care and attention. Did she, Penny, remember the morning after her own wedding day, when a night-old bride might find succour in the understanding of an older woman? No, it wasn't that, he felt sure, for the radiance on Joanna's face was brighter than ever. Could it be that these two women from different walks in life had found that magic bond which only exists between mother and daughter? Nothing would please him more if this were so.

However, Penny had organised everything so well, that by 10.15 a.m., they were ready to leave. The goodbyes were said, and a wealth of affection was in their embrace as they kissed her. Then, out onto the road, that winding narrow strip that they would travel to their destination. Already they were in that wonderful state of elation, where a sense of adventure marked each milestone on the way; for in their hearts they were not fenced in by hedges and trees, but going forward into a future that stretched out wide and exciting before them. The whole world was theirs, and if joy, happiness, love and devotion were what made the world go round, then the safety of mankind was guaranteed during their lifetime. Thus, for mile after mile they went, with the same vision of bubbling happiness before them, a vision which would flame into reality at each tender clasp of the hand. And so it was by their being in this wonderland of love and beauty that time became the loser, for just as they realised that several hours had gone by, they were pulling up on the forecourt of the hotel Phil had chosen for lunch.

'Do you think three-quarters of an hour will be long enough, my love?' he asked.

'It should be ample, my darling,' she answered.

'Only, if we have two more stops after this, we should reach our hotel at 6.30 p.m.,' he said, catching hold of her arm.

Giving him one of her loveliest smiles, she replied, 'I was hoping it might have been 7.30 p.m., for the farther down we go, the more it feels like the start of summer, not its end, and at times it seems as if it is only you and I, my darling, in the middle of all this beautiful countryside.'

'It really is wonderful,' he agreed, 'but I want you to have a good hour's rest before dinner if possible, my love.' Then he continued, 'Besides, I'm already longing for the next wonderful kiss, and there doesn't seem the slightest hope of stealing one here.' His face was beaming with delight, as for a second or two, he put his arm around her.

'Don't worry, my darling, I'll keep a lookout for a quiet spot, where we can pull off the road and share a minute of heaven in each other's arms,' she answered, squeezing his hand.

The lunch was delightful, and not just a few of those present noted with admiration this elegant pair who only had eyes for each other; but it was only Phil who saw and caught her, for the second time, gazing with that faraway look that seemed to go right through him.

'A penny for them,' he said.

'Worth more than that,' she answered with a whimsical smile.

'A kiss, then,' he replied.

'That's more like it,' she answered, 'but if you must know, I was trying to fathom out just how wonderful you are, my darling, and how desperately I love you, so that will mean one extra special kiss when I find the right place for us to stop.'

His answer was not in words, but in the caress of his hand as he placed it on hers; just one little touch, yet she could feel the joy of his perfect wonderful love for her surging through until it embraced her completely.

But now, as could be expected, their thoughts were out on the road, wondering how far they would have to go before the hunger on their lips could be satisfied. But luck – or fate – was on their side; for within twenty minutes of leaving the hotel, the winding road suddenly rose very steeply, and, once at the top, they were faced with a straight two miles of open ground. He motored on until they were about halfway, pulling on to the wide grass verge before coming to a halt. He took one look back and another forward, then they were in each other's arms. All that they had meant to each other since they had met, the gateway to heaven they had been about to enter twenty-four hours ago, which had led them on a path to ecstasy divine, took complete control of them. All this rolled into one and instantly swept aside all other thoughts. Only one thought, one feeling, rose through the haze which now enveloped them; that the love, the desire, which flowed from their yearning lips, would only find expression in the burning passion they felt for each other. But this kiss, the kind whose birth he had first been aware of only a few hours ago, left him almost breathless; most of the time he was like a half-drowning man, clawing himself to the surface through the mist that her wonderful love deluged upon him.

No longer did her lips surrender and respond just so far at the first touch of his, and no longer did he feel just a tender crush from those bewitching arms. For those few hours ago in the moonlight, she had held him as she did now in an embrace of a sanctified and blending love, where the glory and wonders of all things known seemed his alone, an embrace that never tried for one second to veil its reluctance to relax, or to let him go. And those lips, supple and alive, matched his in each move on their silky path to ecstasy, spelling out to his pounding heart the true depth of her pure and wonderful love for him, telling him that she was his partner now, the other half of him, and also emphasising that those two halves were already moulded into one for all time.

This was no flight of fancy, but a true feeling of heaven, where each and all are more glorified in giving than receiving. As soon as he had breath enough, he whispered, 'You know, my darling, you are learning fast, for in every kiss you become more wonderful than ever.'

Opening her eyes and returning his loving smile, she answered, 'It's not just a question of learning, my darling, for when I spoke my vows to you almost twenty-four hours ago, it wasn't simply that at last my desperate longing to become your wife was over. At the same time, I was willingly pledged and committed to love you perfectly, purely, and with all I have at my command, no matter what time of the day or night.'

Still with that deep loving smile upon his face, he replied, 'If that is so, then it looks as if I am in for a very exciting time, my angel.'

Kissing him gently, she said, 'I believe you are my own true love, just as I am yours.' She paused, then continued, 'I know you will never mind when in the future, no matter how busy you are, I shall steal up on you for one swift kiss, and as our lips brush and press together, fleeting though it may be, my darling, you shall know the full flood of my love for you, a love that needs no kindling now, but one where the very thought, sight or sound of you, brings it rushing to the surface in the twinkling of an eye, a love that stretches forth to delight and embrace you, just as yours my darling, does to me.'

'How could I ever mind, my love, when it is only a love and devotion such as my own, which finds its life blood in a kiss and caress at any time?' he answered, giving her one more long wonderful kiss that would help their eager and longing hearts over the rest of the journey.

Then, as their lips drew back from this overflowing cup of heavenly joy, and as the senses cleared once more, he looked into her eyes, saying, 'From the moment we met, my love, my whole being cried out for you, knowing that there just couldn't be anyone else in my life but you, my darling. Whether our meeting was the direct will of God, or a master stroke of daily fate, I have no idea; but whichever it was, I am lost at its perfection, and overcome by all its wonderment. There were times when just to hear your voice on the phone made my heart beat so fast that I had little control of it; and then, there were the times we were together and life meant being in paradise, when just to hold your hand was heaven itself. It was then that I asked myself, "How can there be so much unhappiness in the world?" Surely if two people fall in love and live their lives for each other as we do, they can bring nothing else but a wonderful happiness to each other. I know that something isn't wrong which told me so, for we are a pair, an inseparable pair, whose lives are dedicated to bringing all the goodness of this world to each other, my darling.'

'I have often asked myself that same sad question, my love,' she whispered, 'but there's one thing – nothing is more certain than that we were meant for each other. For even as I was growing up, whatever it was that guided me, must have grown steadily stronger, moulding me and keeping me content in what would be to most people a very restricted way of life; and yet in all those years I never had any desire to break away. Then, in a flash, that old way of life was suddenly swept aside. That was when your eyes and mine met for the very first time, my darling, when they revealed the love, devotion and happiness that was ours together.'

She snuggled closer into his arms for one more last kiss, a kiss that would have to satisfy their love for the next few hours.

True to his hopes and calculations, and after having to ask the whereabouts of the hotel a mile from it, they entered the drive a few minutes after 6.30 p.m. Already they had passed beneath the shade of trees that were strangers to their part of the country, and now the road was flanked on both sides with clusters of hydrangeas. The flowers, which had been as blue as the sky, or as pink as the most delicate sunset, were almost faded now. But to those in love, all around seemed to send out its special charm, as if to welcome them. Hardly had this autumn beauty revealed its best then they reached the hotel, a building that was much larger than first impressions had given them. Marooned in its own expanse of well-kept grounds, it overlooked a most beautiful bay, from where it stood aloof, high on the headland.

Fifteen minutes later they were settled in, and already they had known the joy of each other's arms, and the spell of a kiss which had seemed so long overdue. But now they are standing before the open window, with arms still around each other, as they gazed out upon a perfect sea, so blue, so calm, so fascinating.

'Won't it be wonderful, my love, if we are lucky enough to have this beautiful weather all the time? Just imagine it, a real Indian summer for our honeymoon, when all the places we want to see will look their perfect best under a cloudless sky.'

'It will be more than wonderful, my darling,' she answered, 'but do you remember what I said two weeks ago? No matter what the weather is, as long as we are together then everything is perfect, for you are my whole world, and I know I am all of your world also.'

He half turned, and, as arms closed around each other, the glory and wonder of the future flashed before them; love in all its heavenly meaning was theirs, absolute and in abundance.

Could they but have seen into the future, they would have known that an unimpeded sun would shine over them each day. But whatever extra delight such perfect conditions could bestow, nothing could have added to their sacred joy at being together. So they enjoyed dinner and dancing, and in the five days that followed, they visited all the quaint and beautiful places within easy reach. But on three out of those five days, after they had found a secluded beach where it must have been almost as hot as in the middle of summer, they spent most of the afternoons swimming and sunbathing. He would always remember the first sight he had of her in her costume. Whether it was her golden hair which blended perfectly with her pale blue costume, or vice versa, he had no idea; all he knew was that she looked divine, while the natural shade of her skin looked as thought she had already been kissed a little each day over the past few months by a tender sun.

She was a dream, and he loved her more than his own life, and for the thousandth time he realised just how much he adored her. Her angelic beauty, and the perfection of her figure, were blessings beyond all dreams, but even those two great wonders took second place, when compared with the sweetness of her nature and the heavenly ecstasy of her pure and desperate love, which she almost overpowered him with. Inwardly and outwardly, he was so proud of her – for to him, wasn't she nothing short of a gift from heaven?

So those first few heavenly days just drifted by; then it was on further down the coast for three more stops, with a couple of trips over to the north for good measure. But this would not be the end of the honeymoon, for they had fallen in love with the place where they had spent those heavenly first days, and had decided to spend the last three there on the way back. He had already phoned and booked the same suite, so that those wonderful memories would be there to greet them. But love, their undying love, was with them always, and when they phoned Penny, or her father and Marie-Ann, even if they had tried, they could never have disguised the perfect joy and happiness that was theirs to overflowing. For each day was the start of an ever-increasingly wonderful and joyous time. And each night stealthily let down its blanket of mystery around them, closing them up in a world of their own, opening the door of ecstasy and togetherness, then smiling over them as they slumbered as one.

As day followed day, so too did the soft placid perfection of this late summer and the hard rugged beauty of the land, which fought its relentless battle against the might of wind and ocean, hold them spellbound. Often they would stand with arms around each other, silently gazing at all before them, but the grandeur was mostly beyond the full meaning of any known words. Usually it was 'wonderful', 'perfectly beautiful', or 'fantastic, darling', and often all three; but always they realised the inadequacy of their words. For that which can hardly cause an eyelid to flicker in one man can wring the heart of another, even as he beholds it for the thousandth time. No wonder they never seemed to tire of feasting upon Cornwall's beauty, for this was a beauty quite different from that of the Cotswolds. There, the big hills always seemed to guard and comfort the countryside around; but here it was one mighty foe against another, and the blessing was for their sakes that they were seeing them only at peace. But they were true lovers of nature, who, even as they looked upon the beauty of this peaceful scene, could quite well imagine the reverse; leaden skies filling up the gap from earth to sunshine, almost completely; angry seas surging forth with the strength of a mountain, fearless in their bid for victory; and those rugged cliffs and rocks hanging grimly to the motto of a million years, that they shall not pass, only as misty spray in the wind.

So much in love, so much to see, and so much beauty to be seen, through happy eyes that were the lights of heart and soul. Snapshots of each other were taken whenever the background offered its perfect best, and at least twice a day Phil would politely ask some friendly stranger to snap them together.

'One more for the family album,' he would say, as he thanked them, knowing that these would be the ones they would treasure most, when this happy and wonderful time would spring to life again, during the winter evenings to come. But there was one picture he especially hoped would be a success. He had snapped her just as she was landing a fish, and he wouldn't know until it was developed whether it was delight on her face, or a touch of fright; however, they would laugh about it whichever way.

But now there are just three days more, and they are back in that very room from which their wonderful honeymoon started, and just as before, arms are entwined around each other as they gaze out of the window. The few moments of silence between them are only a sign that they are once more under the spell of all that stretches out before them, but never for one tiny second does the closeness of each other diminish, or falter in the slightest. More and more they have become nearer to being one, and more and more each thought is known and granted before a word is spoken. In constant touch in mind and body, and in heart and soul, they are no different one from the other, but are perfectly in unison, perfectly in love and thought for each other, and with so great a love, why shouldn't they, like most others, expect only a future with no real black clouds, and plain sailing for most of the way?

Yet life is like the placid sea and perfect sky that their eyes are feasting upon at this very moment. A change of wind can bring a change of fortune… when, as seas run high, and winds are at their tempest height, thundering in to scatter the golden fringe from the feet of Mother Earth, being blind in their fury, they leave all before them scarred and bare; where even time and friendly tide, in the aftermath which follows, can never quite heal all the ugly wounds. So too in life, when the storms of trouble no longer hurry by, when the dark clouds of despair cry 'Halt!', and hover overhead; when the world, our world, seems really at its end. The pangs of unrequited love... those lips quivering after an unkind word... the loss of one who meant so much... a wounded, or broken heart. These are the scars that life and time can never erase entirely. Even when the span of a life has passed, a sudden thought and a tear will fall, and a word is something which remains unsaid, for the choking feelings won't allow it. This is the jetsam that ill fortune leaves upon the human sand; this is the worldly price we pay for all the ill that might have been good; this is the price of human love.

So, as Phil and Joanna still stood before the window, there was no pang in their hearts about what trouble or sorrow the future might hold for them; for, like all others in love, their future looked so secure and so exciting. It was a time when in their sublime happiness they would live each day to the full, and welcome the dawn of the next with an ever-increasing sense of joy, and open arms.

Squeezing her more tightly to him, Phil said, 'We must try to come here again, my love. Before the winter is over would be lovely – it would be wonderful to feel the first touch of spring, which comes much sooner here than we are used to at Spring Farm.'

'I'd love it darling, as long as you don't work too long and hard to make it possible. But I forget,' she continued, turning around to him and giving him one more of those lovely smiles, 'that is a part of my duty now, to take great care of you, and you can rest assured that I shall, my love.'

Kissing her lightly on the lips, he said, 'I know you will my love, but if I work that little bit harder for anything, it's funny, I always enjoy its fruits that much more; and besides, you like helping me with the paperwork, so you will be doing your share of the extras also.'

'I'll help you all I can, my love,' she whispered, 'I'll do

anything just to be with you, my darling, anywhere.'

Before another word could be spoken, their lips met, gently at first, then the full force of their love took command, and it was a far more beautiful picture that flashed before their love-closed eyes than the one they had a moment before been admiring. There was no limit to the depth of a kiss now; from the start she had fallen hopelessly in love with him, and he with her. But now, since they had knelt before the sacred alter of everlasting life, they had belonged to each other, and in that time the inward joy of heart and soul had fashioned another sense, an infinite one, which communicated between them in the intimacy of a kiss, 'that there never could be an end to this wonderful love, that was their blessing.' Moreover, there was something which it was determined to instil into their minds; even at the end of this earthly life, no matter how long it was to last, they would only be on the threshold of a timeless life together, where the love and joy which they know now would be magnified a million times in its heavenly glory and wonder.

Those last few days held just as much fun and happiness as the ones before; there was not the slightest remorse because their honeymoon was coming to its close. They had had a wonderful time, with perfect sunshine, and had fallen in love with all the beauty and the quaint little places they had seen.

Soon they were going home, back to their love-nest that lay in the comforting arms of the Cotswolds, where they would pick up the golden thread of that heavenly first night together, and they would know the sort of joy that can only spring from a marriage of perfect true love.

On the way home, it was no more than could be expected of them, they just had a pull onto that grass verge, at the very same spot where they had snatched a glimpse of heaven on the way down. After their first wonderful kiss, Joanna withdrew her arms from around Phil's shoulders. Then, looking into his eyes and caressing his face in her hands, she whispered, 'You're so wonderful, my darling, but the disappointment is, there just aren't words wonderful enough for me to thank you for giving me all this heaven. Only with my love for you can I hope to show you just how much you mean to me.'

'Then you've really enjoyed every minute, darling, and you've no grumbles having me as a husband?' he asked, with a loving smile.

'How could I, when everything has been so perfect and heavenly? For no woman could have known more joy than I have, and I pray that I have given you the same amount of heaven also, my darling.'

'You have, my angel,' he answered. 'To me, you always have been and always will be the very last word in all things that are perfect, heavenly and wonderful.'

So before they started on their homeward journey, they spent two more minutes in each other's arms, and, going along each of those miles towards home, whether they were talking, or remaining in that crowded silence which two people so desperately in love have the gift to know, cherishing the unspoken word, they were in heaven, for now they were together for always.

Whatever it was that overflowed from their loving hearts, it would keep flowing on, making each second of their lives nearer to living as the major part of each other. So that long before the first anniversary of their wedding arrived, as each day came and went, it was filled with a love which knew no bounds, whether they were being serious, or in their many moments of play. Smouldering always just below the surface was the desperate will to please, the pureness of a heavenly desire, and the offering of many a silent prayer, for a bliss that could only stay as such as long as they had each other.

One More Star is Born

It was almost five o'clock. The preparations at Spring Farm had long since been completed, and the air of excitement and expectancy which had prevailed for most of the day was now almost at fever pitch.

'They won't be much longer now,' said the colonel, as Penny brought the eatables in and put them on the tea tables. Then he continued, 'It will be lovely to see them again, Penny...' He got no further, for the sound of a motor horn, faint at first, then louder as the car came out of the bend to enter the yard, caused a mad scramble to the door.

'We've had the most wonderful time,' said Joanna, as she kissed them all in turn.

'Well, you certainly both look on top of the world, and with all those smiles one would think you were just going off on honeymoon, instead of the end of it,' said her father.

'There's no end to our honeymoon, Daddy,' she answered, as she kissed him once more. Then, putting her arm around her husband, she continued, 'There just can't be, can there, my darling?'

'Not if we can help it, my love,' he answered, bending down to kiss her with all his sincere affection.

It was happiness unbounded they had brought home with them, and a wonderful joyous welcome they received in return, so much so that it was another ten minutes before Penny could break away to make the tea, and in her thoughts was a never-ending joy, for the couple she loved were home, and everything would be just too wonderful for words now.

That was exactly how fate had meant it to be, too wonderful for words; but could it be too wonderful to last? That was one question which only the future could provide the answer to. But as day followed day, outshining the glory of its brother of yesterday, there was not, and there never could be, any retreating for the love that was theirs. The caress of a hand, the intimacy of a kiss, and the times when they shared the realms of heaven, all this was no different from when they had been on honeymoon. But the inward force which controlled the very depths of them was a limitless power, ever surging on and bringing to them each day an ever-increasing need for each other, a deeper meaning to all understanding, and a love which would go on in its search to give its ultimate best. This was theirs as the weeks went by, a time when all this happiness and joy was never for one second taken for granted, for in all their doings, and in their hearts, were the unmistakable signs that they were forever thankful for their blessings.

So, after four visits to Northwood, it was a must that they should spend their first Christmas in their own home, a home which could only be described as paradise; and it was to her father's supreme delight that he and Marie-Ann had been asked to spend it with them. How their eyes shone when they arrived that afternoon, and saw what a wonderful display Joanna and Penny had made of the Christmas decorations.

'You're two very artistic girls,' her father said, and Marie-Ann had agreed emphatically.

From that moment on, the spirit of Christmas never flagged, even when it was bedtime, for she thought her father and Marie-Ann would never finish their goodnights, so that her heart's desire could help her bring down the presents and place them around the Christmas tree. They were all sizes – large, small and in between.

'I love Christmas as much now as when I was a boy,' Phil said. Then, smiling, he continued, 'I should think there's enough here for twenty people, for this is my fourth journey.'

Seven or eight for everyone,' Joanna answered, as their lips met; she was feeling very pleased that he was as excited over Christmas as she was.

'All those different shapes and sizes, and yet you've arranged them perfectly, my love,' he said as he handed her the smallest one of all, then added, 'that's the last one, darling.'

She placed it in its special slot. Then, standing up, she turned round to him, and at the same time slid her arms over his shoulder and said softly, 'Not quite, my love. I've still got one very special present, for you alone; in fact the most wonderful present any wife can give her husband.'

'Oh, my darling, if it's what I'm thinking and hoping, then you are far more wonderful than ever,' he answered.

Before she could reply, their lips met in a kiss that opened up a vast new joy to them.

'Can I ask when?' he whispered.

'Of course you can, my darling! If all's well, I'm going to present you with a son and heir, I should think early in August... and I'm not the only one who is wonderful, for there's one thing I can never grasp – just how wonderful you are, my love!'

Once more they sealed their new-found joy in the depth of a heavenly kiss and, once more, two hearts beat as one.

'You're quite sure, my love, it's going to be a boy and not a girl?' he asked.

She hesitated a while, and then that sort of look came over her face, as though she had never considered that possibility whatsoever. 'It's got to be a boy, my darling, in fact I know it will be,' she answered.

'Well, if you are that sure, my love, we shall only have to think of a boy's name,' he said.

'Oh, I've thought of that already, and the one I like best is Jamie, if it suits you, my love.'

'It's lovely – sounds nice too; so Jamie it shall be, my treasure,' he replied.

'Thank you, my darling,' she whispered, as her arms tightened around his neck once more.

Christmas morn, and already the seasonal spirits of the night before are making their presence heard; snatches of songs could be heard in one direction, and carols in the other, plus the sound of happy laughter in between. All this made it a certainty that one would hardly be able to get a word in edgeways at breakfast time. That was how it was; everyone was in top form, and later, when they were gathered around the Christmas tree opening the present with the same sort of glee, when thanks and kisses were given all round, the two young ones, the two with a secret, knew as they kissed and held each other close why a new light was shining in their eyes, and an extra glow of tenderness seemed to radiate all around them.

They knew the reason why; they knew that this was a joy, a tenderness, that only the start of a new life could bring, and in their supreme happiness their thoughts had already flown to the Christmas beyond, and they could visualise a special pile of presents under the tree, presents of a different sort; while in their arms would be the comfort of a bundle of joy, their final step to being one in all things.

Not once during those two weeks did Joanna's father or Marie-Ann, or more especially Penny, show even the slightest sign or drop the tiniest hint that they had guessed their secret. They were so used to seeing them so full of life and loving that the slightest suspicion never dawned upon them. Only to each other was their new-found joy so plain to see. But this was the wonder of all wonders, a blessing which they felt like letting the whole world know, a joy which they could keep no longer from the ones who were near and dear to them. So the day before the colonel and Marie-Ann's visit came to a close, the great moment came at tea time, and Joanna deliberately waited until Penny came to take the tea things away, so that she would hear the glad tidings at exactly the same time as her father and stepmother.

Bubbling over with excitement, but trying to be as casual as she could be, she said, 'We've got something wonderful to tell you.' Then, sliding her arm through her husband's and looking into his eyes, she continued, 'We've had many a laugh, silent and otherwise, haven't we darling? For neither of you mentioned in your fun that perhaps there would be someone else to buy presents for next Christmas.'

Before she could finish all she wanted to say, her father, his face beaming, blurted out, 'Are you trying to say that I'm going to be a grandfather?'

'Yes, Daddy,' she answered, as he rushed over to kiss and congratulate her.

'I'm so thrilled,' said Marie-Ann.

'I'm delighted,' said Penny joyfully, then added, 'that's made it the happiest end to a Christmas ever! Just think of it!'

While Joanna was receiving the full force of Marie-Ann's affection, and after the colonel had congratulated the father-to-be, Phil turned to Penny, saying, 'I hope you, of all people, are satisfied now.'

'Well, for a while,' she answered, and they could hardly kiss each other for laughing.

After a while, when things had calmed down a little, Joanna was able to continue. 'I felt sure that one of you would have noticed, when I refused a drink on so many occasions, as well as being a little more choosy in what I ate.'

No, none of them had.

'That was probably due to having too much to drink ourselves,' said Marie-Ann amid more laughter.

'There's one thing, Phil,' said the colonel, 'This calls for a drop extra tonight.' Then he shook his son-in-law once more warmly by the hand.

By the time Jane's wedding day arrived, Joanna's once perfect figure had taken on a more motherly appearance, but, with her wealth of knowledge, and her natural gift for dress design, she knew exactly what would pass her off as a radiant matron of honour, rather than a glowing mother-to-be. Hardly a soul would have guessed the truth of her condition as she glided up the aisle a few steps behind Jane. Heads turned, so that eyes could catch the first glimpse of the bride of the day. But there was one pair of eyes which stole a much longer look than any of the others, and only afterwards did he feel a slight touch of guilt. For he realised his eyes had hardly flickered over the radiant bride, who took pride of place in front. They had been drawn and held in the spell of the woman who walked behind, the one who, as each day passed, grew more lovely, more wonderful and – though it seemed to him impossible – more loving and tender. The woman who six months before had walked up a different aisle to be his bride, today, these six months later, was still his bride, and she would go on being his bride, no matter how long the future stretched out beyond.

It was like their own wedding at Northwood. A big marquee covered most of the lawn at the Court, but even with the warm atmosphere, the talking, the general excitement, and the one glass of champagne Joanna had allocated herself, plus the bundle of joy she carried inside, she never seemed to flag for one second. If, as on a few occasions, when she and Phil were no longer together, whether it was two yards or ten which separated them, no longer than a minute would go by before their eyes met, and in that flash, their love for each other and the heaven which that love surrounded them with at all times, was transmitted and understood, each to the other. When they were side-by-side, or face-to-face, when only the clasp of a hand could be given in front of so many, the whole flood of their wonderful love enfolded them, and the glories of heaven blotted out the gaiety going on around them.

So the weeks rolled by, and to the three of them as well as the colonel and Marie-Ann when they came to visit, if ever there was a heaven on earth, then it seemed Spring Farm could surely claim the title. What sadness this friendly house had known in days gone by had been dimmed as time passed by, and what scars there still remained were transformed into sacred memories by the joy and happiness and the unquenchable love which abounded on all sides.

The beginning of June brought the first clear skies for two whole weeks, also the last time for a while that Phil would let Joanna take their favourite walk to the top of High Ridge. There were other walks which branched from the Ridge itself, so in the cool of the evening, along these he walked her. Handicapped though she was, never once did her arms forget to enfold him under the old chestnut tree, and never once was the vision of that first time dimmed in the slightest.

The chasing and romping in the fields were over for the moment, for the plight of a woman who labours with her unborn child is a sacrifice to the time when, in her joy of motherhood, she is bestowed with those heavenly instincts, so deep, so loving and protective, and with a soft rare tenderness that bears no resemblance to her relationship with man. For she has, with God's help and blessing, performed the miracle of life; the whole world is at her feet, and it is all hers.

But even as she was, there was one day that just had to be

remembered to the full, one day when Joanna's condition would have to take second place. For she was determined to have a wonderful party to celebrate the first anniversary of the day they had met. The day, when in a second or two, the life she had known had withered into emptiness, and, at the end of an hour, the future, though uncertain, had blazed into a raging fire of expectations. And now, a year later, a year which had so completely overflowed with joy and happiness that she had hardly known one heavenly day from another, she was within weeks of realising the living proof of her creative powers. Pleasure, gratitude and pride would know no bounds when the time came for her to present her 'own true love' with his son and heir; while for herself, a rapturous joy lay within, unknown so far, but a joy unfathomable once she had heard that first tiny cry.

Her father and Marie-Ann were an automatic choice for the party; then there was Major and Mrs Marchant, Jane and Gerald, and she had also invited Bob and his new-found girlfriend, Clare.

'It's not too many, is it?' she asked Penny.

'No, certainly not,' came the reply. 'We've had more than that before, and you know I can manage quite easily with the help I get.'

Over the past few months, these two, who had been like mother and daughter almost from the very start, had grown as close as could be, so much so that even as she was, and much against Penny's wishes, Joanna still liked to help her all she could, especially with the extra work of this party. That was why, and unbeknownst to Penny, she had already asked Jane, and she would ask Clare when she arrived, if once dinner was over, they would all set about clearing the table and finishing the washing-up, so that Penny would be able to join them for coffee and drinks to celebrate with them on this lovely June night out on the lawn.

That was the plan, and that was how they carried it out. The men were not allowed to stay in the dining room for their usual half-hour or so; even Marie-Ann and Mrs Marchant wanted to play their part, and were the ones to rise first after their excellent dinner, telling the men that a stroll around the garden would do them good.

So the five of them descended on the kitchen, and were surprised that except for the dining table which they were clearing, everything was finished and Mrs White and Mrs Dodds had already departed.

'We are going to finish what there is to do while you go upstairs and change,' Joanna told Penny, then continued, 'you're going to celebrate with us over coffee and drinks.'

'I can manage quite well,' Penny replied, 'Besides, you've got all your friends to talk to.'

'That's why we want you there as well. When we are here on our own you wouldn't call us strangers then, and whoever is here makes no difference to Phil and me, to us always you are our Penny, our friend.'

'Besides,' said Mrs Marchant, 'the major wants to congratulate you on the excellent dinner.'

That was almost the first thing he did as they walked out, taking the coffee with them. In fact they all did, each in turn.

Phil, Bob and Gerald had the job of seeing to the drinks, and it was just as they had served the second round that the major remarked, 'You would never think that it was a year ago today that my old car broke down for the last time.'

'Why, have you sold it?' asked Bob, who had never been quite in on the picture.

'No,' answered the major, 'not a thing wrong with the engine from that day to this! That was how these two came to meet, because it spluttered to a halt and just refused to go when we were on our way to meet Joanna at The Junction.'

'That was one factor,' replied Joanna, looking delighted, 'but there was also the other one; if Penny hadn't been going on holiday, Phil wouldn't have been on the road that morning, and I would have been left at The Junction not only waiting for you and Jane to arrive, but to this day, I would still be in my narrow world, and not know how perfectly wonderful love really is.'

'You know now, then?' asked the major teasingly.

'Yes,' she answered, standing up and sliding her arms over her husband's shoulders. 'Right from the moment we met, wasn't it, my love?'

'Yes, my darling, and not a moment too soon,' Phil replied, as their lips met.

True to her first calculation and their unbounded joy, young Jamie was born on 7th August, a little before three in the afternoon. From the moment that first tiny cry ushered into the room memories of the past, a new world, a mother's world, was born – of sacrifice, pain and a love as deep and strong as any love could be. How the pride shone in the eyes from two proud faces as Phil tiptoed carefully (and needlessly) across the room to see his son for the first time, as he slept peacefully in his cot by the side of the bed.

'He's absolutely wonderful, my love,' he whispered.

'He's a real treasure, my darling,' she answered, 'and just like that photograph of you when you were a baby.'

'Can't be my darling, he's far too beautiful for that; must be exactly like his mother,' he whispered.

'Impossible, for I have done my utmost to make him just like you my love, all because I love you more than my overflowing heart can measure,' she replied, as he made his way round to the other side of the bed.

Once there, and with the happiest of smiles all over his face, he took her tenderly in his arms, and gently his lips transferred the depth of his love to hers, telling her that she was everything in the world to him, and just how wonderful she was. Then with one hand caressing her face, and with the other stroking her golden hair, he looked into her eyes, saying, 'I shall always be eternally grateful to you, my angel, for this precious gift, our son.'

'What else could I do for one was wonderful as you, my own true love?' she whispered, then continued, 'if Daddy had been like most, and had been against us seeing each other, I would have walked barefoot, rather than be parted from you, my darling.'

'If that had been the case, my love, we would have met somewhere along the road. As it was, it was absolute torment for me, and you were only over the other side at the Court.'

'Yes, we both suffered, my darling,' she answered, 'and since then you have made me not only the happiest girl in the world, but the happiest mother as well.'

'Not only me, my love, but having an understanding father like you have has put that extra bit of sunshine on everything. He's the best sport that could be.'

'I know,' she answered. Then, smiling, she went on, 'But it's not every girl who is lucky enough to take a young man home as wonderful as you my darling.'

Five more minutes of tender love and gentle kisses followed before Phil hurried downstairs to get Penny, five more minutes of real heaven, while Penny gloated over his son and fussed around his queen. He had no worries there; they would have the very best of attention, and already he could see that same old glitter in her eyes that had been there when he was a boy.

The first place to hear the glad tidings was Northwood, where the colonel and Marie-Ann were both overjoyed, and more so when Phil said, 'I've got a message for you from Penny, to say that your room is ready when you are.'

'Won't it be too much work for her?' enquired the colonel.

'No,' answered Phil, 'I think she and her helpers are raring to go after a quiet time, and we know you must want to see Joanna and your grandson for the first time.'

'Wonderful!' came the reply. 'Say, the day after tomorrow?'

'Lovely, and we all send our love to you and Marie-Ann.'

Next came the Court and then Bob, and all sent good wishes and congratulations from the well of the heart. Poor Jane was so excited and wanting to know everything that in the end she said, 'I can't wait until tomorrow to see them, Phil! Promise to give me a ring as soon as Joanna's awake, even if it's in the middle of dinner – I'll drop everything.'

'I will,' he answered.

But as things turned out she didn't have to wait quite as long as that, for a little after 6.30 a.m., Joanna awoke, either from the instincts of motherhood, or the excitement of that ray of sunshine who was sleeping peacefully in his cot by the side of her bed.

So Phil phoned Jane as promised, and it was only the space of minutes before she arrived, bringing Gerald also. What a wonderful half-hour they had together! And, in the days to come, with the colonel and Marie-Ann – not forgetting Penny – all in a state of unmeasurable delight, Jane would arrive, usually without Gerald, and her eyes would light up as never before, every time she had a glimpse of young Jamie.

The Sun Sets on Peace

What a world of love this child had been born into, a world of joy that day by day he would become a little more a part of, but a world that on the outside had already braced itself for a course of madness on one side, and survival and freedom on the other. So, on that fateful day, 3rd September, 1939 a month after Jamie was born, the place of origin of this little innocent, and the birthplace of millions more like him throughout the world, took up the sword of war against each other; a war in which, before its end, not only the flower of youth would give their all in untold numbers, but the old and not so old, and far too many like him just born, would cease and wither, before the bud of knowing could show a small petal.

What madness, where so many, so young, had to pay the price for the folly of a grown-up world! But just as almost two thousand years gone by, when a multitude of innocents perished before a tyrant's sword, so that one, the Holy One, would live and grow, to show humanity the way before being crucified, so would these modern martyrs return as angel hosts, some before one foot could leave its print upon the friendly earth. Their loss, their sacrifice was made, so that His word could echo round the world to give mankind its one and only hope.

So this was the future – a future unknown, a future which only in a few minds bore the impending burden of sorrow and sacrifice barely dreamed of; a future where Fate put all names into a huge sack and picked them out at random for her sport.

The party for their first wedding anniversary was just as grand as if it was in peacetime, and at Christmas there was very little difference either; that extra pile of special presents were in the most prominent place under the Christmas tree, and joy and happiness was theirs to overflowing. Their love, their sacred love, had blossomed to this everlasting peak of fragrant beauty, rare, pure and wonderful; but the only thing which stopped the flow of Joanna's happy world was when the thought crossed her mind, which it did little more often as time went by, 'What will I do without Phil if he's called up to go to war?'

He had reassured her all he could by telling her that with three farms to run, he wouldn't have a chance of joining up, even if he pulled all the strings possible.

But there were times, even though he was completely unaware of it, when she could see those signs of restlessness about him, and she understood; yet she knew nothing would make him leave her of his own accord. He would never be the willing instrument to pierce her heart with emptiness, hopelessness, and, worst of all, that dreaded loneliness. The joy and blessing of young Jamie did more than anything else to keep the horror and dread of war in the background.

However, there was always a deep sense of feeling for the men who had to face the enemy through this bitter winter. Phil and his men on the farms knew all about being cold and wet, but what must it be like to be under fire and bombardment, under those awful conditions? He knew his job was as vital as any, so he had made his plans for the year ahead, making sure that not one square yard of all those acres was being wasted. If there were no hope of him being allowed to fight, he would do his utmost for those that were.

Besides, war or no war, nothing could prevent their love from being the biggest joy in living; and now, as the dreary cold of winter gradually gave way to the first hints of spring, it was time to start their longer walks up over the Ridge. But now there were the three of them. Phil would carry young Jamie mile after mile with all the ease in the world and, under the old chestnut tree, it now meant two lots of heaven for them, for he would 'pop' them each in turn, and in their eyes were not only the lights of this wonderful love of theirs, but the thanks for this precious blessing which that love had given them. It was times like this when in his heart Phil thought of the double wrench that those other husbands and fathers had known – and what sort of hell were they going through at this moment?

Three more weeks slipped by, then, one morning towards the

end of April, when he was rather later than usual going back to work after breakfast, he suddenly had a glimpse of Joanna standing by the bird bath out on the lawn. Going closer to the French windows to get a better view of what she was doing, the sight before him seemed at first as nothing unusual. She had in her hand what he assumed was a dish of bread and milk, but he then received the shock of his life, for feeding out of her other hand were two fully-grown jays. Quietly he called Penny.

'Oh yes,' she said, 'that's been going on for ages. Some mornings if Joanna is a bit late, they're out here waiting.'

'What, wild birds like that?' Phil exclaimed, 'Usually you can't get within a hundred yards of them.'

'I know, and I can't understand it,' she answered.

'Well,' he said, 'I've lived here all my life and that's the first...' He stopped short. 'No it isn't! I forgot the first jay I ever saw in this garden was the first time Joanna came here... it was when we were having our coffee outside, two came and perched on the bird bath.'

'Well, they're regular visitors now, but only to Joanna; they won't come anywhere near if I'm out here,' Penny explained.

Busy though he was, he waited until Joanna's feathered friends had gone before going out to kiss her goodbye.

'That's a couple of really exotic friends you've got there, my love, isn't it?' he remarked.

'Yes, my darling,' she answered, sliding her arms around his neck.

'It's really beyond me,' he said. 'As wild a bird as any, is the jay... and yet they feed out of your hand.'

There was a lovely smile on her face as she answered, 'Jays they may be to you, my love, but to me they are God's blue birds, and they're perfectly beautiful.'

'Not half as beautiful as you, my darling,' he whispered, as he gave her one deep long kiss that would last her until lunch time, leaving her with those two lovely eyes brimming over with stars.

But if God's blue birds came to see her each and every morning, how was it that as soon as she went to Northwood, there was never sight or sound of them? It was as though by some instinct they knew the very moment she had departed from Spring Farm, and appeared the very moment she returned. How this was puzzled them all, but no one knew or was likely to know; they could only wonder.

What a rare time, what a time of joy, when the rain and sunshine comes as it is required, to fit each season of the year. Hence, none can be more exciting or exhilarating than the onset of summer. A refreshing shower, or a thunderclap; a blazing sun that won't be denied; the heat comes down and the stream will swell and nature grows before your eyes. The early summer of 1940 was one of those times, fantastic and wonderful, when each day is a joy unto its own, and the paramount instinct of man is to be outside. That is how it was with Joanna and Phil on this lovely June eve. Leaving Jamie sound asleep under Penny's watchful care, they had strolled, still so much in love, to the top of High Ridge; and there, with arms around each other, they were standing and looking out over all this beauty, a beauty which gave no sign of anything other than peace, perfect peace.

The joys of their home, and the wonder of all this countryside around them made it impossible for anyone like them to realise that soon, perhaps in a day or two, this island home of theirs would be standing alone – alone against an enemy whose ruthless philosophy was set to enslave the whole world.

If one could only have seen into the future, just a few weeks ahead, when the hearts of the free world saddened at the total horror which seemed about to burst inevitably across our shores. There would arise in the cities, the towns and the countryside a will to stand up, a will to fight and, if the need came, to resist the surrender of each precious inch down to the last drop of blood.

Thus came the birth of a determination to fight with all we had at our command, until the day when, perhaps not alone, we would go forward seeking victory, to bring freedom to so many across that narrow strip of water.

But on this lovely summer eve, who in any corner of the world could even dream that before that great day would dawn, there would not only be those multitudes who would die in the heat of battle; but many more than them, with no chance or hope at all, would meet their untimely end in the cold hell of extermination...

Fear and degradation would walk hand in hand, not only in the darkness of the night, but on a day like this, when the glory and wonders of all around are beyond man's comprehension, and the nearness of God's hand is known as it stretches out to take the hand of all who need and believe in Him.

To the people of these islands, just having the benefit of their right to pray was worth a mighty army to them. Had they, with all their faults and folly, been chosen as a bastion, to stop the forward march of evil from trampling the beauty of the whole earth underfoot? Were they just the tools in the hands of the divine right, taking in their girth and arming themselves for a fight that had to be won at all cost? Were they being made an example, to show mankind once again that no one man, nor one country, either by destructive power, word or pen, could ever hold the destiny of the world in the hollow of the hand? So far they may go in their forward march of conquest, but only so far; then the tide shall turn against them, and they shall lose all for defying that which belongs to their Creator alone.

So, as those weeks and months went slowly by, faith became like so many straws to drowning men. Perhaps they had prayed before, as they went about their daily work, as they looked across the pleasant countryside, or at a clear or rainy sky; perhaps they had prayed just as seriously then, only now they prayed more often, and found their comfort in the house of God. Prayers were said for their loved ones, prayers for those who would never return, prayers for their daily bread and prayers for safety in the night; but, from the depth of all hearts came that one beseeching cry, for they prayed for survival first and last, survival for their island gem, so that the flickering light of hope would soon burn more brightly, not only for them, but for all those who were no longer free.

Man at all levels, as he has stumbled down the path of history, must have asked himself a million times, 'Why must man be so inhuman to man, and must he mar and ravage the beauty of this earth, when all is here for his good alone?' But now in this age, when he should have known better, he has entered into a new and terrifying era, defiling the very lap of God to rain down death and destruction, not only on those who were prepared to do battle, but on the unprepared, and on helpless women and children alike.

Thus by mid-September, this island home had already had its first baptism of death from the skies, and a whole nation knelt in prayer and gratitude for the boys who flew; for only by their dauntless courage and fearlessness were they snatching victory from impossible odds. Inwardly and outwardly the whole nation rejoiced at the feeling of still being free, and they would go on rejoicing, never knowing until a long time ahead, just how thin that line of determination in the skies really was – a line that, had it broken, would have meant not only the end for this island, but for the rest of the free world as well.

No longer was there that frightful thought that this green and pleasant land would tremble under the foot of a conqueror. Death, destruction, trials and tribulations had to be accepted as part of the future, but at least their island jewel would still be home, undefiled, clean and free.

All the time that those great aerial battles had been going on, at Spring Farm it was happiness for the victories and sadness for the losers; but it was on that great day, 15th September that something happened which made it a day never to be forgotten, even before they heard of the resounding victory on the radio. Their extra joy started just after lunch time when they were having their half an hour together out on the lawn. Suddenly young Jamie took his first few steps – and what was more, he seemed to have all the confidence in the world. Calling Penny, his parents watched with fascinated pride as he managed to stay up on his feet until he reached her. There was no giving up now; it was walking all the time, for, in his determined little mind, he had discarded crawling like an unwanted toy.

'It won't be long now before he is going round the kitchen table, trying to peer over the top to see what is on there,' said the proud father.

'He tried that this morning when he pulled himself up by the table leg, and he's got all the same little tricks that you used to have,' answered a very happy looking Penny.

'I bet he was a real handful then,' said Joanna teasingly.

'He was, and the most loveable as well, and his son is exactly like him already,' Penny answered, as young Jamie reached her once more with open arms.

'That means that there'll definitely be another lucky girl like me in a few years' time,' said Joanna, as she leaned sideways into her husband's arms, only for him to bow his head until their lips met.

Almost a Victim of the Storm

Life can hold no greater blessing to the rich or mighty, to the poor or weak, than when two people are so much in love that they are literally a part of each other, so much so that a heartache shared is a heartache halved, and happiness shared is all joy let loose.

For Phil and Joanna, the latter was their lot. They savoured each precious moment as one more winter gave way to another, and each new summer seemed far more wonderful than the last. Thrice more, making four times in all, the honeysuckle and the orange blossom had cast its magic spell, scenting their nights and sweetening their dreams, either as they slumbered close, or in the heavenly joy of each other's arms. Thrice more, since the year young Jamie had been born, the snow and frost had come and gone and the sun had journeyed on its longest path. Thrice more had the wonders of spring burst forth anew, and the crowning glory of autumn had shown pride in its jewelled head.

Once again those tiny flecks of yellow are peeping from their leafy hiding places, and once again the yearly race is nearly three parts gone; soon the glowing warmth from log and coal will stem the chill, as darkness takes its share of time, growing with each and every day. Soon there will be that awful clinging fog, when sight is limited to a few yards hence; or a heavy storm which stings the face, or the fury of a full-blown gale.

This is what could be expected by any man who worked outside at this time of the year, but as Phil, after kissing the two loves of his life, got into his car to go back to work after lunch, not one shadow of doubt was in his mind that the rest of the mid-October day would finish just as it had started, not too cold, but dull with heavy cloud.

'You'll be home at the same time my darling?' Joanna asked, as always.

'Yes, my love, 5.30 p.m., as usual; you know I couldn't wait any longer than that without seeing you,' he said, smiling his happiest smile as he waved them goodbye.

He was on his way to the top farm, for although there wasn't nearly as much work in the fields at this time of year, there always seemed plenty of other things which needed attention. This afternoon he would be working in one of the barns with a couple of his men, fitting new parts to the farm equipment. The afternoon wore on, and, owing to the dullness of the day, the lights had been on from the very start. So engrossed were they in their work that neither of them had noticed that by half past four o'clock it was as black as ink outside. But had they gone outside it wouldn't have been only the darkness that would have registered but the stillness. It was like just before a violent thunderstorm breaks, when there is no motion whatsoever, and you are touched by something uncanny that seems almost inhuman. That was how it stayed until five o'clock, then the first small blasts of a gale of unknown force rattled the barn doors.

'I think you had better make for home, Mr Phil,' said Jim Preston, as his brother, Ted, went to the doors to see how things really were outside.

But as Ted lifted the latch, a blast of hurricane force hit the building, literally throwing back the door and almost sweeping him off his feet in the bargain.

'We'll have to go out the side door, we'll never have strength enough to close this one from the outside,' gasped Phil in the teeth of the gale, as the three of them struggled to close the door and only just managed it, before another mighty blast shook the whole building.

Phil gave them a lift to their home some five hundred yards from the farm, and even with the three of them inside the car rocked and swayed like a little toy. But when he had shouted goodnight to them and started on his way, once more did he realise just how much this was going to be a ride of caution, strength and any amount of luck that was going. Branches of varying sizes were strewing the road already, or flying by as if they were thistledown; sometimes he was being blown almost into the hedge on one side, or almost scraping the wall on the other, and by now he doubted whether he would be able to hold the car at all once he hit the high and open stretch of road to the east of High

Ridge. Should he risk the shorter route known as the Ruts? It was a little more sheltered, but nothing much more than a track, lined on one side with tall sycamores. He weighed up the two possibilities a couple of times and finally decided he would take his chance down the Ruts.

But time had raced as fast as the wind during his nightmare drive and it was already a little after six, when like a drunken man he managed to clear the entrance to the Ruts unscathed – but only just.

Meanwhile, at Spring Farm, from the moment the first shock of this mighty wind had made its presence felt, Joanna had become restless, and, as each minute ticked away, so did her agony increase; and the first signs of worry showed not only on the beauty of her face, but in the very depths of those lovely eyes.

At 5.30 p.m., she rang the top farm.

'Yes, he has left,' Dave Williams told her. He explained how he'd seen Ted and Jim getting into the car, and had felt a bit concerned, so he watched from the lee of one of the buildings and calculated that it must have taken four times as long before the white fence around their house showed up in the lights from the car.

About the time that Phil was negotiating the Ruts, Joanna felt she could stand the strain no longer. Just waiting and waiting was torment; she had to do something. It was no good ringing Top Farm, she knew he had left there. Could he have taken shelter at the middle farm? She rang to find out.

'No, I haven't seen or heard him, Mrs Fraser,' John Bates said, 'but I'll pop out to see if there is any sign of him.'

A few more agonising minutes went by before he came back.

'No, Mrs Fraser, there's no car in the yard, and not a suspicion of a light to be seen anywhere.'

'Oh dear,' said Joanna in a tone full of despair. Then she declared, 'I'm going to pick up Percy and start searching.'

'I think that is what we had all better do,' said John, 'so I'll round up the lads, some to take the road to Top Farm, and the rest of us to meet up with you, ma'am.'

'Thank you, John,' she answered with all the gratitude she

could muster.

Penny, who had been standing by her side and had heard all that was said, tied to calm her anguish by saying, 'There could be a tree across the road, my dear, and he is having to walk.'

'I know, my dear,' answered Joanna, picking up the big torch, 'but I just can't wait here to find out.'

'Well, do be careful,' implored Penny, 'and I do hope you'll find him soon, and safe and well.'

Phil was almost three-quarters of the way down the Ruts. His arms had hardly any strength left in them, and it was one terrific battle to hold the car against the hurricane, which seemed hell bent on snatching the wheel out of his hands. Even so, he was just thinking that he had made the right decision after all, when *crash* – a thousand stars broke before his eyes, instantly followed by total darkness over his conscious mind. A huge limb from one of the sycamores had fallen on the rear of the car, while the lesser branches had battered the rest of it into something almost shapeless.

How long he had been unconscious he had no idea, but as his mind began to focus, the first thing he realised was that the lights were out and that the gusts from that cruel wind were cutting him like a knife. Next came the pain and the throbbing of his head, and the feeling of something sticky running down his right cheek. He couldn't move his legs; they were trapped by the shambles that had been the front of the car. But even in his semi-conscious state, he became horrified when the thought struck him that his left hand seemed almost useless and, as he painfully felt over it with his right, his heart missed several beats at the hopeless mess it felt to his touch. It wasn't the pain, or the mess that was his worry now; it was his ring, the one his angel had slipped upon his finger as a symbol of all her pure and perfect love.

No, came the thought through his fuddled mind, they weren't going to cut that off his finger, that had to be preserved above all else!

Weakly but desperately, he tried to get it off, but flesh and gold moved as one, and only so far, as once more he slipped over the border into the realms of unconsciousness.

By now, the searchers had, at considerable risk, covered most of the roads. If they had uncovered their headlights it would have been ten times easier, but this was wartime and with those narrow slits of light it was possible to miss a car gone off the road in certain places. Going over the road once more, into gateways and any buildings along the way, they had fanned out in one desperate attempt to find Phil soon.

Percy drove to the limit in the circumstances, for the wind had begun to slacken now; but another hazard took its place, as spots of rain as big as pennies spattered the windscreen.

'There's only one more place in our area now, Mrs Fraser,' said Percy. 'It's probably what Mr Phil would do in a gale like this – he'd get off the high ground, and the quickest way to do that is down the Ruts.'

Joanna was silent, praying from the depth of her heart for his safety and to find him soon. However, as they turned into the Ruts and started along its bumpy path, neither of them said a word. Both wondered what they would find if Phil happened to be here. It was only trees that could stop him for this length of time, and that was an outcome that didn't bear thinking about. On, over one bumpy yard after another, through teeming rain and a wind that was only a sigh now, they strained their eyes as they searched the blackness beyond those narrow strips of light, and often those little tricks of fantasy sparked a false hope inside.

Then suddenly there was something unfamiliar ahead, and, as the lights brought it into detail, the car lurched over a bigger bump than the ones before; and from the middle of those tangled boughs and branches Joanna caught a glint of metal, a glint that induced thankfulness, hope and dread, all at the same time. Before Percy had brought the car to a standstill, she was out running and searching for a way through the debris, clawing her way through to the passenger side where the door had burst open on the moment of impact, and was now totally unrecognisable. She crawled the last few yards to get to the opening, fear gripping her heart as she swung the torch into what was left of the inside of the wreck. A blood-spattered face was the first thing the torch picked out, bringing tears that swept aside the rain lashing her face.

Was it the light, or was it her presence that lifted the heavy shadow from Phil's mind? For his eyes flickered open as he made his second return to consciousness. The sight sent relief and thankfulness flooding through her like a tidal wave.

'Oh my darling, thank God we've found you!' she whispered tenderly, as she supported his sagging head in the comfort of her arms.

By now Percy was a witness to the scene.

'I shall have to get the others, Mrs Fraser, it's hopeless without a lot of help.'

'I know, Percy,' she answered, then continued, 'get one of the others to go and ask Penny for at least six pillows and a mattress from one of the spare rooms, and the first aid box as well, while you go straight for Doctor Snell and bring him here, he'll never find us otherwise.'

Hardly had she finished than Percy was gone. Vaguely, she heard him make only one reverse before he roared off in the darkness, and then every few seconds came the sound of his horn as he called the others to meet him.

Tears still ran freely down her cheeks as she wetted her handkerchief in the rain which streamed on to them from a dozen places, and gently swabbed blood from Phil's face, whispering those loving endearments which were a part of their daily life.

'My angel,' he whispered.

'My own true love,' she replied, kissing him tenderly. Then she asked, 'Tell me how you feel, my darling, and where you have the most pain.'

'It's not the pain that worries me, it's my left hand, my ring, the one that you placed there, my angel. I won't have it cut off, it's far too precious for that, so see what you can do, my love.'

Gently she lifted his right hand, which was covering his left, and the sight of it made her shudder; it was a hopeless task, for every time she moved the ring, the flesh moved as before.

'I can't, really, my darling, it might do all sorts of damage and hurt you unnecessarily. Besides, I can buy you another one exactly the same.'

'No, my love,' he whispered a little desperately, 'you hold the flesh and I'll try the ring, we can manage that between us.'

For three whole minutes, and with the fingers of both hands, as gently as she could she held the flesh as firm as possible while he wriggled and pulled, until his priceless possession was free – and, in his mind, out of danger.

'It isn't damaged is it, my love?' were the first words he gasped, for it wasn't only rivulets of rain which ran down his face.

'No, my darling,' she answered, holding it up in the light of the torch for him to inspect, not knowing how she had stood the weight of all that pain which she had felt for him.

'Keep it safe, my angel,' he whispered. 'Then, when the time comes, you shall return it in the same room and just as before.'

'I will my own true love, and I pray that that day is not too far off,' she whispered, putting her arm around him once more and pressing all her love and devotion into a gentle and tender kiss.

'I won't disappoint you, my love, I'm quite tough really,' he answered, showing the first suspicion of a smile.

Gently she started to mop the rain and blood from his face again and had almost completed it when the sound of more than one vehicle could be heard coming up the track.

John Bates found his way in, asking how things were. Then, taking stock of the best and quickest way of clearing a big enough path before the trickiest part of all, taking the weight off the front of the car without endangering or causing their boss any more injury.

'We'll try to get it cleared before the doctor arrives, Mr Phil.'

'Thank you, John – and thank all the men too,' he answered feebly.

For already they could hear the saws going to work, and the lights from the storm lanterns reduced Phil's feelings of helplessness quite a bit; but above all this activity, they could hear the heavy throb of the big truck with the winch running.

'They've even got Matilda here, all the way from the saw yard at Top Farm! I wonder how they knew,' he whispered.

'News travels fast, even on a night like this, my darling,' Joanna answered, but at the same time she wondered herself.

Only later would she learn from Penny about everything that was needed, and how every man from the three farms was there to play their part in finding him and setting him free as soon as possible. She, Penny, had rung Top Farm and had even suggested that Matilda should be with the searchers.

So feverishly and carefully did they do their job that by the time the doctor arrived, all that stood in the way had been cleared, with only the branch which trapped Phil's legs needing to be raised. Already Matilda was in position and the chains were being put around it, and many eager hands sought to gently ease the weight and swing it to one side.

'I don't want a jab to knock me out,' was how he greeted the doctor.

'We'll see about that when the branch is off, there's still parts of the car that have to be removed,' answered the jovial Doctor Snell.

Twenty minutes later Phil was free and lying on a soft bed of pillows, with the mattress on top, in one of the farm trucks, a task that had only been accomplished by hard and careful work, plus Joanna's gentle care and loving encouragement. She thanked the men with all her gratitude, then told them to get home and change as quickly as possible, for there was not one among them who wasn't soaked to the skin.

'Shall I follow you to the hospital now, Mrs Fraser, or shall I change and come after?' asked Percy.

'You change first, Percy,' she answered, 'for I won't leave the hospital until I know how things are, and I'll ring Penny from there.'

Now she was in the back of the truck, her arm caressing Phil's head and the rest of her pressed close to him, so that he couldn't sway or roll about while they were on that bumpy track, for no one knew as yet the extent of the injury to his legs.

'You should have gone home and changed, my love,' he whispered.

'I'm not all that wet, my darling, and even if I was, you know I couldn't leave you until I knew you were all right.'

But it wasn't until they had arrived at the hospital, and he had been wheeled away from her and out of sight, that did the cold from all those streams of rain which had found their way down the back of her neck while she had been comforting him in the shambles of the car, and the teeming rain that had soaked her feet and legs, strike her for the first time. In her hour of anguish for him, she had been completely oblivious to her own feelings; now she shivered and only found temporary warmth from the cup of tea that one of the nurses brought her. But even so, her whole thoughts were in that other room, wondering how her love was, and going through the agony of his wounds time and time again.

What a welcome sound of relief there was in Penny's voice when she had phoned her, also the same amount of concern as to what sort of shape she was in too, asking if she was wet and cold; but that was forty minutes ago.

Joanna got up once again, and was pacing to and fro to bring a little warmth back into her feet and legs, when in walked Percy.

'Is there any news yet, Mrs Fraser?' he asked.

'No, Percy,' she answered, 'just a lot of coming and going.'

'Just as I imagined,' he replied, 'and I guessed you would have a long wait in wet clothes, so I called in at the Seven Bells, had a quick one myself and brought you this little bottle of rum – it's the best there is to keep the cold out.'

'Thank you very much, Percy, that was very thoughtful of you,' she answered, as he handed her the bottle ready for her to drink.

'Try and drink it all, ma'am, I'm going to sit in the car and have a smoke, and I hope we shall have good news when they come out.'

'So do I, Percy,' she replied, with a worried look upon her face.

One sip after another she took, and gradually she could feel the warmth returning to her, and the wet cold stickiness of her clothes ceased to be quite so uncomfortable.

She thought to herself, by all the laws of nature she should be in for a real chill; if she escaped after being so wet and cold for so long, it could only be the rum, the first she had ever tasted. If so, she would get Phil to keep some in, and make him have a glass whenever he came in wet or cold.

For the tenth time she took his ring out of her pocket and, for the tenth time, she lovingly ran her finger over it, and dreamed of that happy time when she had pledged her love with it; but, just as she slipped it safely back into her pocket, the door opened and Doctor Snell came towards her.

'It could have been a lot worse, Mrs Fraser,' he said, as jovial as ever. Then he went on, 'Owing to his perfect physical condition, he has weathered the shock and pain much better than most; there are no bones broken, and I think we shall have a job to hold him here beyond a week. Of course, he will have to have attention to his left hand for some time, and I did my very best with the stitches to his head and down the side of his forehead – just to keep him as handsome as ever.'

He gave a chuckle, which brought the first suspicion of a smile to her face.

'However, you can see him for a few minutes; a few will be enough for him, for he is very drowsy.'

'I'm so grateful, Doctor, and thank you, everyone has been so wonderful,' Joanna replied as he opened the door for her to enter.

Doctor Snell was quite right; Phil was very drowsy, his eyes flickered open and shut as though he was hanging grimly on to consciousness until she came to him, so that he could carry this one last look of her through the sleepy hours of night and beyond.

The sight of his bandaged hand and the thickness of those around his hand struck a chill to her heart. Yet the tears which rolled slowly down her cheeks were tears of thankfulness, for her inward prayers had been answered. He was going to be all right and would be back home with them sooner than she had dared hope a few minutes before.

'How are you feeling now, my darling?' she whispered.

'Much better, my love… hardly any pain now, but very tired,' he answered, slowly and softly.

'Well, have a good night, my darling, for I shall be with you in my thoughts,' she whispered, bending down and concentrating her undying love in a tender kiss.

He nodded and, in a whisper just loud enough for her to hear, said, 'And you in mine, my love, always.'

No longer could he find the will to fight the tide which was sweeping over him, but for a full five minutes Joanna knelt, prayed, and watched, holding his right hand in a tender caress as the merciful mist of sleep took command and carried him beyond on its painless ride.

Back home, after telling Penny what the doctor had said and what she thought of him herself, was as far as she was allowed to get.

'You can tell me the rest later,' interrupted Penny, 'There's a lovely warm bed up there, so I'll run your bath while you get those wet things off; then after we can talk while you are having whatever you fancy to eat and a glass of hot milk and whisky. Phil would never forgive me if you got pneumonia through staying in wet clothes a moment longer that necessary.'

How different she felt now as she slipped between those warm and welcome sheets! The hot bath had made her feel so much better physically that when she had crept into Jamie's room for her nightly last peep, what had been a sad and heavy weight on her heart almost disappeared at the sight of their son. As gently as possible, she had kissed his tender brow, and her love, true mother love, found the utmost difficulty in subduing the burning desire to gather him into her arms.

He was the perfect likeness of his father at that age; one was her big love and the other was her little love, and she wondered was it the all-consuming power of her love for the big one that had fashioned his son unto his own image. She could never know this for certain, but what she was sure of was that she would never be completely alone again, not now she had the living evidence of all that they were to each other, which could only be classified as 'heavenly'.

It was almost an hour that she spent eating and telling Penny all that had happened.

'Dear Percy,' said Penny, when she heard about the rum.

'Yes,' Joanna agreed, 'everyone was wonderful, so much so that I feel awfully indebted to them. Phil will definitely make it up to them when he is well enough, but I can't wait to show them my thanks and gratitude, so I shall draw enough out of my own account to give every man an extra week's wages. They must have been absolutely soaked, and dead beat as well.'

'Just like your husband,' said Penny smiling. 'Sweet, kind and generous!'

'I hope I am like him,' she replied sleepily, 'for that is the greatest compliment you can pay me.'

An Innocent Dream, or a Grim Warning?

Phil's stay in hospital lasted precisely eight days. He limped quite badly, but that was only to be expected after such injuries. In pain though he was, he wouldn't think of having the use of a stick. His left hand had responded wonderfully, but his finger, the one his precious ring had encircled, would never be quite the same. Just as Doctor Snell had hoped, the scar down the side of his forehead lost its angry look, and faded more and more as each day passed. By the time Christmas came, he was back to almost as good as new, and in Joanna's great joy her heart offered up many a silent prayer for bringing him safely through that awful night, when it seemed that only a miracle had saved him.

It was this nightmare thought of life without him which made her shudder every time she dressed his finger, which even now was still painful and distorted. No, there was not the slightest hope of her slipping that ring back to its rightful place for some time yet; he had hinted that way several times already, only for her to reply, 'Not for at least another month, my darling.'

On this night, the last one of the old year, when they are arm in arm with her father, Marie-Ann and Penny, dancing round and round celebrating the birth of a new year to the vocal strains of *Auld Lang Syne* and wishing each other a happy new year, they wondered if this year – the infant 1943 – would bring hope and happiness in a greater measure to all those who were parted from their loved ones than the year which had just faded a few moments before.

For over three years there had never been a day go by without them counting their blessings for being together; and, deep inside, they had already resigned themselves to the fact that the rest of this year would go by, leaving them untouched by its tide of death and destruction. Work they would have to, but it was a source of great comfort to think that they would never know the pain of two aching hearts desperately needing each other, with not the slightest hope of covering the great distance which separated them.

Had their thoughts, their instincts, been blinded to the fact that it was beyond any one man to know his fate one day from another? Or was it because of their wonderful love, a love that filled them with a sensation divine, in which they were only aware that two pounding desperate hearts were there inside? But it wasn't just the pure red blood which made them beat, nor the passion which made them beat faster, but a deep heavenly love which had welded them into one, making their happiness so sublime that they were oblivious of anything tragic which might overcome them. If that ever came, that one joyous pounding heart left would shrivel and die to a tearful whisper.

It was the beginning of February before the time came for Joanna to slip that precious ring back onto Phil's finger and, if it was possible, there were more stars in her eyes now than even on that first occasion. Over four years of perfect wedded bliss had left its mark on her; she knew her way along the path to paradise now, but what mystified her most was that it seemed a different path each time, and each more glorious than the one before. No wonder as their lips parted she snuggled into him cheek to cheek, whispering, 'My wonderful love, my own true love,' only for him to reply, 'My wonderful darling, my angel.'

Gently she slipped the ring over his mangled finger, only for a look of concern to cross her face now there was not enough flesh where there should be. The ring with its engraved shield was top-heavy and would no longer stay in its proper position. At the slightest movement of his hand, around it slipped to the inside of his finger, the very place where it would do most damage if he happened to clasp anything too strongly.

'Darling,' she said with a pained expression on her face, 'will you let me have it made smaller?'

'No, my love,' he answered tenderly, 'I want it to stay just the same as when you gave it to me; besides, the knuckle is still about the same size, so as long as there's no fear of me losing it, I'm quite happy.'

'Then promise me, darling, to be very careful when you catch hold of anything, for it would be so easy to open those wounds again.'

Phil smiled to himself, for she looked every bit as anxious as she sounded.

'I will, my darling,' he answered, sweeping her into his arms once more and along that dreamy path that was so much a part of their lives.

Spring came round once more, and once more the countryside is born again. Her 'blue birds' never failed to make their rendezvous each morning when she was home, but whether it was still the same two, Phil wouldn't know, for even after all this time, if he showed himself at the open door they were gone in an instant. What an exciting time this really was! The snowdrops and the daffodils had already said 'hello' – and to think that soon they would be in the scent of rose time, walking arm in arm around an Eden of their very own. Then there were all the other flowers and shrubs that gave to them a wealth of happiness; but none took pride of place over the honeysuckle and the orange blossom, as each year their sweet fragrance either drifted on the daylight breeze, or settled in the stillness of the night, making their room seem just like an island in paradise.

Things had gone as usual through March and April. They had made several visits to Northwood, and the colonel and Marie-Ann had returned the same, only now it was always by train. Whenever they were alone at weekends, either on the Friday or Saturday he would take her out for dinner or just a drink, and usually they would meet one of his lifelong friends, now married like himself; but there was always that extra bit of excitement when Jane was home, for she would make up the trio now that Gerald was in Scotland.

But oh, the joy of young Jamie – a perfect half of each of them – and, as was only natural, worshipped by both of them, with Penny as an equal third.

'Not half as mischievous as his father,' she would say, doing her best to cover up for any mischief he got into, and always they would have a good laugh over it when Jamie was out of hearing, or tucked up in bed. The joy he gave them was something out of this world, making their joyous home sublime, with happiness unbounded.

The morning sky on 1st May was heavy with cloud and, contrary to expectations, continued the same the whole day-long. It was a low-lying blackness that threatened a deluge at any moment, yet not a drop fell. But the next day, the second, was a different story. Rain fell as though there hadn't been any for months, from early light until the last vestige of an invisible sun was swallowed up in the darkening gloom. What a day Phil had had! And, with so much to attend to at this time of the year, the fact of having to change out of wet clothes twice in a matter of hours didn't exactly lighten his load. Yet he smiled to himself, thinking that he should know better than to expect the weather to suit him at all times. But days like this always seemed to sap more of his energy. He felt really tired, but whether it was the frustration, or the lack of a cheery sun, he didn't know; but whichever it was, he was more than ready for bed at their usual time. Always they would have a little talk as she lay in his arms, but this night she must have been equally as tired as he was. They had talked a little while only, but the silence between them was no more than two minutes old before they had lost their wakening touch with the world. Then suddenly he came to; he had kissed her a dozen times or so, but he couldn't remember having kissed her goodnight – well, not properly. Gently he turned her, kissing her firstly on the lips and then on the forehead. She didn't stir, not even when he drew her close and whispered, 'God bless you, my angel.'

She had drifted off so deep, so peacefully, perfectly content in the arm which held her as its most priceless possession. A minute or so more, and he was in the same world as she was, and sleeping so soundly that it seemed impossible for anything to wake him until his usual time. But some time in the middle of the night the sound of sobbing awoke him with a start. She was crying a deep cry, just as though her heart was breaking.

'What is it, my love, what's the matter?' he asked anxiously, realising as he did so that she was still in the deepest of sleeps.

Gently he caressed her, hoping that the presence of his arm would bring comfort to that art of her unconscious mind which was in torment.

But no, in a voice, a tone that can only come from the unconsciousness of sleep, and with sobbing in between, he heard these words of despair all too clearly.

'My love, my love, do not fret too much when I am gone, for I shall come back to you, my own true love, and to our ray of sunshine.'

Then he heard more sobbing and a jumble of words that he couldn't understand. Then clearly once more, but still shaking him with those sobs, she continued.

'Take heed, my love, outside the little red house among the trees, beware my love as you cross the humpbacked bridge and turn right.'

A few more sobs followed, before silence and peace returned to her as if my magic.

That was the end; her only movement was what he knew she had done a hundred times before, and mostly in her sleep. Gently her hand went down his arm until it reached his ring, and just as gently she turned it round away from the scar on the inside of his finger.

What did it all mean? Was that age-old curse rearing its ugly head once more, to wipe out this heaven on earth and to leave him with nothing? This was what kept going through his mind. He felt stunned and helpless as tears rolled slowly down his cheeks, and for the rest of the night that dreaded thought pierced his heart a thousand times, with only a few snatches of sleep to relieve him of his torment.

What a blessing for him that the sun was shining brightly in the morning. At least the amount of work to be done would help keep his mind off the nightmare that had shaken him so. He wouldn't dare say a word to her about it; this would be the one and only secret he would hold from her, for her sake. For he knew he could never bear to see that vacant, faraway look of premonition eating away her happiness and her beauty and devouring this heaven that was theirs, only to leave them broken in mind and body. He would bear this cross alone until her father came, and then he would only tell him when just the two of them were out in the fields somewhere.

For three whole weeks, unbearable though they were, Phil never let his inward feelings show in the slightest. On the surface he was all life, love and laughter as usual, and she, never dreaming of the fear which gripped his heart, returned to life, love and laughter in the same ultimate measure as always. It was the second day of the colonel's visit that the opportunity came for Phil to open his heart. They were walking across the fields, and he watched his father-in-law's face as he unfolded the most worrying story he had ever told. He saw a frown cross his brow, only to disappear in an instant.

'It could be just a bad dream, you know, Phil, for as far as I'm aware, none of the others before ever had, or gave any signs of, impending disaster, and I know Joanna's mother didn't. I can well imagine how it appears to you, but please don't look upon that nightmare as a sign that something dreadful is going to happen. If you do, sooner or later you are going to show it in your face and actions, and everything that makes life really worth living will disappear for both of you unnecessarily.'

Those reassuring words already made him feel so much more relieved, and that arm across his shoulder gave him more comfort that he had dreamed possible.

'Perhaps I have been worrying needlessly. However, my heart and my mind are more at ease now that I have shared it with you, for you have given me more peace of mind than I had hoped for, so for that I am more than grateful.'

'Well, I don't want you going around with a dark cloud over your head, and a heavy weight in your heart. I know that both of us would lay out our lives down for Joanna, but in this world we have got to face up to it; what is to be will be, and it would be wrong of both of us to try to meet something which might never happen. That would be tempting fate.'

As each day passed, so did a little more of his anxiety disappear; for with a life like theirs, there was no room or time for anything else other than their burning love for each other, a love which was a blessing from the unknown.

But to her father, it was a different story. The worried frown which had crossed his brow and had disappeared all so suddenly had left an open wound upon his heart. He just had to smooth things over at the time for Phil's sake; he dared not let him think that he was the slightest bit perturbed by what he had just been told. Being older, he had the experience to cover up what he was feeling inside, and to do all he could to put his son-in-law's mind at rest. But he didn't like the omen one little bit.

June was almost out before they made their return visit to Northwood, it being the busy time of the year. Phil could only spare a few days from the Thursday to the Monday, though she and Jamie could have stayed a week or two. But no, Joanna just wouldn't hear of being parted from him, even for one night. Yet sometimes fate takes a hand, and man and woman too must tread the path which is laid out before them.

Those first three days were wonderful days, and in her extreme joy she recalled the happenings on his first visit to Northwood. At that moment they were in each other's arms, almost hidden on all sides in a nook of rambling roses, when she said, 'I didn't think at the time, my darling, that it was possible to be any happier, but little did I know that the joy and happiness of each second piles up day after day, so that now I am completely overwhelmed by it.'

'That is my blessing too, my love,' he answered. 'It is five glorious years since we met, five wonderful happy years which have simply flown by, and yet, each time as I take you in my arms, it is just as the first time. You and your wonderful love, my angel, are all that is life to me.'

'Don't forget Jamie as well, my love,' she said with a little smile.

'Of course, Jamie as well, for he is the ultimate of our perfect love, a love whose joy and beauty never ceases to baffle my understanding,' he replied, as their lips met and they clung to each other, just as desperately as if they were in the intimacy of their own room.

The End of the Beginning

It was just after Sunday lunch when Joanna complained of not feeling well, and several times in the next two hours she was violently sick. Everything they tried brought her no relief, and Phil had visions of her having to have her appendix out.

'Sure it is nothing else, my love?' he enquired, gently stroking her pale face and giving her all the comfort he could.

'No, my love, I would have told you even if I had only suspected it... I'd welcome that sickness compared to this any day, my darling.'

By tea-time the doctor arrived, but after a thorough examination he was as mystified as they were.

'It can't be anything she has eaten, or you would all be like it. It's just one of those things with no explanation. However, she must stay in bed for two or three days with complete rest. I'll call again on Tuesday, but if you are at all worried, ring me at any time.'

Once the doctor had departed, Phil made straight for her room, saying as he closed the door, 'I'll give Penny a ring, my love, and tell her what has happened, and say we won't be back until you are well again.'

'No, my darling, don't do that,' she said, as her arms went around his neck, 'I know I shall miss you as though darkness has descended over my world, but if you stay all your work will get behind. I know it is because there's a war on that you work so many hours, and if you get behind now, you'll be cutting short the holiday next month, and I'm insisting that we have that for your sake alone. No one can push themselves as you have without suffering for it, so please, my love, take things a little more steady; for you are Jamie's and my whole world, and I love you more than I can tell, my darling.'

'All right, my angel, anything you say, but I shall miss you both so much, and I promise to slow down a little. For after all, it is you and Jamie and the never-ending love I have for you both that gives my world its sunshine,' he replied, with all the sincerity in the world. Then, bending down, he took her tenderly in his arms to seal those words, which came from his very heart.

Back home, Phil found a place he knew only too well, but a place that couldn't be home without the two loves of his life. Joanna was forever in his thoughts, and so were her words of warning. Consequently he checked himself more often from doing too much. They rang each other many times a day and, when he was near at hand, young Jamie would come on the phone and would have talked to his father for hours if only there had been time.

By the Wednesday, Joanna had regained most of her strength and vitality and was allowed to get up. It gladdened his heart to think that in two days' time he would be reunited with them once again. She missed him desperately, and her absence left him alone and seemingly without hope. There had been no sight or sound of her 'blue birds' now that she was away, and that was one more small part of each day that made life so empty without her.

Thursday went and Friday dawned. It wasn't the sort of day that was welcome in July – no sun and no hope of any, for the low ceiling of heavy cloud looked as level as a lawn turned upside down, and seemed to stretch outwards and have no end. On the phone her relief and excitement was as great as his, knowing that he would be with them by lunch-time.

'I can hardly wait to be in your arms, my darling,' were almost her last words. After having left his car at the garage just outside The Junction, Phil found a corner seat on the train and read the daily paper – or pretended to, for inwardly he was very impatient to get going. Once they began to move he became a little more relaxed, but he always had that heavy hand of sadness upon him when he passed along the stretch of line where those two trains had thundered into each other and robbed him of so much; but today, as always, that vision of sadness would melt into a treasured memory as he progressed further up the line.

In fact, at this very moment, even before that transformation could come about, when a tear seemed always ready to trickle down his cheek, unknown to him the cruel hand of fate was already poised to deal him one more stunning blow, one where his whole world would be like a darkened tunnel, with only a chink of light in the distance, where hope would diminish to nothing and loneliness rear up to the size of a mountain.

The cloud cover over Northwood was exactly the same as it was over most of the country. Jamie was out on the lawn and playing in and out of the summer house. It was almost twelve noon, and just under three-quarters of an hour to go before the car, after picking Phil up at the station, would arrive with her heart's desire. Joanna was in the drawing room sitting on the sofa with her father. They were both reading, but it was all too plain to him that now she knew Phil was on his way her powers of concentration were almost nil. Up and down she went, first looking at Jamie, then scanning the bit of the drive that was visible, seemingly to will the vision of the car that was bringing her love to her arms once more.

Once more she picked up the paper as Marie-Ann, turning around from her desk, said, 'He won't be long now, my dear.'

'No,' she replied, 'just thirty-five minutes, if my watch is correct.'

It was correct, but before one more minute had ticked away, she was up once more and looking out at Jamie. Almost immediately the sound of an aircraft was heard as it broke through the cover of that thick blanket of cloud, on a course which would take it almost over the house. Twelve seconds away, and the metallic clatter of guns shattered the peaceful scene on the earth beneath.

Joanna was gone like a flash; Jamie was by the summer house but still in full view.

'Quickly, Jamie, run into the summer house!' she shouted as she raced across the lawn.

Jamie did what he was told without a moment's delay, and, just as he scampered to safety, the German gunner caught the flash of Joanna's yellow dress against the dark green which surrounded her. Quickly he swivelled his guns and fired.

Her father, not being so quick off the mark as she was, just managed to get to the doorway as the last score of bullets viciously kicked up tufts of lawn around her. He saw her halt, then stumble on a few more paces, before crumpling in a heap almost two-thirds of the way to safety.

As if from nowhere, everyone seemed to be on the scene in the matter of seconds. Someone whisked young Jamie away, so that those tender eyes would not behold his beautiful mother spattered in blood. For that age-old curse had struck for the last time, and her nightmare dreams had become reality. Her poor father, so dumbstruck was he at this terrible blow, that not even a tear could force its way to trickle down his cheek as he tenderly cradled her head in his arms; but no words could come from her, for she was already unconscious, and may have already gone so far that there might be no returning.

It was Marie-Ann who phoned for the doctor and the ambulance with desperate urgency. It was she who told Henry to break the tragic news to Phil when he met him at the station.

'I know I can trust you to break it to him as gently as possible, and to get him to the hospital as quickly as you know how.'

Twenty minutes had gone by before they were on the way to the hospital, a journey which would take another twenty minutes; and, by that time, thought Marie-Ann, *Phil would be on his way also*. But no, because of a special train carrying military equipment, he had spent an agonising twenty-five minutes out in the country.

Poor Henry, knowing what he did, and with the thankless task he had to perform, found out for the first time in his young life that a half an hour's suspense such as this was like eternity. Yet with all the things that had to be done at one and the same time, no one had panicked. Everyone's aim had been to make Joanna as comfortable as possible, and to get her quickly into the only place which might save her life.

It was only natural, then, that no one had thought to ring Spring Farm. Not until Marie-Ann was actually getting into the ambulance did she turn to the butler, saying, 'Oh, Briggs, I think you had better ring Spring Farm and tell Penny. Explain to her as gently as you can, won't you, and tell her we still have hope.'

That is what he did immediately. Poor Penny, one minute she was overjoyed at hearing his voice, as he asked how she was, and the next she was frozen to the spot until he had told her all. Then, giving a single cry, she crumpled in a heap on the floor. Briggs heard her cry, the thump and the crash as she dragged the telephone down with her. He kept calling, and luckily Mrs White heard the cry and crash and rushed to see what had happened. She heard Briggs calling and, picking up the receiver, she told him, 'Penny's fainted.'

Briggs then explained quickly what had happened and asked her to ring him back as soon as Penny came round. 'I think you had better stay with her, if it's possible,' he added.

'I won't leave her,' Mrs White answered, her voice much more shaky this time.

If anything, it was Henry who had the greatest shock, he knew there was not a minute to lose, so he met Phil as he stepped out of the train and gently told him the news as they hurried towards the car. He saw Phil's square shoulders sag at each step they took, and that ever-ready smile slipped so far away, almost to the point of no return; but it was the eyes, those perpetual laughing eyes that told the full depth of his anxiety, for they were fixed hard as stone, and completely lifeless.

Hardly another word passed between them as Henry gave the Rolls full power. Only when they turned into the hospital did he say, 'I hope and pray, sir, there is better news awaiting you.'

'So do I, Henry, thank you,' Phil replied, as he ran from the car.

Marie-Ann was waiting for him just inside the door. Tears had long since reddened her eyes and stained her cheeks.

'How is she?' he asked pleadingly, as she put her arm around him and led him towards that fatal room. No words came, only the shaking of her head as tears now fell uncontrollably. Silently, he opened the door and entered alone, but hardly had he crossed the threshold before Joanna opened her eyes for the first time since she had been struck down. Then, before either her father or the doctor could help or restrain her, she had struggled into a sitting up position, smiling a wonderful smile and holding her arms out for Phil as he hurried towards her.

No one would ever know how she knew of his presence – the one and only thing that could bring her out of unconsciousness – and certainly no one would ever know the agony and pain that this last desperate yearning for his comfort had cost her. For a few priceless moments the advancing shadow of the angel of death was halted in its measured tread.

'Hold me close, my darling, hold me forever,' she whispered, as her arms closed desperately around him.

'I will, my love, I'll hold you forever,' he answered, holding her as firmly, yet as tenderly as he could.

What else could he say, what else could he do? The quick flash he had of the faces of her father and the doctor had told him the worst, and already his world, their world, was tumbling down around him.

Through watery eyes, his gaze moved slowly over the loveliness of her face, as once more she seemed lost to this world, and he wished a million times in those few seconds that he could put the clock back to the time when his eyes were privileged to behold all her beauty for the very first time, a beauty and sweetness that had given his heart no rest, until she had dispelled his fears by returning her love, a love that was as a shining light, a love so perfect, so true. Tears now ran at will down his cheeks as he kissed her tenderly on the lips, whispering as he did so, 'My angel.'

Was it those magic words, with all the depth of what they meant to each other, that made her struggle back to him? What an effort she had to break through the encroaching mist, from that far-off land. For the last time she opened her eyes and, tenderly looking into his, she managed to whisper, but only in spasms, 'Do not fret too much, my love, I know I shall come back to you, my own true love.'

Those were her last words. He felt her arms tighten around him, then that loving embrace relaxed for the last time.

This was the end; there could be no sun, moon, or stars, or beauty of anything in his life from now on. All would be dark, bleak and hopeless, something which at this moment made him dread the thought of living, even for one more day. Then, through the sorrow and torture which ravaged him, there came to him just one gleam of light. He remembered he had young Jamie, half of himself, and the other half more precious than the whole world.

He still held her in his arms, he just had to. That last smile, that last tender kiss, given to him in his greatest moment of sorrow, had to last him for the rest of his life; this would be how he would remember her until they would meet again.

Only when he felt a comforting hand upon his shoulder did the existence of his physical being remind him to go forward, on a life that would be a weary journey, always hopeless, and often unbearable. Gently he laid Joanna down and lovingly caressed her golden hair, before giving her a heartbroken kiss.

Between them they led him out, only a shadow now of the man he'd been an hour ago, and through the torment of his mind there came a cry – to know why, oh why? Theirs had been a life and love so good and true and each day a perfect happy day, so it was a joy to face the next. Was it just the blink of an eye in the march of time, when this world is granted to know perfection? So why, oh why? Came that cry. Why should a cruel fate take her away from him, leaving him as an empty shell, to endure a life utterly bleak and desolate; a desolation where no flower would bloom, where no bird would ever sing; with no spirit left to face each new dawn, and worst of all, his lonely grief in the silence of the night.

Driven to War

How the rest of that day went by, no one could really tell, and if it hadn't been for the doctor calling in at ten o'clock, staying until eleven o'clock and giving them a strong sedative, there was every possibility that the night would be an endless night. Shocked, stunned, and overwhelmed with sorrow they all were, but Joanna's father and Marie-Ann knew they would have to take a grip on their own feelings for Phil's sake. He was in a terrible state, and only by their comfort and understanding would he make even half the man he was before.

Two more days of agony ensued, when all the arrangements had to be made, but the only thing he did was to ring Penny.

'Out of the last crash we had nothing,' she told him tearfully, 'but out of this one we've got young Jamie. And as black as the future is, we've still got to do our duty, so that his future will be as bright and as happy as possible.'

Phil found a bit of comfort in her words, but it was when he had to face young Jamie that he had to fight to stop the tears from flooding down his face. For it was always, 'Daddy, I want my mummy,' or, 'When are you going to bring my mummy back to me?' And having to answer questions like that was like sticking a knife into his already stricken heart.

But all through this terrible time, the Reverend Brown had been a constant visitor, doing all in his power to bring light into this time of darkness. He had prepared Joanna for confirmation, married her, and now he would be going with them tomorrow to Spring Farm to officiate at the funeral service on the day after. Gloom was the one thing he had to fight; he talked about any trifle as they drove towards the station, anything, just to keep their minds off that big motor hearse which followed about a hundred yards behind.

It was a ten-minute wait at the station, and, when the train did arrive, it was packed as usual; but after going up and down they found there were just two vacant seats in one compartment, and two more at the other end of the coach.

'I'll go with Phil and Jamie, shall I?' asked the vicar.

'Yes,' answered the colonel, as he followed Marie-Ann to the other end.

The Reverend Brown opened the door and stood back for Phil, with Jamie in his arms, to enter first; but as Phil entered, the thought struck him of something he had often experienced. Sometimes you can enter a carriage and sit amongst strangers and, hardly before the journey begins, but always before it is anywhere near its end, you are all friends, you feel you have known these people all your life. Then, as you alight and say goodbye, there comes a tug at the heart, for deep inside you know you will never meet again. Then there is the other kind, where the journey, no matter how short, seems far too long. Now here he was, overwhelmed by his terrible grief and, as he sat down with Jamie on his knees, he sensed that they were in one of the latter sort.

Opposite Phil there were two couples, all somewhere in their mid-forties, either relations or friends, while on his side were two soldiers. Suddenly the train began to move, but instead of going forward, it moved backwards for some fifty yards.

'Whatever are they doing?' exclaimed a fussy little blonde. 'We shall be late for our luncheon engagement with Sir George.'

'It's an absolute bore,' answered her dark-haired companion, 'they're probably putting some troops on the train, when it's got far too many already.'

One of the soldiers sighed an exaggerated sigh, but never answered, while the vicar thought to himself, *Why don't you shut up, you silly self-centred woman?*

Whatever had gone on between the four opposite and the two soldiers before they had entered was only guesswork, but as soon as the train started, it seemed to be the signal for it to recommence.

Hardly had the last coach cleared the station, when an overweight man in a black Homburg glowered towards the soldiers and shouted, 'I told you before, if the guard appears I will report you! You've got no right to be in a first class compartment.'

'I don't suppose they have enough money to pay the difference, either,' chimed in his insignificant friend.

'That's because we're fighting for the likes of you!' the soldier in the corner shouted back.

Then the soldier next to Phil said, 'We don't care two hoots if the guard or the ticket collector comes along. If he orders us out we shall have no alternative, we shall only be standing out in an already overcrowded corridor after being on guard all night. Call yourself British? You make me sick!'

All this was too much for young Jamie, who had never heard voices raised like this before and, with tears rolling down his cheeks, he clung to his father.

'I want my mummy!' he cried, 'I want my mummy, Daddy.'

Any attempt to try and console him seemed futile, especially as the ticket collector arrived and the argument started all over again. There was nothing for it, the soldiers had to go; but not before the one who'd been in the corner turned and, looking defiantly at the fat man, said, 'If you were just half a man, and as young as I am, I'd give you a taste of what I've got saved up for the Jerries.'

Phil was doing all he could to pacify young Jamie, but no, he would keep taking a frightened look at the quartet opposite and continue crying, 'I want my mummy, Daddy!'

So it was not surprising that before long the black looks were directed at them, and the two females said, quite loudly, 'Absolutely wicked,' and, 'Really shocking.'

After a while, with no success and more black looks, plus the showing of open resentment, Phil carried young Jamie out into the corridor. Hardly before he was through the door, the perky blonde said, louder that was necessary, 'It shouldn't be allowed! The mother's place is with him, not just leaving him with his father.'

All this time the Reverend Brown had been reading his paper, or pretending to; but now he could stand it no longer, and, putting the paper down he glowered at them each in turn before he said, 'In all my years of meeting saints and sinners alike, I have never had the misfortune of facing anyone so smug or so interfering as the four of you. First it was those two young soldiers, who were doing you no harm, and then secondly it was my young friend and his little boy. Compassion, which is the greatest gift of all, is something which you cannot have heard of, but it is something which before long you will have to find, or you will either have retribution from above, or a taste of what that young soldier promised you.'

He paused, then, with a little more conviction in his voice, he turned upon the fussy little blonde, saying, 'And you, woman, you who asked more than a little indignantly why my young friend never had the little boy's mother with him, I will tell you. She *is* with us, but she is in her coffin in the guard's van, shot by a strafing German bomber while she was trying to protect that same little boy. And I'm sure, knowing her as I did, she would be awfully sorry if you are late for your luncheon engagement, just because the train had to go back some fifty yards to put her on board...'

Four very red-faced, silent people hurried from the train at the next stop.

Meanwhile, out in the corridor, Jamie stopped crying almost as soon as the troublesome four were out of view, and it was only the matter of a minute or two before he was on quite friendly terms with the two soldiers and a group of Waafs. It did his father a world of good to see his young son happy again, like he always had been until these last three days; yet that fatherly smile which hardly fell from his face was only a disguise for his breaking heart.

On reaching home, Phil allowed no tears to fall in front of Jamie. It was only after some little while, when Marie-Ann asked Jamie to show her around the garden that he broke.

'I know I have Jamie,' he sobbed, 'but there's nothing else in life now. It seems that everything is for nothing.'

There were no words that the colonel or Penny could say. They both knew how hopeless life looked to him, for their own lives had been shattered in the same way. All they could do, knowing the measure of their own sorrow, was to comfort him.

How could he carry on without her? That was the one thought which kept drumming through his mind. He had heard that time heals all wounds, but he knew if he lived to be a hundred, his sorrow and that empty void could never change.

But time, the blessing of time, was gradually marching him over the greatest crisis of his life; for once more the night falls, and with it a tearful age to bear alone, when precious sleep won't come and banish the torment of his mind and his weeping heart. Not until there are no more tears to shed, and no more strength to battle on, do those sleepy shutters fall.

So time goes on, and time brings yet another day. For morning comes – fresh, warm and beautiful – and only from his faith does Phil find the strength to face the greatest ordeal of his life. For this is the day when he must say farewell to his one and only one, his angel; she who was spending this last night in their little church... but not alone. In fours, the men from the farms had kept a solemn vigil the whole night through, paying their last debt of gratitude to one whom they knew could never be replaced.

And time goes on to that pitiful moment when she is lowered down and almost out of sight, when his heart cries, 'No!' and his body shakes convulsively, as he fights his greatest fight to keep control.

Time has brought his sorrow to its greatest depth, where not one small part of the world that was theirs can be recognised now; their dreams, their hopes, their love, his life, are split asunder, and the ruins stretch around, and out of sight.

But time itself cannot always mend a broken heart, or put a smile back on the face; so everyday routine steps into the breach by giving man his work to do, and time, as it goes on, sees that he becomes more involved. No hope there may be for his weeping heart, as sorrow strikes so many times a day; but in between there are so many things that he must do, and life becomes just bearable once again.

However, as time progressed, so did Phil find that there were moments – unnecessary, unbearable moments. Why was it that a voice, and above all, a sweet young voice, always seemed to taunt him whenever the occasion arose? It was his son, his own sweet innocent son; yet the heartbreak of it was, the boy never mentioned his mother in front of his grandfather, Marie-Ann or Penny, but as soon as he found his father alone, or if they were out together, it was always the same.

'Where is Mummy, Daddy?'

And he would answer, 'Up in heaven, my love.'

Then would come the familiar second question.

'When are you going to bring my mummy back to me, Daddy?'

Always it would be said so full of emphasis, as though he, his father, had no right to be here, but ought to be out in the world somewhere searching for her; and he would answer, 'Sometime soon, my love,' giving a quick shake of his head to stop the tears from rolling down his cheeks.

These were the times he ought to cherish above all, instead they were the ones he dreaded the most. His working hours were full enough to lighten a little the darkness of that cloud which was forever upon him. But each time, as he made his way towards home, that feeling of being lost, hopelessly lost, came back to him and overwhelmed him.

His nights were as he expected they would always be; too long, bleak and lonely, and no matter how elegant were the mornings, there was never a sign of her 'blue birds'; they too, it seemed, had gone forever. It was only as the shadows fell, when he made his nightly visit to stand in a lonely vigil at her grave, only then did he find some peace of mind. Small though it was, it was his only consolation, for he could feel her presence as though she was standing beside him; and this, a happy reminder of their wonderful life together, was all that kept him going from one day to the next.

Yet as time went on, so too did this one gleam of light fade gradually into the background. It wasn't the same incessant questions from young Jamie that was now driving him to despair and away from home; worst of all, those nightly visits ceased to give him the strength to carry on.

Something had happened. No longer could he feel her nearness, it was as though some total stranger was lying there, just as though there never had been a bond between them; and, try as he might, not one part of him found the response that was the daily bread for his sorrowing heart.

He just couldn't go on like this. He would have to get away from it all, if only for a while. Then the thought came to him, *either by inspiration or a whisper from above, that they might let him join the army.* Well, the colonel and Marie-Ann were coming down the day after tomorrow; he would pour his heart out to him and see if he could pull a string or two, to get him away for a complete change of living.

As things turned out, there was no need for him to try and convince his father-in-law that something would have to be done soon, very soon. For when he met them at The Junction, it didn't need the colonel's expert eye to see that Phil was in a far worse shape than when they had last said goodbye. The smile vanished as quickly as it came, and his face looked so gaunt compared with that which he remembered. But it was those eyes that worried the colonel most. They had sunk too far back for a young man who had been so full of vitality and was still in the prime of life.

However, neither of them had long to wait. For, after lunch, as was their usual practice, they, just the two of them, were in the car and on their way to the top farm.

This time there was an unusual silence between them. Both men in their minds had something to say, but neither knew how to start. Then suddenly they both began to speak at the same time; but it was the colonel who listened as they stopped in one of the gateways.

He heard all there was to be told without uttering a word. Then, putting his arm around Phil's drooping shoulders, he said, 'As soon as I saw you at the station, I knew something would have to be done for you soon, and personally, I'm sure you are doing the best thing in the circumstances. It's a complete change you want, so I'll put the wheels in motion as soon as we get back, and I'll pray for you then, as I do now, just as if you were my very own son.'

Tragedy is always an unwelcome visitor, yet it now seemed in the colonel's case to have been a blessing in disguise, for he had been but a few years older than his son-in-law when he had lost his own wife. Over the years, as he had watched his lovely daughter grow from a beautiful child into the loveliest flower of womanhood, there had always been that fear and uncertainty if, or when, that curse might fall again.

So he had steeled himself at the loss of his daughter, creating a buffer inside against the shock and sorrow that was slowly destroying this young man by his side.

There was nothing anyone could do or say which would bring her back, but by holding on to the future, he became the main tower of strength to his son-in-law, for Penny had told Marie-Ann how near to rock bottom he always was.

'All we can talk about is the farms, for I daren't mention the past, and, in his sorrow, he has no interest in the future.'

A New Life and a New Friend

Just before the autumn was halfway through, things started to turn out for Phil a little more on the happier side. He had chosen not to become an officer, wanting to be one of the men and he had had his medical two weeks before, then he received his calling up papers; he would be going to a training camp on Salisbury Plain, then would be posted into one of his county's regiments. Up to the moment of reading his instructions, he hadn't minded where he was being sent, or what regiment he was joining; but after he had read them over two or three times, he knew things could not have turned out better. This suited him more than anything else could possibly have done.

Right up to those very last three days, young Jamie had kept his searching questions going whenever the opportunity arose, but as soon as he realised that his daddy would soon be a soldier, like the others he had seen, and would soon be leaving them, those questions stopped, and not once in those last three days, even though they had been together and alone much more than usual, did young Jamie mention his mother. What was the reason? How could an innocent child of only four suddenly find calm and contentment, and only because his father is about to leave him and for no specified time? Is there a reason, or is this the end? Is it that almost all that has gone before has counted for nothing, or is it that which is to come is the real and only beginning? Whatever fate had in store for Phil during his six weeks' training, and also for the rest of the war, when often the chance of survival would be so remote that it wouldn't bear thinking about, nothing in that immediate or distant future would match this tense emotional strain, as the minutes ticked by towards his final hour of parting.

Both Penny and Marie-Ann had shown traces of tears long since, and the colonel was lost for words for the first time since the two men had known each other. Only Jamie showed any happiness, as he marched up and down, shouting, 'My daddy is going to be a soldier!'

Phil, on the other hand, hardly knew the thoughts which ran through his mind, or whether he had a heart or not, for the numbness inside was completely overwhelming. This was the second time that the happiness of his home had been turned completely upside down; the first time he had faced his sorrow with a young heart, and had only found a cure when he had met his one and only love. But this time there was no cure, there just couldn't be; he had known what it was like to love and be loved beyond all dreams, he had known what it was like for two lives to be so intertwined that there was no difference one from the other – so close, so infinite, that whatever stretched out before him now was only time and emptiness. There was not one thread of his life before that he could ever pick up again. It was gone, gone forever, and now he seemed to be severing the very last link with all that had been heaven to them, and with the place of his birth. He knew that, all being well after his training, he might be lucky to come home for a day or two; but after that, who knew what the early part of 1944 might bring? Not every man who went into action lived to see the sun rise on the following day; some were found to pay with all they had. What if he was one of these? Perhaps in a few brief months there might be no returning. And, as he took one last look at the faded beauty of what had been their dream garden, the thought sent a greater shiver down his spine than any of the horrors he would see in the battles to come.

From the moment Phil arrived at the camp and settled in, it became the start of a long process that would make him not a *new* man, but a different one. There was not much chance for his thoughts to wander, to brood, or to dwell upon his sorrow, there was just not time; and only as he closed his eyes at night and prayed did it all flood back to him. But as day followed day, each one more energetic that the one before as they marched, trained and raced across the countryside, so the weariness that followed took a little larger bite from that awful loneliness that had made his nights so long and so unbearable.

Gradually he fell into the way of things, probably much

quicker than most of them, and he thanked his lucky stars that he had been brought up to a tough open-air life, as even his strength was often taxed to the hilt. How some of them managed – men who had worked in shops and offices – he could hardly imagine. They had his sympathy, yes, all of it. Hard though it was, like most things when first attempted, if you press on, suddenly, before you realise, it is at your fingertips and becomes as second nature to you.

Here they were, having their daily baptism of mud, and often a fair share of rain, and learning what aching muscles are really like, from the incessant chasing over that rough and hilly ground, and finding out that there was no excuse for a step which faltered.

Trained to take the worst of all in their stride, the cold, the wet, and the never-ending weariness, which all too often they were more sure of than breakfast, lunch or tea. Yet as they went one, each man's face formed the same expression, the grimness of determination to go forward, on and on; conditioned to fight and not give in, conditioned to suffer without one cry, conditioned to die and not count the cost; this was a soldier's lot in the time of war.

Most things have some form of compensation, and judging from the rumour that was going around the camp – if it was really true – then those six weeks of agony would be worth every bit of the suffering. More often that not there is no smoke without fire, and this case proved to be no exception. Five day's leave, spanning over the Christmas period, was what they were told three days before their training finished. This was because it was the usual practice for the instructors and most of the other staff to have Christmas leave, so the camp would be almost empty. Owing to this wonderful news the hardship of those last three days was taken in their stride, and most of the men could hardly believe their good fortune.

Only those who have had the privilege of pitting their strength and conquering all that is put before them under such tough and awful conditions, and come through with flying colours, can ever hope to understand their relief at the end. They had won, now they could really believe in themselves. The privilege had been theirs, a challenge which had made so many men real men.

The colonel and young Jamie were at The Junction to meet Phil, and what a welcome they gave him! The feel of that fatherly hand gripping his, then patting him on the shoulder with all the sincere affectionate pride, as if he were his own son, and, at the same time, those young tender arms squeezing him around the neck so tight, and planting kiss upon kiss all over his face. Phil was so overwhelmed with it all that it took quite an effort to stop his emotions from showing, but one thing he couldn't keep from view was his excitement at coming home. This was the first time that the colonel had seen those sad eyes shining since the weekend before the tragedy.

'It's wonderful to think that you'll have five whole days with us, and we all jumped for joy when we received your letter,' exclaimed the colonel.

'Yes,' chimed in young Jamie, 'and Penny has been making all sorts of nice things for you, Daddy, and I've been helping her sometimes.'

'Bless you, you're all so wonderful,' answered his father, hugging him once more.

On reaching Spring Farm, he saw Penny and Marie-Ann were already standing at the door to greet him, and even before the car came to a standstill, another wonderful welcome awaited him as they both hugged and kissed him almost together. How happy they were! There were no tears now, only three pairs of eyes that were trying to analyse him without him suspecting; he looked in perfect health, they all told him so, but to themselves they were thankful that their prayers had been answered, for at last something new had brought more interest into his life.

But at a time like this, there were bound to be some moments when those dark clouds of sadness were all too visible, and all too near; someone very special is missing at all times, and that empty place can only be looked at for a second or two. His love, his shining light is with him no more, and there is no Christmas present he can buy her this time, there are only the lovely flowers which he had asked them to get for him. So a little more than an hour after his arrival, he was on his way to the church. Twilight was already creeping in, as alone he knelt beside her; the memories of a year gone by flood back to him, half of it heaven in all its glory, while the other half just made him grit his teeth and shake his head to stop the tears that were rolling down his cheeks becoming a flood. He had asked himself a million times the reason why – why had she, who was so perfect and so angelic, been taken from him? He knew now that those million questions were all in vain, for the million answers were all so empty and just as hopeless. If only, as he knelt with his eyes closed beside her, if only he could hear her whisper 'My own true love', or just to feel the tender touch of her hand upon his face; but no, she seemed as far away from him as she had before, and inside, one more drop of blood was squeezed from his weeping heart.

Why, when they had been as one in heart and soul, was the bond not strong enough to reach out and take his hand, and guide him as a blind man through the dark and loneliness, even unto his life's end? That was what he had expected. But the tremor which went right through him was the warming hand of faith, touching the coldness of his empty heart and bringing to him the thought that she, his life, his angel, was in heaven alone, and that he would have to go on, even if only for Jamie's sake; for only thus would they be together, and hand in hand for always.

So quickly were the shadows falling now that, for a moment, Phil had fears that he had left it a little late to arrange the flowers properly. He managed it, however and, after covering them with a large paper bag, until his visit in the morning, he stood quite still and prayed; he hardly knew for what he prayed, except for the blessing of their son, and for them to meet again.

As he walked slowly down the lane, then out onto the road, passing a couple of cottages before he crossed over, the sound of happy children's voices came to him from within. Yes, he almost said aloud; then his thoughts ran on. He would have to play his part so that everyone would have as happy a time as possible. They knew that life for him could never be the same again, but this was a time for rejoicing, a time when he must cover his sadness with a smile.

Bravely, and to a great extent, this is what he did, but the other three realised beyond all doubt what an effort of strength and self-discipline he was making, for they knew what his true feelings were. That first evening he was the same as any happy father as he played with his son, and, after he had given him a pickaback upstairs to bed, kissed him a dozen times, and tucked him up for the night under Penny's supervision. Phil was impatient to know what presents they had been able to get for Jamie, and if they had been able to get the train set which he wanted to give him.

'As a matter of fact,' said the colonel, 'we've been very lucky. We've all got for him what we set out to get, and the train, it's a second-hand one, but in perfect condition, and with everything there. Penny has not wrapped it up yet because we thought you would like to see it first.'

'That's wonderful, and I'm so grateful to you all for doing so much in these hard times, and I hope you are not overdoing things looking after the farms,' Phil answered.

The colonel laughed at that. 'Do you know, Phil,' he went on, 'I'm only allowed to do so much and no more. I remember often hearing you and Penny say what a wonderful lot of men you had, and these last few weeks I have found out why both of you were so unstinting in your praise for them. They know exactly what to do and when, I'm not allowed to soil my hands in any way. I'm fully convinced that they could run the farms, except for the paperwork.'

'I know,' answered Phil, smiling. 'Often one or the other has said to me, when I've finished this, Mr Phil, it'll be time to do so-and-so either tomorrow, or the day after, or next week – and they're always right too, it's funny. Dad often said there might be places in the world that grow more and better crops than we do, but none of the things upon the earth comes forth with more loyalty than we have.'

'I'm sure he had something there,' added the colonel.

'He certainly did,' answered Phil, 'and that is why we have always looked after them, in good times and bad.'

Christmas Day dawned almost like the beginning of spring. Phil rose early and had already shared in young Jamie's excitement as he opened all his presents, then, before breakfast, he slipped out quietly to take the paper bag off the flowers. There had been very little frost, leaving them as perfect as the night before. How she would have loved this beautiful display, and he would have given the whole world if only they had been together in their own home, and she was doing the arranging. To think that a year ago, already by this time in the morning they had known the joy of each other's arms, and the wonder of each other's lips, sometimes under the mistletoe, but most likely anywhere. He knew that on this day of all days, he must not let his grief get the better of him, but as he walked away, every few steps he took, he turned around for one more look, seemingly afraid that each one might be the last. Not once so far had Jamie mentioned his mother, not even when just the three of them had gone to church. Grandfather caught father's eye as they saw him gaze towards his mother's grave as they went in, and the backward stare as they came out on their way home. Jamie had removed the twin leather holder with her two beautiful photographs from his father's room to a place by the side of his own bed, and often when either Penny or Marie-Ann looked in to see how he was, he would be sound asleep with those photographs held tightly in his arms, yet never once did he mention her to anyone. As young as he was, it seemed as though he held some secret all on his own, and also, something that appeared a little more obvious, that he had no intention of sharing it with anyone.

Could it be that the powers above had cushioned his mind with the thought that all would be well, and all he had to do was to whisper a few words in his father's ear and wait? Could it be that a small boy like him, untouched by thought, word or deed of worldly sin, might be granted the only sign that all is not lost, and there is still hope ahead?

Not only on this day, Christmas Day, but also during the three days that followed, there was more happiness in Spring Farm than there had been in the whole six months before. Not even when Phil had to leave did he appear to be downhearted; he knew he would only be at the training camp for three days at the most, and he felt a touch of excitement at not knowing where he would be posted. Penny and Marie-Ann might have been near to a tear or two as they hugged and kissed him goodbye, but at least it wasn't like the last time. They were more able to hold their composure now, because he did.

While at the station, the colonel once more revealed the happiness in his mind by saying, 'I wouldn't care if I were coming with you, for I know you will enjoy it even more now that you are joining a unit.'

But young Jamie clung to his father, smothering him with kisses just as he'd done when he had arrived, saying after he had got his breath back, 'Come again soon, Daddy, won't you?'

'Yes, my love,' he answered, 'just as soon as it is possible, and I hope for much longer.'

After a roundabout journey Phil arrived back at camp at 20.00 hours, but there was no need for him to go and see what orders were on the board, 'the gen' was already around the camp. All personnel were to be on parade at 10.00 hours the next morning. By now he'd got to know a few of the lads quite well, and inwardly he was hoping that he would be going to the same place as one or more of them. But twenty minutes after the parade had begun, he had his first taste of disappointment; twos, threes and fours seemed to be going here, there and almost everywhere, but when his name and number was finally read out, it was alone; he had to join one of his county's regiments near Ashford in Kent, and to be ready to be taken to the station the next morning at 09.30 hours.

Long before he went to bed that night, he had consoled himself to the fact that it might be all for the best in the long run, so what was the use of worrying over it... The last thing he was going to do was to try and work fate to suit himself, as he had always been a fatalist; what is to be, will be, and any man who dared to try and alter it, especially in these times, could be taking a short cut from this life into the next.

After saying goodbye to the few lads who were still there, he was soon on his way; even though he had a change at Reading, it was still a fast journey to London, but definitely no faster than his exit from the station. Too many memories were there for him to stand still and ponder, the sight of those milling crowds would have disappeared from before his eyes and only she would have been standing there, radiant, beautiful, and with her arms full of heaven. It was all so vivid in his mind, and all so cruel to his heart, he dared not stay a second longer and dwell upon it. He had enough food with him, but he would have dearly loved to have lunched in some really nice place, especially not knowing when he might get the chance again; but there was the problem of all his kit, and then again the memories, so across London he made his way.

By 1.15 he was at Victoria, walking to and fro as he finished the last of his sandwiches, and feeling a little impatient to know what he was going to. He was also realising that, after those weeks of comradeship, his own company was not exactly the best thing for him. Phil had to admit to himself he felt lonely.

He enjoyed the journey down, and by four o'clock he had been picked up at the station and was on his way to the camp.

'You'll like it here,' the driver told him, 'they're a grand bunch of lads and there's not one stuffy officer among the lot.'

Before they were halfway to the camp, Phil was in a much more light-hearted mood. It was more than comradeship that made this driver go out of his way to make him feel welcome and one of them, it was a brotherhood among men, real men, men who lived for the day, the hour, the minute, the second, and joked about what tomorrow or the future might have in store for them. No wonder he thought as he got out in front of HQ. If they are all as friendly as you, then they must be a grand bunch.'

There was only a corporal present when he went in, and from the very start he felt at home as they laughed and joked as he went through the usual formalities, and once more he thought, *the driver must be right, for here was another fellow who couldn't be more friendly.*

'You're in hut 16, straight up the road and the first turning on the right, but if you'd like to wait for a few minutes, I'll get one of the lads to help you with your kit,' said the corporal.

'Thank you very much, but I think I can manage after all the sitting about I've had in the trains,' Phil answered, smiling.

'Well I must say, you look strong enough – and don't forget, if there is anything you are in doubt about, I shall be only too pleased to give you what help I can,' replied the corporal.

'Thank you very much,' Phil replied, 'I don't expect you will have long to wait, as I'm a raw recruit.'

It was to the sound of a good laugh that he left the guardroom and made his way up the road. He had gone a hundred yards before he turned right; the huts were not in lines, but staggered at different angles; fifty yards he had gone down this road and still the hut numbers were in the twenties. Suddenly he noticed a soldier coming out of one of the ablution rooms. He was in shirtsleeves and had his towel rolled up under his arm; both were about the same distance from where the path met the road, so they met almost face to face. Before Phil could ask where No. 16 was, the soldier asked.

'Are you our new replacement for hut 16?'

'Yes,' answered Phil, 'and I was just wondering where to find it.'

'Well, your problem's solved now, and let me have that kitbag, it's a long way up from the guardroom.'

It was no use protesting, in fact he didn't have time to, for his companion had it off his shoulder and on to his own before he could say a word. Then, stretching out his free hand, he announced, 'I'm Charlie Legge, appropriately known to all the lads as Chesney... and yours?'

'Phil Fraser,' he answered, returning as much friendliness in his handshake as he could muster.

While they walked slowly towards the elusive hut, Chesney wanted to know if he had come from another unit or straight from training camp.

Phil told him about some of the hardships on Salisbury Plain and how it was much colder there; that was as far as they got as they reached the door of No. 16. Chesney opened it, calling out as he did so, 'Stand to attention and salute our new replacement!'

They didn't salute, nor did they stand to attention, but one moment they were sitting around the stove, or on the beds close by, and the next they were all standing, ready to shake his hand and welcome him, as Chesney introduced him.

There were three Scots, three Welsh, two Irish, and the rest a mixture from different parts of England; in the matter of a minute Phil's kit was taken from him and put by his bed, and he was ushered into a chair in front of the fire.

'Have a warm-up for ten minutes before tea, Phil,' said Robby Drysdale.

So for the next ten minutes he sat there, entering into some of the conversation, but always laughing, as they mostly wisecracked; yet inwardly he was completely overwhelmed by a sort of comradeship he had never met before.

Tea-time came, and by the time he had fished out his mug and other utensils from his pack, the others had gone. But Chesney had remained, more from a point of comradeship than just to show him the way to the dining hall.

'Have we got batmen here?' Phil asked, 'only I'm wondering who made my bed.'

'No, nothing like that!' answered Chesney, laughing. 'Your blankets were sent up from the stores not half an hour before you came. Paddy – he's the taller of the Irish lads – and I made it up at once; we always do this for anyone coming off leave like you today.' He paused. 'You'll sleep well in it. It's what we call the pocket bed, once you get in, you've got a heck of a job to get out.'

'Thank you very much,' said Phil, 'and I mustn't forget to thank Paddy too.'

Only Two out of Four Left

During the next few days Phil settled down to things much quicker than he had dared to hope; if there was anything he didn't know, Chesney would soon put him into the picture. Nothing seemed too much trouble for any of them, so that he would feel at home as much as possible, and also know that he had been accepted into their little band. A handful of men, whose unspoken word and quiet confidence were a law unto their own, they had a comradeship which, if it was put to the test in the battles to come, meant they would fight to the death for each other, without bothering to know the reason why.

But it was one more act of fate, quite unforeseen, that had brought Chesney and him together. They sat together at meals, stood side by side in the ranks, and off duty they talked, went to the cinema or had a couple of drinks together.

Phil had known almost from the start that Chesney was married, and his home was in London, but it wasn't until he had been there a couple of weeks, when they were walking along the road towards the town one evening, that he learnt the main part of the story that was Chesney's life.

Like himself, Chesney had been born a country boy, and from the time he had left school he had worked in the office of the big estate on which his father was employed.

He had met Grace, his wife, at one of those friendly village hops, when she had been on holiday from London.

'You know Phil, when I walked into that dance hall and caught the first glimpse of her, I knew that was the girl I wanted to spend the rest of my life with. So we were married in just over a year, that was eighteen months before war started. The first twelve months were like heaven, for we were together in our own home, a picturesque cottage with roses hiding most of the walls.

'Then Grace's mother was taken very ill, and her father, a long-suffering victim of that other war, was quite incapable of coping with anything as strenuous as that, so there was only one thing we could do. We sold, or gave away, most of the home that we had cherished so much, and hated every moment then and after. I got a job in an office in the city and Grace nursed her mother as far back to normal health as she will ever get. But as soon as it hit me that war was inevitable, I wished with all my heart that my in-laws had joined us in the country and not the reverse, for there's not a night goes by when I don't get that sick empty feeling in the pit of my stomach, and inwardly I cease to live between the last letter and the next. Six months before my parents died, I could have got them a cottage almost next door, but no, the old folks wouldn't leave their battered and beloved London, and now my Grace has lost the tint of all those lovely roses in her cheeks.'

He sighed a sigh of regret, and almost in the next breath he asked, 'You've never said if you are married, Phil. Are you?'

'Outwardly I was, until six months ago; but inwardly, I am and always will be married to that same and only girl, who can never be replaced.'

Chesney's pace slackened as he caught the tone of sorrow in his voice.

'I'm sorry, Phil, I wouldn't have asked if I had known there was something you didn't want to talk about.'

'You weren't to know, Ches. It's not your fault, and in any case I would have to have told you some time.'

They turned into a field gateway and he leaned over the gate gazing out across the fields, while Chesney stood with his back against it. This was no time for eyes to meet as he unfolded his story, a story where a pause came only too often. He told all there was to know about heaven on earth, until six months ago, then all that changed so quickly, and so tragically, leaving him with a life before him as barren as a desert under a perpetual and scorching sun.

'I'm deeply sorry, Phil, and I'm sure I am not the first to say that to you by a long chalk. Probably you are tired of people saying it, when nothing anyone can say or do can ever make your life the same again. But I want you to know that you have my deepest sympathy, and my most friendly understanding, and I hope this will not only carry us through the rest of this war as friends, but also into the better times of peace.'

'I appreciate that very much, Ches,' he answered, recovering his composure 'for now you will understand and know the reason if I'm not quite my usual self sometimes.'

For the next five minutes they looked at photographs that were very dear to them; firstly it was Grace outside their cottage in the country, then a studio portrait taken after four years in London.

'I can see what you mean, Ches, she's nowhere near as bonny in this one.'

'I know,' answered Chesney sadly, 'I'd have her out of town tomorrow if I had my way, but it seems that we're like a lot of other people, we must suffer solely for doing our duty.'

'This is my son, Jamie,' said Phil, showing him a large snapshot taken eight months before.

Chesney studied it. 'He's a lovely boy, Phil, and I can see quite a bit of you in those tender features. Bet you're awfully proud of him! I know I should be if he were mine.'

'I am desperately proud of him, in fact he is the only reason why I hope I shall come through this war all right.'

'The mob we are in isn't exactly one of the safest, but I hope both of us come through it without a scratch,' said Chesney, as he took the other photograph that Phil offered him.

'Oh, Phil!' he exclaimed as soon as he saw it, 'this is a picture of the most beautiful girl I have ever seen.'

'That's what I thought the first time I saw her, which was only a matter of weeks before that was taken. And the strange part was that over the few precious years which followed, she seemed to grow younger and more beautiful every day, and I know our joy and happiness couldn't have been more perfect... and that is why there seems so little to live for now.'

'I can really understand how you feel,' replied Chesney. Then he added, 'I may only go to church now and again, but deep inside, Phil, I am a believer without any reservations. Just looking at this picture, if I were in your place, every time I looked at this, this face of an angel, I should find my comfort in the thought that God took her because she was far too good for this world.'

'That is what I often think when I am in that frame of mind, but then there are times when I don't know, I just don't know, and I can't find any logical answer.'

'Well, for the sake of your little son, and yourself, don't try to seek it, for we know we can never find the answer to those sort of problems in this world. Face the future, Phil, and hold on to your faith with both hands, for a man without a faith is a man lost. He sees no real beauty in the heavens or on this earth and in the end he is nothing.'

He paused for a moment, then went on, 'This is how my silent but burning faith affects me, whenever I am confronted with the wonders of this world. Be it a tiny flower that I am holding in my hand, or gazing out over a vast panorama that stretches as far as the eye can see, I stand in awe, for I know then that I am in the presence of "The Creator of All Things", and for those few moments I am down to my real size, and I marvel at the miracle which is me. We shall never know in this world why these things happen, Phil, for we are not meant to know; we can only believe that there is a better reason than what we can think of, and one which we, in our human form, are incapable of understanding, but one which I am sure we shall all know that answer to one day.'

From that moment on Phil realised more and more just how good Chesney was for him; if that cloud of sadness started to envelop him, Chesney would spot it in an instant, and either start some interesting topic, or say, 'Put you Sunday best on, we're off to the flicks, then, on the way back, we'll call in the Whistling Robin for a game of darts and a couple of pints.'

What an understanding friend, he thought. Even if he could never forget all that had gone before, there was one certainty, Chesney wasn't going to let him brood over it a second longer than possible. How lucky he was to have met someone like Chesney, someone not only so full of life, but someone whose thoughts seemed to be focused more on him than on himself.

But was it only sheer luck that had made their paths cross, even before he was settled in the camp? Or was it something with a more definite plan for the future, something which was determined that Chesney should play his part in making him hold on to as much of life as possible? He didn't know, but for the first time, he wondered.

Out of the eight weeks that followed, only two of them were spent in the camp that was home to them. The rest was taken up at different places, a toughening-up course in Wales, another on small arms in Essex, with the inevitable long cold dreary day's exercise. This was new to him, but the others had been on several before and hated them.

'Phil, the worst of these damn exercises is that it's only the top brass who know what it's all about; it puts me in mind of when we were kids, playing fox and hounds, only now there is no fox.' That was how Ginger Brown, one of the Yorkshire lads, summed it up.

'Yes, and you didn't get as blasted cold at that game either,' chimed in the East Anglian voice of Johnny Clark.

It didn't bear thinking about; seven days of this at the end of February, sometimes wet and hungry, always cold, and not knowing where you were going to rest your weary head – that is, as long as you weren't on guard, then you didn't have to worry much where you slept...

Yet through it all, they were an education to him. For the bigger the privation, the bigger the wisecracks, and the louder the laughs. *These were real men*, he thought to himself; yet some were only mere boys, who in heart and outlook had long since attuned themselves to overcome any hardship or danger that they came face to face with; and he himself was enjoying all, or most of it.

The one big thing he had against all the moving around was that he didn't get his mail regularly, neither did he have the opportunity to write his usual amount. However, after the exercise was over and they had arrived back at Ashford, there were quite a few letters waiting for him; he sorted them out according to the dates, and it wasn't until he came to the last of both the colonel's and Penny's that he received the shock.

Jane had been having trouble with Gerald – woman trouble. No one had known until she could stand the strain of it no longer and, according to what the major had told the colonel, divorce proceedings had been started already.

Poor Jane, he thought; it didn't seem so long ago when the four of them had the world at their feet. Now there were only two left, two who had loved and lost; but in his heart he would rather have his type of losing than hers. For he could and would go on loving his angel for ever, knowing that the years they had had together were perfect and heavenly, and what small comfort he derived in his loneliness was made up of all those treasured memories. Nothing could ever take them away from him, and nothing would ever dim or tarnish them in the slightest, for, apart from Jamie, they were all he had to hang on to, and, above all, they were most sacred.

Once more he and Chesney settled down to the usual routine and, as with all pals, it was more than a pleasant surprise to them when they learnt that they were going on leave at the same time.

'Think of it,' said Chesney, 'nine wonderful days' leave at the beginning of April! And from now until we go, those nine days will seem like eternity, but once you step inside the door, they'll be gone hardly before you can take your coat off. So have as happy a time as possible, and make every minute count, for I've an awful strong feeling that this will be the last nine days we shall get this side of the water.'

'I wouldn't be surprised if you're not spot on,' answered Phil, 'for it's the right time of the year coming now, the springtime.' Then in the next breath he added, 'I wonder what it will be like in reality,' with a look on his face that showed he was trying to visualise something he had never experienced.

'Your guess is as good as mine,' answered Chesney, 'but one thing you can be sure of, it will be hell upon earth, and we, the PBI, will be sure to know as much about it as anybody!'

'It's bound to be grim,' added Phil, 'but even so, I shall be glad when we've tasted the real thing for the first time, for no matter how much training we get, we can never be sure of our reactions until we have been in action and under fire. Only that way will any man know if he can stand up to it, or if it will slowly break him.'

Chesney got up and replied, 'This time next year, if we're lucky, we shall not only know more about our inward selves, our hopes, our fears, our strengths and our weaknesses, but we shall know how to pray with our faces pressed down into the mud or dust, and cursing Jerry at the same time. That's a soldier's privilege,' he went on, 'saint one minute and a sinner the next!'

Phil laughed.

Two mornings before they went on leave, everything so far had gone as usual. It was wash and shave, breakfast, then out on parade. Nothing had ever invaded the sanctity of the parade ground before, nor did it actually do so this morning; but right at the moment the RSM handed the parade over to the CO, four squadrons of Spitfires appeared as if from nowhere. If they had carried on it wouldn't have been so bad, but unknown to them the RAF was once more taking over the airfield, a mere mile from their camp.

They looked skyward, and in no time those four squadrons became one large circle. Then they all watched as in three the planes took their preselected turn to land.

'Let 'em all come!' said a voice behind Chesney and Phil.

'Hope they'll do this every morning,' chimed in another.

It was about ten minutes before the air was clear enough for an order to be heard.

Then the CO took over; after giving the order to 'stand at ease', he laughed and continued, 'Don't think you are going to get away without an inspection every morning just because the RAF are now our neighbours. If this happens often, I shall have to hold parade before breakfast, or have the RAF grounded from nine to quarter past.'

The roar that greeted the CO's laughing face and words would have drowned the noise of the aircraft had they still been overhead.

'Smashing fellow.' 'One of the best.' Sayings like this could be heard all through the ranks.

He was the type of man that they would go through hell and high water for, and, what was more, he had gathered around him officers as near to his way of thinking and acting as possible.

But if they were dismissed from the parade without it fulfilling its purpose, there was no hope of escaping the next duty, for it was straight back to the huts, on with the kit, and out for a route march. Not that this was looked upon as something to dislike, for when the weather was fine the men loved it. Swinging along those country roads and singing their favourite songs was quite a pleasant way of spending a day in early spring. How many miles they marched they didn't know, and neither did they care, for not one of them would dream of spending the night in camp; tired, weary or footsore, it made no difference, they would be in town in force as usual, enjoying life as it came.

Being in no desperate hurry, Phil and Chesney were almost the last two to leave the camp that evening, and it was just as they reached the outskirts of town that Phil turned to Chesney saying, 'They say, Ches, that an army marches on its stomach, and how I feel now I must have left mine somewhere along that route march.'

'Hungry, then?' enquired Chesney.

'I should think so! I could eat a horse and chase the rider,' was the reply.

'Well, I know a place where we can get a good meal... might be a bit expensive though,' said Chesney.

It's a deal,' answered Phil, 'but on one condition, that the meal and the drinks are on me.'

Chesney protested.

'It's no good, Ches, you'll want all the money that you have to take Grace out with next week. I've no one special like that now, and money isn't a thing that I'm exactly short of.'

Ninety minutes later the eating was over, but they would be there for a while yet, drinking their coffee and talking, for out of the blue Phil suddenly said, 'I've been wondering, Ches, do you think it would be possible for Grace to leave her folks in the care of someone else for a few days?'

'I should think so,' answered Chesney, 'but why ask that?'

'Well, I've been wondering if you would like to come and stay with us for a few days, say, four days before we have to report back. It would be best for you to travel down as early as possible, then have three whole unbroken days in the country, and then the last day we could all go back to London together after lunch.'

'Oh, Phil, that would be something out of this world as far as Grace is concerned, and I should be a million times happier myself, knowing that she is loving every second of it.'

'That's settled, then,' replied Phil.

'I'm absolutely thrilled, and grateful to you, Phil, but are you really sure it will be all right with your people at home? Only there is a war on, you know.'

'I know all about that!' answered Phil smiling, then continued. 'I casually mentioned it a week ago, and by return I had a letter from my father-in-law and his wife, and one from Penny, making it a must, and saying how much they were looking forward to seeing you both, and also the food problem was being taken care of; satisfied now?'

'I don't know how to thank you, Phil, for I know Grace will be like a little child going on a Sunday school outing for the first time,' answered a very sincere Chesney.

'All I hope,' said Phil, 'is that Grace and you won't get tired of chicken, pheasant and all the other eats that can be got on a farm, for I expect the colonel has been out for the last few days making sure that we won't starve.'

'Lovely!' exclaimed Chesney, 'that is what we have missed most by living in London, plus the lovely fresh vegetables out of our own garden. I think we have almost forgotten what the real thing tastes like now.'

'Well, let's hope the colonel's shooting is on target,' added Phil.

'I'm not worried about that,' answered Chesney, 'I'm just dying to see Grace's face when I tell her the wonderful news the day after tomorrow.'

The Calm Before the Storm

So time went by, and that great day, the day of departure, dawned, and brought with it a magic spell, for as Phil sat at breakfast, he could quite easily pick out almost every man who was going on leave. Eyes sparkled and shone with a different light, and the entire world was theirs to laugh at; they were going home to the ones they loved, to those who had longed and waited as patiently as they had themselves.

Yet wasn't it cruelly true that among that happy band, there were some for whom this would be the last time ever, the last time to know the welcome and joy of home, and the last time to feel the clinging of loving arms?

That was one worry Phil didn't have if anything happened to him. He would be mourned, no doubt, but Jamie would be well provided for, and in one so young, time would heal his distress that much quicker. He would leave no one in the same empty void that he himself had accepted as his prison for the rest of his life.

He wondered, if his 'angel' had still been with him, would he have been as brave as any of those in nine days' time, when that last goodbye just couldn't be delayed a moment longer? He doubted it, that last desperate hug and bruising kiss would have torn his inside into little pieces, and he would never have known a moment's peace, leaving her alone, and seemingly so helpless without him.

'There's about enough time for you to come and meet Grace and the old folks and have something to eat and drink before your train goes,' said Chesney, just as they arrived in London.

'Thanks awfully, Ches, but I'd better not risk it. I've got about fifty minutes to get to Paddington and catch my train; it's plenty of time for that, I know, but I mustn't miss it, as the colonel and Jamie will be at The Junction to meet me.'

'You know you are more than welcome, but I suppose it

would be a bit risky, and I wouldn't want you to miss that train for anything. And please remember what I told you the other night, make every minute count, and once again, I'm most grateful to you for asking us down for a few days of heaven.'

'Think nothing of it, Ches, we'll meet you at The Junction on Friday at 11.45. Give my best regards to Grace, and have a good time.'

'I will, and thanks again,' answered Chesney, as two strong right hands clasped each other in a bond of true friendship.

On the way down he was in one of those compartments that was blessed with a friendly atmosphere, yet there were moments when his sorrow and loneliness swept right over him. He was going home, that one spot on earth where every yard seemed to pierce his heart with memories of days gone by; but there were also moments when he felt impatient to get there as soon as possible. The thought of his son, and the awful dread that these next days might be the last that they would have together, made him desperate to catch the first glimpse of him waiting on the platform. He would have to try to be a little bit more like his old self, for all their sakes. He knew they realised just how much had gone out of his life, never to return; so he would do what Chesney had told him to, make every minute count. He would have to, for it was only when he was at Spring Farm that life held any semblance of reality, and whether the memories were good or bad, he would have to bear them and put on a bold front.

His thoughts got no further, for the train had just passed under the bridge two hundred yards from The Junction. He was in the front part of the train, and in the space of a second he was out in the corridor and looking out of the window. His heart jumped for joy as he caught the first sight of grandfather and grandson holding hands. They saw him and waved as he passed by, and hardly had the train stopped before he was out on the platform. Jamie, leaving his grandfather behind, ran towards him, never heeding the crowds as he picked his way between them.

'Daddy, Daddy!' he cried, as his father swept him into his arms.

'I've been longing so much to see you, my love,' he just managed to get out as the kisses were planted all over his face.

'How is everything?' enquired the colonel as they greeted each other.

'Fine, thank you, Dad, and I hope you and all at home have kept in trim these last few days.'

'Yes,' answered the colonel, beaming. 'I've managed to look after them all right, and I must say it's a real pleasure to see you looking so fit and well.'

'Army life,' replied Phil, laughing.

Going along the road, there was no lack of conversation, for Jamie kept up an almost never-ending story of this and that and what had happened at the house or on the farms, almost as far back as when Phil was last on leave; and the look on that young angelic face as they roared with laughter at something he had said only made his father hold him more desperately close.

'Bless you, my love, you're a lovely boy and growing up fast,' he said, squeezing him tight once more, and, just for a second, he let his thoughts run away with him; his son, their son, was claiming a bit more of his mother's beauty, as well as her sweetness.

Penny and Marie-Ann were at the door to greet him as usual, the happiness on their faces telling him just how much they had missed him. What a welcome, just like the last time; and before he knew it, the colonel had thrust a whisky in his hand, while they toasted his health, and eventual safe return.

'We're awfully glad you asked Chesney and his wife to come down,' said Marie-Ann.

'Sure you can manage all right?' Phil asked.

'Perfectly,' answered Penny, 'we may be short of some of the things that were plentiful in peacetime, but for good country food we are well stocked up.'

'You're all so wonderful,' he replied, 'and everything looks just as it always did.'

'That's just how it should be,' answered the colonel, 'and I must say for myself I feel much fitter walking around the farms and trying to lend a hand here and there.'

'Well, don't overdo it, will you?'

'I'm enjoying it too much for it to do me any harm,' replied the colonel, laughing.

'How is Jane… is she at the Court?' enquired Phil.

'Yes, she's at home, and quite well,' answered Marie-Ann. 'We saw her yesterday, and she's invited us all over for tea tomorrow. You'll come, won't you?'

'Oh yes,' he replied, 'I'd get shot if I didn't go to see the major as soon as possible.'

All this time young Jamie had been sitting on his father's knee, eating some of the sweets he had brought him, and most of the time looking up into his father's face, with an expression on his own which, if it were put into words, would have spelt out, 'This is my daddy, my hero, the one who is going to bring my mummy back to me.'

By the time tea was over, the three of them, who had all worried so much about him, and also wondered if he were making the best of what life had left for him, found at last the ray of hope they had been looking for; already he had shown that he had more fun about him, and, even if his face changed to a look of sadness when various things were mentioned about days gone by, at least now he seemed to have the strength and determination for the shadow to be only a passing phase.

Could they but have known, to himself he had already resolved that if he came through the war all right, what was left of his life would be dedicated to his son. He would not let the world share more of his sorrow than he could help. Only when he was alone, or in the stillness of the night, would he let his lonely heart cry out for her, and the tears flow at will. Service life and discipline had done that much for him, it had enabled him to condition himself, to subdue his thoughts, and not let his feelings show in the face of whatever might be before him.

That night, after he had made his lonely vigil and knelt beside her, the atmosphere in Spring Farm was a far happier one than it had been for a long time, and the next morning it carried on where it had left off the night before. Young Jamie had crept into his father's room quite a half an hour before Penny was due with the early tea, so there were bursts of boyish laughter and shouts of glee almost until they came down to breakfast.

By nine o'clock, they were ready for a quick run round the top farms, all three of them, for toys, train and tricycle were all forgotten now that Daddy was home, and Jamie would listen and take it all in whenever his grandfather asked his daddy if they had done this or that as he would, and if things were up to his usual standard.

'It couldn't be better,' said Phil, 'even if I were looking after things myself. You've done wonders, and I am most grateful.'

'Can't go wrong with the kind of men you have,' answered the colonel, laughing.

Actually, deep inside it wasn't the work that gave Phil any concern, it was his men. He had missed a few familiar young faces, and their down-to-earth country wit. He understood, for had he not himself known the feel of itchy feet, even when he had been surrounded with all the joy and happiness in the world? But, by the time they had started back for lunch, he had had his usual friendly chat with all of them, plus a word of thanks, and hope for better times in the future.

Once back home, they had their lunch, then a quick trip around the home farm to meet the two of his men he hadn't seen so far, then just as quickly back to change for an early walk to the Court. Penny had been invited too, and, in the early spring sunshine, it was more of a saunter and a nature walk than anything else.

'There's no need for England to tremble when we've got soldiers like you,' said the major, laughing. Then, in the next breath he added, 'How are you, Phil? I'm so very pleased to see you.'

'Fine, thank you, Major, and I trust you are in the best of health also.'

Before the major could answer, Mrs Marchant interrupted, saying, 'Yes, we're all fine except that we want this war to end, so that all you young people can come home again; it's not the same, you know, for we miss you more than you think, coming up to see us at odd times.'

Just at that moment Jane entered the dining room, and, making straight towards him, said, 'It's wonderful to see you, Phil, after all this time.'

'May I return the compliment,' he answered, smiling, 'and also how glad I am to see you looking so well, Jane.'

It was quite a gay and happy two hours they all had together, but it was only during the last half-hour that he and Jane were far enough away from the others that they could hold a different topic of conversation on their own.

'It's all over, Phil,' she said. 'I became a free woman once more on Tuesday.'

'I'm very sorry, Jane, that something like that should have happened to you; when I heard about it, I was really shocked, and I still can't understand what came over him.'

'I know it's wartime,' she said, 'but it wasn't as though we were apart for ages; I was actually working at the local hospital only two miles from his camp when it all started. I think,' she added, 'that's what hurt as much as anything.'

'Apart or not, there's still no excuse for that sort of conduct. I don't suppose,' he went on, looking down at her hands, 'that there's another woman in the whole world who could cause one of my eyelids to flutter, let alone my heart.'

'I know that,' she answered, 'but all men aren't like you, and come to think of it, I've never met another girl like Joanna. I always said that you two weren't just born for each other, but made for each other, and I still believe it.'

She saw the signs of grief spread across his face and added quickly, 'That's enough of that subject; it's all right to remember the past, but it's fatal to dwell upon it. As a matter of fact, I've been waiting for you to invite us over for tea tomorrow, only I'm leaving the day after, making a fresh start at the Military Hospital at Salisbury.'

'You know very well the door of Spring Farm is open to you at any time, and I'm pleased to think you are going to Salisbury. It's a nice place and you'll find it very pleasant there... but do be careful not to get hurt again, won't you?'

'I will,' she answered, smiling. 'The only way I can be sure of that is to find someone as near to you as possible, but I realise what a hopeless task there is before me.'

'Don't you believe it,' he answered. 'Mind, I can't vouch for the officers, but I know some real nice fellows in the other ranks – they're as straight and trustworthy as you could wish to meet anywhere. In fact,' he went on, 'my pal Chesney is one of them.

It's a pity you are leaving before Friday, because I've invited him and his wife down for the remainder of our leave, then we shall all travel back to London together.'

'Is that where they live?' she asked.

'Yes, and much against their will,' he answered, and then proceeded to tell her the rest of the story.

'Poor things,' she said with her face full of sadness, 'and the trouble is that they are only two of thousands. It's when I hear things like that that I realise just how lucky I am; from the time I can remember I've had most of what I've wanted in life, and only twice in the whole of that time have I known what trouble and sorrow are really like.'

'Yes,' he answered, 'when we stop and look around, it isn't hard to find someone either as bad off as ourselves, or a little bit worse.'

No more words passed between them for quite a few moments.

'Well, don't forget to bring your mother and the major over for tea tomorrow,' Phil said finally, rising to his feet, 'and if it's a nice day, we'll have tea on the lawn.'

'Delightful,' she answered, as she swept Jamie into her arms and covered him with kisses.

Tea on the lawn it was, for the last of the patchy cloud had disappeared, leaving a clear blue sky and a sun which was making its presence felt a little more every day. To Phil, a man bred of the country, there was every sign that they were in for a spell of perfect sunshine; he hoped for Chesney and Grace's sake that he was right, so that the few precious days in the country would be perfect and lovely.

Time proved that his hopes and wishes were on the threshold of being granted, for as they were on their way to meet them at The Junction it was so perfect that even he could have mistaken it for a day in the middle of flaming June.

Yes, Chesney was quite right; Grace was badly in need of the fresh country air. That was his first thought when he met her.

'It's awfully kind of you, Phil, to ask us down,' she said, as he shook her hand.

'We're all very pleased to think you could come, and I've

prayed hard for this lovely sunshine for your sake,' he answered, smiling.

'You say you're pleased we came,' interrupted Chesney, 'from the moment I broke the good news, these few days of heaven have not been out of the conversation more than ten minutes at a time.'

'That's quite right,' Grace chimed in, her eyes shining more brightly already.

A really nice, sweet girl, Phil thought, as he drove back along the road. He listened to her speech as she talked to the colonel and Jamie, and if he hadn't known, he could never have told what part of the country she came from, and what he knew of her already he liked and admired. They were a good pair, as close to each other as he and his love had been, hard working and with not much to spare; but what little they had, and what opportunities for or against had come their way, they had certainly made the most, and the best, of all of it. He listened more than he talked, but the colonel, who was sitting next to him, was half turned around, and holding the friendliest of conversations with their guests.

It was the same at Spring Farm. In no time at all, they were one big happy family, and, after lunch, Grace would insist on doing her share by helping Penny and Marie-Ann with the clearing and washing-up. Spring Farm had at last sprung to life again; the absolute joy on her face as they walked around the garden, and the look of unbelieving when she saw the view from the top of High Ridge, were a pleasure to watch.

Here was someone else, he thought, *who saw the beauty and wonder in all things*. And, as he looked at her a second time, a sense of guilt came over him. How far had he slipped off that road which had been their life; had he gone so far where the wonders of all around were not only taken for granted, but ignored almost completely? His love, his only love, would understand that he could never wish that he should cut himself off from the joy of all the beauty that surrounded him. Almost every yard and every view they had shared and found a glory in that was magnified a million times, because of that wonderful love of theirs, so from now on he would try to find a little more of that joy and happiness that had been theirs to overflowing. He missed her more as each day went by, and his love for her was just as strong and true as on that wonderful day when he had led her out into the sunshine as his bride, his queen. No longer would he let himself hide behind a curtain of self-inflicted misery; that was a duty he owed to their happy years' together, and to her sacred memory.

Although completely unaware of it, Grace had, in a few short hours, brought him back to the realisation that his life still had to be lived, and as happily as possible. He had seen the joy spread over her face as the breeze on the top of High Ridge had ruffled her hair in all directions, and a radiance reborn from the warmth of the sun emerge, as they had strolled across the rich green grass in the valley below.

She reminded him in lots of ways of his Joanna, kind and sincere to everyone, and with a love which was all bound up in Chesney.

Even before the golden sun had dipped behind the trees along the Ridge, the first hint of fresh air and sunshine were already on her cheeks; she was like a rose, poised on the brink of showing its fragrant loveliness, soon to burst forth and bloom in all its natural splendour.

So as long as each following day held the promise of its predecessor, the agenda for each one of them would be carried through as carefully planned. Good food in plenty they were assured of, but Phil planned to take then round the farms and to a few other places of beauty, so that they could see the most and best of everything, and for this there had to be only blue skies and sunshine. Yet, in the end, it turned out that they might just as well not have given the weather a second thought, for it saw the close of those few remaining precious days, and beyond, as perfect as it could be.

Then, on the Sunday, it was church first, and secondly lunch and tea at his favourite spot near the Severn, The Calling Seagull.

After the service, and just as a bunch of pilgrims would, they all slowly made their way over to where that white marble cross stood as a symbol of heartache and sorrow. Hardly a dozen words were whispered between them, until young Jamie, who was holding Grace's and, suddenly looked up into her face and said, 'This is where my mummy was, Auntie Grace, but not any more, for she is up in heaven now, and one day Daddy is going to bring her back to me.'

'Of course he is, my love,' she answered, in barely a whisper, and the uncontrollable tears that rolled down her cheeks were seen on others too.

One hour later they were in somewhat different surroundings, and all during lunch Grace and Chesney could hardly keep their eyes off the beautiful scene which stretched out before them; the flowing waters glittered and danced their tantalising rhythm so fast and so unpredictably, while the hills beyond were full of elegance and majesty.

'I shall find it hard to settle in London again, after these few wonderful days,' said Grace, looking quite despondent.

'Well, this need not be your only visit,' said Marie-Ann 'We'll be only too pleased to have her, won't we, Penny?'

'Can't think of anything nicer, in fact I've been thinking how lovely a real country look would suit that pretty young face,' answered Penny, smiling.

'We mean it, Grace,' said Marie-Ann, 'any time you can get away, you are welcome to stay a week, or a month, or as long as it suits you.'

'You would have that country look all the year round then, my love,' remarked Chesney.

Would it be possible for you to arrange for someone to see to your mother and father at odd times?' asked Phil.

'Oh yes,' answered Grace, 'even before the war there was never a lack of really good friends, people who would share what little they had, and do anything to help, and now in our part of Lewisham with a war on, it's like one big happy family. It's often tragic, but when they climb out of the shelters in the mornings, they are ready to face the day in the only way they know, with a cheery word, a happy face which often hides their own sorrow, and always a helping hand for anyone who needs it. Yes,' she went on, 'I could safely leave them at home and know they would be well looked after.'

'It's "yes", then?' enquired Phil.

'Yes,' she answered, looking absolutely radiant, 'I'm completely overwhelmed with your kindness and your wonderful offer, thank you'

From that moment onwards, Chesney felt as though he had been given a million pounds. There would be at least one week in every month when he would be able to close his eyes without the gnawing worry of wondering if Grace was all right. No wonder that during the rest of their stay his gratitude seemed endless, for he would never be able to repay this act of kindness which meant so much to both of them. For them, those few days in this lovely spot, which was heaven on earth, had been the happiest and most carefree since they had left their own little cottage home in the country. But time, this precious happy time, seemed to be flying by, and the end was all too visible.

Only two more hours remained before the first step back to stark reality; two hours, when all sorts of different heartaches would rise almost to boiling point; two hours, when the tiniest thing looked big, and becomes so sentimental; two hours when the thought of home serves only to kindle the embers into a flaming fire of emotion; two hours, two fast diminishing hours, when the thought that a fleeting glance, or a tender word, a loving embrace, or a lonely vigil by her grave might be the last forever.

That was the thought that was uppermost in Phil's mind as he knelt beside Joanna's grave arranging the flowers; he had not missed one evening without either taking fresh ones, or rearranging those that were already there. But in all those times, and in the depths of his solitude, he had never captured once again the feeling that she was near him, nor did he this afternoon. He knew the loneliness was something that he would have to bear, but knowing what dangers he would soon have to face, when the first five minutes of battle could be his last, was a thought he dare not dwell on. He had only one consolation if that happened. She, his love, his angel, must need him more than Jamie did; and yet it was Jamie, and only Jamie, whom he so desperately wanted to hang on to this life for.

This last agonising time was no different from all the others when he left her grave; he would go so far, then turn around. He knew each special place to the very inch, where that white marble cross would stand out best in all its clarity. He had just got to the last spot where he would have his final view, where the wall dipped and the gap in the trees made it look like a picture in a frame.

He turned for his last long look, but it wasn't having this last vision of the cross which made his already troubled heart miss several beats, it was the sight of two jays, perched one on each side of the cross, and absolutely motionless. So long did they remain thus that he thought his eyes were playing him tricks, and it was only when the one on the left joined the one on the right that he was quite sure he wasn't seeing things. He watched as, side by side, they acted more like two loving doves than jays. He just couldn't fathom it out; the first time he had ever seen a jay in the garden was the very first evening his love had visited Spring Farm; then there were the years which followed, when they would call and wait for her each morning to feed them. What was he supposed to think now? There hadn't been sight or sound of them while he was at her graveside, and why should they choose her cross to alight on just at the moment when his last look would be the vision he would carry into a future unknown? Could it be just coincidence? He just couldn't bring himself to accept that this was the answer. *No*, he almost said aloud, somehow there was a link between his angel and her precious birds. It was an omen, of that he felt sure, an omen either for good or ill; but how, when, and in what form, he was as completely in the dark as ever.

Saying goodbye to Marie-Ann and Penny at the house was a mixed affair; there was some happiness, to think that Grace would be seeing them again within a month, but also very deep sadness in not knowing when would be the next time they would see Phil and Chesney again. Penny was the most upset; it was that awful dread that life for her would be at its end if fate struck again, and took for the third time one whom she looked upon as her very own.

'I shall be all right, so don't worry, we shall all be here hardly before you know it. Now take care of yourself,' Phil whispered as he kissed her goodbye.

He felt the master of himself then, with not even the suspicion of a tear, and not the slightest thought crossed his mind of what peril the future might have in store for him. But at The Junction, as he held young Jamie in his arms, and when only seconds now remained for that last goodbye, it was a different matter; those few seconds were the only time in all his leave when he had to fight to stop his emotions getting the better of him. It wasn't just those young tender arms around his neck which almost choked him, nor the flush of kisses which seemed to have no end, it was what Jamie said, and the way he said it, that made Phil's heart come up almost into his mouth, and gave him his greatest fright.

'God bless you, Daddy, for I love you so, and I shall miss you lots and lots,' he said. Then his voice went down to a whisper as he went on, 'And when you see my mummy, tell her I am waiting for her, won't you?'

'I will, my love, and God bless you also,' he just managed to get out, giving him that one last desperate hug.

But at that moment it wasn't the tears blurring his vision which gave him the most concern, it was the terrible thought that this could be last time that he would ever hold or see his son again.

No one could be sure of anything, especially in wartime, that he realised; but it was a heartbreaking thought when one's life, one's future, and the happiness of others hung solely on the slender thread of prayer and hope.

The parting was over, the last kiss had been had, and, as they gathered speed, the last silent message of his frantic waving arm told its own sad story. It was as if he was willing himself never to lose sight of them, thinking of nothing else except keeping contact with them, even after they had disappeared from view.

At that moment he was only thankful for one thing, he had Grace and Chesney for company, for he dreaded to think what he would be like if he were left to his own thoughts at the present time. The wound in his heart was as wide and as painful as ever, he knew that could never alter while he was in this world, but it was leaving young Jamie, their precious son, that had seemed to cut his legs from underneath him. He felt much worse over this parting than any before; the last straw, or almost the last, was the pitiful way he had mentioned his mother, really believing that he, his daddy, was about to meet her and would bring her back to him. Then one more troubling thought flashed into his mind. What would he do if he got through this war all right and returned home alone? Would Jamie, with his childlike mind, look upon him as a failure? But one more thought from out of the past flickered through the darkness. Twice his love had said she would come back to him; the first time in her tortured sleep, and the second time as he had held her, and knew not what to say, when the light that had been his world faded before his eyes. Then, later, it was Jamie who never gave his breaking heart a chance to dry its tears, for it was always, 'When are you going to bring my mummy back to me?'

That task which his young son had set before him was greater than if he had to win the war all on his own. It would be nothing short of a miracle, and to him as he was, a fighting man standing on the threshold of battle, a battle where no quarter would be given on either side, to think of miracles now was something which was as far out of his reach as the most distant star.

That was the extent to which Grace and Chesney allowed his thoughts to wander, and what made matters even better, it was one of those compartments which he always felt at home in. Once they reached Paddington, it was a quick rush for a taxi to take Grace home first. Then five minutes were spared for Phil to meet the old folks, and for those last 'goodbyes' to be accomplished.

'I shall always remember these wonderful days of heaven which you have given us, Phil,' said Grace, as they shook hands while standing by the side of the taxi. Then she continued, 'You've all made these last few days the happiest we've had in years, and Chesney and I are most grateful.'

'I'd be a poor friend to Chesney if I didn't help you a little, so think nothing of it, for it's a great pleasure to me to see you together, and so happy and carefree – and, what is more, to see quite a few of those roses that have returned to your cheeks!'

'Yes,' she replied, 'and I've got you to thank for them, and now that I am invited down for at least a week a month, there's a good chance that I shall keep them, and I promise you I'll do whatever I can for them when I go down, and also see that Jamie has lots of fun.'

'Thank you, Grace, but you won't get away with doing much,

you'll be there for the fresh air and a holiday! I know them, and in any case they have all the help they need, but as long as you and Jamie have lots of fun together, I shall be that little bit happier and grateful to you at the same time,' he answered.

Just then, Chesney said, 'We shall have to go, darling, or we shall miss the train.'

Phil got into the taxi as Chesney and Grace clung to each other for those last dying seconds.

'Take great care of yourselves,' she said as Chesney got in, 'and God bless you both.'

'And you too,' replied Phil just above the noise of the engine, while Chesney held her hand until the taxi started on its forward motion.

Still Waiting

For almost the next four weeks, camp life as they had come to know it was changing daily. The routine of parades and training was as strict and as serious as ever, but the atmosphere which prevailed both day and night, one of great elation, couldn't be suppressed or disguised by the officers or any of the men.

The show would soon be on, that was the feeling; all the toil, the sweat, the mud and the dust that had been their lot for so long, was soon going to be tested for what it was really worth.

Are men fools who are thus? Men who look forward to do battle, men who fight for what they believe to be the truth and right, men who in their last visions of earth have dreams and hopes, and die in the arms of the sublime, so that the world will be a better and happier place... a heaven on earth which never comes, even though they have given their all.

Those kinds of thoughts never entered their heads these days; the expectancy, the excitement, acted as a blindfold against the hell which they were about to enter. Only on the last night, the night before they moved one step nearer toward their final rendezvous, did they as one come face to face with stark reality. The sun, a golden one, had less than two hours to run before the pale shades of a starlit night took command of the heavens. The whole regiment was assembled for the service of veiled preparation for the blessing of themselves and the great venture that was before them.

Facing the padre and looking towards that mellow sun, they looked like a band of Indian warriors, ready and looking forward to do battle. With their bodies, arms and unflinching faces a golden bronze, trained for battle, strong in arm and leg, alert in mind and body, how could they be expected to conjure up the real feeling of fear?

It was only as the padre addressed them as man to man did they see behind the veil of some of his words, for he was saying not only prayers for them as they were now, and for the success of what was before them, but for the ones who would fall, and those they would leave behind. Then at the last they knelt as one, and nothing could have laid before them a picture of what they might expect more clearly than those age-old words of the twenty-third psalm. As they knelt with eyes closed and hands clasped and pointing to the heavens above, they heard the words which above all others carved their ultimate meaning on each man's mind, 'Yea, though I walk through the valley of the shadow of death, I will fear no evil, for Thou are with me.'

Yet even though each man's lips spoke the remaining words to their heavenly end, each man's thoughts went back to those two all-important lines, and inwardly each man asked himself that same searching question.

'Would he himself get safely through the valley of the shadow of death and into the sunshine on the opposite side? Was it possible that God would look after him in some special or mysterious way?' There was no way of knowing, only time would reveal to the ones, the lucky ones, those who were destined to pick up the threads of life again, almost the same as when they had dropped them.

Then there would be those who would know time, cruel time, as in pain they would linger on in a tiny world of their own; and only time, patient time, would clean and smooth the earth again, over those who had found eternal peace, down in the valley.

Thus was the beginning of doubt, of resigning oneself to good or ill, for this was now the thought – what will happen? – that flipped through the mind of every one of them. A few of them would dwell upon it, and perhaps feel it much deeper than the rest; but generally it was a thought which would more likely present itself by a letter sent, or one received, a photograph or a special tune, which brought back those treasured memories that now seemed an age away.

By the next afternoon they were in somewhat different surroundings; the camp, somewhere in East Ham, was squalid and unfriendly; all mail was censored, and, worst of all, they were confined to camp. It gave them the feeling that they were more like prisoners of war than soldiers in their own country, but it was from here, on the fourth day of the five they were there, that they had their last few hours of heavenly freedom.

From 10.00 a.m. to 23.59 p.m., seemed long enough to go anywhere within reason. Chesney begged Phil to go with him, but Phil, adamant for the first time since Chesney had known him, replied, 'No, Ches, your last few hours together – not likely. But I'll tell you what, I'll call for you and Grace around 9.30 p.m., to go out for a drink, and just in case I can't make it, I'll meet you just inside the underground, and if I fail there, don't wait for me, I'll bear my own punishment if I'm stretched that far.'

'You're trying to get home, then,' said Chesney, knowing full well that that was the only thing he would risk being overdue for.

'I must try. I just couldn't stay in London all day thinking that I had missed even as little as a couple of minutes at home. If there's an earthly chance, no matter how small, I feel I must see young Jamie once more.'

'I hope you manage it, Phil, so the very best of luck; if you do, give them all our very best regards and a big kiss for young Jamie.'

'I will,' answered Phil, as they parted in a hurry.

Paddington was quite a different place from the station he had known just over four weeks ago. Phil's heart sank almost into his shoes when he enquired from the first porter he met about the departure of the trains.

'Well, mate,' replied the porter, 'your guess is as good as mine, this morning! It's only them up there,' he added, indicating to the loudspeaker, 'that knows what's going on, and I don't think they are very sure.'

Just then, a list of late arrivals and departures was announced, but worst of all were the cancellations, including two that should have been in Phil's direction.

'Where did you want to get to?' enquired the porter.

'The Junction on the Gloucester line,' Phil answered, 'not only to get there, but I have to be back here by eleven o'clock tonight.'

The porter winced, saying, 'I shouldn't think there's a hope, but come with me just to make sure.'

The man at the office was shaking his head before the porter had finished asking him, then looking at Phil, he said, 'There might be a train going your way in three, four or five hours' time, but how long it would take and whether it stops at The Junction I just wouldn't know; and as regards getting back here by eleven o'clock tonight, I should say that was impossible, for so many passenger trains have been taken out of service, both yesterday and today, that we hardly know the position ourselves from one minute to the next.'

Phil thanked him as he walked away with the porter.

'Sorry, mate,' said the porter as he saw the look of disappointment on Phil's face.

'Well, we tried, and thank you very much,' he answered, as he turned to make his way towards the street, while the porter stood there lost for words, and staring at the one-pound note that had been slipped into his hand.

There was nothing to hurry for now, so Phil quietly picked his way through the crowds to Praed Street. Sometimes he would gaze into a shop window to see if there was something special he could buy Jamie. He just had to keep himself occupied, it would have been fatal for him to keep looking at his watch, and thinking that he would be at such-and-such a spot along the line if things had turned out as he had hoped. He turned into Edgware Road towards Marble Arch, crossing over as soon as there was a lull in the traffic; once again, as he entered Oxford Street all his thoughts were on finding a book or something else for Jamie. He noticed Lyon's restaurant as he went by, thinking to himself, after he had explored the shops he might return there for lunch.

Not since he had joined the army had he made one of his usual visits to the office, and today he still had no desire to, nor to lunch in one of those expensive places which had once been his practice. As regards the office, he had no worries there; it was all in good hands, and besides, the colonel had been calling there every fortnight.

By 12.45 p.m., he still hadn't found anything that was suitable for Jamie, and was already retracing his steps back to the restaurant; this would be the first time he had been there and he wondered what he was going to find as he went down the steps. The thought that struck him as he went in was that one wouldn't have dreamt that there was as nice a place as this tucked away down here, and with an orchestra playing such lovely music. For wartime, the meal was excellent, and the cold lager most refreshing. The only thing that was wrong was being surrounded by so many happy people, all laughing and talking. He felt a thousand times more lonely, and somewhat out of place; it wasn't that he was jealous of their happiness, far from it, it was his own happy memories that today of all days he couldn't bear to think of.

There was no need for him to linger after he had finished his coffee, and, ten minutes later, he was walking towards Hyde Park Corner via the park, still determined to see what he could find for Jamie in Brompton Road. The bigger shops seemed hopeless, but in the first small shop he looked in, he found the best book for a boy between the ages of five and seven that he could have imagined. He felt happier now, especially knowing that Grace would take it down in three days' time. From then on, he walked or went by bus, just as the fancy took him. Tea time saw him in a somewhat more elegant place than he had looked for, and by 6.15 p.m., he was making up quite a large number of people just inside Downing Street.

Luck was with him, he had never seen the great and famous man before, yet he had hardly been there more than a couple of minutes before the cheering started, then the waving, and from where he stood he had a first-class view as the car went by at a little more than walking pace. There wasn't only cheering and waving, for there were shouts coming from the crowd of 'Good Old Winston!' – only to be returned with a whimsical smile and his famous sign for victory.

There was nothing else Phil wanted to see now, and all he wanted to do was to get over to Chesney's as quickly as possible, so he hailed the first taxi he saw.

They were overjoyed at seeing him, yet disappointed and sorry that what he had set his heart on had been impossible.

'You'll have to write a few lines for me to take down... they'll be as disappointed as you are,' said Grace.

'Yes, I will,' he answered, 'that's the next best I can do, and I wonder if you would take this book for Jamie? I'd be pleased if you will, it's the best I could get for his age, and his wanting to know this and that.'

'Of course I will, and I'm dying to see his face when I give it to him,' she answered.

He smiled, but they couldn't tell whether it was sadness or just disappointment that he tried to cover up by only meeting their eyes fleetingly.

Chesney hadn't seen him down like this for some time, yet somehow had expected it. How pleased he was that he had scouted around that morning for a drop of the right stuff from one friend, and a full bottle from another. He'd been lucky, and what a blessing, for he knew that Phil in his present state would much prefer a drink in the peacefulness of their home than in the noisiness of a strange pub. Gradually, as the Johnny Walker took effect, so too did the cloud of depression drift further into the background. The lights were back in his eyes again, and his conversation was once more back to normal. He was back to the limit, the whole ninety per cent, the self-imposed outward and visible sign which made him appear happy and carefree; yet inwardly his weeping heart cried out incessantly for his one and only one, writhing in its sorrow, and knowing the hopelessness in those tears of blood that were his loneliness.

There just couldn't be any relief for him, even as they said goodbye, when Grace planted a swift kiss upon his cheek; that kiss was more like the stab of a knife than the gesture of admiration which she intended. Yet he said light-heartedly, just as they were getting into the taxi, 'Don't worry about Chesney, Grace, I'm big enough to look after him as if he were my little brother!' He paused, then added, 'As a matter of fact, I often do.' He chuckled in an easy-going way Chesney replied, 'To hear you talk like that, anyone would think you were my batman!'

This little bit of banter as those last tearful seconds ticked away was the best thing that could have happened. Grace laughed between the tears, then leaned into the taxi for that one last kiss.

'Take care of yourself, my love,' said Chesney, 'and keep your chin up.'

'I will, my love,' she answered, 'and God bless you both and keep you safe.'

In less than sixty seconds, the gulf before they would see each other again was already stretching out before them like eternity; she would be like millions of other wives, mothers and sweethearts, hoping, praying and knowing the dampness of a pillow far into the night; while he would be going out into the unknown, where often in the heat of battle the thought of home would be the farthest thing from his mind, but in the lull which followed, his heart would cry out for all that was near and dear to him, and he would know the bitterness of sharing loneliness.

There were two reasons why it felt good to be alive when they awoke the next morning; the perfect spring sunshine was a joy all on its own, and almost to the last man they couldn't say goodbye to the dreary place quickly enough. The joy of setting forth to find new pastures and more pleasant surroundings seemed so exhilarating, but a few hours hence they would realise just how foolish they were to anticipate anything which lay before them. It was the unknown that stretched out before them, total and unexpected, not only in the hours remaining of this beautiful day, but in the weeks and months that were to follow.

By eleven o'clock they were in full marching order and on their way, sometimes marching along untouched streets, where life went on as theirs had done before this deadly war had claimed their liberty. But they only had to make a turn to the left, or one to the right, and the grimness of total war would come face to face with them. Mountains of rubble lay on both sides, and the once clear smooth road nothing more now than a dirt track.

A blessed house, nay hundreds more, lay in ruins, where no longer would the joy of a child's voice ring, nor the soft, almost silent delight, when whispered words of two people in love had fashioned bliss. All that was over now, the blessed house, nay hundreds more, were blown into dust as far as the eye could see, but the cry of joy, and whispered love, were hand in hand in eternity.

Those heaps of rubble, stretching much too far from the pitying eye, had been bombed, blasted out of this world. People whose only thoughts were of precious life had found an everlasting tomb just where they stood, or where they crouched in fear and prayed.

What reaction went through their minds as the men passed this desolation, no one knew? It would have been one of horror, shock, or a will to win the war at all cost; most likely it was all three. However, scenes like these were about to become commonplace to them. Worse than that, they were destined to be a part of their daily lives for the next two weeks. It was only when the message had travelled the whole length of the column that they realised they had entered Canning Town.

Canning Town had had more than its share of unwelcome attention from the Luftwaffe. The amount of desolation they had seen so far had been frightful, but even that seemed a pinprick to the vast area of emptiness up in front and on the left. Getting closer, they saw that this great expanse was fenced in with barbed wire, all eight foot tall, and a foot or two wider than it was high, while soldiers patrolled outside and within, guarding the hundreds of troops already there.

Was it a prisoner of war camp? was their first thought. No... they were only a matter of seconds away from learning the truth, for this was where they would spend their last remaining days upon their native soil. There was nothing else for it; to accept their lot was the only way forward, and with the inborn tradition of the British army, they set about the task of making the best of what seemed hopeless. First came the job of levelling the rubble before the tents could be erected, then it was a case of helping each other, for there was no soft earth here to knock the tent pegs into; the ropes were strained out and anchored by the weight of large chunks of brickwork, of which there were a multitude.

It was a fantastic scene of desolation. Only three pubs, empty ones, stood on an area as big as a small town.

'If we have a few nights sleeping on this, we'll be able to sleep on the side of a mountain after,' said Chesney.

Phil laughed as he replied, 'Even the fellow on the bed of nails would turn his nose up at this!'

'That's a fact,' answered Chesney, 'and don't forget the daytime, there's nowhere comfortable enough for a fellow to take his ease; if you walk around you're in danger of tripping over anything from a seven-pound brick to a hundredweight of shapeless rubble.' Then, with a whimsical chuckle, he went on, 'Rubble, rubble everywhere! I wonder what Grace would say if she could see us now. Think of it,' he said as he let his mind wander, 'we're so near, and yet we might just as well be a thousand miles apart, for there's not the slightest hope of letting her know where we are.'

'Looking at that wire, and the way the outside guards order everyone to keep moving who shows the slightest sign of lingering, I should say there's not an earthly hope,' added Phil.

But although this was the case with Chesney, (though it was nothing short of a certainty that Grace knew the place existed, allowing for the way news travelled from one friend to another), there were a few of the troops, perhaps twenty or so, whose wives or girlfriends would stop mostly on the other side of the street and wave, two or three times a day. Perhaps a packet of cigarettes was thrown over occasionally, and whatever could be gleaned in the way of eatables; and a few, either the smart or the lucky ones, were able to exchange a few precious words, and that was only when the guards were preoccupied at some other spot of the fence. But gradually, as long as there was no danger to security, they were allowed to buy bottles of milk, soft drinks, or ice creams; mostly over the top it would come, and back would go the money, and never once did they witness a disaster.

It was the wonderful good nature of the East Enders that struck Phil most of all. He just couldn't imagine being brought up in these sordid surroundings, with nothing else than a lifetime of hard work to look forward to. But they must have been a breed apart from most men, endowed with an inborn cheerfulness and a willingness to share what little they had. It made a mockery of the dinginess around them and the struggle that they seemed to accept as a part of life. Life to them meant the enjoyment of every minute they could call their own; life was for living, helping, and that meant giving, so there was not the slightest thought of counting the cost of the multitude of bottles of beer, cigarettes, or anything else which they thought would relieve the boredom of the men beyond the wire.

'Can you catch, mate?' was always the phrase of those who risked throwing goods over the top, while some, with the help of a guard, would push the item under the wire by means of a long stick, until it reached the eager grasp of those on the other side.

Boredom turned out to be their worst enemy. Sometimes there were a few bouts of boxing, and on two occasions one of the celebrities from the West End gave them an hour's entertainment; other than that, it was a short letter to write with nothing new to write about, or a game of cards, and after that, it was only watching the people go by, and time dragged by endlessly.

Chesney would sit there, hoping and half expecting to see Grace suddenly come round the corner on the opposite side; whether his thoughts were on the past, present, or the future, only he knew. Phil kept his vigil too, but with a difference, he knew for sure that there would be no one for him to come suddenly round that corner, who would put a light to the present, and bring back to him a yearning for the future. All he had was his everlasting memories of the past, memories that have given him the whole world in one hand, and almost destroyed him with the other. Joanna was forever in his thoughts, and the gulf of a year had only served to make her memory more sacred to him.

The tears still fell whenever he entered that private world of his own, but there was no bitterness now, no asking the reasons why; for some time now he had accepted the feeling of being alone inside as the price of his grief, a grief that had brought him to the realisation that even though she was gone, they were never parted in every sense; for she had taken far too much of him away with her, making it impossible for a love as strong as theirs to be severed for all time, and to leave no trace whatsoever.

Committed at Last

Except for the boredom, and the difficult ground on which their days and nights were spent, the men realised just how lucky they were. Not once during their two weeks' stay on that island of rubble were they confined to the cramped shelter of their tents through rain of any sort; if they had, it would have been absolute misery; to have been bored and uncomfortable was one thing, but to have been half drowned as well would have been the last straw.

Those two weeks ended in the same glorious sunshine as they had begun, and on 1st June they marched out and turned left towards the docks, the only difference now being that each man carried his pound's worth of Allied currency on his person, a sure sign that the reality of combat was not too far in the distance. To these men, who were trained and in the peak of condition, and more than capable of eating up mile after mile on a hundred marches, it seemed that they had only stretched their legs before they were filing up the gangplank of the SS *City of Canterbury*. She was a fine ship of some twenty thousand tons and, according to her crew, had a record second to none. This was their new home, but for how long? The answer to that could only be in the lap of the gods. Once again they would make another step towards their destiny, for in the evening sunshine they lifted anchor and made their way down the estuary, only to anchor once more off Sheerness. There they would wait again, but at least they had a change of scenery, and something level to walk on.

All ships have a character of their own, and the feeling on this one was one of well-being and excitement, and as an extra blessing, there was a canteen which sold almost anything they needed; it opened at 7.00 a.m. This suited Phil and Chesney admirably. The first morning was the pattern for the start of each day that they would be afloat; up at 6.30 a.m., so that they were all spruced up by a little after 7.00 a.m., then up to the canteen where they would enjoy that early cup of tea; and from then until breakfast time, it was a leisurely stroll around the ship.

By the fifth day the novelty of their surroundings had almost exhausted itself; the trouble wasn't boredom now, it was restlessness. Out here on the water, life seemed so peaceful, and they couldn't remember the last time they had heard the wailing of a siren; yet there were many more ships like theirs, just waiting, and, like themselves, sitting ducks if the enemy had been strong enough.

But as the sun went down, dimmed by the thickening atmosphere over the metropolis, unknown to them, their fate, and the fate of thousands upon thousands more, had already been cast into the melting pot of total war. This would be the last sunset they would see over their homeland for the remainder of the year, and for some it would be the last for all time.

The next morning the sound of unusual activity could be heard, and as the early risers washed, shaved and got ready for the day ahead, the only topic was whether the show was really on, or about to start. Little did they know that the answer to their questions would be provided very soon. Even that early cup of tea was going to be delayed this morning. Not a man moved, not a sound was heard, as the announcer on the seven o'clock news told of allied landings along the coast of Normandy. The men were transfixed, intent, and more than a little degree fascinated. This was it, this was what they had been waiting for; but, even as they listened, they tried to picture in their minds the scene of battle at the first shock, and how the lads were doing at that present moment.

What brought them back to earth wasn't the end of the news. For suddenly they could hear the throb of mighty engines, and the feeling of vibrations tingling throughout the ship from end to end, reminding them that they were on their way, and were even now already part of the great struggle that they had been trying to visualise a few moments before.

By five o'clock, on the starboard side Dover could be just seen in the distance, but on the port side a great blanket of smoke screened them from the enemy, as the destroyers rushed here and there, making sure that those in their charge would pass this danger spot as safely as possible.

But it wasn't those long-range guns which occupied their thoughts. Everything except home was forgotten as one voice led them into the only appropriate song for the moment. Soon the entire company were singing 'There'll be blue birds over the white cliffs of Dover' with all their might, a song which at that time was immortal to them. Eyes might have been shining, and voices clear, but those words, and the sight of old England gradually fading away in the distance, showed the inner thoughts on each man's face. No doubt Chesney was thinking of Grace, but poor Phil was never before more desperate than at this moment to come through this war all right just for his son's sake. Jamie would need him more than ever once this war was over. And who could tell, he himself might find more comfort as the years went by, by watching the sweetness and beauty of the one who had been his whole world grow once more as their son grew, and bloom as perfectly as it had before.

The next morning, though they searched as far as the eye could see, not one trace of land could be seen on either side. The rest of the convoy was still with them as before, and the escorts were as busy as ever, searching and probing.

There was nothing to cheer about concerning the weather; it had already rained a good deal during the night, and the flat, dark grey ceiling above didn't seem to promise any improvement for the day ahead. Yet all this, and the fact of not knowing just what they were going into, didn't seem to dampen their spirits one bit.

Just before ten o'clock a grey smudge could be seen in the distance, and it was to that smudge that they were slowly but surely going forward to; hardship, weariness and death lay before them, but not one would have taken a step backward as the unknown grew closer.

Then came the order to get ready, and as they all filed on deck, each man surrendered his kapok lifesaver with torch attached to one of the crew.

'Pity,' said Chesney, smiling, 'could have done with one of those, made us a couple of lovely pillows.'

'More likely to get worn out as an elbow rest than one for

your head,' answered Phil with a chuckle, as one of the destroyers came in close and wished them 'Good luck and good hunting.'

As they drew closer, it wasn't only the land, which could be seen quite clearly now, that held most of Phil's attention. His gaze was more heavenward than to the earth. For directly above that coastline, as if separating the sea from the land, that dark blue blanket suddenly ended in a long straight line, just as if it had been sliced along the edge with a giant razor, and on the other side was clear blue skies as far as the eye could see.

Part of him watched the battleships sending their red-hot message of death to an unseen enemy, while the other part wrestled to keep his eyes fixed on the skies. He wondered was this an omen, these beautiful blue skies in front of them? Was this a sign that this great venture, which they were already committed to, was going to end in final victory? Or was there something special for him? Did it mean he would be going back to Jamie all right? For that he would be eternally grateful; but afterwards, there was nothing for him that could make his life worth living. Jamie would be his one and only joy. In that respect he was probably alone on the ship; for him there would be no letters with that special kind of love to ease the strain of battle, and to help him look forward to a life of happiness once it was all over. There would be no dreams of loving arms and tender lips to ease his pains of loneliness; he was alone, desperately alone, for he had given his heart once, and that once was for all time.

It had only been a few moments that he had let his thoughts wander, and what a feat that had been with all the noise and excitement going on around him, for now there were ships, large and small, near them in their hundreds. It was a sight no one could believe without seeing it in reality. He felt for the first time in his life that he was a part of history, just one tiny word on a single page somewhere; for it wasn't only that they could see, but they could feel history in the making.

For the first time speed was now essential. The tide had already been on the ebb for some time, in fact, too long for the crews of small boats who had to ferry all those troops as near to the shore as possible.

Chesney and Phil were in the first wave down the scrambling

nets, timing their jump perfectly as the landing boat came up to meet them on a four-foot swell. Someone's rifle took its last plunge to the bottom of the sea, but that was the only casualty. The sea came up a little more than waist high on Phil, but on the shorter ones it was almost up to their armpits; their only fear was in case they waded into a shell hole, but no one did. They reached the shore safe and sound, and glad to be on dry land.

Before them, dotted about here and there, could be seen the grim evidence of that first assault, those who in one mad long rush had tried to get away from the bareness of the beach, and had not quite made it. They lay where they had fallen, each a grim reminder that right had at last come to grips with evil. How tragic, and almost unbelievable was the thought that went through Phil's mind. To think that only yesterday they had been in the full flower of youth and manhood... Somehow it didn't seem right to him, it looked as if it depended on the luck of the draw, and that was a slim shield in wartime. Then he had a horrible thought. If things had worked out differently, he could have been one of those lying there, with all those preparations, all the hopes and fears, all come to an end at the outset.

Suddenly something caught his eye, something which seemed to draw his attention and hold it against his will. It wasn't the sight of someone's white lifeless hand that had slipped from the cover of the gas cape which brought his own world of sadness back in an instant; it was the golden ring around the third finger, a ring almost like the one his own true love had placed upon his. Pain, or some unconscious fear, compelled him to look at this own ring, and for those few moments his only concern was for his own weeping heart. How he would have loved to have torn that gas cape away, and to have given that young face all his sorrowing sympathy, but his thoughts turned to the man's other half, the living half, to whom that gold band was still a symbol of love and happiness. What was she doing at this moment? he wondered. How would she stand up to life once she had learned that she was alone? His heart went out to her, knowing that she would be anxiously waiting, hoping and praying. But she would soon be sorrowing; hers would be another life like his, and she'd be only too willing to let the world go by, without taking more than a token part in its joy and pleasure.

In those few moments the burden of his own sorrow was forced into the background, with the fallen victims of battle around him; his heart was full of pity for all those whose lives would soon be like his own, the ones who were left, living, yet with nothing, or very little, to live for; for they too would soon know the dread of facing each night, and the endless desperate urge to hide during the day.

Scenes like these, and worse, were ones he would often experience in the coming time, and even as the weeks and months went by, when the toll of war would stamp itself in some way or another upon every man jack of them. No matter whether it were their own lads or some from another unit, or even the fallen foe whom he saw in their last peaceful sleep, the bulk of his sympathy was always for those unknown faces who flitted across the screen of his imagination. They were the wives, the children and the not so young – the innocent ones. These people always bore the brunt of this human sacrifice in war, the ones whose lives, for good or ill, would be suddenly shunted on to a different path. Always he prayed that he would be spared for Jamie's sake. The thought of Jamie growing up without a mother or father was something that he daren't dwell upon, and he pushed it as quickly as possible into the background. He just had to come through this war all right. To watch Jamie grow up, that was the only task that life had left for him; to see him grow into a man, and old enough to hold the reins of life in his own hands.

Even though he was a countryman, three months in and out of action had left Phil very much wiser. Far too many familiar faces had disappeared during the fighting on the beachhead, and the helter-skelter race through France to the liberation of Brussels. He had always prided himself that he knew the countryside, but being a front-line infantryman for the best part of those three months had sharpened him tremendously. It was not only making the use of every bit of cover, no matter how small, but you always had to try to put yourself in the place of the enemy; taking an unnecessary chance made all the difference between life and death. The loss of all those familiar faces was a heartbreaking thought, but he had one thing above all to be thankful for. Chesney and himself, though a little weary, were at least fighting fit, and as far as possible, had always remained side by side, both in and out of action.

There was much to talk over when the letters arrived, for Grace would always put a note in Chesney's letter especially for Phil, telling him about her wonderful times at Spring Farm, and some of the sayings and doings of young Jamie; mostly she would finish with something along these lines:

> He's a wonderful sweet boy, Phil, and I'm always put on my honour not to forget to send you a big kiss from him.

It was the same with his own letters; there was so much in them which interested Chesney that they were never at a loss talking over the joy that peace would bring. But it was the scrawly bits which Jamie wrote at the bottom of Penny's letters which touched Phil most of all. Those few short sentences, partly guided by Penny's hand, told him in his childlike way that 'he missed his daddy and wanted to see him very soon', but there was never a mention of his mother.

He would have given the whole world just to be able to clasp his son to him at any one of those moments, but the pain, the awful pain when he thought of the future, and the sure knowledge that the worst was yet to come... How could he hope to satisfy his young son's fantasy for a mother who was no more? He was not only helpless, but even hope would have bordered on the impossible.

However, that wasn't the only sphere where the worst was yet to come, for what they had endured already had been definitely uncomfortable, being half choked with dust and the never-ending stream of sweat that blinded the vision, and saturated every inch of clothing that touched the skin. But that would be pleasantly bearable to what he could foresee in the not too distant future, another three months hence, if they were spared. They would be thinking of Christmas, but how much freezing wind, seemingly endless rain, and of course snow, would they have to drag their weary existence through, before the birth of a new spring brought a little comfort into their primitive lives?

Still, a whole week's rest on the outskirts of Brussels had given them a new life, and a batch of replacements arrived to fill the gaps left by those who had been wounded, or left behind to claim their little bit of France.

Nine Days of Sunshine in Winter

Now they went forward once more, on and on, right to the tip of the arrow, the barb which couldn't quite split the enemy ranks and bring relief to the men at Arnhem. These were hard frustrating days, for they got so far and no further, with neither side seeming to have that little extra strength to push back the other; so it was trenches and foxholes once more, and the possibility loomed of a sniping war for a long time to come.

Slowly and dangerously the weeks went by, until just about the time when they would be preparing for the season of goodwill in normal circumstances. Then came the rumour, a wisp of smoke from a source no one knew, which burst into flame and ran like a bush fire along the whole length of the front.

It was leave – they were going on leave! How their hearts were gladdened and their eyes shone at the thought of a few days at home, a few days of heaven that would blot out this hardship and loneliness. There was even greater joy when it became official, yet even in their awful plight the men could still hardly believe it, for this greatest thing of all had come so unexpectedly. But there was just one thing which didn't work out quite right for Phil and Chesney; for them, like so many others who had fought side by side and had shared the good and bad as only brothers could, the fickle draw had given Chesney 22nd January and Phil 5th February. It was a pity, and they were both disappointed, but there was nothing they could do about it; all they could do was to take that extra bit of care, now that here was something definite and wonderful to look forward to.

Christmas came and went, and with it not only the disappointment of not going on leave together, but the first hint of snow had threatened on several occasions, and already the biting wind chilled flesh and blood as it swept across the lowlands completely unchecked. Yet they, and those around them, still laughed and joked in their typical British way in the face of all these hazards; for these were men whose daytime hours were a mixture of all things which made life only just bearable, leaving only one phrase as they strained with ear and scanned with eye during their vigil in the blackness of the night; *Hell, absolute hell.*

Every one of them must have asked himself a thousand times, *Why wasn't I born into an age when wars were something which were only talked about in the comfort of a room around a blazing fire?*

But it was not only here that life had its hazards; in the recent letters Chesney had been getting from Grace, reading between the lines it was obvious to him that the V-bombs were, if anything, more nerve-racking and devastating than half of the bombing before, as they came with very little or no warning at all, day or night.

'If only the old folks would leave London, Phil, I wouldn't have the slightest worry then. I get a much worse feeling inside when I think of home than when we are on our way back into the line, for then I know there's no alternative.'

Phil patted him on the shoulder, knowing that nothing he could say would alter anything. As long as Grace was in London, Chesney would worry; there was just one way out, only the one, and the old folks wouldn't take it.

Then, in the final letter he received from Grace before going on leave, came the best bit of news that he could hope for, and he read it out to Phil.

'The colonel, Marie-Ann, Penny and, not forgetting young Jamie, want us to spend as long as we like at Spring Farm, in fact everything is ready and waiting.'

Whether it was the look of surprise on Phil's face, or the matter-of-fact way he said, 'Just the job,' that made Chesney ask, 'I suppose you're in up to your neck in this, aren't you?'

Phil laughed, saying, 'We just couldn't let you and Grace spend half of that precious leave down some cramped and stuffy shelter; besides, they're looking forward to seeing you both, and Jamie has got all sorts mapped out for you already.'

'You're the best pal any fellow could wish for,' replied Chesney, thrusting out his hand.

'That's what pals are for,' answered Phil, grasping a hand as cold as his own.

'I know you would do the same for me if you were in my place.'

No doubt those precious ten days of leave went by far too quickly for Chesney, but for Phil it was just the opposite. Seven of them were spent in the line, and what made every minute seem like an hour was the snow. It had threatened for so long, and at last covered the earth to a depth of six or more inches. If it had been the sticky type, which once it was down, there it stayed, it wouldn't have been so bad; but this powdery stuff gave form to the wind, one moment billowing like an earthbound cloud, and the next rushing on like the spray of an angry sea, which found every crevice, no matter how small, from the neck down to the feet.

Yet not for one moment in these awful conditions was the war forgotten, nor was the resolute enemy they faced treated with familiarity or contempt. Conditions like these were merely a hindrance to desperate and well-trained men, and there were plenty of those on both sides, so the war went on, and not the slightest chance could be taken without paying a high price for it.

Chesney returned, absolutely full of his few days of heaven, and he never ceased to thank Phil for their wonderful time at Spring Farm; there were messages of love and good wishes from all, but there was always that feeling of deep emotion when Chesney told him all the things about young Jamie, and how much he had grown since the last time he had seen him. This only made the time drag even more for Phil, knowing that his son was counting the days almost as desperately in his little way as he was himself.

But like all things, the day which he had longed for, finally arrived, and was just as cold, icy and bleak as the two preceding days. More than one lot of snow had fallen since that first thick carpet of soft light powder, thus making the journey to board the train anything but a quick and easy one. Time after time they were almost thrown from their seats as the truck lurched over ruts of frozen snow, sliding from this side to that. But who cared as long as they were going home? Even the day and night on the train, with the awful sore feeling of being a prisoner on a slatted seat, never dimmed the excitement for one second as they wound their way down towards Calais.

The crossing was rough, even for the time of year, but that was not the only discomfort, for the boat was almost as tightly packed as a tin of sardines.

Phil didn't exactly envy a sailor's job on a boat like this. He wasn't scared, but it was the feeling of helplessness, of being only half aware of oneself or one's identity, that bothered him. It was like being partly in a void, knowing that the gates of heaven were not very far off, if the elements or the enemy should strike that fatal blow in the darkness which enveloped them.

The thought that they were heading for the target area of the V-bombs and rockets never occurred to him, and even if it had, it would never have taken away from him that wonderful feeling as his feet touched the soil of England for the first time in months. Life suddenly became reality again, a reality which took him back to the time when he was around eighteen, when the world was a peaceful, beautiful place, and all its joys and happiness were there for the asking. He daren't let his thoughts dwell on the greatest moments of his life, when the other half of his heart was with him, when his world was not only worldly, but when all things were graced by a touch of heaven.

He took a close look at his watch in the dimness of the train compartment. How the time dragged! Would they never reach The Junction? The thought kept going round and round in his mind. It was already an hour past midnight, and it seemed ages since they had left London, so long in fact that even though he had heard that The Junction was the next stop, there were times when there was that shadow of doubt – had they gone straight through? *No*, he told himself, it was only his impatience to get home as soon as possible, and above all to see his son.

Fortunately he had made use of the few minutes to spare at Paddington. The colonel had been overjoyed at hearing him on the phone. *Yes, he would be at The Junction to meet him, no matter how late he was.* And now at last, with the gradual slowing down of the train, he knew it would only be a minute or so before his feet would be once again on familiar ground.

All the pain and discomfort of those weeks of snow, mud and biting winds disappeared almost completely out of his mind, as the colonel welcomed him with a warmth usually found only between father to son. It was like old times. Home, and all he held near and dear, were only a matter of a mere twenty minutes away; but as they groped their way down the platform in almost complete darkness, the picture that was chiselled on his memory for all time was far different from the one of the moment. Then the world was at peace, and he was walking towards a beautiful lone figure in blue, whose hair glittered like burnished gold in the sunlight. He wondered, *how he'd known at that moment that here was the only person who could possibly give him a life and love far beyond his wildest dreams, a heaven on earth, a heaven which would go on forever.* He felt grateful for the darkness, for even the colonel didn't suspect those tears of sorrow, which were blinding him more than the pitch black surrounding them. Phil shook his head, little realising that one tear fell on the exact spot where she had stood, and another exactly where he had been stripped of all power of speech and thought as he had gazed down at Joanna's angelic loveliness for the first time.

He wondered, now, how far had he seen into the glories of heaven through the mysteries of her eyes. That was one thing he would never know, never able to fathom out; but what he did know was that the he had fallen hopelessly in love with her in that split second. She had disturbed every tiny fibre in his whole body, so much so, that even now after a year and a half without her, he was still as hopelessly in love with her as he had been when they had shared their earthly paradise together. The loneliness was something which he knew he could never have borne without the blessing of young Jamie, but, even here, it was ironical that fate showed him no sign of mercy, for Jamie was so much like his mother in looks and in so many ways, that every thought, sight, or sound of him always increased the pain in his heart and the gap in his life. She was, and always would be, his one and only one; the thought of another woman taking her place in his arms was abhorrent to him, for those few brief years of perfect love were years when every moment shone like a star in the blackness of the night, and he knew that nothing in the future must tarnish those cherished memories, which were priceless to him, otherwise he would be left with nothing.

All this, the fullness of his life as well as its emptiness, took only a few seconds to flash before him, and it was obvious that, even at this late hour, the colonel was in the sort of mood where a moment's silence was out of the question. Having been a soldier in the Great War, there was so much he wanted to know about; then there would be something which Jamie had said, or about the work on the farms.

Time and distance went by so quickly that before they knew it, the gateway to Spring Farm loomed dimly in the darkness, and, as yet, they had only touched the fringe of almost a year-long parting.

Penny and Marie-Ann were still waiting up for him. Their welcome hugs and kisses, and the tears of joy that ran down Penny's cheeks, were more than a gentle reminder that they had missed him more than he realised. Everything was ready for him; he had a quick bath and change before taking his choice of all the lovely things Penny had prepared for him, and of course his homecoming had to be celebrated. But first and foremost he made a silent entry into Jamie's room.

Penny, who had gone up before to run his bath, came in as he was kneeling by the side of Jamie's bed.

'What do you think of him, after almost a year?' she whispered.

'Wonderful,' he answered, 'and much more like Joanna than the last time I saw him.'

She noticed the break in his voice over the mention of her name. 'I knew you would say that,' she told him. I always think the same when I see him asleep each night, and yet in the morning, you will see that there is a good half of you about those tender features.' She paused a moment, and added, 'it's strange, but to me that is how it always is.'

She placed her hand upon his shoulder, saying, 'Now, you hurry and have a quick bath, because I for one can hardly wait to toast your homecoming.'

Phil got up and, leaning over, gently kissed Jamie for the second time upon the forehead. Then those kind arms, which had so often cradled him through his childhood years, now caressed him as tenderly as she had then, knowing that he was desperately more in need of her comfort and understanding in this, his moment of inevitable heartbreak. There he was, home with all that was dear to him in the world, where overwhelming joy abounded one moment, only for utter despair to take its place in the next. And for the first time in months, over and over again in the torment of his mind, he asked himself, why he had been blessed with a love so deep, so pure, so wonderful, where the sunshine of togetherness had been all so heavenly and beyond his comprehension, then in a flash had it snatched away from him, leaving him totally lost and almost alone? He knew he was no longer on the right side of those gates of heaven. He was on the other side now, an outcast, committed to spend the rest of his life without his one and only love; why, oh why, did he have to lose her? Oh God, how he missed her...

What was it that brought him out of the soundest sleep he had had in a long, long time? Was it the fact that it was already light and the winter sun was casting its light a few inches from his face? Or was it the strangeness of a comfortable bed and the unfamiliar sounds which unavoidably came up to him from the daily chores below?

No, it was nothing quite as ordinary as that; it was young Jamie. This was the fourth time he had crept into his daddy's room, and three times he had crept out again. But this time the irresistible longing to see his daddy awake had kept him standing for a full five minutes by the side of the bed. Not once during that time did his eyes stray, even for one second, from that sleeping face. Mostly they were transfixed, gazing on those peaceful motionless lids, his stare trying to bore right through them, willing them to open, while his own twinkled with expectancy, and were ever on the brink of bubbling over at the first sign of success.

Before his father even had time to realise that he was at home, there was one mad rush and Phil was smothered. This was the start and the pattern for nine whole days, when only during the times of school and the hours of sleep would they be out of each other's company. This was the start of another episode, when a young son now looked to his father for the way to the first rung on the ladder towards manhood. Phil was the shining light in that young life's world, the one to play with, the one to watch and always the one to follow, and, becoming more fatherly as the days went by, he became utterly lost in the joy that his young son wove around him; so much so, that it was only now and again, when he seemed to come back to earth, that he realised how the joy of his son would make it so easy to let the rest of the war and all its troubles go by, without even a second thought. But Jamie was young and needed him now. What was in store a few short years ahead, when their paths of life forked in different directions? He daren't think about it.

So far this was the happiest he had been at Spring Farm since Joanna had been taken from him, and only in the solitary silence of his own room each night did the fleeting heartaches of the daytime came back to him in a mighty flood. For no matter where or what his eyes beheld during the daytime, there was hardly one square yard which didn't hold a memory of those happy years, times when they had walked hand in hand, or with arms around each other, or had chased across the fields in hay or harvest time, when her radiance and her love had never ceased to enfold him, and her angelic beauty had fanned him like the softest breeze. Always he had been left wondering, wondering why he had been singled out to be blessed with all that she was, and why had fate caused them to meet in the first place. He knew quite well why he had fallen hopelessly in love with her, but why had she returned his love in equally the same measure? They had, in the form of a perfect love, found heaven on earth, and yet, almost unconsciously at first, from the moment that his world had collapsed around him, when the sorrow, the loneliness, and the darkness became unbearable, when the turmoil of his mind clamoured out for the end, not counting the light that was young Jamie, one more tiny gleam had struggled desperately to the surface. Through the remembered love and joy of those few brief perfect years, through the pain which stretched out ahead – who could say how far? – that little gleam, a faint ray of hope, a split-second thought now gave its message more clearly, for only now was he aware of all that it implied.

Theirs was not only the love which he had known, and now pined for, but theirs' was an infinite love, whose present pain was only a pinprick to the limitless joy which once stretched out beyond. But there was one thing which still bothered him. Providing he got through the war all right, would his weeping heart find comfort enough in only the memory of those happy years? Would he be strong enough to go on living for Jamie's sake, to go on waiting? Or would everything once again become unbearable, when each day he died a thousand times, and what was left of his heart shrank even more? He didn't know, and he was no nearer to finding the answer by the time these few days of happiness came to a close.

Trouble Strikes Behind Both Lines

For Phil, the train had gathered speed all too quickly; the picture of Jamie still waving back to him from the arms of his grandfather would be as fresh in his memory in the months ahead as they were at this moment. As he settled into his seat, he thought of all the happiness those nine days had given him. He hadn't had much time to brood with a buoyant son like Jamie around, and he was grateful for it. One after another, the events of the last few days flooded back to him; there were hosts of them that he would be thinking of to the end of his time, but most important, they would help to keep him going in the immediate future. But there was one thing he still couldn't understand. On his daily visits to Joanna's' grave, he still couldn't feel that she was near, or there at all.

It was this thought which brought to the forefront what Jamie had said to him only a few minutes ago at The Junction. He had sad in an ordinary voice, 'Give Auntie Grace the box of eggs from me when you meet her at Paddington, and tell her they are from my own hens, and God bless you my daddy, and come back to me soon.' Then, lowering his voice to a whisper so that no one else could hear, he went on, 'And give my mummy a big kiss from me when you see her, and tell her I am waiting for her, won't you Daddy?'

He had answered, 'Yes, my love,' and he could still feel how grateful he had been for the hustle and bustle around them, for this was the first time Jamie had mentioned his mother in over a year. It was one more thing the future would have to take care of. He felt safe from that angle at the present, but one day the hard facts of life would dawn upon Jamie. It would be another time of sorrow and dread he'd have to face up to, and console his son with his own heart broken beyond repair. He shuddered at the thought.

As they'd arranged, Grace was waiting for him just beyond the barrier at Paddington; at first sight Phil thought how tired she looked, but the message from Jamie, plus the box of eggs, instantly spread a look of joy over her face.

'Bless him, and thank you. You know I miss him more every time I leave, for we have such fun together,' she said, with eyes shining.

It was the same when Phil enquired of Chesney; her eyes sparkled as he remembered them when they had all been together.

'He's quite all right, he says in the letter I had this morning, but he misses both of us,' she answered, and then continued, 'I'd gladly change places with you, Phil, at this present moment. I'd give anything to see him either tomorrow or the day after.'

Phil did his best to cheer her up by telling her that they might all be having another leave in a couple of months. What else could he do – even though he was certain there wasn't the slightest chance of it happening?

However, he had plenty of time to spare before catching his train, time enough to take Grace for a meal, one which was out of her reach on wartime rations, something to remember, something to make her reluctant sojourn in the city a little more bearable, even if only for a day or two.

She had enjoyed herself, he could tell that, for her normal ever-ready smile only slipped when in the course of conversation either of them referred to anything in the immediate future. Somehow he formed the impression that if only she could wish a year away, she would be satisfied; he wasn't exactly worried about her, but Grace clearly wasn't at her happiest. Yet those precious minutes had ticked away far too quickly. He thought, he had plenty of time, but there was hardly a minute to spare by the time they had found a taxi.

He had her letter for Chesney, and several messages as well to remember, but for the moment all was pushed into the background, as his one and only concern was catching the train. The platform was crowded, and Grace would have lost him if she hadn't clung to his arm as they fought their way forward. The chance of finding a seat had disappeared at the start; it was a gap in the crowded corridor Phil was looking for. Almost two-thirds of the train they covered before finding one, and without a second to spare, for the whistle had already gone, and the green flag was up. He felt her hand slip from his arm as he jumped aboard. He dumped his kit and turned around all in the one movement, his hand was already out to wish her goodbye and the words were on his lips. But Grace was not there, she had vanished. He leaned out as far as he could as the train started to move, searching for a hat of a bright green shade, and suddenly he saw her; she was on the outside of the crowd and seemed in a hurry. Whether she looked to the right or left he didn't know, but she certainly didn't look back, of that he was sure.

To say he was dumbfounded was putting it mildly, for even in his mind he could not find one tiny reason why she should have left without saying goodbye. This was not like Grace, the Grace he had heard so much about, come to know, and to form so high an opinion of. He was sure she would have told him if there had been any trouble at home she couldn't cope with. He had always been so sure of that; he just couldn't imagine her not seeking his help or advice if she needed it, anything rather than let Chesney worry more than he was already doing.

However, it was too late for him to do anything about it, he was already on his way, and quite fast too; a journey on which he would ponder for most of the time either on what Jamie had whispered to him at The Junction, or the strange and irrational behaviour of Grace. One was a secret for his own heart alone, a secret which stirred the very depth of his emotions every time he thought of it, but he cherished it; he cherished the innocent belief that could only come from someone as young as Jamie. But Grace was another matter; he dare not tell Chesney what had happened. That would only be one more source of worry for him. He would have to hold this as another secret, one not to recall, but to put in the back of his mind as far as possible.

Waking from her fitful sleep was fate – untouchable fate, unseen and so unpredictable. Was there at last a hint of impatience as she shuffled the next piece of the jigsaw towards its proper position? On one side was Phil with so many things he didn't know the answer to, and on the other, fifty miles northeast into Germany, was a village, the home of Fritz, Eva and their beloved Chrysta. Upon it descended the largest number of no-goods that the German High Command could possibly gather together. Fear swept the village like a pestilential wind, for these were not like the other soldiers who had stayed in and around the village before, these were the worst of the SS, whose self-imposed ideology was that nothing and no one should stand in their way, and what they wanted, they took. Now every man had his own private fear, yet strangely the fear of every one of those SS was one and the same; it was their Commanding Officer, the Sturmbannführer. That was the name that they called him officially, but whispered among themselves, even to them, he was known as the 'evil one'. Over six foot he stood, over six feet of cruelty, evil… and an uncontrollable lust for women.

It wasn't only those whose homes had been taken over who prayed for deliverance, the whole village did. And all the while fate, smiling icily, knew that there would be four whole days of dread and fear in front of them; four whole days of torment before peace would reign once more; four days before their tormentors would journey on, finally coming to the edge of no-man's-land, where opposite them would be Phil, and the rest of the men in his regiment.

But before that time, almost the whole village would be enduring far worse treatment than they would have received at the hands of a conqueror. Fritz and his farm were one of the exceptions; perhaps it looked too bleak and desolate, with the snow still deep over most of the ground. But his and Eva's worry was as great as anyone's; they could have no peace of mind from the time Chrysta left for work in the morning until she returned in the evening. The radio factory was on the other side of the village, and there was no other way she could come and go except through the main street, which was now the focal point for this dreaded band of ruffians.

What happy years they had been for Fritz and Eva! Every one of the twenty-three had brought them some new blessing in the person of Chrysta. She was their life, their sun, and the stars that twinkled merrily, and if she had been their very own, no greater joy and happiness could she have given them. Often as she helped in the fields, Fritz would pause and watch her working happily away in the distance, and always he would ponder over what Eva and himself had talked about so many times. For twenty-three years they had been the sole possessors of someone who was dearer to them than life itself, a girl whose beauty and charm had gradually ascended to the very peak of feminine perfection. Through the carefree days of her childhood, she had been desperately loved and understood, and was loved just as desperately now, as she took each step up the dizzy and dazzling stairway of womanhood. But they didn't understand that part of her now; girlfriends they knew she had in plenty, but boyfriends were another matter. She seemed to stand alone and aloof, with not the slightest desire to mix with the opposite sex in any shape or form. Yet in all that time, neither Eva nor Fritz could pluck up courage to ask her why. Somehow they could always sense that there was that something different about her, something which set her apart, so that in their eyes she was definitely much higher than they were. That was why they could never ask that question; they would have trespassed into her inner soul, seeking an answer which, if she could tell them, they knew they hadn't the right to know.

Two of the four days went by without Chrysta meeting trouble of any sort, but on the third day, just as she was passing the grocer's on the way home, around the corner and in a hurry strode the evil one himself. Whatever the importance of his mission, it was instantly forgotten as his evil eyes took in the picture of grace and charm walking towards him. It was a blessing that it was bitterly cold and Chrysta had her headscarf on, for this hid not only her golden hair, but most of the dazzling beauty of her face. Otherwise, he would have lost what bit of reason he had, and as he had done to so many others before, he would have done his evil best to take her completely. As it was, he barred her way, saying in a repulsive tone as he did so, 'Ah, Fräulein, you're just the one I've been looking for to keep me warm in bed tonight!'

Chrysta didn't answer, but she acted like lightening, giving him a sharp hard kick on his right shin, then ducked under his arm as he was about to grab her, and was gone before he even had time to turn around.

With so many of his men in the vicinity, he was sure some of them had witnessed the way he had been thwarted for the first time. He held back his seething rage and the urge to pursue her and teach her a lesson, but he couldn't resist walking slowly after her, just far enough to see her turn into the tree and shrub-lined drive towards the farmhouse.

By the next morning, Chrysta had almost forgotten the episode, thinking to herself that it was just one of those things which could only happen once in a lifetime. Yet how could she even dream, after all those years of peace and perfect happiness, that the hand of fate was once more pointing in her direction?

The daily routine of the three of them, she at the factory, and the two people she only knew as her mother and father, went on the same as usual; but there was one member of the household whose behaviour became stranger as the afternoon wore on.

Rex, through age or accident, had now become Rex VII. He was four years old and as human as any dog could be; only when there was a warm sun to lie in did he condescend to spend any of his time outside the front of the house. But today, for more than an hour before Chrysta was due to arrive, he took his place out there, sitting as rigid as a sentinel and with a fixed stare in the direction of the road. The only semblance he gave of being a living thing was when the biting wind swept his fur in all directions, and even then he was motionless.

By the time Chrysta turned into the drive, she had already congratulated herself on her trouble-free journey, but she had hardly left a quarter of the drive behind her, when from behind the largest tree strode the evil one himself.

'It's no good trying to run this time,' he hissed, 'whenever I've wanted a woman – *any* woman – I've always had her, and I'm going to have you now, and you'll get extra tonight for what you did yesterday!'

Chrysta knew it was no good retracing her steps. There was only one way out of this terrible situation, she just had to get past him somehow. The evil one was only a few feet from her now, his anger and his evil intentions were marked by flecks of froth in the corners of his mouth, and the look upon those warped features sent shivers of horror down her spine.

Suddenly and impatiently, he lunged to grab her, but as before she acted like lightning, letting out an awful scream as his hand almost grabbed her. Somehow she was past him; she was in full flight and he ran after her.

From the moment her scream had rent the air, Rex was on his way. Not down the middle of the lawn did he go, but behind the little low hedge on the right. The inborn instincts of a thousand years were in the forefront; he knew the element of surprise was half the business of victory and survival – that was what his ancestors had handed down to him. The evil one was gaining now, only another yard or two and he would have her, when suddenly, and just as silently, something hit him in the rear like a thunderbolt. He was tripped into a rolling, shapeless heap, almost winded, and deeply grazed on hands and face.

Rex stood over him, watching every move, as the evil one came slowly back to reality. Eyes met, and dog became man's equal, fearless and ready to die no matter what the odds, as long as the issue was the right one. Slowly the man's hand started to slide down towards the revolver, but before it had reached halfway, Rex was on him in a frenzy of teeth and muscle.

The picture which greeted Fritz as he hurried forward with his shotgun at the ready could only have had one conclusion. Hands and arms would have been bitten into a helpless shapeless mess, leaving the man's throat wide open.

'Rex! All right, Rex!' he shouted.

Rex stood back, but his gaze never left the hand on the side of the gun. One false move by the evil one, and he would have attacked again without question.

'So this is the way you fight a war is it, trying to molest girls who don't want anything to do with you?' said Fritz. 'If I had been working in the barn on the other side of the house, you would have been dead now, for I couldn't have got here in time to call Rex off! But you'll die for sure if you try to molest my daughter again, for I'll put both these barrels right through you.'

The evil one had never been at such a disadvantage before, but even so, the hatred in his eyes gushed up to exploding point, and the foulness of his language grew more unprintable with every word. Getting shakily to his feet, he dabbed the blood from his hands and face with a handkerchief.

'Now get out of here,' said Fritz, 'and remember my warning, leave my daughter alone.'

For a full thirty yards, Fritz watched the evil one amble slowly towards the road in silence. Then around he turned, and, shaking his fist, he shouted, 'I'll teach your defiant little daughter a lesson yet, and I'll get you and that dog of yours in a different way!'

The next morning, whatever fears they had for Chrysta's safety, or she for her own, were unnecessary, for the news reached them that during the night the evil one and those who cowered at his command had moved on their way towards the front. So those four days of fear had ended, and the tranquillity of the last twenty-three years settled over the village once more.

The dark clouds returned in the second batch of mail since Phil's return from leave. Grace hadn't been to Spring Farm for her usual stay, neither had she written to Penny. Penny was worried because of the V-bombs in London, worried for Grace's safety. But there was no need for Phil to hide Penny's letter from Chesney, for as he glanced up over the pages of his own, he could see that Chesney had some bad news. All colours had drained from his face, and the only expression there was one of dazed bewilderment.

'What is it, Ches?' he asked, hurrying over to him.

'There's nothing left,' he whispered, handing Phil the letter.

It was from a cousin of Grace's. A V-2 had landed far too close to all that he loved; it was just desolation.

'Nothing left,' he whispered in his daze, 'nothing left…'

Phil did all he could to comfort him, even drawing on all the experience of his own sorrow, but at the same time he knew there was no measure of tenderness in a touch, nor kindness in a word, which could penetrate the desolation and darkness which they now shared together. They now had a common bond, something which made the rest of their lives more of an ordeal than a pleasure; only poor Chesney was worse off, he didn't have someone like Jamie to hang on for.

Poor Grace, Phil thought. Was it a premonition of impending disaster that had made her unable to face him to say goodbye? He knew now that was the only explanation possible.

The End Suddenly Becomes the Real Beginning

One month passed, and once again came a time when there would be very little chance to ponder or worry over the past, and the future was something too far remote to even contemplate. Only the present mattered now, not tomorrow, nor ten hours hence, not even one hour; only that vital second in front, which was the difference between this world and the next. For once again they had begun the offensive, pressing forward against an enemy who was just as determined to stop them as they were to go on.

The evil one, and those whom he held under his rule of steel, knew all about fighting. They had gained valuable experience in the art of offensive and defensive fighting during their two years on the Eastern Front. But nothing they could do could possibly stem the advance of forces who never seemed to lack anything, be it weapons, vehicles or simply manpower.

Sometimes they would hold on to a certain position as if every man would die rather than relinquish another inch; while at others, due to the weight of shells, bombs and those terrifying rockets that rained upon them, it was impossible for them to do anything other than surrender miles of their homeland in a matter of hours.

So with only two more days before the month of April ended, one side was still retreating, and only a shadow now of its former self; and the other side was still pressing on for nothing less than total victory. But on both sides, the sight and the shadow of death, the weariness, the lack of sleep or even rest, was clearly visible on each man's face. Bleary eyes looked out from expressionless faces; arms, legs and bodies were ready to crumple, craving for that intoxicating wonder of sleep that would take them into oblivion in a matter of seconds, if only the chance came.

Yet there were still a few more days to go, a few more days when all that's assembled in the human frame would be driven right to the limit of its endurance.

Their objective, and what fate had determined would be their last one, was that peaceful village of Niendorff, a peace that would fade for four whole days, as the noise of battle and its instruments of death filled the air above. Niendorff – that tiny speck in space, where three and twenty years before a lone bright star had come to light the earthly path of an unknown child, with its heavenly light.

How different it is now, as the battle rages all around, and the stubbornness on each side only adds to the weariness on the other! But for Phil and the others, there was one thing that kept their spirits up, even in situations such as this. There were always the rumours, mostly false so far, but this one fired a little more urgency into all they did. They had heard that once the village was taken, fresh troops would take over the fight, leaving them to have a well-earned rest – a real bit of heaven, if only it was true this time.

2nd May, fewer and fewer men opposed each other on each side, and many times a day Phil offered up a silent prayer for the safety of Chesney and himself; he knew the war must be in its last throes of death and destruction, and he didn't want to die or lose Chesney at so late a date. That would be worse than dying in the heat of battle some three or four months ago, when peace and thoughts of home were pushed into the background; not like now, when peace must be only days away, and home leave a matter of weeks.

They still endured the weariness, even though they had snatched a few hours' sleep during the night, and as they now waited for the order to advance, it was hard to imagine what peace was really like, as all hell was let loose once more.

Shells by the dozen screamed overhead, aircraft bombed and strafed on a broad front a couple of miles beyond the village, and the tanks were manoeuvring into position.

At last it was time to go, and each man's life was balanced on the hand of fate, as the firing from the opposite side grew as fierce as ever. Somehow the distance between him and Chesney grew wider as they, like the rest, made the most of whatever cover was in front of them. The line and flight of mortar bombs made him edge well over to the right, but several times he looked to see how Chesney was, and was satisfied. For soon he would have to commit himself to a fifty-yard crawl to a clump of trees. He started out, and arrived there in one piece, but only just.

Was it the weariness or the heat of battle that had numbed his brain? Didn't the sight before him, that little red house, which nestled among the trees, bring something all-important back to him from out of the past? Had the din of battle drummed the voice of his loved one completely out of his mind? He had seen the house and was crouched against it, and still nothing registered. Would Phil pay the penalty for not remembering those words, those solemn words of warning that had been spoken as Joanna lay beside him, uttered in a voice and tone not quite of this world?

'Beware, my love, outside the little red house among the trees.' That had been her first warning, only to be followed by, 'Take heed, my love, as you cross the humpbacked bridge and turn right.'

The chances of him even seeing the humpbacked bridge seemed very remote, unless he remembered and took cover, for he had been spotted by two Germans with a machine gun. Was he to die without even knowing it? For he had not the slightest idea that a gun was trained in his direction; but at that vital second before the first bullet left the barrel, something pushed him swiftly forward and sideways through the open doorway of the house. A hail of lead sprayed the full length of the house, some even through the doorway, but luckily none found their target, for Phil had ended up sprawled across the floor at an angle which had given him ample protection.

His first reaction was to look around to see who had pushed him, who had seen what he had failed to see and had saved his life; but there was no one there, he was utterly alone except for those who were his enemies, and he couldn't spare the time to ponder over that, for he had a job to do. The inside of the house was like all houses that had been looted and ransacked. Furniture lay broken and upside down, and the floor was strewn with something of everything. He crawled halfway across the room on his way to the other door. Papers and books slipped in different directions under his weight as he moved forward, but he had no wish or time to bother about anything other than that machine gun outside. But even so he paused, and looked around to make sure he was safe from that direction. Satisfied, he was about to start moving again, when the book on which his right hand was bearing slipped. He was almost spreadeagled. His face couldn't have been more than an inch or two from the floor when he recovered himself. However, in that split second, a brilliance dazzled him so much that he had to shield his eyes before he could look at it a second time, and see what was lying there before him. Cautiously he peeped between his fingers; he could see quite clearly now where the brilliant light had come from, but how had the reflected light from a six-pointed golden star half blind him? For the sun was still shining on it through the open door, and he could stare at it with hardly a blink now. It was about two and a half inches in diameter, and its chain was of the same precious metal; the few seconds which he beheld it were long enough for him to know that he had never seen gold of such lustre and beauty before. He gathered it up, carefully placed it in his pocket with his field dressings, and then once more started on his way.

He carried two grenades. One would be enough, he thought, as long as he was on target first time; he scanned the foreground in front of the open door from a kneeling position, then, crawling out of sight, he stood up and took his helmet off, so that it wouldn't show round the corner before his right eye took in the situation. Yes, there were two of them; they must have felt sure they had finished him off, and were busy firing bursts in the direction where he reckoned Chesney should be. They were about fifty yards away and made a difficult target. It was no good trying to lob a grenade into those trees, it would have been like trying to knock the wickets down from the boundary. This time he would have to be spot on, there'd be no second chance.

Inwardly, he felt sure he wouldn't let Chesney down. Hadn't he on countless occasions thrown a cricket ball with pinpoint accuracy from much further than this?

Phil yanked the pin out, took one more peep, then stepped into the open and threw the grenade with all the skill he could muster. He was on target, absolutely dead on, for he heard a mighty clang as the grenade caught the nearest German on the side of his helmet. It couldn't have touched the ground before it exploded, leaving a silence from that one spot that stretched on and on.

He crawled forward to see if they were merely wounded, but both were beyond all human aid. *Poor devils*, he thought, but it was Chesney's life or theirs, and it would have been his own if something hadn't pushed him to safety at the very last second. Yet, in peacetime, they were probably fellows like himself, who'd rather risk their lives in saving someone else's than take one. All were a part of mankind, a mankind which now seemed hell-bent on destroying itself and causing as much suffering as possible. *Would man never learn?* he asked himself as he turned away.

Ten minutes later he slipped into the same ditch as Chesney, and the unmistakable look of relief spread over two tired faces, as two grubby hands clasped each other, as brothers would. They were together again, together so that each could watch over the other, for nothing must happen to them now, on this last run in.

The little red house among the trees had been left behind, obviously unrecognised, and as yet unremembered; but a hundred yards in front was the humpbacked bridge. Once again, would the sight of this stir the depths of Phil's memory? Would the din, the excitement of battle, yes, and still the weariness, crowd out the cry of her voice and her warning that was imprinted so deep within him?

Already they had had their orders, and each man knew his final objective; once over the bridge, Chesney, he and four others were to take the right-hand turn, then make their way to the farmhouse and buildings some three hundred yards away, almost beyond the village. There was just one snag at the moment. An enemy machine gun commanded most of the right-hand side of the bridge, so they would have to keep close behind each other and hug the left-hand wall as tight as possible. But they had one thing in their favour. Almost adjoining the bridge was a house; that was one bit of solid cover for them, if they got there, and from then on, each party would be on its own initiative.

'Our biggest danger will be crossing from left to right once we are over, but I'm sure we can make it,' said Chesney.

'We'll have a jolly good try,' replied Phil, and a smile full of confidence spread over their tired faces.

In five minutes' time they would be starting on their last day of actual fighting; in ten minutes' time, some among them would know no more, others would have fired their last shot, but would still live on; yet with their help, those who were left would carry their orders through to the last letter.

Two minutes to go, and by now Phil was one crouching step behind Chesney on the humpbacked bridge. They had gone only halfway towards the hump when a large-calibre shell landed a hundred yards behind them.

'Hope that was only a stray one!' joked Phil, above the roar of gunfire.

Once over the hump they went at the double. Bullets whined and spattered the wall and parapet on the right-hand side, but no matter how Phil tried to keep in line with Chesney, some unseen hand pulled him away until he was completely on his own, and on the side of the bridge which was under fire. How he wasn't hit at least a dozen times was only a miracle. He was running like mad, much faster than he thought he could, so fast in fact that his speed propelled him in such a wide circle round the corner of the bridge that in the process he missed the little low wall, his first bit of cover; but twenty yards on was a hedge which he reached before his momentum had slackened.

He was just wondering what unseen force it was that had pulled him over to the right-hand side, when he had tried with all his might to keep in line behind Chesney, and once again nothing clicked in his mind to bring Joanna's words to him.

But there was no more time for him to ponder, for with a roar like thunder the next big shell hit the house almost fair and square.

'Oh no, God, please not Chesney!' he cried.

He was on his feet in a second, and quite oblivious to his own danger, his heart cried out for all the lads; but his pal, the one who was like his own brother – it was unthinkable, it just couldn't be, they had come through thick and thin together, had faced death more times than they cared to remember, and now this...

He was almost back to the corner of the bridge, when one of

his officers on the other side of the road waved him away and shouted, 'You'll have to do your best, but don't take unnecessary risks!'

So once more he took to the cover of the hedge, and from what he could see of it in the distance, it seemed to stretch almost to the farmhouse itself.

He couldn't concentrate on anything for long; his thoughts kept going back to Chesney, worrying what had happened to him. Was he alive or dead, or badly wounded? That was the trouble, he couldn't know for some time yet.

He had gone about half of the way when suddenly he realised just how careless he had been. One second he was alone, or thought he was, and the next he was almost face to face with an old man sitting under a tree.

If that had been a German lying in wait, I'd have been dead for sure, was the first thought that raced through Phil's mind. Instead, the old man looked up and smiled at him. He had been trying to wrap a dirty piece of rag around a gaping wound just above the right ankle. A blood-spattered boot and saturated sock lay on the grass nearby.

Phil returned the smile. Then, as he looked at the jagged wound with blood still pouring from it, and taking it for granted that the old man didn't understand a word of English, he exclaimed, 'Oh, father, you are in a mess, but you ought to be safe at home, and not out here in no-man's-land.'

Was it his deep concern for the seemingly helpless plight of this old man that caused him to address this total stranger in this way? For he had never called his own father by that name; it had always been 'Dad', and so too with the colonel. Yet that was the name that would slip from his tongue each time the occasion arose; but what was also strange, was that it would be said so naturally and without him realising it.

If he'd had one surprise coming suddenly face to face with someone, he was definitely in for another, when the old man replied in perfect English, 'It probably looks worse than it is, my son, and my home is a long way from here.'

Quietly they had a chuckle together as Phil answered, 'And I didn't think you understood a word of English.'

As quickly as possible he poured water from his bottle, and with a clean handkerchief swabbed around the man's wound. Then, as he wiped the blood from the foot, he saw the mark of an old scar standing out large and white on the top of the instep.

Phil didn't make any mention of this, but as he hastily pulled the field dressing from its pocket, the star, the golden star which had been tucked so tightly beside it, came out as well, and flew a couple of feet to the old man's right, landing in a patch of dust, where it almost disappeared. The old man reached out and picked it up. For a brief space of time his hand was at full stretch, and in that time, which was no more than a flash, Phil glimpsed another scar on the back of his hand.

'I must say, Father, you have been in the wars!' he exclaimed.

'Yes, my son,' the old man answered, 'but it wasn't this one, nor the one before.'

'No,' said Phil, concentrating more on doing the bandaging than what the old man had said.

'No,' replied the old man, as he carried on cleaning the star back to something even better than its former glory.

'You're quite sure that's comfortable?' asked Phil as he finished his task.

'Quite sure, my son, and you have been very kind,' replied the old man.

'I'm only too pleased to think I came along and was able to help you; and Father, if you'll wait here till I return, I'll see that you get much better attention. Leave it to me.'

Just then the sound of automatic gunfire came from the direction of the farmhouse, and at the same time the old man held up his hand and said, 'It is time for you to go, my son. I shall think of you always and bless you, for you as well as I must overcome evil, before we can reach all that our hearts desire.'

Fifty yards further on the thought suddenly came to Phil that he hadn't got the star. Well, it didn't matter for the moment, he knew it would be the first thing the old man would mention when he returned.

The farmhouse was spick and span, and the last bit of tidying up around the barn and buildings had been accomplished. Fritz was

on the outside, Eva and Chrysta in and just around the house;
they had just finished what was to them a very late spring clean.
What with age, and Chrysta working in the factory up to a few
days ago, things had got a bit behind, but they were ready now,
ready for the British to come, ready for them to see just how clean
and tidy the Germans are.

The guns had been busy since first light. Shells had screamed
overhead on the way to an unseen target, and in the village and
beyond, man had pitted his craft and skill against his opponent.
But here they had gone about their tasks not taking much notice
of what was going on around them. Only Rex had done anything
unusual; he was behaving as had on that other occasion. He stood
as rigid as a sentinel outside the front door, and this time, as
before, no one had given the slightest thought about his strange
behaviour. What was he on guard for, why was he totally
oblivious to the noise of battle going on before him and the shells
screaming overhead, was mystifying when any other dog would
have been cringing under the table?

An hour went by, and it was now mid-afternoon. Fritz,
knowing that it was unwise to be working outside, had just joined
Eva in the sitting room for a rest. Chrysta, her chores done, with
not a speck of dust to be seen anywhere, was washing her hair in
the kitchen, she had just given it a final rinse and her groping
hand was on the towel, when suddenly and without warning, the
whole war seemed to have moved up to their very front door.

The vicious snarling that Rex let out as he bounded fearlessly
into attack was blood-curdling, but it all died in a breathless
whimper as a hail of bullets from an automatic gun almost cut
him to pieces. Whether it was the first or last bullet that was the
fatal one no one would ever know, but the fearless dedication of
Rex had carried him so far that his blood spattered the boots of his
assailant.

Fritz and Eva were out of the front door in a matter of
seconds. There, twenty-five yards away, with Rex dead at his feet,
stood the evil one the Sturmbannführer. Without a second
thought they both shouted, 'King Charles, King Charles!' as hard
as they could.

To Fritz, the evil one looked even more evil than the last time they had met.

'I told you I'd come back and get you and that blasted dog, and teach that daughter of yours a lesson! I'll teach her to be nice to an officer; look at your miserable dog now, that's the first part of my threat accomplished!' he shouted, like one possessed.

Meanwhile, inside the house, Chrysta had heard all, and she knew her likely fate if the evil one laid his hands on her. Quickly, she did what her mother and father had impressed upon her so often. In no time at all she was in the darkness of the hideout, kneeling by the little doorway, listening and hoping that they would be able to make their escape and join her. But her fears were about to become reality; she heard them both try to scramble through the doorway, then came a long burst of automatic fire, a cry, and the sound of two bodies falling on the hallway floor.

She closed the little door, and noiselessly slid the iron bar into position. She stood up, hardly daring to breathe, let alone cry aloud, but tears ran down her cheeks in a never-ending stream. So many times she had been in here for practice, now this was the real thing; she knew almost every inch of the hideout, even in total darkness. She could hear the evil one thundering into room after room, then upstairs, doors crashing open, and things being overturned. She was already looking through the spy-hole into the kitchen when he rushed downstairs and into her line of view. Through the kitchen window he could see the barn and buildings, and the leer which came over his evil face as he thought, *I've got her now, made her flesh creep*. He was so sure of himself that he dumped his automatic gun on the kitchen table.

Phil was going more cautiously now. He had heard the second burst of fire, so he was creeping and crawling and making the most of every bit of cover. The barn was the nearest building to him, but there were about twenty yards of open ground to get across; if it was stony, he would have to crawl, but if it was grass, he would make a dash for it and hope for the best.

It was grass, so quickly and quietly, he soon reached the lee of the barn. He was only a few yards from the back end, so, crawling those few yards, he made sure there was no danger coming from that direction. Everything was all right, there was nothing to worry about on this side of the barn, nor the buildings further on. He got to his feet, and, in a crouch, crept slowly and silently towards the end of the barn nearest the farmhouse.

The evil one had by this time searched all the buildings, but without success, and now as Chrysta looked out of the left hand spy hole, she could see him. But he wasn't all rush and haste, as before; now he was creeping silently.

She watched him leave the buildings behind and cross he space between them. Now he was going down the front of the barn and he went out of her line of vision, so, groping, she found the other spyhole. She watched him, and hated him more with every evil step he took. He had only another quarter of the barn's length to travel, when some other movement caught her eye. It was a figure in khaki, an *Englander*, and just about the same distance from the corner as was the evil one. Her heart stopped, for here were two giants on a collision course – but the Englander had a gun.

Nearer and nearer she watched them get, and with her whole heart she prayed that the Englander would be the victor.

Both men reached the corner simultaneously; their noses almost touched as each went to find out what was round the other side. Who received the biggest shock was not in doubt longer than a split second, for with a terrific left hook, Phil caught the evil one flush on the chin. The German went flying and so did Phil, due more to the awkward angle than the force of the blow. Both helmets left their headpieces and Phil's gun slithered yards away.

But that was a mere nothing, for in those few seconds, two thousand years rolled away without trace, leaving two warriors from out of the past, stripped of everything from the twentieth century, back to the days when might was right, and through each brain seared only one burning thought; the total destruction of the one who stood in front of him.

Within seconds, they were at each other like two wild animals; it was brute force and cunning all the way now, a total disregard for what was given or received, a disregard which sooner rather than later was bound to end upon the ground.

Chrysta, with her tear-filled eyes glued to the spyhole, prayed aloud for the *Englander*. First one man had the advantage, then it was the other's turn as they rolled all over the place. But now she prayed even harder, for the evil one was astride the *Englander*, one hand clawing for the throat, and the other about to aim a vicious blow into Phil's face.

Was the Englander weakening? This was the dreaded thought which flashed through her mind. 'Oh God, please give him strength,' she prayed.

In fact, Phil *was* weakening, but at the very last second before the blow fell, or the hand could get a real grip on his throat, from somewhere a surge of strength welled up inside him. Jerking his head to one side to miss the blow, he sent the evil one sprawling with a mighty heave.

But the evil one was up in a flash and aimed a vicious kick at Phil's head. If it had connected, Phil would have fought no more; but all animals have a survival instinct, and his prepared him for his line of defence even before the evil one had got to his feet. Swivelling quickly on his side, he caught that vicious kick on the bottom of his boot. It was action for him now, and calling on all his reserves of strength, he hooked his legs around the evil one's, and sent him crashing to the ground.

Now it was Phil's turn; it was his hand which clawed for the throat and found it, it was his massive fist which fell like a steam hammer into those evil features, a fist that went on pulverising them into a gory mess right up to the time that the last gasp of breath had left the body.

Chrysta desperately wanted to tear her gaze away from the sight before her, for every time Phil's fist came up it became more crimson than ever, but only when she saw the arms of the evil one go limp did she dare to go to her mother and father.

Five minutes it took Phil to come back to the world around him, and a few more while he put the helmet over that awful sight, and washed his hands in a rainwater tank. It was only as he was shaking the water from his hands that he heard a queer sound coming from inside the house.

Going back to where his gun had fallen, he picked it up and made ready for whatever he might find. Cautiously he crossed the kitchen to the half-open door leading to the front of the house. It was a queer sound no longer; it was the sobbing of a woman in deep sorrow.

Going into the hall, he examined the woman first; there was nothing any one could do here, he was sure of that, but with the man, there were the signs of a weak and spasmodic pulse.

Then, suddenly Fritz seemed to rally. His eyes opened, moving first in Phil's direction, then to Chrysta's head of golden hair and back again. With his last remaining strength he gripped Phil's hand with his left, and his right he gently laid upon that head which was bent so low in sorrow. Then, with the greatest difficulty, somehow he forced the words out.

'Were you in time, Tommy?'

Phil nodded, as once more Fritz's failing strength managed to turn his head in the other direction. A beautiful smile was upon his face as his flickering eyes beheld that head of golden hair, eyes that were not only full of earthly good, but all things heavenly as well, as they closed once more for the last time.

It was the end, for as Phil searched for a spark of life, it was only a second or two before he was sure that what he had hoped to find had gone forever. But now, as he looked at the still form of Fritz, and with all this tragedy still around him, the sudden realisation struck him that here was the second man who had spoken to him in perfect English in less than half an hour. It made him wonder.

However, it wasn't the dead who needed his immediate attention, it was the girl, still sobbing bitterly and so full of grief. Gently he helped her to her feet and his arms went around her to steady her. He felt awkward; having a girl in his arms was one thing he hadn't bargained for, and what made matters worse, she was crying too; now he would have to do his best to try to console her, but he didn't relish it one bit.

For a whole minute he just held her close and let her cry. He tried to think about Chesney, how he was and what would he say if he could see him now, for that head of fluffy golden hair was pressed close to his chest. Only the tenderness in his heart made it possible for him to hold her close and try to comfort her, as the sobs shook her from head to foot; only that tenderness made him hold her a second longer than he was bound to. For as soon as he thought she was capable of answering, he asked, 'Do you speak

English as well?'

A nod of the head, followed by a muffled 'Yes', confirmed that she did.

'Only you just can't stay here by yourself… Is there anyone in the village that you could stay with?'

The sobs had died a little now, but there was still the same amount of tremor in her voice as she gave that same muffled 'Yes', as before.

'Well, if you'll get a few of your things together quickly, I'll get you safely there somehow,' he said confidently.

He watched as she walked dejectedly towards the stairs, and saw the depth of sorrow in each step on that upward climb; he understood, for was not his own heart broken and beyond repair? He watched on as she turned the corner at the top, and even then it still hadn't occurred to him that as close as he had held her in his arms, when his heart had matched each tear which she had shed, when every sob had made him die a thousand times, yet she was still a complete stranger to him after all. For up until now, that golden hair had hidden her true identity.

Once she was in her room he got busy. Side by side he laid the man and woman, and did all he could to make them as comfortable as if they were still a living part of this world. Then, taking some coats from the rack, he covered them completely.

When that was accomplished, his thoughts went back to what was happening elsewhere in the village. How was that other war going on? Looking through the siting-room window, he could see that the tanks had already passed through and were disappearing into the distance; the village was theirs. Would he be able to have that long awaited sleep? That was his most burning thought.

He was still keeping a sharp eye on their side of the village as Chrysta came downstairs. He heard her footsteps stop as she took one last long look at her mother and father. The outside seemed to be his sole preoccupation even as she entered the room, but that was about to be shattered completely as she said, 'I am very grateful for the kindness you have performed, and I am ready now if you think it is safe to go.'

Crash! Something hit him like a thunderbolt, for the sound of her voice didn't stop short at his hearing sense but rushed on, on and on until he was utterly consumed by it, even after the sudden shock had almost paralysed him. He was dazed and felt weak as the last bit of his remaining strength seemed to ebb away with each beat of his heart, a heart that, in its confusion, didn't know whether to jump for joy, or to cry out in anguish.

For he had heard that voice a million times, prayed a million more to hear its joy again. Now, here it was, as if from that other world, and his broken heart was torn in shreds.

Somehow he turned around and a far greater shock awaited him as his eyes beheld her face for the first time. Were his eyes playing some cruel trick on him? was the first thought that trickled from the numbness of his brain. Was that perfect life together and the desperate longing for his lost love so great? So powerful, that at last it had taken control of his imagination? No, for no matter how many times he tried to concentrate or blinked his eyes, the vision before him was always the same, for the girl that stood before him was the exact and perfect image of his one and only love.

It was as though he had been turned into a pillar of stone. His face was blank and all the colour had drained from it; he was speechless and motionless, for how long he had no idea, but suddenly he could stand the strain no longer. Groping for a chair he flopped into it and buried his face in his hands.

Instantly, she was on her knees beside him.

'What is it? Have you been wounded?' she asked anxiously.

He didn't answer.

'Were you hurt in that fight?' she asked, even more anxiously.

He shook his head.

'Well, what is it? Please tell me, please,' she begged.

Slowly his hand went to his map pocket and withdrew the precious wallet, which he handed in her direction. She opened it and without hesitating exclaimed, 'It is a photograph of me!' Then, in the second breath she went on, 'And yet it can't be, for I've never had a dress like that, nor a double string of pearls… and yet the face is my face, and the hair is exactly the same also.'

For a few moments she was silent, then tenderly she asked, 'Is this your wife?'

Slowly, and with his face still buried in his hands, he unfolded part of his joy and the awful tragedy that was now most of his life. But before he had finished, Chrysta was well aware of the heaven he had known, and the desolation that he had walked through since his love had been taken from him.

She put her arm around his shoulder to comfort him, knowing all the time that besides her father, this was the only man's shoulder she had ever put her arm around. But the drama of the moment was so over-powering that little did she realise just how much love as well as tenderness was in her touch. She was being drawn towards him, hopelessly, if unconsciously, for everything about her other than words was shrieking out, 'Don't let him vanish out of your life, hold on to him, hold on!'

But the time was bound to come when unconscious thoughts were turned into words, for, just as they were preparing to leave, she said, 'Will you promise me something? If you get moved from the village, will you promise to come back and see me?'

He saw the tears in her eyes and the utter loneliness on her face as he answered, 'Of course I will... How could I go away and never see you again? If I did a thing like that, it would be like losing a part of my first love for the second time.'

She put her hand upon his arm, and with the suspicion of a smile touching her face, she answered, 'Thank you, that could be the only bit of sunshine that I shall have to look forward to.'

Going across the yard, he took her by the arm and shielded her from the sight of the evil one. It was the same procedure on the return journey; keeping out of sight as much as possible, and not taking the slightest risk. But he was in for a shock, for when he got to the place where the old man had been, there was not the slightest sign of him, nor the golden star either.

Well, that's that, he thought, but even so, he was more than a little puzzled.

He was just starting to move on again when she said, 'There's no need for us to go down to the bridge and up the road. If you think it is safe enough we could keep behind the hedge, it runs right up to the Schmidts' back garden.'

He smiled as he answered, 'It couldn't be better! That was the one thing I was a bit worried about, having to explain what we are doing together. Now there's no need for anyone to see us.'

Before five minutes were up, the back door was reached, and, taking him by the arm, Chrysta led him gently through the kitchen to the sitting room beyond.

The Schmidts were very old and looked at him with more than a little apprehension, but after a conversation of some length, all in German, during which the tears fell quite freely, suddenly he was ushered into a chair and a cup of steaming ersatz coffee was placed in front of him. These were friendly people, he could sense that; these were people with the same outlook on life as his own. He watched as the old man took his pipe and proceeded to fill it with some horrible looking stuff.

'Chrysta,' he said; he had heard the Schmidts call her that.

'Yes,' she answered, as a brief but beautiful smile covered her face.

'Tell Herr Schmidt I've got some better tobacco than that, only he must keep the tins out of sight because of the non-fraternisation ban; you know that really I shouldn't be here.'

She spoke to old Schmidt as Phil fished two tins of tobacco from his small pack. The look on the old man's face as he gave them to him was as though he was giving him a million pounds. This called for a real outburst from him.

'He thanks you very much, and no matter how long you stay in the village, you are welcome to fresh eggs at any time,' she translated.

There were smiles all round as Phil got up to leave; the old man held out his hand for him to shake, and he took it, and that of the woman too. But the smile on Chrysta's face vanished completely when she led him to the back door to see him go. There were tears in her eyes as she stood before him.

'You will take great care of yourself, won't you?' she got out somehow.

'I shall do my best,' he answered, feeling a bit awkward, then continued, 'I must go, but I am going feeling much happier knowing that you are among real friends, and never fear, I will keep my promise to you just as soon as it is possible. So keep your chin up, for I shall think of you often and pray for you in your sorrow.'

With his one free hand he drew her towards him, he held her

tight just to give her reassurance. Then he kissed her lightly on the forehead, and was gone.

She watched him out of sight, knowing that more than one little bit of her heart went with him. Fate had taken so much from her in so short a time, and she wondered, was fate going to give her back more in return, in other ways? The life that stretched out before her could now be one far more wonderful than she had ever visualised, a life full of love... but she would have to have him to share it.

Most of the Darkness is Swept Aside

There were more strange faces than ones he knew when Phil arrived back at the bridge. It took him a long time to find out what had happened to Chesney. There had been eight killed, double that number quite badly wounded, and as for Chesney, it was almost definite that he would lose a leg.

Poor Ches, Phil thought, *no wife, no home, no anything.* And what worried him most was how could he learn how he was getting on, and where he was going to live once he left hospital. It would take him ages to find out, and during that time poor Chesney might discover what another sort of hardship was really like.

He would have to see his colonel as soon as possible and get as much information as he could, for he could never let Chesney drop out of his life just like that; to him such a thing was unthinkable.

There seemed no respite from the duties needing to be done, no relief from the tiredness and weariness, and the hours stretched on. But when the time finally came for Phil to crawl into the tent for that overdue and long awaited sleep, deadbeat as he was, still his mind kept flitting over the crowded events of the last twenty-four hours. But no matter what thought came uppermost, or what mental picture flashed into his mind, all were soon dimmed or pushed into the background; for superimposed over all was the vision of a beautiful face.

She stayed with him as he drifted towards oblivion, and she brought him halfway back as he saw her lips move and utter those words of long ago…

'Beware, my love, as you cross the humpbacked bridge, and turn right.'

Only then did he remember the little red house, and the humpbacked bridge he had encountered that very day; only then did his thoughts struggle to find the answer as to who had pushed him to safety through the doorway of that little red house, and who or what had led him against his will, yet safely, over the humpbacked bridge.

But once more the desperation for sleep swept over him. He drifted on, unable to know and too tired to wonder. Then once more she brought him halfway back, and this time her vision grew as if she was really there in front of him, and the smile upon her face was one of sublime happiness, and once more she repeated words which he had heard before.

'I shall come back to you, my love.'

But the toil and hardship of the last days and weeks finally became too much for him to fight any longer. He drifted on to the end this time, so quickly in fact that in a matter of seconds he was dead to the world.

Yet for the first time in two endless sorrowful years, there was the suspicion of a smile around his mouth and a look of contentment upon his face.

There was one more thing that he hadn't realised or remembered, and that could be expected, for in a war hardly any soldier knew the day, let alone the date. The last twenty-four hours which had been so full for him was the fateful and all-important 2nd May.

Three days had gone by without the slightest sign of Chrysta, but on the fourth he noticed a lot of people dressed in black for what he guessed was the funeral of her mother and father. He kept a lookout, and from a distance he saw her accompanied by the Schmidts on their way to church. Her head was bowed, and oh, how he wished he could be by her side to comfort her.

This was the second time he had known three days to seem like eternity, only he was at a greater disadvantage this time. It wasn't just the difference on the social ladder now, but a High Command order which stated, 'No fraternising with the Germans.' He dare not risk that, for instead of being close to her, he would be charged and sent to some detention camp miles away, and not able to see her again for ages.

But fate was all too strong, and just as determined that war and all its implications would not keep them apart a moment longer. For on the day after VE day, the end of the war in Europe, what he had prayed so very hard for – just the chance to see her –

literally fell into his lap.

'Would you go around collecting fresh eggs in exchange for tins of meat?' the sergeant had asked him.

'Certainly,' he had answered, thinking to himself that of all the avenues he had explored, this one he hadn't dare dream of; yet this was the one, the only one that would give him the legitimate chance to see her.

He hadn't been able to find anything out about Chesney, and this alone had worried him more than enough; but knowing that someone identical to his one and only love was just up the road, yet so far out of reach, had even caused him to lose many precious hours of sleep.

Would he, if the chance came, gladly give her that little bit of his heart that he had left? He knew he could never give her that same depth of love that he had given his angel. But outwardly, he couldn't tell one from the other; there was not an atom of difference in looks, the way she spoke, or in her mannerisms. She was his Joanna in everything but name, and because he knew she couldn't be.

The angelic beauty of her face, and the sound of her voice, had haunted him almost every second for a whole week. He had thought of those words, 'I shall come back to you, my love', a thousand times. Was this the way that those words were meant to come to pass, that someone else would be fashioned in her likeness down to the very last detail, someone else who would gather up, and try to mend the awful mess that was his broken heart, to try and make the rest of his life before him at least a little more worth living?

So as he started out upon his egg-collecting mission, no one could point the finger of scorn at the happiness in his eyes, and the smile upon his face, for was he not going forward up that road to his only chink of light, to a light as yet so small, but one which, if it were meant to be a new life for him, would save him from a darkness that was so very slowly destroying him.

One dozen eggs he got from the second of the first three houses he called at, in exchange for two tins of meat. He then ambled on towards the Schmidts', little realising that in the last seven days, another lonely heart had eagerly awaited, yearned, and yes, cried a lot more desperately for him than he had for her.

He was only halfway up the path when the door opened. She stood there, and the smile upon her face was a mixture of relief, welcome, and a love that had blossomed to its fullest in the shortest possible time.

The sight of her loveliness, that familiar loveliness, once more brought him to s standstill, for those few brief seconds it was as if he were being blinded by a dazzling light, a light that for two long sorrowful years he had yearned for, but a light that was so very unexpected, and above all, so unbelievable.

That old and ever-ready smile was at its very best as he greeted her.

'We're really in luck's way, I was asked to go round exchanging tins of meat for fresh eggs, so as long as I make a success of it, we shall be able to see each other two or three times a week – that is, if it's not too often for you.'

'You know there is nothing that I have longed for more desperately, in fact that is what I have prayed for day and night for a whole week, first that God keep you safe, and secondly, although I didn't know how it could possibly happen, I prayed to heaven to bring us together soon, just as we are now.'

'Where are the Schmidts?' Phil asked, seeing no one else in the room.

'They are visiting friends just up the village,' she answered.

'It's been a terrible week for me also,' he said, 'a whole week of waiting and wondering, but now...' He got no further, the rest of the sentence died on his parted lips, as his eyes once more dwelt on the familiar beauty of that face before him.

Unknowingly, she had placed him in an awful dilemma. The joy and happiness of those wonderful years seemed to urge him forward and take her in his arms, but the faithfulness and sorrow of the last two indicated a much more cautious approach; she was all his Joanna was in one sense, but in another she could never be.

Only their eyes seemed capable of any physical movement, eyes which searched out one heavenly joy after another, for the rest of them were almost completely spellbound. In those lovely eyes he saw a heaven which he had known, and a greater part of that heaven was now within his grasp, if only he had the courage to take it. In his, she saw the same heaven, a heaven which was all so new, and oh so wonderful, a heaven which she had only glimpsed in a dream, a flash on the mind which had vanished almost as quickly as it had appeared.

They were now just one step apart. Would his courage fail him, or would he take her in his arms? Would be present her with a little bit of that heaven which would set the seal on a new life for both of them?

The breaking point had to come soon, and the step which he took forward had all the confidence which he could muster. Gently his arms glided around her and at the same time so did hers sweep over his shoulders, only to end in an embrace that was very little short of desperation. She was as fantastic as she was beautiful, for as pure, innocent and as unkissed as she was, she poured all those years of dormant love into a long, deep, breathtaking kiss.

However, it was different for him now, for somehow he just couldn't return quite the same measure as he had with his first love. Yet it was almost the same picture as the first time, for as he looked down at her, her eyes were closed and over her face was the same look of sheer contentment. Only one thing differed, she moved her lips as though she was tasting something exotic, something which she had unconsciously known before and was now relishing again for the second time.

Time after time they savoured the heaven that was each other, and time after time, just the joy of holding her would almost sweep those two years of darkness from out of his mind. She was not only the perfect replica of his Joanna in everything down to the last detail, but in this first kiss, it was as though she was beginning where his first love had left off.

But his thoughts were not allowed to wander any further, for out of the depth of her first taste of ecstasy, she suddenly whispered, 'How is Jamie, or haven't you heard this last week?'

'No, we haven't received any mail so far,' he answered.

'You'll let me know as soon as you do, won't you?' she said, opening her eyes and looking into his.

'Yes, I'll let you know, in fact I'll let you read them, for he always sends a special message in them for me.'

Five minutes later he had exchanged the amount of food tins for the eggs he needed, and there was no lack of pleasure on her face as he gave her a handful of boiled sweets and two bars of chocolate.

'For a girl in a million, or should I say a million millions,' he said, knowing that the latter was nearer to being correct.

'Oh, thank you, an almost forgotten pleasure,' she answered, turning her head so that her lips would once more come in contact with his. It was one more deep and lingering kiss, one more which broke the chains of being earthbound, and one more step towards the realisation that the earthly life could once more bloom again as long as they had each other.

She was a mixture of joy and sorrow as she watched him disappear from view, sad because so many things could happen which they had no control over. She shuddered as she thought that he could be a hundred miles away from her tomorrow, she dare not think about it. She would have to concentrate on the happier side, the joy of when they would be in each other's arms again, or thinking of each other, wondering, waiting, but always hoping. She didn't expect to take the place of his first love, but second best in his arms was a heaven far more wonderful than she had ever dreamed of. It had washed away those years of emptiness and waiting, and had smoothed her sorrow into something which was bearable.

Phil was her prince in golden armour, a knight who had overcome the evil which had sought her. He had brought unto her his loving tenderness and compassion, and by their first embrace, he had opened the door to a love which would know no bounds. For heaven had already decreed that theirs was a love which would last forever, a love which would still only be in the infancy of its infinite bloom, long after the light of the world had disappeared.

For the next few weeks, the situation just had to be endured; if the Schmidts were at home it meant a quick embrace as she let him in, and a minute or two longer when he departed. But long or short made no difference, for the hand of fate had already woven a web which would bind them ever closer together. Then suddenly the non-fraternisation ban was lifted. What joy – he could now whistle his favourite tune, 'Starlight Serenade', to let her know when he was coming up the road, while outside the beauty of the world was theirs to be shared together. They strolled the lanes, the fields and through the pine forest and she read his letters as he received them. But there was one dark cloud looming on her horizon; it was when he told her he would be going on leave at the beginning of August. She was overwhelmed with joy for his sake, but two weeks without him seemed to shatter her. Yet as the time approached a state of calm seemed to return to her.

'I want it to be a lovely long holiday for you, but I want it to go by as quickly as possible for me,' she said, snuggling closer into his arms.

'Long or short, I shall be thinking of you all the time, and you know I love you very much; that alone will help you a little over your loneliness,' he replied, kissing her.

'That is the most wonderful thing in the world, to know that you love me,' she answered, holding his face in her hands, while her eyes travelled from hair to chin; she seemed to be making a mental note of each tiny part of his face, so that she could picture him vividly, and imagine that he was always in front of her.

Desperately she loved him, and she knew that while he was away, her longing to feel the comfort of his arms, and her ultimate joy of a heavenly kiss, would be just as desperate, and probably more than she would be able to cope with.

So time slipped by, until it became their last evening together before he went on leave. He had managed to get old Schmidt some extra tobacco, a double ration of sweets and chocolate for his new love, plus the same for Jamie.

For the last half-hour they had been standing under one of the pine trees, talking mostly, but when their lips finally met, it was deep, deeper than he had gone so far. She was in her greatest state of ecstasy, and also inside, overwhelmed with joy, knowing that his love for her was a love that was lasting and real.

'I love you with all my heart,' she whispered.

'And I love you too,' he replied, holding her a little tighter.

'I shall have to steel myself, so that when you have another leave, I shall be able to bear it with more strength,' she said quite softly.

'Well,' he answered, 'if the war in the Far East is finished soon, I would probably be demobbed before I was due for another. The only worry then would be getting you to England – that is, if you want to come…'

Her arms tightened around his neck as she replied, 'At the moment, almost all of me is selfishly hating the thought of being without you for less than two weeks, so what greater joy could I possibly ask for, than to join you as soon as I am able?'

'I hope that is not the greatest joy you're looking forward to, I hope again that it will be the first of many greater joys that you and I will share together; yet that is the one thing which has caused me more anxiety than anything else these last few weeks. I have worried and wondered whether you could possibly accept what is left of me, whether I have the right to ask you what I have wanted to for so long.'

'We have very little time before we must part, and I know that I just couldn't stand the strain of knowing that I am still in the wilderness, and on top of that, not being able to see you for almost two weeks. Could you, or would you, in the not too far distant future, do me the greatest honour by taking my hand in marriage?'

She didn't answer, and because she couldn't, she clung to him all the more, and the unashamed passion on her lips transferred the very depths of her emotions until they seemed to sweep right over her. He felt the trickle of hot tears as they wetted his cheek, and the tremors as they shook her from head to foot, and he held her tight for a little while longer, before he spoke.

'Have I upset you in any way? Is it that you don't want to marry me?'

Her tear-filled eyes looked into his, and from her trembling lips came their first endearment of loving possession.

'Of course I do, my darling! Everything is so wonderful that I just can't realise that it is happening to me. What have I done to deserve all the joy which you have brought me? To know that you love me, and now the nearest thing to heaven that I have ever known – to have the honour of being your wife.'

Tenderly, he comforted her and dried her tears before he answered.

'Whatever joy I have brought you, you have repaid me a thousand fold. To me, you are like a light that draws me through the darkness. Where before there was no light, you have given me the will to stand up and to face life again, and my eyes are once more open to the wonders that are all around us. No, my love, it is what I have to offer you that will fall desperately short of what you give to me. Mine is the honour, and I shall try, try with all I have, to be worthy of you; for at the back of my mind I know, it is only because you as my Joanna was, down to the very last details... Can you still love me, knowing that that is the reason?'

'I have known that for a long time, my darling, I have known that whatever love you will have for me, most of it will only come to fulfilment through my own endeavours, yet my heart has cried out for you, ever since the day of sorrow when I thought my world was at its end. There we were, two lonely strangers, two sorrowing souls, yet in a very short time together it seemed that I had known you all my life, and I knew then that there would be no joy or happiness in the future for me unless I could be by your side for always. Since then my love for you has grown out of all proportion, so much in fact that its size and intensity dominates the whole of my waking hours, and beyond, for you are forever in my thoughts and in my dreams. It is not only that I am honoured to give you my hand in marriage, my darling, but I am privileged beyond all the joys of this world, knowing that you have chosen me to walk beside you through the years ahead.'

'Well, I am still greatly honoured and also deeply grateful,' Phil answered, as his lips found hers and sealed the pledge of their love, which at the moment was overwhelming on her side, but not quite so strong on his.

But fate, unpredictable fate, was smiling now, for was not their spoken bond of marriage the last giant turn of the wheel? It would turn again and again, no doubt, but only as a guide and never as a maker of their destiny. For as always the greater milestones of their lives would be in the hand of the 'power over all', while in between fate, that obedient servant of good as well as ill, would be daily administering whatever had been allotted to them in the years to come.

It took them a quarter of an hour to reach the house, another five minutes for him to say farewell to the Schmidts, and now they are out in the porch and in each other's arms, holding each other tight for the last time. Once again, he feels her tears wet his cheek, and for the first time he realises just how much of his thoughts, his hopes and his new-found life he was going to leave behind him.

Once again Phil comforted her. 'It won't be for long, my love,' he whispered.

'I know, my darling,' she answered between the sobs, 'but I shall feel so all alone without you, and my life will never start again until I feel the comfort of your arms, as I do now.'

'Well, try to keep the picture of this moment in the forefront of your thoughts, and keep your chin up just for me, darling.'

'I will try desperately my love,' she answered, then out of the blue she softly said as she still clung to him, 'You won't let Jamie know about me, will you, dear, for he is so young and it might be above his comprehension.'

'All right, my love, if that is how you wish it, that is how it shall be,' he answered.

But just as he was about to give her that last kiss, she whispered, 'And God bless you, my love, and remember you will be forever in my thoughts, for my home will be home once more to me, knowing that that face which has haunted me almost every minute for two long years, will soon be there again in reality.'

The last kiss was one that she would remember; he made sure of that. They waved as far as the moonlight would allow, and she watched on until the dark blur that was him vanished in the distance.

Overjoyed

Early next morning he was on his way; his route wasn't Calais to Dover this time, but the Hook of Holland to Harwich. He thought of all that had happened from the moment he had overcome the evil one; it was just like something come true out of a dream, and yet it was far more out of this world than anything he had ever dreamt of.

As each mile took him farther away from Chrysta, the more he struggled to reassure himself that anything as fantastic as this had really happened. Yet he could still feel the crush of her arms around him, and the silky strength upon those beautiful lips as she fought so hard to let him know how desperately she loved him, and at the same time to overcome her inexperience.

That, plus the vision of her face that was now a part of his world again, should have been enough; it was in one sense, but in another it didn't seem right. It didn't seem earthly; that was the part which he couldn't explain, and neither could he fathom it out.

He thought of home and wondered if Jamie was getting excited already; he also thought of Chesney – he still hadn't been able to find out how he was, or where. Back his thoughts went to home, and he wondered if he would be able to make them believe what he could hardly believe himself. It would be one thing for them to try to imagine, or to look at his first love's photograph and try to convince themselves, but it would be another thing altogether when they came face to face, Would they be as dumbfounded as he was, as shocked, as unbelieving, even when the proof was there in front of them? Only time would give the answer to that.

It was going to be a night crossing; at the 'gift shop' Phil managed to get a small bottle of perfume and two pairs of nylons; he was well pleased, thinking they would make her eyes sparkle when he returned. He slept quite well going over, but was more than ready to leave the ship when they docked around 6.30 a.m. On Parkeston Quay a wonderful bit of news awaited them, for the headlines on the early morning papers blared out, ATOM BOMB DROPPED ON JAPAN! His first thoughts were, If Japan surrenders, then I could be demobbed by January or February. There was only one dark cloud; when would she be able to join him? Anyhow, that was an obstacle they would have to face when the time came. Meanwhile, it would be just wonderful to get the fighting over.

In London he bought a couple of books and a model aeroplane for Jamie; his would be another pair of eyes that would sparkle, and oh how he longed to see him and hold him close again. All these months he had waited quite patiently; now it was only a matter of a few hours, and the longing to catch the first glimpse of him was growing more desperate minute by minute.

He arrived at The Junction at 3.30 p.m. He had been so sure that he would have to phone the colonel to pick him up that he hadn't bothered to lookout of the window as the train came into the station. But as he alighted, he saw the colonel further on up the platform, and with him was young Jamie. How his heart raced as he saw his son let go of his grandfather's hand and run towards him. He dropped everything and gathered him up in his arms in one big hug, and kisses flew in all direction.

'I've missed you so much, Daddy,' were his first words.

'It has seemed like years to me, my love,' answered his father, 'especially when I can see how much you've grown and how heavy you are.'

'This is the moment I've been looking forward to,' said the colonel, giving him a hearty shake of the hand and a pat on the back.

'Same here,' replied Phil, with his eyes shining more like they used to. Then he asked, 'How is everyone at home? I hope you've not overdone things just for my sake.'

'We're all right,' replied the colonel, laughing. 'Everyone's in top form – mind you I wouldn't say we look as fit as you, but then we're a little bit older.' Then he continued, 'We've had one bit of disturbing news these last few days.'

'Oh, what's that?' Phil enquired.

'The major is not at all well,' answered the colonel.

'Nothing serious, I hope?'

'I'm afraid it could be,' replied the colonel.

'I'm very sorry to hear that... What about Jane, is she at home?'

'Yes, she's at home. I see her most days; naturally she's very upset, but otherwise on top of the world.'

'Not courting again?' asked Phil.

'No, I was teasing her about that when she came over the other day and she said, "One bad dream is more than enough in one lifetime, I shall be far more choosy if there is a next time."'

That was about all the chance they had for that sort of news, for the rest of the journey was taken up with Jamie telling his father all about school and what had happened on the farms while he had been away.

Penny and Marie-Ann were not only overjoyed at seeing Phil looking so fit and well, but they were deeply grateful that the happiness on his face was much more permanent than it had been the last time they had seen him; his whole manner seemed much freer, and for the first time there was more than a suspicion of his old self.

Jamie was having more fun in that one hour than he had in all the time his father had been away, and in the days to come there would only be the odd thing which would keep them apart for any length of time.

'That would just about finish me off, all the chasing you two have just had!' said the colonel, laughing.

'Well, I must admit I'm a bit out of breath myself,' answered Phil, 'but it's all so lovely up here, and I must thank you for all you have done; you only need half an eye to see how well you have managed things.'

'I've enjoyed every minute of it, and I know I shan't look forward to going to Northwood one bit.'

'If and when you do go, it will only be because Northwood is calling you, and not Spring Farm kicking you out.'

'I know that, Phil, for here there's so much which seems to hold me, while back at Northwood, I'm afraid I have sadder memories rather than happy ones.'

'I understand perfectly, and that is why I want you to remember that this is as much your home as Northwood, and I should be very put out if your visits became fewer and fewer.'

By the time they reached the house it was almost Jamie's bedtime. Marie-Ann supervised the bathing and Penny saw to his eats and drink, but it was his father who had to pickaback him upstairs and read him a short story. Questions there were aplenty, but not once did Jamie mention his mother or refer to her in any shape or form, and yet during that quarter of an hour, his father saw him take several quick glances at her photograph by the side of his bed; it was as though he knew that everything would come right in the end, and that that end was not very far away.

Once downstairs, Phil asked Penny how long he had before supper was ready, only if there was sufficient time he would take flowers to the church before instead of afterwards. He had picked the best of what was on offer, and arranged them, as he knew Joanna would approve, but he still couldn't feel as though she was close to him. He might just as well have been kneeling at the grave of a total stranger, for all the response he got. Was it possible that all he had loved, all he had lost, had been spirited away from here, and transformed into his second love all those hundreds of miles away? He shook his head to bring his senses back to reality, for a concept like that was definitely impossible in earthly terms.

The meal was over, and now the four are having their coffee outside in the cool of the evening. Chesney – or to be more precise, the total absence of news from him – had been one of their main topics of conversation.

'I shall have to find him somehow,' was Phil's conclusion.

'Perhaps I'll be able to help,' remarked the colonel finally.

What had gone before was nothing to the drama that Phil would scatter around them, when he could find the right words to unfold the story which still left him spellbound. However, he had to start sometime, and luckily the right moment came sooner than he had anticipated, for he knew the longer it was delayed, the harder it would be for him to start.

So, drawing his chair round so that he faced them, he said, 'I hope you will be pleased to know that I have found a new girlfriend. Yes, she is German, but she speaks English perfectly.'

He then went on to tell them almost the whole story, and he saw the expressions on their faces change from relief at the start, then to horror, then to sadness.

'Now I will tell you the rest of the story. When I said I had found a new girlfriend, I was wrong. It is only God who could ever arrange what's happened, for it wasn't a case of me finding her, or vice versa; it could only have been the hand of God that guided our destinies so that we would meet, for I can truthfully tell you that if Chrysta – that is her name – walked through that doorway now and said, 'Would anyone like more coffee?' None of us would know the difference between her voice and Joanna's, for she is the perfect living image of the one we loved with all our hearts, in looks, figure, and even the same mannerisms.'

Tears welled up in his eyes as he went on, 'When I heard the voice that had been ever fresh in my memory for two long, lonely years, the shock was so great that to this day I couldn't tell you how I found the strength to turn around. But that first shock was only a fraction of the second; you can imagine what it was like to be suddenly confronted with the one you had loved, as if from the other side of the grave! Out of all the questions and answers that tumbled from the confusion of my mind, there was only one thing which I was conscious of from the start, namely that I, as strong as I was and had been for those two whole years, was now absolutely powerless to let this girl drop out of my life. Standing there, she was, is, and always will be, my Joanna in everything but name, and because I know that is impossible.'

He had hardly finished the last word when they were around him; there were handshakes, kisses and a hearty pat on the back from the colonel as he said, 'It's the happiest news that you could possibly give us, for it is what we have all prayed for, for a long time.'

'Life has to go on, Phil, and it's wonderful to see you looking so much happier already,' said Marie-Ann.

'When would she be coming to England?' was what Penny wanted to know most.

'I only wish I knew,' Phil replied.

But they weren't going to rest on that note, not as far as the colonel was concerned, for almost immediately he said, 'I'm sure this calls for champagne. Will you come and help me, Penny?'

They had hardly got inside the door when Marie-Ann said, 'If I told you that this is one of the happiest moments of my life, Phil would you believe me?'

'Really?' he answered.

'Yes,' she replied, 'we have all worried over how you would face up to life once the war was over, and now I can hardly wait to see Chrysta... or should I say, Joanna the second?'

Just then, with four glasses clinking on a tray, came Penny, followed by the colonel with one of his prized bottles, which he had brought from Northwood.

Standing, he filled the four glasses and handed them round. Then, raising his own to each of them in turn as they stood up, he said, 'To Chrysta, for I can't help wondering whether this girl is going to return to us most of what we have all grieved for.'

'To Chrysta,' they replied.

The next morning Spring Farm awoke to the sort of happiness it hadn't known for over two years; of course Jamie was his usual buoyant self, but snatches of song could be heard coming from different parts of the house. Summer was at its height on the outside, but a touch of spring had entered them all.

After breakfast, it was a quick tour of the two lower farms, then back at 11.30 a.m., to visit the major. It was quite true, Phil could see how ill he was but the major, being the major, and with a will of iron, left them in no doubt of his extreme pleasure at seeing Phil. But it was only for a limited time that he could keep his thoughts in focus, and he drifted off.

'He won't come round again for some time,' said the nurse, in virtually a whisper.

Jane, who had been in Tetstone when they arrived, now returned. How delighted she was to see him after so long, and he thought, *what a difference there was in her now, compared with her character before I had known Joanna.*

While the colonel and her mother talked in the drawing room, Jane took him by the arm and led him out into the garden.

'Wouldn't it be wonderful, Phil, if we could only turn the clock back, just to those days when the four of us were so full of happiness, that for a second, we seemed afraid that it was too good to last; but little did I think that mine would end so quickly, and the way it did.'

'Yes,' he answered, 'we have both known the joys of loving and the emptiness when there was no joy at all, but now perhaps life will turn again in our favour, and you, like me, may soon meet someone who will once more give your life a purpose.'

He then told her all about Chrysta.

She was silent for a few moments after he had finished.

'It's unbelievable Phil – exactly like her, you say, in everything?'

'Yes,' he answered, 'I'm sure even you who had known Joanna much longer than I had, won't find a jot of difference anywhere.'

Her eyes had a faraway look as she replied, 'It's not often, Phil, that one female will heap praise upon another, but even when we were at school together, and later on, I must have stated a thousand times that Joanna was the most beautiful, the most perfect, and the most sweet girl that could ever grace the face of this earth. To me she was something so rare, someone to whom mother nature had picked the very best of everything, and mixed them all into one.

Even though I don't doubt that you have told me the truth, I still can't imagine that it is possible to happen a second time. It's beyond me, for one; Joanna was a rarity, two can only be a miracle caused by the hand of God.'

'I know,' he answered, 'even now I myself am no nearer to the answer of how or why. I know everything I have told you is fact itself, but as soon as my thoughts start to delve below the surface, I become as baffled and bewildered as you are. I can only be thankful for what fate has put before me for the second time, for deep inside something tells me that I must accept the challenge of life again, and my duty lies to that end.'

In the days that followed the happiness at Spring Farm was at its peak. Jamie was in his element, full of energy during the day and out like a light each night. The glorious sunshine had given them a wonderful opportunity of spending nearly all their waking hours in the world outside.

Jane had been over for lunch one day and dinner one evening, while Phil had popped over to visit the major every day so far; he certainly wasn't any better, in fact, there seemed very little change.

The war in the Far East came to a sudden close, and on every face there were the signs of relief; for soon a husband, a father, a son or a daughter would be homeward bound. Gone was the fear of another battle to face on the other side of the world. Hope and the longings of the heart ran high, for the future stretched out like the early morn, when the first rays of the sun peep over the hill, before warmth touches the cheek and its message is known; when you know by the birds and you know by the sky that it's ushering in a glorious day.

That was the picture before the eyes of millions, for peace was here at last, a peace which had only been won by a terrible price in human sacrifice, a sacrifice which must never be dimmed before man's eyes, for if that day ever came, man would be treading a downward path and would never survive.

So time marched on until the morning came when Phil had to depart. He was more burdened with luggage going back than when he came; somehow Penny had mustered up all sorts of things, mostly those which she knew Chrysta hadn't even seen in years. Tears were not in abundance this time; the old dark clouds had gone and in their place was a silver lining, stretching out as far as their imagination would allow, and, for good measure, he would soon be back home with them.

All this time Jamie had never once mentioned his mother, but on the platform as he kissed his father goodbye for the last time while his grandfather held him up to the carriage window, he whispered, 'God bless you, Daddy, and my mummy too, and give her a big kiss for me when you get back, and tell her I want to see her soon, please Daddy.'

'And God bless you too, my love,' was all he had time to say, as the train started in motion; they waved as frantically as always until they could be seen no longer.

Only then did the full impact of Jamie's words hit him, just as on their previous partings. When there had been no mention of his mother in nine whole days, why, why should his young son choose the very last moment? Was it that this was the most vital time to give his message, so as to make sure that his father would remember, or was his young son one jump ahead of events that had happened so far away? He had no idea. But there was one thing he did know, he'd had a wonderful leave, and naturally his thoughts kept going over all the exciting times he and Jamie had together, and how he hated leaving him. But despite the heartache, no matter how painful, this was one parting which was of the greatest importance to both of them. For out of a few more months of waiting and longing, there would come the only chance of a new life for himself, and that vital mother love for his yearning son.

All through his leave, he had hoped and prayed that Chrysta had not known too much gloom and despair without him. However, he felt quite sure that she had known little else, for only now would her hopes and the light in her eyes rise and shine again, only now as each hour ticked away would her heart start to beat faster again, and only when she was in the sanctuary of his arms would her life start to begin again.

On arriving at Paddington, the thought of having any refreshment never occurred to him, it was a much more important mission that was on his mind, something which had been almost an obsession to him for weeks. So he took the quickest way by taxi to the same jewellers where he had taken his first love, only this time he knew exactly the ring he was looking for. He used one of Joanna's personal rings as a pattern for size, so that was no problem, but what worried him was he desperately wanted this second ring to be as nearly identical to the first one as his new-found love was to his lost love. After twenty minutes he had chosen the one that looked like the twin to Joanna's. It had one large diamond in the centre, with two smaller ones on each side, beautifully set in platinum. He was on top of the world as he waited the ten minutes for his cheque to be cleared; now the rest of the journey could take care of itself.

Exactly at three o'clock the next afternoon he arrived back at his unit, and before it was time for tea to be served, he had gone through all the preliminaries, bathed and changed, and enjoyed twenty minutes' chat with some of the lads.

At 5.30 p.m., he was on his way, his small pack slung over his shoulder, crammed to capacity. He was about to whistle their favourite tune to let her know he was coming, when he saw old Schmidt standing on the front path surveying the garden. The old man was so preoccupied that he was totally unaware of Phil's coming until he reached the gate. The ageing lights in the old man's eyes suddenly flickered into a flame as he saw and recognised his visitor; the quickening of his faltering step was just as though he was greeting his own son, a son who had been away for so long, and so far. Slowly, he led the way into the house. Frau Schmidt was sitting in a chair by the window. For the second time she called Chrysta, as Phil entered the room, and she pointed to the ceiling indicating that she was upstairs.

What seemed ages was less than a minute before he heard her hurrying downstairs.

'My darling,' was all she had time to say. With the Schmidts looking on and with her arms outstretched, she rushed into the ones that were waiting for her, in a desperate embrace.

There were tears of joy and thankfulness in her eyes as she looked at Phil and said, 'I'm sorry, my darling, I have waited desperately for this moment ever since you left me, and when you arrive I'm not ready to greet you, and I never heard our special tune either.'

On his face was a mischievous smile as once more he kissed her.

'You know I'll forgive you, my love,' he answered, still smiling, 'for there was no special tune to hear, and actually I'm a good half an hour before my usual time.'

Just then, Frau Schmidt spoke to Chrysta and Chrysta translated.

'I've got to tell you that they are very pleased that I've got a young man who loves me very much and who is worthy of me, and that they have always thought the very best of you right from that very first day.'

'Tell them that I am honoured for having you, deeply grateful to them for giving you a home, and that my feelings towards them are as high as they possibly could be.'

She translated back while he undid his small pack. There were all sorts of things; tea, sugar, a 2lb tin of coffee, one tin of golden syrup, three jars of butter, three jars of home-made potted pheasant, a tin of Spam and half a ham, which he had carried under his arm. How their eyes shone, and even more so when he gave Frau Schmidt two bars of chocolate and the old man two tins of tobacco; while for Chrysta there were the bars of chocolate, the bottle of perfume and two almost forgotten pairs of nylons.

What joy, as she undid the package and realised what it really was! Throwing her arms around his neck and giving him a wonderful kiss, she said, 'Oh, thank you, my darling! I know now that I am the luckiest girl in the whole of Germany, having two pairs of nylons, but I have known for a long time that I am definitely the luckiest girl in the whole world having you, my love.'

Once more there was a burst of German.

'They are very grateful to you for everything, and they only wish they could repay you somehow.'

'By having you here, my love, they have repaid me a thousand fold, and besides, if you can't be kind to the innocent or the unfortunate, you've no right to call yourself a human being.'

Chrysta translated once more, and the look and smiles upon their faces told him more than all the words in the world.

At 6.30 p.m., they had started on their favourite walk. Sparingly, she had dabbed some of the precious perfume on, but the nylons had to be saved for a greater occasion, should it ever arise in this war-torn country of make do and mend. That was one thing he had always marvelled at, how industrious she must be, for the condition of what she wore was always tip-top; she looked the perfect lady at all times, and her beauty, that familiar beauty, was now radiating its dazzling charm to its full extent.

They had just reached their favourite stopping place and, as she looked into his eyes, she said, 'You can tell me all about Jamie now, my love, and the rest of the family, and what you did on leave.'

He told her all there was to tell and at the end he said, 'So he wants to see you soon, darling, and you'd better have that big kiss from him now.'

'That was Jamie's,' he said afterwards, 'now here's mine, for the loveliest and most wonderful girl in the whole world, for I have missed you terribly, my love.'

Once again the loneliness which she had known was edged a little further back by the tide of joy from his kiss, and heaven was descending upon her once more.

'You're quite sure the perfume and nylons were what you wanted, dear?' he asked.

'Of course, my darling, just as much as if you had given me a million pounds,' she replied.

'Only I hope what I have got here will mean even more to you, my love,' he said, taking that small but beautiful box from his pocket.

This was something which she hadn't even dreamt of. It was one thing to see the expression of wonderment on her face as she opened it, but it was another thing altogether when the lights in her eyes put to shame those dazzling diamonds before her.

'I hope it is the one you would have chosen if you had been with me, my love,' he said.

'Oh yes, my darling, yes!' she answered, throwing her one arm around his neck and holding that precious box in the other hand.

'It's so beautiful, so wonderful, my darling, that there just aren't words whereby I can express even a tiny part of my grateful thanks and joy,' she said as he took the ring from the box and placed it on the third finger of her left hand.

Then he blessed it with a kiss, saying as he did so, 'This is the first outward visible sign that you belong to me, and I belong to you, my love, something which we have known in our hearts since that very first day.'

The beautiful box fell from her grasp and bounced a yard away from them on the cushion of pine needles, where it would lie almost forgotten for a full five minutes. Chrysta surrendered completely to the joy of his lips and the strength of his arms, while reality floated away like thistledown; she was in a world which was only theirs, a world where only the right time would make them one in all things. Desperately she loved him, so much so that her whole being was exalted by the joy of his love. But the sudden change from that utter loneliness without him, to this heavenly joy, had its anticlimax. He felt those hot tears wet his cheek.

'What is it, my love? There's really nothing to cry over,' he said.

'I know, my darling,' she sobbed out. 'It's just that you're so wonderful, it's just that I've come from the depth of despair and walked straight into a heaven far more glorious than I could ever imagine, in a matter of an hour or so. Then there is Jamie... How I wish I could see him soon, and I wonder how he knows that you have met me?'

'Heaven only knows my love,' he answered, and little did he realise that it was only heaven that did.

Good and Bad News in Equal Measure

In the weeks and months to come, the pattern of their daily lives was almost the same day to day. Only when Phil was on guard duty was the joy of each other's arms missing, but even then they were never out of each other's thoughts. She could tell the time almost to the minute as she heard him coming up the road, whistling. It was always the same tune, their tune; he had taught her the words, and she loved it, yet whenever he sang it to her, inwardly she trembled.

Happiness was almost theirs to the full. Only two dark clouds ever crossed their horizon, and they both added up to one and the same thing. What would they do if he were moved to some other place, and how long would it be before she could get to England when he was demobbed? The uncertainty of the former was always there, but it was the latter that made him feel far more helpless.

As much as he would have loved to be home with Jamie on the one hand, on the other, he hoped that his being a farmer wouldn't put him in line for an early release. That could mean months and months before Chrysta might be able to join him, if it happened. A parting of a few days had been terrible for both of them; month after month would be more like a disaster.

Christmas came and went, and up until then neither of those dark clouds had descended any lower. Had they worried in vain? That seemed the case when he told her that he had heard of two German girls who were waiting for their passage to England.

There was only one thing to do now. He would have to see the colonel about two problems; one was Chesney, of whom there was still no news, and the other was getting his future wife to England.

The colonel, one of the toughest in the heat of battle, proved to be one of the most humane and helpful men he had met.

'I can't promise you a date or anything like that, corporal, but

I'll do everything in my power to get your young lady to England as soon as possible. It could be before you are demobbed or after.' He paused for a moment then went on, 'And by the way, how is your father-in-law?'

'Quite well, thank you, sir, but I didn't even know you knew him.'

'I know him all right. We met several times before the war, but it was only through the grapevine that I found out he was your father-in-law.' His eyes saddened as he went on, 'I know of your great loss and its tragic circumstances, in fact I know far more of the men's backgrounds than they think I do.'

The sad look in his eyes gave way to a twinkle as he continued, 'I know how many times a lot of them went to church, and how many times a lot of them went to prison. But getting back to the issue, you realise that there are complications taking a German or any other girl back to England; it's a new country for her, a new way of life, and a new language to learn. Can you give me a reason why you should face all these things, just to take a German girl home?'

'Yes sir,' answered Phil, taking his wallet out of his pocket. 'This is a photograph of my late wife, and I can't tell one atom of difference between the wife I know and the girlfriend I have now. They are identical in speech, looks and everything else.' He looked at the floor as he went on, 'If it hadn't happened this way, sir, I could never have married anyone else.'

Silence reigned for quite a few moments as the colonel went on looking at the photograph, then he said as he handed it back to Phil, 'It would be a good idea if you could get your young lady to come here as soon as possible. Do you think she could manage within half an hour?'

'I should think so, sir,' answered Phil.

'Quicker the better,' said the colonel. 'I'll have the papers brought here while you are gone, and I should be able to carry a mental picture of that photograph for half an hour, just to see if things are as fantastic as you say.' The last sentence was said with a whimsical smile upon his face.

Fifteen minutes later Phil returned with Chrysta, and although she had had very little time to change, she looked absolutely breathtaking. After the introductions, the colonel looked at Phil, and without any hesitation said, 'In looks, one and the same.' And that was all.

Then came Chrysta's turn, and while the colonel was asking the questions and she was giving the answers, Phil had the impression that the officer was more in awe than being just a gentleman. He knew just how he felt, for although her arms and her lips were ever ready for him, for some time he had had that feeling that she was something much higher than he was, so high in fact, that just to see her and to be in her presence was like being privileged to behold something which the human eye had never witnessed before. Yet with her sweet nature and gentle manner she showed not the slightest sign that she was aware how she subdued and at the same time brought the very best out of the people around her. Only the evil one had tried to do otherwise and cross that forbidden barrier, and he was no more.

'That's about all I can do for the moment,' said the colonel, getting up and coming round to their side of the room.

'Thank you very much, sir,' said Phil.

'Well, I can't promise you dates or anything like that, but I'll use all the influence I have to get you together in England as soon as possible… and we may meet there sometime, for my wife and I often tour the Cotswolds.'

'You should make that a must, sir! My father-in-law spends a lot of time at Spring Farm, and I know that he, as well as ourselves, would be more than delighted if you and your wife would stay with us.'

'Yes, I should like to meet him again. So, thank you for the invitation, and hopefully we shall all be under happier circumstances then, for my wife, like the majority, doesn't like me away from her a moment longer than possible.'

He then shook them both by the hand, saying to Chrysta as he did so, 'Now don't worry, young lady, if by chance Phil is demobbed before your time comes; even though you may not hear anything, always remember that I shall be keeping those wheels turning.'

Once more they both thanked him gratefully and departed.

'That's the best bit of luck we could have hoped for, my love,'

Phil said as they walked up the road. 'It's much better to have someone in authority on your side than against you.'

He received two letters in the next batch of mail. In the one from Penny there was the usual news, and a lovely long note from Jamie, but in the one from the colonel, posted a day later, there was sad news and good news too. The sad news concerned the major; although he had lasted much longer than had been expected, when the end came, it had been all too sudden. It had happened just before the colonel arrived on his daily visit almost a week ago.

Phil had always liked the major and they had got on well together, but, unbeknown to him, the major had wished many times that Jane had cast her eye in his direction, or at least to someone who was as much of a gentleman by nature and as manly at the same time.

However, the good news to some extent helped him over the sad. The colonel had found out through the Red Cross where Chesney was living. He wrote:

> I have tried to get in touch with him, but I think it better if you went and saw him at the first chance available. From what I can make out, you'll be much more likely to get him to leave London than anyone else. Apparently he is in a frame of mind brought on by his disability which makes him afraid he is imposing on other people, so he seems to shun everybody. We shall have to alter that, Phil.

'We shall,' Phil said aloud, as his mind pondered whether Chesney would prefer, after a stay at Spring Farm, to lodge with Mrs White, or have a cottage of his own at some time in the future. But whatever happened, he would never let his friend pine away his life in some half-bombed-out hovel in a grimy city, knowing how much he loved the countryside.

In these benevolent musings, he had utterly forgotten that what the future held was still a mystery to man and woman alike, and he might not have believed what he saw if he had been privileged to have a peep. For in seven weeks' time, to the very day, almost to the very hour, he himself would be in a world full of happiness, a world which not so very long ago he had given up all hope of ever knowing again. But there he would be, just as though he was standing on the top of High Ridge, looking out into a clear and sunlit sky with all the dark clouds swept behind him.

Had he been given a second peep, he would have received a pleasant but unexpected shock concerning Chesney. Chesney would come to stay at Spring Farm, but his future would be finalised before those seven weeks were ended.

Eventually the date for Phil's demob came through. It was 21st February, and that was in two weeks' time – two agonising weeks when the scales would bump on one side, only to seesaw and bump on the other, for despair would outweigh joyfulness on one side, and joyfulness would outweigh despair on the other.

It was the feeling of being so helpless which made matters worse for him. He would have paid Chrysta's fare ten times over if only they could have made the journey back to England together. All they could do was to pray that their parting lasted but a short time, and that the loneliness was not too hurtful to bear. But it wasn't only the thought of leaving his love behind that caused him concern; it was the old couple as well. With Chrysta's help he had gathered all the wood available, just before the cold weather had begun. Though enough was one thing, not enough made all the difference between life and death, to a couple of their great age. The cold of winter was really taking its toll, and the news that Phil would be leaving soon seemed to make them relax their grip on the last bit of life which they had been hanging on to.

Yet even in their feeble state, they were more than certain over one thing. They knew Phil had to leave when his time came, no matter what, and so must Chrysta when her time came too; in that they were adamant. For the two young ones, life was about to begin. A whole lifetime lay in front of them, which made love and belonging so wonderful and exciting; they had everything to live for, everything to grasp and hold on to. While the Schmidts themselves, they who had lived for so very long, had known the joy of loving and being loved; they had known the full measure of happiness and not too many tears, and they also knew the comfort of each other as they walked down the path towards life's end together. What is there better in life than what we have known? What more can we ask, than in the end we should die together?

So time went by, and each night, one more one less, only served for the tears to fall more readily, and each time Phil would comfort and console her, and in the end she would promise him that when he was gone, she would look forward to the joy which might come on the morrow, and not dwell on the disappointment of the day just ending.

'I will try very hard to do as you wish, my darling,' she would answer.

But on the last night, during those last few precious hours together, when only a few tears fell this time, looking into his eyes she said, 'I will try to be brave for your sake, my darling, so please don't worry. I shall find that extra strength, knowing that this will be our last parting, and I shall know that when the sun shines for me again, it will be for always.'

Looking down at the dazzling ring upon her finger she continued, 'It will only be this beautiful ring which you have bestowed upon me that I shall be able to look to for any comfort when you are gone, from tonight onwards until we meet again, my darling. This ring, this symbol of our everlasting perfect love, which God has blessed us with, shall shine for me and sparkle as it has never done before. Always as I look at the four smaller diamonds sparkling out like twinkling stars, to me they represent all the love, the joy and the compassion which you have showered upon me. But always I feel lost, for this beautiful world which you have woven around me is far beyond my most vivid imagination; the glory of it all dazzles me, and I am in awe at all its wonders.'

'Then, as I gaze at the large diamond in the centre, whose sparkling brilliance is so many times greater, this to me represents the heavenly future which God has in store for us. For soon I shall be by your side, and you will have placed a plain gold band upon my finger. What joy shall be mine, as I am about to enter a world which up till then is unknown to me; and, my love, on that same night, when you take me in your arms and tenderly guide my faltering innocence on to the most wonderful path of womanhood, I know nothing less than the glory of all heaven will be before me, for my heart has told me so, that all that heaven will be mine only because of you, my love, and because I love you far more than life itself.'

Whatever endearment he was about to say was only a muffled tone as their lips met. How long they stayed thus, neither of them had the slightest idea, for they were in a heaven which was only theirs, a heaven which could be felt as well as seen, but one into which they would not dare to trespass.

Tenderly he whispered, 'You know, my love, you are more precious to me than my own life, and that I am longing for that wonderful day just as desperately as you are, for I know only when we belong to each other in all things will the happiness of the future start to wipe out most of the sorrow of the past.'

Half an hour later he had said his farewell to the old couple; they were happy in their way, but more than a little sad, knowing that this would be the last time they would see him. Outwardly, he was his usual cheerful self in front of them, but inwardly he was quite unhappy. For the present they were in good hands, but only as long as Chrysta was there to look after them.

Out on the porch they clung to each other, putting off that last farewell at least a dozen times, but finally he had to go, and her parting words to him were, 'God bless you my love, and I pray that He will take the greatest care of you, for Jamie's sake and mine, and that we shall all be together very soon.'

'I shall pray for you, my darling, a thousand times a day, and only when I am hurrying towards you to take you in my arms again will the suspense which grips my heart vanish into thin air.'

Just one last very deep kiss, to help bridge the parting which was before them, and he was gone; and, as always, she watched him until there was no more to see in the darkness.

It was an early departure again this time, and, as on his first leave, Phil went from Calais to Dover. He barely had time to gather his thoughts after leaving one half of himself behind, with the other half looking forward to seeing Jamie and the others he loved, when he was on his way to London.

Once he arrived and had gone through the procedure of being

demobbed, his first port of call had to be Chesney. He had very little difficulty in getting a taxi, and going along he asked the driver if he would wait once they arrived at the address.

'Only too pleased, mate – in fact, I'll wait all day as long as you pay me,' he replied, with real cockney humour.

'I shouldn't think it will be that long,' Phil answered, laughing.

It was about half a mile from where Grace and her family had been killed, and if anything the place was a little more dingy. He couldn't help giving way to a shudder, thinking to himself, I just can't have Chesney cooped up in these surroundings, it would be the death of him in no time.

He knocked at the door of 66 Garton Street, not knowing what to expect when the door opened. However he didn't have long to speculate before his knock was answered. Soon, a middle-aged woman stood there glaring at him.

'Good afternoon, ma'am, is Mr Legg at home?' he asked.

She didn't bother to return his greeting, but answered in a very ill mannered tone that suggested that she couldn't be bothered with anything, 'How should I know? He might be, or on the other hand he might not be.' So saying, she turned her head towards the stairs and screeched out, 'Are you in, number seven? Wake up number seven.'

From that Phil came to the conclusion that this was some sort of a boarding house, and a very poor one at that. No reply came from upstairs.

'You'd better go up and find out,' the woman snapped, 'and it's no good you asking for a room because we ain't got any.'

I wouldn't if you paid me to, he thought as he climbed the stairs.

Number seven was more than halfway down a long passage; he knocked, and to his pleasure he heard movement inside. The door opened, and for a few seconds the two men, who had once been so inseparable, just stood and looked at each other.

It was Phil who broke the silence first.

'How are you, Ches? I have wondered so much about you, and it's taken me all this time to find out where you were.'

'I'm fine, Phil, and pleased to see you,' Chesney answered.

He might have been pleased to see him, but he couldn't disguise the lack of life in his eyes, or the despair on his shoulders as he hobbled across the room.

'You're about that last of the few people I know who I expected to knock at the door,' he said as he slumped into a chair.

'Surely not, Ches, surely you guessed that as soon as I knew where you were, I'd be here post-haste to give you all the help I can? We've been through too much together for me to let our friendship vanish without trace.'

'I'm very sorry, Phil. What with this—' he tapped his artificial leg as he spoke '—and then not having a home or anyone to come back to, plus these dingy surroundings, there doesn't seem much left in life for me; but in any case, you should be the last person in the world I'd show any ingratitude to, please forgive me.'

Phil could see he was almost at the point of breaking down.

'There's nothing to forgive, so let's forget all about it. What I did come here for was to take you down to Spring Farm now... There's a taxi waiting outside, so let's get all your things together. For one thing is certain, you're not coming back to this place.'

'I can't impose myself on you indefinitely, Phil.'

'Well, you can stay with us until Primrose Cottage is ready for you, you always liked it and it's still empty.'

A bit more sunshine crept back on those downcast eyes as he asked, 'Do you really mean that, Phil?'

'It's all yours, and for as long as you want it; now let's get your things packed, and by the way, how much will you owe the battleaxe?'

'Somewhere around six pounds, I should think.'

Phil handed him twenty pounds, saying, 'Pay your bill out of that and keep the change.'

Chesney was about to protest, as Phil continued, 'And no arguing!'

Less than ten minutes later they were on their way downstairs, and while Phil carried the luggage out to the taxi, Chesney went to find the landlady to settle his bill.

'She wasn't at all happy over losing a boarder,' he told Phil, when they had settled into the taxi. Then, taking a last look at the house, he went on, 'All I hope is that I shall never have to live in a place like that again.'

'You won't, you can be sure of that,' Phil answered.

Happiness Unbounded for All

Partly in the taxi, and partly in the train, the greater happenings of the months they had been apart were unfolded to each other; Chesney had had a difficult and rough time, that was certain. But as Phil told him all about his new love, those haggard features, which pain and loneliness had chiselled without a fight, started to become a living thing once more.

'It's absolutely out of this world, Phil, it's so unbelievable that it doesn't seem true, but I'm so happy for you, you know that.'

What with that, and the sight of the countryside that he loved so much, Phil could see a remarkable change in him already. But it was when they arrived at The Junction that the greatest transformation occurred. After Jamie had almost smothered his father with kisses, Chesney's turn came next.

Phil watched his friend's face. Despair fell away from him, only for happiness and joy to take its place, and when young Jamie, with his face beaming, said, 'I'm so glad you've come, Uncle Chesney, we'll have lots of fun, and I've so much to show you,' Phil was sure that Chesney looked years younger already.

It was the same with the colonel. He was overwhelmed with joy, knowing that Phil had come through the war all right, and was now home for good, and he extended the same amount of welcome and pleasure to Chesney also.

What a homecoming they both had when they reached Spring Farm. It was a place of gaiety now; gone were the days when the postman was looked upon with some reluctance. The one they all loved so much was home at last, physically fitter perhaps than before he went, and definitely more fit to face the world once more. For his second love would be coming to join them soon, whose face they would all know so well; but deep inside they all wondered, was it possible that they would be seeing that selfsame face once more?

Yet as that first day of happiness ended, unseen and unknown the wheel of fate had begun to turn once more. Chesney, except for his few belongings, had nothing else in the world, but the pleasure upon his face had a much firmer foundation than that of Phil's. The broken heart which they had both suffered was mending faster for Chesney; but for Phil, his would be an open wound until Chrysta was safely by his side; she was never out of his thoughts and, except for Jamie, she was each smile upon his face, and the last touch of her lips was ever present upon his. He would laugh and joke, and play around, but just below the surface was the greatest longing to be able to stretch our his hand and caress the face of beauty that was forever before him.   ·

The next morning, a bitterly cold one at that, they had a quick run around the farms; it was a morning of renewing old acquaintances as they met all the men at their different jobs. How glad they were to see him back, and not one missed the happiness which was now on his face, where before there had been so much sorrow.

It was too cold to stay in any one place for very long, but before they made their way back to a warm house and lunch, he thought it best to take Chesney to Primrose Cottage at the earliest possible moment. How the lights grew in Chesney's eyes as they noted down the things that needed doing; he could imagine it all looking lovely, and himself so comfortable. He could see himself on a day like this with a blazing log fire in that lovely stone fireplace. Three days ago, all this, plus the offer to help Phil run the farm, which he had jumped at, would have been beyond his wildest dreams; yet here he was standing on the threshold of a new life, with Primrose Cottage as the centrepiece.

Everything seemed to be going far better than planned – apparently everything, that is; but only as far as man was concerned. How could they possibly know that at that very moment the hand, the gentle hand of fate, was pointing in Chesney's direction? How could they know that this was not what fate had in store for him? For Chesney would never live at Primrose Cottage, and neither would he help Phil run the farms.

'I should think you're both frozen,' said Penny, as they walked into the hall.

'We are,' answered Phil, 'and I'm hoping your kitchen is the quickest place to thaw out in.'

'It's quite warm, so you shouldn't take long to get back to normal.'

Chesney followed her in, while Phil got them three whiskies.

'All the best,' he said raising his glass and looking more at Penny than at Chesney, and thinking to himself how happy she looked and hardly a day older, for all her sorrow.

'I knew you would be cold, so you're having soup for the first course.'

'Lovely!' they both answered. Then Phil put his arm around her shoulder and went on, 'You know, Ches, she's not only the best cook, but she's even one step in front of the weather, for you can bet that that soup was being got ready last night, am I right?'

'You mostly are,' she answered, laughing.

As expected, the soup was delicious, and so was the rest of their lunch. The colonel wanted to know how they had got on, where they had been, and so forth.

'We've had a brisk walk over to the Court,' he added, as Marie-Ann chimed in, saying, 'I've invited Mrs Marchant and Jane over for dinner tonight.'

'Just as well it's tonight,' answered Phil, 'or they might not get here, for I'm sure we're in for a heavy fall of snow very soon.'

'I wouldn't be at all surprised, for I'm sure it was colder coming back from the Court than going,' replied the colonel.

From the time Jamie got home from school, his father devoted every minute of his time towards his son. They were inseparable; son looked up to father for all things, while father looked down upon son and was well pleased.

Yet Jamie's father couldn't help wondering as he kissed him goodnight for the third time, why the boy hadn't mentioned his mother, for he had whispered his message for her, all those months ago at The Junction. Not one little word, not one little hint, yet every now and again he took those quick glances at her photo by the side of his bed. That swift action, and whatever thoughts went on in his little mind, were still as big a mystery as ever, even to his own father.

At 7.50 p.m., Mrs Marchant and Jane arrived. Phil was waiting for them and had popped out to open the car door and to escort

Mrs Marchant inside.

First he introduced her to Chesney, and after the usual greeting she went on to say, 'I've heard a lot about you, and I must say that I am very pleased that you are going to stay here, it's a much healthier life in the country.'

If Mrs Marchant was pleased and showed it unstintingly, that was a mere nothing to the pleasure upon Jane's face when her turn came to meet Chesney.

Her greeting was nowhere near as clear-cut as it should have been, and the handshake lasted much longer than was necessary. It seemed that Chesney had not only brought back to life all her feminine charm, but had awakened all her other assets as well, ones which Phil had never seen her display towards Gerald.

He was sure that not one of the others had noticed, but he knew the symptoms only too well to be mistaken, and during the wonderful dinner of Penny's, he was sure again that they were only half conscious of the never-ending stream of conversation, and the look on Chesney's face showed clearly that he was as deeply under Jane's spell as she was under his.

Often those fleeting glances were all that was necessary to transmit the topic which was uppermost in their thoughts; it was another case of love at first sight, only this one was born out of pain, sorrow and disillusion. Not quite like Phil's own, where the whole world had been his for a few short years, then empty except for Jamie; but now once again he was looking out over that realm where the sun was looking down from a sky, unimpeded and glorious.

It was the same in the drawing room. The flow of conversation went on and the time went by, almost unheeded; but it wasn't just the time that had taken second place, the weather outside hadn't been given a second thought either. It was a little after twelve o'clock when they were preparing to go that Phil went to the door, only to be greeted by a flurry of snowflakes, and a carpet of four inches covering everything in sight.

Going back into the drawing room, he announced, 'Chesney and I will have to act as pathfinders for you, it's quite thick outside and about four inches down already.'

Quick as a flash a different suggestion came from Jane. 'You take Mummy in your car, Phil, and Chesney can come in mine.'

'All right,' he answered, 'but I'll lead the way.' He thought to himself, *after the way you used to help Joanna and me, I'll do anything to oblige...*

The car behind took a while to follow whenever his speed was down to a walking pace; he could well imagine the love scene that went into operation each time they stopped. 'Good luck to them,' he almost said aloud, and wished that his own love was sitting here beside him too.

Once they arrived at the Court, Phil took Mrs Marchant up the steps and inside as soon as possible, while Jane drove round to the garage.

'You can shut the door, Phil,' said Mrs Marchant. 'They'll come along the covered way and in through the other door, so help yourself to a drink while you are waiting; and if you'll excuse me, I must go to bed.'

'Thank you, I think I will accept your offer of a drink, even if it is only an excuse to keep the cold out.'

'That's right, Phil, and thank you for a lovely evening and a delicious dinner.' Then, with a twinkle in her eyes she went on, 'Wish Chesney goodnight for me... and Phil, I like him very much.' Then, with a quick glance at her watch, and with even a bigger twinkle, she said, 'And it looks as if I'm not the only one, unless it's further along the covered way than I've imagined all these years.'

What a laugh they had together!

'You noticed, then?' Phil said.

'Couldn't miss it, Phil, right from the moment they set eyes on each other. I could sense it, and look how their eyes have been glued to each other all evening!'

'Actually I didn't think anyone else had noticed. What do you think, are you pleased about it?' he asked.

'It wouldn't be any good if I wasn't, but actually I am, for anyone who has been your friend for as long as Chesney has is bound to be all right, and that is more than I can say of Gerald. In fact, if Jane had asked me if I had liked him the first time we met, I would have been bound to tell her the truth, and that would have been no, but she never asked me. Well, I'm off, and I hope you won't have too long to wait. So goodnight, Phil, and thank you again.'

'Goodnight, Mrs Marchant, and you know it's always a pleasure to see you,' he replied as she disappeared through the doorway.

Five minutes later, in they came, and it was just as if the heavens outside had been laid out before them; for in their eyes a thousand stars twinkled merrily, while happiness was written all over them, and in their hearts they were walking on air.

'Mummy gone to bed?' Jane asked.

'Yes, about five minutes ago,' Phil answered, raising his glass to them.

'Phil,' she said, coming over and putting her arms around his neck, 'we've never had any secrets, have we?'

'No,' he answered.

'Only I want you to be the first to know... Chesney and I are in love.'

Phil put one arm around her and signalled for Chesney to join them with the other before saying, 'I have known your little secret all evening, and so has your mother, and while you were outside we've been talking about it.'

'What did she say? Is she pleased about it, Phil?' she asked, slightly concerned.

Phil kissed her on the cheek before answering.

'I would say she is very pleased about it, myself.'

'Oh Phil, you are a darling,' she cried, kissing him full on the lips, before turning to Chesney for a much longer embrace.

Her eyes were shining even brighter now, as she went on, 'There'll be no need now for me to break it to Mummy little by little. It's all in the open, Phil, and it's all thanks to you, something for which I shall be eternally grateful.'

Poor Chesney was so happy that he was almost speechless, until Phil said, 'I'm as pleased as punch, in fact I can't think of anything nicer to happen to two very nice people, and above all, two people I'm deeply fond of.'

'Thanks, Phil, for everything, for I am another person who will be eternally grateful, for it seems only a few hours ago when you knocked at my door, and brought the chance of a new life for me. Little did I know then, or even dream, that in so short a time my whole world would once again be overflowing with so much joy and happiness. Once again I thank you for everything, but most of all for what I have in my arms at this present moment.'

Jane returned his embrace in the same eager measure, as Phil walked away to wait in the hall.

'Goodnight, Jane!' he called back, but he received only a muffled reply. Out in the hall he was not alone, for as he stood inside the porch, in his imagination she was there before him. He recalled the day all those years ago when he had only half held her in his grasp, and had given her not much more than an ordinary kiss; then, in the height of her purity and in her sublime ignorance of the art of loving, she had reckoned their little caress and their stolen kiss were almost the last word of all that was beautiful in man's relations with woman. Not until that night at Spring Farm, when, as promised, he had given her first real kiss, only then had she been aware of the turmoil which had lain dormant inside her. The thought of her, and the perfect happiness that she had given him, held him in that selfsame world for a few more moments. Then he remembered the awful shock when he had lost her and the pitch-black void which had engulfed him.

Would he, if it were possible to take that same chance again, would he grasp with both hands those few years of heaven, only to know the depth of a hell which obliterated the beauty of the years before and left him with no will to go on? His lips formed the word 'yes'; hell or no hell, a broken heart, or a living death – he would face that all again, for had he not tasted of the finest wine at the touch of her lips? Had he not seen the wonders of a whole world when she was in his arms, and had he not lived in a heaven on earth only because they had been as one, and had opened those gates of heaven together?

Just then the two lovers came in and broke his thoughts.

'He's all yours, Phil, but not for long, I hope. For if Mummy agrees, and you also, I'd like Chesney to stay here; would you mind?' she asked.

'Not in the slightest, you know I'll do anything to help where either of your happiness is concerned.'

'You're a dear, Phil,' she said as he opened the door.

Once in the car, it was a case of two friends who could laugh, no matter what was said.

'Doing quite well for yourself, aren't you? From a back room to a country mansion all in a week, takes a bit of beating!'

'It's really fantastic, Phil! Falling in love again was the furthest thing from my mind, and yet from the moment you introduced us I had that feeling that here was a girl who could help me over my sorrows, and probably I could help her over hers. As the night wore on, whatever barriers there were between us just vanished one after the other; oh, I'm in love Phil, faster and deeper than I ever thought possible – and I think she is as much in love with me also.'

'I know she is,' answered Phil, 'and just between us, I've never seen Jane look as radiant as she did tonight. She loves you all right, and more than she's ever loved anyone before.'

'You won't mind me going over there so soon, will you? Well, that is, if Jane's mother agrees?'

'Of course not, what do you think I would do if I were in your shoes? But bang goes Primrose Cottage,' Phil answered, laughing.

'Yes, it's a pity,' said Chesney, 'but I can't very well turn down an offer like I've just received, not unless one of the fairies in the garden of Primrose Cottage grows up to be as wonderful as Jane.'

'I can't guarantee that,' said Phil, 'so I think you had better stick to the offer you've just had, I feel sure that's the most reliable.'

Less than a week later, and no more than an hour after breakfast, Jane arrived to pick up Chesney and his belongings. They were all sorry to see him go in one sense; but in another, they were delighted that things had turned out the way they had for him. At least this way he had found a happiness which would have been impossible to find elsewhere.

For about two or three minutes the others were talking together, which gave Jane the opportunity she was looking for. Turning to Phil, in little above a whisper she said, 'Guess what Mummy said that night when I asked her?'

Phil shook his head and replied, 'I've no idea, knowing your mother.'

'I'm absolutely delighted, the sooner the better, it will be like old times to hear another artificial leg clumping across the hall... and before I forget, when is the wedding?'

'Trust your mother to come right to the point,' said Phil, laughing. Then in the next breath he went on, 'Yes, Jane, when is it? The wedding, I mean.'

For a second or two the glitter faded from her eyes as she answered, 'I've had such a lonely time Phil, that I wish it was today. It won't be long, you can be sure of that, but what I am praying for is for Chrysta to come soon, then she can be a bridesmaid at my wedding, and I can be a matron of honour at hers – just the opposite of the last time.'

'Thanks, Jane,' he answered, 'it's very kind of you to have thoughts of our dilemma at the height of your own happiness.'

'Don't ever imagine, Phil, that I haven't thought of you often, for I have.' A whimsical smile came over her face as she went on, 'But it's too late now for you to get the slightest big-headed, when I tell you that I have thought more of you than you'll ever know.'

That was as far as that conversation got, or ever would, for Chesney was ready to go, but they would meet again very soon, for there was lunch at the Court on Sunday for all of them, Penny included.

For the next two weeks, sometimes with the colonel and Jamie, but mostly by himself, Phil pushed himself into the work on the farms almost relentlessly. He just had to, with the awful waiting and wondering; how he wished he had told her to write, it might have got through to him, but the situation was such, that there was practically no chance of letters between civilians reaching their destination.

Had he known just how Chrysta had fared, his anxiety would have been all that much greater. The Schmidts had both taken a turn for the worse the day after he had left. For a day over two weeks, she had ceaselessly struggled to do all that was possible for them, but in the end their condition deteriorated so much that the doctor had them removed to the hospital.

Each day she had visited them, and each day they had slipped a little deeper into a coma. If the call came for her to leave for

England, she wouldn't be half as worried over them now; for in mind they were already out of this world and no longer knew she was beside them, and the end could come any time.

Chrysta had risen at seven o'clock that morning as usual, and for the first hour the pattern of the day was as each morning before. At eight o'clock she heard the sound of a motorcycle as she busied herself in the kitchen, but with so much on her mind she was only half aware of it; consequently the knock on the door was quite a shock to her.

She hurried to open it; a young soldier stood there, his crash helmet gleaming in the early morning sun.

'Good morning, miss,' he said, 'the colonel sends his compliments, and if you can be ready by nine o'clock, you'll be picked up here and taken to the airfield. The colonel has managed to get you a seat with the RAF.'

'I'll not keep them waiting one second,' she answered, 'so please thank the colonel and tell him how grateful I am, and thank you also.'

The waiting had been terrible enough, but it was not knowing how long which took its toll, for he had seen her face grow pale as he had given her the news.

'Do you feel all right, miss?' he enquired.

'Yes, thank you,' she answered, 'it's just that I can hardly believe the wonderful news that you have brought me.'

'You'll be ready by nine o'clock then?' he said, edging back awkwardly down the path.

'Yes, you can be sure of that,' she answered, as the first smile crept over her face.

'Oh, by the way,' he called out as he sat astride the motorcycle, 'I know you will like England, and please tell Phil that Zip sends him all the best – and that goes for you as well, miss.'

She hardly had time to thank him, and say that she would certainly give Phil his message before he started the engine and was gone.

At 8.45 a.m., Chrysta was ready. Leaving her two cases in the porch, she ran up the road to give the keys of the house to friends of the Schmidts'. She had only been back a minute or so before the truck arrived, and down the path she went, carrying her cases, but before she had even reached the gate the driver was out and greeting her.

'Good morning, miss, I'll take those,' he said. 'The colonel thought it would be warmer for you in the van at this time of year.'

'Thank you,' she answered, 'I expect it is rather cold in a jeep during the winter.'

'It can be, and wet too,' he replied.

For a second or two she looked back at the house, then shifted her gaze sideways to the farmhouse and beyond. Whatever her thoughts were, they were soon dispelled as the driver said, 'The colonel wants to see you before we leave, I think it is to give you your papers.'

But it wasn't only about papers that the colonel wanted to see her for, for as he handed them to her he asked, 'Have you got any English money? Only you'll want some to get to London from Manston in Kent, then across London to Paddington, then on down to Gloucestershire.'

'Yes,' she answered, 'Phil gave me fifty pounds; he seems to have thought of everything, but thank you very much for asking.'

'I was hoping that I would have to lend you some, then when I am in England for three days next week, I would have a good excuse to bring my wife and call in for tea one day and collect it,' he said, smiling.

'You know, Colonel, Phil would be very put out if, after all you have done for us, you have to find an excuse of any sort to come and see us. Besides, he has invited you and your wife to come and stay any time you wish, and I'm sure his father-in-law will be more than pleased to see you after so long.'

'I know, but I don't expect we shall have time to get that far next week. However, later on, perhaps in two or three months, we'll definitely stay for a few days. Now you must really go, mustn't miss that plane for anything,' he said, smiling and holding out his hand.

She took it, saying, 'I am deeply grateful for everything, but most of all for this wonderful day.'

'Safe journey!' he shouted, as they moved off.

Fifteen minutes later they pulled up before a wooden building on the airfield, everything seemed to have been laid on perfectly, for no sooner had they stopped than the driver was told which aircraft was hers and its whereabouts. Around the perimeter they sped, finally pulling up by the side of an aircraft whose engines were already warming up. Chrysta took six pounds from her handbag, saying as she did so, 'Here is three pounds for you for all that you have done for me... and do you know the motorcyclist called Zip?'

'Oh yes, miss,' the driver answered, 'as a matter of fact we are in the same billet together.'

'Well, would you kindly give him these three pounds; when he brought me the wonderful news this morning, I'm afraid I was in too much of a daze to think of anything other than going to England.'

'I will, miss, and thank you very much; and we're all about the same, up in the clouds as much as a week before going on leave, so I know how you feel, and tell Phil that big Jock wish you both all the best.'

'I will,' she said, 'and thank you very much.'

Just then two airmen and two Waafs walked towards them. The two airmen took Chrysta's cases, and the two Waafs took her into their charge, making her feel as if they had known her for years, and doing everything to make her feel as comfortable as possible.

How extremely kind everyone was, she thought, as about ten minutes after take-off, while one Waaf was talking to her, the other brought a thermos and poured out three steaming hot cups of coffee; she hadn't had coffee as delicious as this, not since the last of what Phil had brought.

Time went by very quickly, for even above the roar of the engines, there was never a very long space of time without conversation of some sort; she couldn't have asked for more to help her over the ever-increasing desire to catch the first glimpse of Phil.

Suddenly the Waaf who had brought the coffee said, 'I'll pop up to the cockpit to see if it is all right for you to have your first sight of England from there.'

She was back in no time, saying, 'When the green light goes

on, that will be the sign that the channel's in sight, and on a lovely day like this, you should have a wonderful view of the coastline.'

Five minutes later Chrysta was ushered into the cockpit, and she returned the smile and the greeting from the two friendly faces which turned round to welcome her.

This was not just a wonderful view, she immediately first thought as her eyes scanned below and beyond; that was a gross understatement. 'Fantastic' was a word far more suitable. But what she didn't know was that today was one of those rare occasions when the channel was so calm, so blue, and the view stretching out appeared endless, only to be barred by those cliffs of shinning white chalk. Beyond those cliffs, and capping them, were the rich green fields of England.

What better sight could have awaited her? What better omen could she have prayed for, for was not her future home greeting her as if she came from its very soil? No wonder she had to fight to stop her emotions from taking over. She watched the towns and villages and the patchwork quilt of greenery appear and disappear; she watched the scars of war and felt pained, for had not this land, this fair and peaceful land, captured her heart already?

For the first time she was alone, as both of the Waafs busied themselves preparing for landing, and for the second time she counted six pounds from the bundle, three for each girl, when the opportunity arose.

'It's a little appreciation for your kindness, she explained, 'and for making my journey anything but lonely, and you can guess how much that has meant to me.'

They tried to protest, but it was no good, and even then they didn't leave her, not until she was safely in the bus to take her to the station. The bus was about half full of Waafs and, judging by their conversation, they were going on weekend leave. Chrysta was in one of the front seats with her cases beside her. She was alone, but not lonely, for each second was taking her nearer to all that life held for her.

Once at the railway station, everything was easy, for as she went through the barrier the ticket collector said, 'This side, train in five minutes.'

She had hoped to phone her love, but five minutes would soon go by, and she mustn't miss this train for anything, as it would be almost two hours before the next. On the journey, she watched the Kent countryside go by, but her thoughts were miles away. What was her love doing now? How happy and excited he would be if he only knew that she was steadily creeping towards him! Gone would be the gnawing uncertainty, and she knew how devastating that was, for it took the sunshine out of life, no matter what the weather. So her heart went out to him in his misery, and the overwhelming longing to be in his arms had to be held in check, for tiny tears had already formed in the corners of her eyes. But her thoughts went on. Would she be so emotional that she would hardly be able to speak to him when she rang him from Paddington? She would have to take a grip on herself for his sake.

She saw the bomb damage grow in extent as the train nosed its way through the suburbs of the metropolis, and in the distance she had a glimpse of many buildings which were part of man's priceless heritage.

There was one thing she didn't see, or even feel; yet it was there above and all around her, and still she knew it not, for that guiding hand was there, guiding her through the massed throng, so that she would be in the arms of her loved one without a minute lost.

How wonderful! she thought, as she alighted from the train, to find a porter standing in front of her, as if waiting for her alone on special orders. So it was with the taxi outside, and so too with the porter at Paddington Station.

'We shall have to step on it, miss,' he said when she told him she wanted The Junction. 'Hurry up and get your ticket, your train leaves from number one at 2.30 p.m., that's in three minutes' time.'

There was only one person in front of her at the ticket office, and she was attended to and away before two of those precious three minutes had gone. Down the platform they raced, and once again she knew she was unable to phone her love; it would just have to be The Junction now.

In the compartment were two ladies and one. elderly gentleman, so for the second time she was able to have a corner seat.

'Oh, thank you, miss,' exclaimed the porter, when he realised that she had given him an overgenerous tip.

'It's my thanks to you, for I would never have caught my train if it hadn't been for your help,' she answered smiling.

As they travelled down, the only conversation was between one of the ladies and the gentleman. Chrysta was pleased about that, for now her own thoughts were more than enough to keep her occupied. She could watch the countryside going by, knowing that The Junction was ninety miles away, she could calculate by her watch how near she was to the man who was so extra special, the one she loved more than life itself. Desperately she wanted to see him, in fact to meet them all, but for a second or two she wondered, How would Jamie greet her, and what would he think about her taking his mother's place?

It was all so strange, having to meet the colonel, Marie-Ann and Penny for the first time, when she was already engaged to marry the one they all loved so much. But strange though she thought it might have been, deep inside she knew she had no qualms on that subject, for he had told her a hundred times that they were looking forward to seeing her, just as keenly as she was them.

Even so, there was still Jamie, who up till the last letter his father had received before being demobbed, still hadn't mentioned his mother to Marie-Ann, Penny or the colonel; and even up to this very second, still hadn't to his father either. Her very existence was still unknown to him. This young boy, who had literally driven his father to war for the sole purpose of bringing his mother back to him, was now utterly calm and contented, calm up to the point of being mysterious. Was he still one-step in front of events, or had he known each and every step right from the very start? Only when they met for the first time would the answer be there, but even then, it wouldn't be completely realised.

With so much to see, and with so many thoughts of the past and the wonderful future that was in front of her, Chrysta had forgotten to look at her watch for quite some time, and when she did, she realised that there was less than ten minutes to go. Now, with so little time left, the urgent longing to hear Phil's voice and to feel his arms around her became overpowering. How she wished those last few minutes were no longer than seconds! But inevitably the slow remaining minutes ticked away, until for the first time the tempo of the train took on a different note. It was slowing down, so she made her preparations to leave; through a short tunnel they went, then out into the sunshine again, and before her eyes was the board with THE JUNCTION written in bright bold letters. Only a handful of passengers got off, and only a handful got on, consequently she had a clear view of everything. Then, picking up her cases she made her way to the phone box at the top of the platform.

Meanwhile, at Spring Farm things had gone on as usual. All the morning and right up to the present time, Phil had been at the middle farm overhauling the farm machinery. He had been getting on famously until a little before 3.30 p.m., when he had suffered a bout of frustration, not realising until he wanted a certain new part that it was still in his study, still in the box on his desk where he had left and forgotten it. It was not much more than a handful, but small or big, he would have to go back and get it.

But that was not the only frustration; he was about to discover in the next fifteen minutes that first there was valuable time to be wasted in cleaning his hands before taking the wheel. Then he found out he was almost out of petrol, which meant another delay, filling up before he started.

If he thought that that was the end he was still mistaken, for halfway towards home, his progress was brought to a halt by a large flock of sheep – his own, so he had to bear the waiting without a word. All this added up to the fact that it was a few minutes after four o'clock when he reached Spring Farm.

Out of the car he raced and made straight for his study. He picked up the box containing the part and was hurrying on his way again, when, as he entered the hall, the phone rang.

'I'll take it!' he shouted to the others. Then, picking up the phone he said, 'This is Spring Farm,' only to hear a voice on the other end which rooted him to the spot.

'It's me, my darling,' said the voice. 'I've got as far as The

Junction and oh, how I'm longing to see you and to know the comfort of your arms again.'

'It's wonderful, my love, there is so much I want to say, but I can't delay having you in my arms a second longer than possible. I'll be with you in ten to fifteen minutes, can you wait that long?' he said, blowing her a kiss.

'Forever, my darling, if I had to,' she replied.

'Ten to fifteen minutes will seem like eternity, so I couldn't wait forever, darling, see you much sooner than that.'

So saying he slammed the receiver down and was gone. The spare part he had come all that way to get was totally forgotten now, and in the rush finished up on the floor.

He hadn't even thought to tell the others, so desperate was he to see her; only through Tetstone did he slacken speed, but once out on the open road, he drove as fast as safety would allow. At the end of ten minutes he was turning off the main road, with only another half a mile to go. Down he went under the first bridge, then along and up over the brow to go down once more and under the second bridge; he braked hard, as two council lorries completely blocked the way in front. He couldn't wait, he reversed quickly, he would have to stop at the side of the up line and walk over the bridge. All in one, he stopped, yanked on the handbrake, and was out of the car, racing into the station; but the view of the platform opposite was completely shut out by a stationary goods train, and what with the smoke and steam, he couldn't see a sign of her.

The train started on its way as he raced towards the bridge, but his view from there was even more hopeless, for there was more smoke than ever between him and what his eyes searched for so desperately. Quickly he crossed the bridge, on down the other side, he was two steps from the bottom when he had his first glimpse of her, but his foot never continued on its downward tread, but hung motionless in mid air.

No wonder he had been brought to a sudden halt at this first sight of her, for not only was she standing on the selfsame spot as his first love had, facing the other way, as she had done, but her golden hair, just like Joanna's, glistened like liquid gold in the sunlight. What had taken almost the last ounce of strength from him was the fact that she was wearing a pale blue costume, making that picture before him now exactly the same as when he had first met his first love.

How long he stood poised thus, he had no idea, but suddenly he gathered enough of himself together to put those last two steps behind him and hurry towards her. He had covered a third of the distance before he was sure he could whistle their tune, and before the first line of 'Starlight Serenade' had left his lips, she turned towards him.

They ran towards each other, completely oblivious of everything around them.

'My darling!' she cried.

'My love,' he replied, as arms and lips extinguished the torture they had known without each other.

Liquid diamonds were in her eyes as she said breathlessly, 'Oh my darling, how I've missed you! But now I know what heaven is really like, now that I am in your arms again.'

'It's all happened so fast that I can hardly believe it!' he exclaimed. 'There I was longing desperately to see you, my love, worrying over you, and suffering for you, then I heard your voice on the phone, and it all disappeared in an instant. Heaven is ours again, my darling, now that we are together for always.'

As they walked back up the platform to get her cases, she hurriedly told him everything about the Schmidts, and how this wonderful day had started, how everything had gone so perfectly for her, and how exceptionally kind everyone had been.

Phil said, 'I shall have to write to the colonel tomorrow and thank him for everything, and insist that he and his wife come and stay with us the first chance available.' Then, laughing, he went on, 'You, my love, get here in a matter of hours, and it's always taken me the best part of two days. But that was one thing I used to worry over a lot, picturing you with your luggage going from train to boat, then back to the train again. It couldn't have happened better for both of us, my darling – a quick journey for you, and for me, peace of mind.'

'I would have flown all the way if I could have given the orders, just to have had three or four more precious hours with you, my darling,' she answered.

He was like a boy going on his first holiday as he opened the car door for her to get in, and once he was there beside her, it was one more wonderful kiss and caress, given with all that she possessed and almost all of him.

As they drove along the road, she told him in more detail all about the Schmidts.

'To think I wasn't there to help you, or to hold your hand when you needed me most,' he replied.

'Perhaps God meant it that way, my love; perhaps my loneliness would have been too unbearable if I hadn't been worked to the point of dropping each day.' She paused for a moment then went on, 'But now it is the future, *our* future that we have got to look forward to.'

Home Coming

Tetstone had been left behind; Chrysta had liked what little she had seen.

'This is home,' Phil said as they reached the beginning of Beversbury; his companion fell in love with the picturesque stone-built cottage as they went by.

'There's the castle, or what is left of it,' he told her.

'Lovely,' she answered, 'and what a perfect setting...'

One minute later they turned into the drive of Spring Farm, and he went slowly so that she could see High Ridge in the distance, and home – their home – looming ever nearer.

Penny was just getting the tea, and the colonel and Marie-Ann were talking to her in the hall as the car pulled up. It was Marie-Ann who first noticed and realised who it was.

'It's Chrysta!' she exclaimed. 'Phil has Chrysta in the car. It must have been her when the phone rang – I wish he had told us.'

But it wouldn't have made the slightest difference if they had known before he departed, whether the warning was long, or short, as it turned out to be; emotionally they would have been just as full either way.

Phil was out of the car and went quickly round the other side to open the door; by now they were all there, and the colonel, who was nearest the car, had a look of apprehension upon his face as he watched Phil take Chrysta's hand to help her out. Suddenly they were face to face, and even though Phil introduced them, both of them seemed oblivious to all else around them, for two pairs of eyes searched each other, as if delving for something of which they knew not.

Phil had warned them that they wouldn't know the difference, yet there was no mistaking the look of disbelief on the colonel's face. Though he had been warned, the preparation to face Joanna's perfect double, who now stood before him, had been an utter failure; for here was his daughter, surely, down to the last eyelash.

Then she said, 'I have been looking forward to meeting you for a very long time,' and at last he seemed to shake himself out of the trance which was gripping him.

'It is the happiest day I have known in a long time, now that you are here, my dear,' he answered, as he kissed her cautiously, only for her to return his kiss in a far more confident manner. Not only was she the perfect replica of Joanna in looks, but what she did was the start of being Joanna in all things; for as she kissed him, her left hand went to his shoulder while her right hand held his, just as Joanna, his daughter, had always done.

All three if them had witnessed this, and even the colonel, shocked though he was, was fully aware of it. If there were a score of different expressions upon his face, they were mere details compared with the multitude of thoughts which raced through his mind. It was the same with Marie-Ann and Penny; even though they had had a little time to take a grip on themselves, disbelief showed as much on their faces as on the colonel's, and once or twice Phil glimpsed a handkerchief put to the eye as quickly and discreetly as possible.

Yet a few tears or a torrent made no difference now, for she who had come by the light of a star was here at last, and the last link in that chain of happiness was once more under the roof of Spring Farm.

'Where is Jamie?' his father asked as they reached the hall.

Penny turned to him saying, 'Can't you guess? He's up the garden. Only a few minutes ago he ran in for a glass of orangeade... couldn't hardly wait for me to get it because of those planes flying around. He loves watching them doing their tricks.' This last remark was directed at Chrysta.

'A proper boy, I can well imagine it,' she answered.

Through the French windows they went, and there was Jamie, right at the top of the garden, the untouched glass or orangeade still in his hand, with his face uplifted to the skies; he was watching three training aircraft doing all sorts of stunts.

'Hi! Hi, Jamie,' his father shouted.

Slowly and reluctantly he turned his head towards them, but only for a split second, before turning once more to the display which was holding all his attention.

Then, sudden realisation of what he had glimpsed registered. Like a flash he turned towards them this time, and the untouched glass of orangeade dropped from his little hands, spilling the yellow contents on to the young green grass where his feet had just stood.

'Mummy, Mummy!' he shouted as he raced towards them.

Without a moment's hesitation, Chrysta hurried forward and went down on one knee, ready to receive him when he reached her.

'Mummy, my mummy!' he cried as he swept into her arms.

Whatever tears the onlookers had held in check now ran freely down the cheeks of Marie-Ann and Penny, and dropped intermittently from the colonel and Phil's eyes. The heart rending scene before them went on with a host of hugs and more hugs, a bevy of kisses and more kisses, but not one of the onlookers could bear to watch the full drama that was going on before them. They were like the cast upon a stage, almost shutting their eyes and ears completely as the principal actor and actress went through the most dramatic scene they had even witnessed.

'I'm so happy, Mummy, now that you've come back to me. I knew you would one day, but heaven must be a long way away, for you've taken so long to come.'

'It is a long way, my darling, but I knew I'd come back to you sometime,' she answered, wiping his tears with her handkerchief, and brushing her own away with the back of her hand.

For almost another five minutes they comforted each other, and all the while the onlookers, if not unwanted, seemed to be totally forgotten, while for the two before them, the whole world was their world alone.

'She is our Joanna, it's impossible for her to be anyone else,' whispered Penny, with the tears still rolling down her cheeks; but there was only silence from the other three, for it seemed that none of them had the power to agree or disagree.

There seemed no answer to what they had seen and heard already, and there was definitely no answer to the next few words they would shortly hear her say.

'I've been hoping you would come soon Mummy, for I've got

eight lovely daffodils in my garden waiting for you,' Jamie said, leading her in that direction.

'Thank you, my darling, they'll look lovely in the two silver vases on my dressing table,' she answered.

As best they could, through tear-filled eyes the four onlookers looked at each other, and each one's expression asked the same question; how did she know that Joanna had two silver vases on her dressing table, and that those two vases were still there and in the same position where she had always put them?

For another five minutes, the onlookers just stood there, waiting patiently. Then down they came, Chrysta with eight beautiful daffodils in one hand, and holding Jamie's hand with the other. Emotionally the onlookers hit rock bottom, but there was no place for that now; for the joy and happiness on the two faces coming towards them were a joy and happiness that was not only everlasting, but the start of a wonderful future which would affect them all from the moment they reached them.

It was wonderful, and quite out of this world, the difference her presence made in so short a time, for Spring Farm had found its old way of life again, and even though there were many things far above their understanding, they were prepared to accept them, even though there was no known answer.

There would be champagne for dinner, that was definite, and Jamie had been allowed to stay up half an hour longer. Penny and Mrs White soon shifted most of Phil's things into another room, so that Chrysta could have the one which had been his and Joanna's. Phil had rung Jane and told her the wonderful news, and had invited them over after dinner; Mrs Marchant was away, so there were only the two of them.

He was the last to go up and change for dinner, but he found the room was different, for on the table by the bedside stood the leather holder with the photographs of his first love. Jamie hadn't wasted any time in giving him back one of his most cherished possessions; Jamie had no need of a photograph now, to him she was here in reality and that was all that mattered.

He smiled to himself as he thought of his son, but the smile died as he walked around the bed and picked up the photograph and studied those beautiful features one by one. He could imagine those blue eyes smiling into his, and as his gaze went down to those wonderful lips, his eyes closed at the memory of all the heaven which she had given him, and even now she was and always would be, his first and his only real love; no wonder he sighed deeply as he put the photographs back on the table.

He had heard the colonel and Marie-Ann go down five minutes ago, but not Chrysta, so he knocked at her door.

'Come in, my darling,' she called, she was ready and waiting as he entered.

If he thought he had left most of his heart in the other room, he was mistaken, for the sight before him was just as angelic as his Joanna had been.

'This is the only gown I've got, darling. I hope you like it, for I made it myself.'

The gown was off-white, but where she had got the style from he never had the power to ask her, for so fantastic was it, it was one of those wonderful creations you dream of, yet can never shape in reality.

'It's wonderful and fantastic my love,' he answered, 'and above all, you look divine.'

Those blue eyes smiled into his as he took her in his arms.

'This is only the third time today that I have known the joy of your arms, my love,' she whispered.

'I know, my darling, but so much has happened in so short a time, and if you had been in my arms every time that I had wished it, it would have been at least a thousand.'

Once again his eyes closed as those wonderful lips touched his, only this time it was in reality, and once again he felt swamped by the heaven that she heaped upon him. There was no sigh at the memory this time, for not only was she the perfect image of his Joanna, but her soft smooth suppleness had exactly the same intoxicating effect upon him. So far did her closeness and its heavenly charm take him that the memory of his first love faded farther than he would have dared to admit, even to himself.

Was she, or was she not his Joanna? the thought flashed through his mind over and over again; how could he be expected to hold on to the sacred memory of his first love, when the second one was claiming more of him every time they were in each other's arms? If she had been someone else, it would have been so much easier, but she was a second Joanna in all things, which left him so confused, and with no comparable experience to relate to.

Of course he loved her, but his was a love which was split down the centre; should he tear half of himself away to be buried in the past forever, or should he concentrate all the love he had on a future which was only just beginning?

What brought him back to reality was when their lips parted and she whispered, 'We shall be late, my love, if we don't go now, and I must see Jamie before we go down.'

Into Jamie's room they crept. The little boy was fast asleep with one arm up on the pillow; Phil watched the tenderness on Chrysta's face as gently she put it under the clothes.

'He's wonderful, and just like you my darling,' she whispered.

Before he realised what he had said, he had whispered back, 'And just like you too, my love.'

Quickly she turned around to him and put her arms around his neck all in the same movement. Her eyes looked into his, then went to each part of his face in turn, then back to his eyes again. The look on her face was one which he had never seen on a face before, it was a look which seemed to be delving so deep that it was almost submerged in the unknown. Was she going to say something which would make his words seem ridiculous, or was she going to say something which bore no relation to what he had said whatsoever? What she did whisper was, 'That which seems impossible now, my love, heaven will make possible as the future unfolds before us.'

Then they had one more wonderful kiss, before each in turn bent down to kiss Jamie lightly on the forehead.

At dinner, two things were the highlight of the conversation; first, the beautiful gown which Chrysta wore, and second, the fantastic meal which Penny laid before them. Champagne and other choice drinks, which hadn't seen the light of day for six years or more, flowed abundantly in the dining room and the kitchen alike. Nothing was too good, or too much trouble, in order to make the long-awaited addition to the family feel loved and at home. The gay atmosphere was as it used to be, and once again life was for living with not a worry for the morrow.

At nine o'clock Jane and Chesney arrived; poor Jane, it was one thing to imagine, but no matter how vivid one's imagination, it was another thing altogether to come face to face with reality. Jane just couldn't believe her eyes, and those watching knew exactly what she was thinking; they could tell by the expression on her face that she was almost sure that the woman who stood before her was not a stranger called Chrysta, but her best friend, Joanna; she just couldn't be anyone else, and it was only when they embraced and kissed that Jane found her powers of speech. Of course it was difference with Chesney; he had never known Joanna, but he could quite well remember seeing that beautiful face as a photograph, and he knew that Phil hadn't exaggerated one little bit.

In no time at all, the two future brides were like old friends, everything seemed to fall into place between them, and all the time Jane was under the strong impression that this was Joanna to whom she was talking. So it was inevitable that those two all-important days were soon decided upon. Phil and Chesney seemed to have little choice in the matter, though their delight was none the less. The great day for Jane and Chesney would be in a fortnight, and Chrysta and Phil's in four weeks' time. Both pairs sealed it with a loving kiss, and if the delight on the faces of Marie-Ann and the colonel, and Penny who had just joined them, were anything of an omen, then they were on the threshold of a long and very happy life together.

In the two weeks that followed, every new day brought more and more happiness to Spring Farm. Getting ready for Jane and Chesney's wedding, as well as their own, was of course a top priority. But in between Phil showed Chrysta round the farms and they walked miles together, and quite a lot of those times Jamie was able to come with them, making their heaven even more heavenly.

However, they were alone one day, the first time he took her over the Ridge, and, as before with Joanna, it was under the old chestnut tree where he took Chrysta in his arms. He could tell by her reactions that that was what she was expecting him to do, it was as though she knew all the little things as well as the big ones that had been such an important part of his happiness before.

Right to the foot of High Ridge he took her, where he explained that it was far too muddy to climb to the top that day, but he would show her the world from up there just as soon as the conditions were right.

On the way back, they savoured once more the joy of each other's arms when they reached the old chestnut. Then quite suddenly she said, 'Darling, tell me what went through your mind the first time you saw me?'

'Apart from the shock, a thousand and one things, I should say,' he replied. He paused and then went on, 'But out of all those things that flashed in and out of my mind there was one which came and stayed, as all the rest flitted on. I, who had solemnly promised myself that no other woman would ever know the comfort of my arms again, suddenly knew that the promise would have to be broken. What chance did I have of keeping that promise as you stood before me? You not only brought all the sorrow of the past back in a few seconds, but you were the only hope I had for the future, my love.'

'That is what I hoped you would say, my darling, for what greater love is there than the love I have for you and that which you have for me? I'm so wonderfully happy, my darling, for in my heart I know I belong to you, just as if we had been made man and wife that very first day.'

The Start of the Real Beginning

It had been a wet night, and the rain had continued up until ten o'clock in the morning. Then, from the south a warm breeze had drifted in, drying the earth almost as quickly as a hot iron over a damp cloth. By the time they were ready to set off for the ceremony the sun was quite warm; Chrysta was the only bridesmaid and Phil the best man. Both of them thought, *it was a great pity that Jane and Chesney couldn't be married in church, especially as the breakdown of her first marriage was no fault of hers*. But the few times Phil was able to see Jane's face, he couldn't help thinking how much more radiant and happy she looked this time; she was everything that Joanna had been, and the look of adoration that she gave Chesney was more than enough to mend a dozen broken hearts.

Back at the Court, where about sixty guests were waiting to greet them, everything that could be obtained in those days was there in abundance, and the best of champagne flowed like a river of happiness. Phil introduced Chrysta to the people he and Joanna had known, and Jane took them round to meet those guests he had never met before. *But how ironical*, Phil thought, when later on several of the people he had known had quite unconsciously, and yet as was to be expected, called her Joanna. Yet her face never gave the slightest sign that this was not her name; and unbeknown to him, Penny, Marie-Ann and Jane had been guilty of the same slip on many occasions, and the colonel on two.

It didn't matter whether she was near him, or on the other side of the room; the sight of her looking so near to a bride, without actually being one, made him wonder how would his emotions stand up. Would he be able to choke back the lump in his throat as she walked up the aisle towards him two weeks from now? Only time would tell.

The next two weeks were as the two before, seeing to this or that in preparation for the great day, and in between it was more trips round the farms, or walking over the fields. These would often end in a race between them. Chrysta loved to pit her running skill against his, just as Joanna had, and more often than not he was hard put to beat her. Breathlessly, she would throw her arms around his neck, and the kiss which followed would sap the last bit of breath before it was very old. What fun they had; even when Jamie came with them, the kissing went on the same, only then it was three in each other's arms, and three lots of lips pressed as close to each other as possible.

Sometimes they went out to lunch, and sometimes tea, and once a week Phil took Chrysta out for a meal in the evening. That, and the perfect, pure love they had for each other, carried them along on a heavenly cloud day after day. It was two more days to go to their own great day when they heard from Jane and Chesney. They would be back in good time for the wedding, and although they would have liked to have a longer honeymoon, they wouldn't miss the wedding of the man who made all their joy and happiness possible for anything. Jane's letter went on:

Whether it was intentional or not on your part to bring Chesney and me together, either way, we are eternally thankful to you. If you hadn't been a true friend to him when he needed help, there could have been no way that we would ever have met, and neither of us can bear to think of a future other than how it has been since the first night we met; once again, Phil, we both thank you with all our hearts.

So the great day drew nearer. Jane and Chesney arrived home the afternoon before and Phil would be sleeping at the Court that night. Again, they both thanked him, and with half an eye he could see that theirs was a real love match, and one that was not going to lose any of its brilliance as the years went by. They lived for each other, and he knew that was the most important step towards a happy and lasting marriage.

So it was earlier to bed than most nights for him – not that he would be driving to Cornwall on the following day this time; they wore going by train to Torquay, and then only for a week. Chrysta couldn't bear the thought of leaving Jamie longer than that, and, like Joanna, neither could she bear the thought of their sacred night belonging to anywhere else than Spring Farm.

The next morning, and with expectations of a beautiful day in abundance, even before Phil had gone down to breakfast at the Court, over at Spring Farm it had been a hive of activity for the last two hours.

There were only fifty guests this time, but by ten o'clock, an hour before the ceremony, the inside of the marquee out on the lawn looked as though they were catering for double that number.

Now all the preparations are over, and they are all getting dressed for this great and happy occasion. Penny will be staying behind until the last minute, making sure that everything about this bride would be as perfect as the first one; once her duties are over, she will be driven to church.

Once again the colonel, with utter delight upon his face, is ready and waiting, waiting to give what, inwardly he felt sure, was the same bride to the same bridegroom, for the second time. Marie-Ann and Jamie are going to walk the shortest way, so there is one last tender kiss for the lovely bride from Marie-Ann, and a whole lot more from Jamie.

Off they went hand in hand; up the drive they walked, down the road, and then up the lane. At the top the lane turned to the right; they had just turned the corner, with the church gates some sixty yards away, when they saw, coming from the opposite direction, an elderly man limping along with the aid of a stick.

'Poor man,' said Jamie.

'Yes,' answered Marie-Ann, rather vaguely, for her thoughts were on the more important things concerning the wedding than why should a complete stranger be going into the church for the ceremony.

However, the thought of him went completely from her mind, as he had already disappeared inside before they had reached the gate.

Phil and Chesney were waiting patiently. Chesney had poured him a stiff brandy before they left the Court; Chesney had found out two weeks before that you didn't get two lots of joy while you were waiting for your bride at a second marriage. What you did get was all the joy of the second one, and all the sorrow of the first. It would be a hundred times worse for Phil than it was for him, for there was no difference between his first bride and the one he was waiting for now; how he would react at the first sight of her depended on which way his loyalties went.

They smiled at Marie-Ann and Jamie when they came in, and did the same for Penny when she arrived a few minutes later; now they knew it was only a matter of a minute or so before the first part of his ordeal would be over. The organ, which had been silent for the last few minutes, suddenly burst into the Wedding March, and the first thing Phil became aware of was a great temptation to steal a glance at his bride. He half turned, and the sight of Chrysta walking slowly towards him, on the colonel's arm, almost froze him in that position. Except for the colonel looking a little older, the picture of them now and the mental image he carried of his first bride were one and the same.

He would have to keep his emotions in check for her sake, no matter how he felt inside. On no account must he let any other than a happy smile appear upon his face.

But was he so numb inside that he failed to realise that she was well aware of what a time like this could do to him? Her heart went out to him, pitying him in the sorrow which she unavoidably brought upon him. But as she reached the end of her journey towards him, the unquenchable torment which had almost torn him into little pieces suddenly became a calm. The smile which he greeted her with held all the love and tenderness that he was capable of. He felt almost his old self again, and when her smile returned the same to him, plus all the reassurance that she could cram into a few seconds, and the tender but firm clasp, as briefly her hand held his, he felt that sort of strength flow back into him, the sort which he had almost forgotten had existed.

So for the second time he pledged his vows, and, as Joanna had done Chrysta spoke hers confidently and clearly, just as though she was sure of the future that they were going to share together. Had she unconsciously been let into a heavenly secret? For as the vicar pronounced them man and wife, it seemed as though her innermost thoughts were transferred to him, thoughts which said that this was the greatest moment of her life, this was the moment she had been born for and lived all her life for, for a moment like this could only come once in a lifetime.

Once again they were in the vestry, and just as happily as the last time, the colonel kissed the bride, and congratulated Phil in the same excited manner as before; and once again, arm in arm and with a smile for everyone, a smile which seemed to defy all that a cruel world could throw at them, they walked down the aisle, ready and willing to face the outside world together.

Penny had hurried out in order to arrange the gown and veil ready for the photographer. Marie-Ann and Jamie followed, but Marie-Ann was so full of the joy of this happy occasion, and in such as haste to feast her eyes upon the happy pair once more, that she didn't notice that Jamie wasn't with her when she got outside. He had gone back, having just remembered that the beautiful lucky horseshoe for his mother was still in the pew where he had carefully laid it. By the time he neared the doorway for the second time, he had to stop and shuffle behind the crowd in front. What else could he do but gaze at the lovely horseshoe in his hands? The crowd in front shuffled on a bit further, and he was about to look down at the precious horseshoe once more when a hand touched him on the shoulder. It was the old man he had seen limping up the road and going into church in front of them.

'Jamie,' said the old man, in a kind and gentle voice, 'when you take your lovely horseshoe up to your mother, will you please give her this star also.' He handed the boy a most beautiful golden star and chain.

'Oh yes, sir, and thank you very much,' Jamie answered, his young eyes shining almost as much as that of the star itself.

Once more the old man bent down, saying as he did so, 'Do you think you could remember to give your father a message from me, Jamie?'

'Yes sir,' answered Jamie, nodding his head at the same time.

'Then say to him, that it is I who am here today, and this is only a small part of the promise I made to him when he tended my wound, and bless you too, Jamie, my son.'

'I'll remember, sir, and thank you very much,' replied Jamie.

By now they were almost clear of the doorway, and once through, Jamie turned to thank the old gentleman again, but he had vanished.

'You can give Mummy the horseshoe now, dear,' said Marie-Ann, with one eye on the bride and groom, and the other only half on Jamie.

Jamie walked sedately forward and handed the radiant bride the horseshoe and star together. She bent down and kissed him lots of times, and hugged him equally as many.

'You're the most beautiful bride in the whole world, Mummy,' he said as she thanked him. Then his father kissed him, and thanked him also, but neither of them as yet had noticed the golden star, and, in the excitement, Jamie had forgotten to give his father the message.

But as they stood there, arm in arm, man and wife, both of them the very last word of joy and happiness, waiting while the photographer made his final adjustments, suddenly Phil felt a mighty tremor shake his new bride from head to foot.

'Are you cold, my love?' he asked with some concern, putting his arm around her at the same time.

'No, my darling,' she answered, 'I just can't explain what happened to me or how I felt at that moment; anyhow, I don't feel ill, so there's no need to worry, my love.'

Finally, the photographer was ready. Everything and everyone was placed as he wanted, and for the next ten minutes he took shots of them alone, then the groups, and a special one of them with Jamie standing between them; but in all that time there were no more signs of the tremors.

Soon they were in the warmer atmosphere of the marquee, and after they had greeted the last of their guests, it was Jamie who came in for the whole of their attention for the next few minutes. Kissing and hugging him once more, Chrysta said, 'I'm so thrilled, my darling, with the lovely horseshoe and that beautiful star which you gave me, they're both wonderful.'

'What star?' asked Marie-Ann.

'It's the one the old gentleman you and I saw limping into church gave me to give to my mummy,' replied Jamie. Then, looking at his father, he went on, 'And he told me to say to Daddy that it is I who am here today, and this is only a small part of the promise I made to him when he tended my wound.'

Jamie had remembered the message word for word.

'Did you see which way he went?' asked his father.

'No, Daddy, he was there beside me, and as I stepped outside, I turned to thank him again, but he wasn't there.'

'Was it someone you helped during the war Phil?' asked Marie-Ann.

He didn't answer, for at that moment some of the other guests interrupted the conversation. He was saved in the nick of time; he could have patted them on the back for that interruption. For the last thing he wanted to do was to try and explain something which had no earthly explanation whatsoever.

His lovely bride never pressed him for an answer either, but as their eyes met he was sure that subconsciously she was aware of more than he himself was.

This was the second time Phil had held that beautiful golden star in his hands. He had found it, and in a sense lost it, and he had long since given up all hope of ever seeing it again. Now, as if from nowhere, it had been returned to him. Amid all the noise that was going on around him, somehow his thoughts took him vividly back to the day when he had knelt and bandaged the old man's wound. Doubt crept across his mind as he thought of what he had said to this stranger, and what this stranger had said to him, yet only the loss of the golden star had left him wondering on that day. But now, all those happenings of almost a year ago seemed highly important, and the message that Jamie had just given him was like a key to the realms of heaven. Wonder and speculation turned over and over inside him; the picture before him looked a little bit clearer now, yet there was still a great deal which was beyond his knowing and his comprehension. However, there was one thing that he was sure of now, one thing that took his thoughts through the gates of heaven one second, and the next, back to that day when he had knelt and tended the old man's wounds. That old man, that ageing wounded traveller, was not an old man, a wounded traveller such as we on earth would know; that he was doubly sure of now. But was it really possible that he had been granted a heavenly blessing of such magnitude? And if he had been privileged that day to have seen the other foot and hand, would his eyes have beheld two more of those scars of Calvary?

Who else could have known that he would have to overcome evil before he could meet his heart's desire? Who else could have brought about everything as it was, and made everything so perfect that his heart was almost mended? And who else could have brought back the golden star from a far-off land, and then vanish into thin air? Was it this star, this sacred star that had caused his lovely bride to tremble from head to foot? Had she somehow been graced by a touch of heaven, a touch that would light their future path as near as possible to the one he had once known? Would he ever know the answer to these things for sure? He might one day perhaps, but right now, there was no more time to ponder.

The next morning the colonel wouldn't hear of anyone but himself driving them to The Junction, and of course Jamie travelled with them, while Marie-Ann and Penny went with Jane and Chesney. What a wonderful send-off they had, and how Chrysta clung to Jamie for the last embrace.

'We'll ring tonight and every night, my darling,' she said, 'then you can talk to Mummy and Daddy before you go to bed.'

'I shall stay up until you do,' he answered, his eyes twinkling.

The train started on its way, and both of them leaned out of the window and waved until the little dot standing on the platform vanished completely. The hotel was all that could be desired, and once the bedroom door was closed to the world outside, they enjoyed one deep long beautiful kiss after another.

'Another long day, my darling, when I have yearned so many times to be as we are now.'

'And I have too my love, desperately,' he replied, crushing her to him once more.

How he loved her? How could he stop loving her, when for the last month she had picked up the threads of Joanna's daily life where she had left off? Everything that Joanna had done, she did in exactly the same way; now all that stood in the way for him to accept her as Joanna was his loyalty to his first love.

So seven glorious days and nights they had, days and nights when love, laughter and happiness pointed the way to the future that was before them. No matter whether they were on a coach trip, or on a boat, or just walking, the whole time they were to each other as if they were in the seclusion of their own room. The merest look was as the deepest kiss, while the slightest touch was as though the joy of each other's arms had enfolded them. No wonder she was overwhelmed by it all, and no wonder the sorrow of the past seemed to slip a little further away from him. There were no heavy hearts as they boarded the train for home, for this wonderful week had been but a peep into the heaven that was to come, and the future looked everlasting.

The colonel and Jamie met them at The Junction; father came second now, for it was to his bride that Jamie ran first. He saw the tears of joy in her eyes as they kissed and hugged each other.

'Leave one for me,' said the colonel, laughing.

Within five minutes they were on their way, and some time later when the conversation had switched to everyday happenings, the colonel said, 'I didn't say anything to you on the phone about it, but Northwood is ready for us to go back to, so we'll be leaving you the day after tomorrow.'

'Oh, can't you stay a little longer?' Chrysta asked.

'You must,' added Phil.

'No,' replied the colonel, 'the time is long overdue when we should entertain you, for a change; and besides, it's better for me to get things back to normal sooner than later, and I'm sure Joanna will want to see Northwood.'

Joanna... he had called her Joanna and hadn't even been aware of it.

What a welcome awaited them at Spring Farm, especially for the bride; how attentive Marie-Ann and Penny were to her. To Penny's question, 'Was everything really splendid?' she replied, 'We've had a most heavenly time thank you, dear, but I am pleased to be home.'

So, two days later, the colonel and Marie-Ann departed, and for the last few days of April, life at Spring Farm became as Phil had known it with his first love, so heavenly, so sublime.

Was he so much in love that he was completely unaware that the fateful and all-important anniversary of Joanna's death was drawing ever closer? But fate had not been in charge of events for a long time, and fate, ordinary fate, would definitely hold no power over the events to come. They were, and would be, far too great to be brought about by any other than divine intervention straight from heaven. Things were now moving along more quickly towards the climax, things which had been ordained over one hundred and fifty years before, and in all those years, 'The Creator of All' had watched and waited, waited for the time which is almost at hand when the answer to those hundred and fifty years of foreboding and sorrow would soon be known. How ironical it seemed that on the morning of 1st May they decided to invite Jane and Chesney over for dinner the next evening, to celebrate the first anniversary of their meeting. He seemed to associate 2nd May with nothing else but joy, forgetting completely that was when he had his first warning of the tragedy to come.

Then, after lunch, something happened which should have jolted him out of his unpreparedness and made him realise that things were not quite normal yet. She had just brought him the daily paper, tasted the joy of a real special kiss, and was on her way back to help Penny, when three or four feet before the door she stopped, hesitated, then turned round slowly. For those few seconds all sorts of things flashed through his mind.

'What is it, my love, don't you feel well?' Phil asked more than a little anxiously. He let the paper fall to the ground, then held out his arms as she came towards him. She sat on his lap, putting her arms around him, and her lips met his in one long heavenly kiss before she answered.

'Physically, I'm feeling on top of the world, my darling, but there is something that I must tell you, yet I hardly know how to explain it. No doubt you have heard that when someone has a bad accident, or is very ill, God – through nature – draws a curtain across their mind to numb the senses, so that they don't know how badly they are injured, or how ill they really are.'

'Yes, my love, I have heard of a few cases of it,' he answered, tightening his arms around her.

'Well, my darling,' she went on, 'there is a curtain something like that almost across the whole of my mind. What little of my past life I can remember, and that's not very far back, will be gone by tomorrow, I'm sure.'

'My love, how long has this been going on?' he asked anxiously.

'A week or so, darling,' she answered.

'What is the farthest and most vivid memory you have? Try and think my love,' he pleaded.

'That is not hard,' she replied. 'The farthest and most vivid memory I have is having hold of your arm my darling, standing outside the church, knowing that at last I had become your wife. Beyond that the memories seem to come from out of a haze, one which is getting ever more dense and obscure.'

'You're quite sure you're not worried over anything, my love?' Phil asked, still quite anxious.

'No, my darling, on the contrary; why should I be, when you are all my life? For memories without you are only meaningless to me.'

He drew her down, and the joy and ecstasy in the kiss he gave her would last in her memory for all time; but the one thing in his was the thought of the golden star and the tremor it caused when she had received it. Was that star, that sacred star, about to wipe out the last vestige of all her thoughts before their wedding day? 'Why?' he asked himself, 'why should a thing like that be so important?'

'What time does Jamie get home from school, my love?' he asked.

'Usually around 3.30 p.m., darling,' she answered.

'Well, I'll be back in time to change and take you all down to The Calling Seagull for tea.'

'You're a real love, I don't know which is the most wonderful part of you, your love or your kindness, or both,' she said smiling. 'But what I do know is that you are the most wonderful husband in the world, and I am the luckiest girl for having you, and please don't worry over me, my darling, I'm not ill really.'

Down by the river, all was beautiful and a wonderful time was being had by all, but for a few moments Phil's mind went back to the first time he had brought Joanna here. That was the time when she had first told him of the gypsy curse; little did he realise then what power that curse had, and little had he dreamt that the curse was stalking their wonderful happiness day and night, relentlessly, and would never let go until she was no more and he but a shadow of his former self.

What did he see in the future now? Was their happiness so strong that it would drive all signs of sorrow and tragedy away? It had better be, for there would be no coming back for him a third time, if anything happened and he lost this love; he would be finished, finished with a world that he'd be sick and tired of. But there was one thing that seemed to add up as a wonderful omen for the future. The golden star was in residence at Spring Farm, and the person who had brought it had returned it with his blessing.

'Will you bring us here again some time my love?' she asked.

'Once the petrol situation becomes easier, as often as you wish, my love,' he answered.

'It's so lovely here, darling, and so peaceful,' she replied, gazing all around her.

The next day was born just as beautiful as the one before; from the moment the first rays of the sun paled in the eastern sky, until long after it had disappeared leaving behind a fantastic red glow in the west, the scene was one of perfection.

This was 2nd May, the day when so much of Phil's life, for good or ill, had been decided; yet as they talked and laughed with Jane and Chesney, not one thought of doubt had crossed his mind about whether a deluge of sorrow or a pinch of happiness lay just round the corner. Perhaps it was as well that the joy and happiness of his new-found life completely dominated him, for it was only time, perhaps only a matter of hours, before he would know which of the paths he would have to travel; for the power behind that golden star had set the scene once more, and almost as it had been on the first occasion.

Jane and Chesney had departed around 11.30 p.m., and before the big hand of the clock had glided over another fifteen minutes, Phil and his bride were lying side by side, and had kissed and caressed at least a dozen times. Just as on that first occasion, only that time it had been his first love, sleep now overcame them before they had said a proper 'goodnight' and, just as before, he came back to this world only to find her in a sleep so deep and peaceful. Kissing her tenderly, and whispering, 'God bless you, my darling,' he settled down once more. She never stirred, for the sleep she was in was far too deep; no whispered word or tender kiss could penetrate even the outer cloud of oblivion. Soon he was in that same world himself, but whether it was one hour, two, three or more, he had no idea, for suddenly all sleep left him, and he became fully awake.

Instinctively, the first question that came into his head was what was it that had brought him out of the deepest sleep to his present state of alertness. But there was no time for a second thought on that subject, for in that same unworldly tone as he had heard from his first love, she called, 'My love, my love!'

'Oh, please God, not again,' was the anguished cry which came from his heart. He just couldn't face another two days like the two years he had known, with so much sorrow. He dare not wake her, but as he tenderly put his arms around her, only then did he realise the violent stress that she was under. Her arms, legs and body were as rigid as though she was encased in ice, while her breathing rose and fell, first to its very peak, then down to its shallow depth. Then, slowly and intermittently, she began to speak once more.

'My love, my love... I have come back to you... my love... and to my firstborn... I shall always remember... the first sweet stolen kiss... that took my breath away... and left me completely yours... I stood beside you... outside the little red house among the trees... I held your hand... as you crossed the humpbacked bridge... and turned right. There with my one hand... still upon the gates of heaven... was I waiting for you, my love. Only vaguely do I now remember... the comfort in your tender touch... as you consoled me... in my great grief... a stranger. But I understood, my love... the shock on your weary face... the doubt in your tired eyes... as once more you beheld me... I have come back, my love... back to this room... our love nest... where the fragrance from the honeysuckle... and the orange blossom... drifts... heady on the night air... I have come back, my love... to be greeted by God's blue birds... on the morrow. I shall not leave thee again, my love... for I have overcome the unknown... that took me away... and left you with a weeping heart... I have come back, my love... to love and cherish you... till long after... the allotted years. And when God calls us… for that heaven-bound journey… together… I will hold your hand, my love… I will open those golden gates… and guide you… for I… know the way. My love… my love… I have come back to you… my love.'

The tears which had run down his face on that previous occasion had been tears of sorrow, of foreboding and fear for the future, but now they were tears of joy, for already he could feel the last piece of a heavy cross being lifted.

Those words would be imprinted on his memory for all time. He knew in his heart that he shouldn't have the slightest doubt now. Ninety-nine per cent of him was sure that she was his Joanna, yet even with all the proof he had just had, something deep inside him clung on to that other one per cent as desperately as ever. But if she wasn't his Joanna, how did she know that the honeysuckle and orange blossom scented their room to such a degree? And besides, he had never told her that that was only their local name for syringa; and another thing, how did she know about God's blue birds if she wasn't his Joanna? How could it all be possible? That was the one per cent talking. Could it really be, asked the other ninety-nine, that this beautiful girl sleeping deeply by his side was anyone but his one and only Joanna?

With so much joy and happiness in his heart, sleep was once more creeping over Phil very quickly, but he was not quite over the borderline when she stirred, and he received one more reminder that all was as she had just said. Gently her hand touched his left shoulder, then went slowly down his arm until her hand touched his; then just as gently she found the ring upon his damaged finger, and turned it, just as Joanna always did. She was now relaxed, but still in the deepest of sleeps, and that last bit of contentment was enough to send him over into the same unconscious world as she was in.

He was up as usual the next morning to have his early run round one of the farms. She never stirred when quietly and as gently as possible, he got out of bed. He bent over her, and as he gazed into those beautiful features he was sure of one thing. She not only looked like an angel, but she was one; ninety-nine per cent of him accepted all that she was, and the miracle which had happened during the night should have swayed him completely.

He shouldn't have had the slightest doubt, knowing that the man who had returned the golden star had given her back to him from the unknown. But still one per cent of him still belonged to his Joanna, his first love. A question mark hung over so little; but what it was, was like searching for a needle in a haystack.

He was away almost two hours, but he arrived home just in time to kiss Jamie goodbye before he went to school. There were no early morning blues where she was concerned, and he never suffered that way either; they were a match where kindness, consideration and, above all, love, were concerned. The early morning kiss was as sweet and as fresh as the morning dew, and held all the rapture of the last long lingering one at night.

'Did you have a good night, my love?' he asked.

'Yes, darling, so wonderfully deep that you must have been gone an hour before I woke up; did you sleep well too?'

'Fantastic,' he replied, kissing her again and taking her on his arm in to breakfast.

They had just finished breakfast when the phone rang.

'All right, Penny, I'll get it!' she called, racing into the hall.

'Hello, Daddy, how are you? And how is Mummy?' he heard her say; then a pause. Then, 'I'm sure he would, I'll get him.' But he was halfway there when she called, 'Darling, it's Daddy, they want to know if we can go to Northwood on Friday for a long weekend?'

'Delighted!' he shouted down the phone.

'Did you hear that, Daddy?' she asked, laughing.

By the time she had talked to Marie-Ann, and Phil had spoken to both of them, there were ten minutes gone.

'We're both looking forward very much to seeing you all on Friday,' came the colonel's voice from the other end. 'The same room?' he enquired.

'Yes,' answered Phil, 'everything the same.'

'I'm very pleased to hear that,' the colonel replied.

After putting the phone down, Phil went into his study to deal with the mail. He could only have been there a minute or so when Penny came to the door and in a loud whisper called him. She held up her finger in a gesture of silence. He followed her quietly into the lounge, where another shock awaited him as he looked in the direction where she eagerly pointed. There stood his wife by the bird bath, and perched thereon, feeding out of her hand, were two jays. He watched fascinated as she stroked the head of each in turn.

'She *is* our Joanna,' whispered Penny, brushing a tear away quickly, 'only when she was here did they ever come. There were none for three years, and now they're back again because she is also – and who else could get anywhere near them?'

Phil didn't answer, for in his mind he could hear her voice in that unworldly tone saying, 'I have come back my love, to be greeted by God's blue birds on the morrow.'

What else did he need to convince him that she was his Joanna, his first love? But no, that one per cent of him still lingered in the past, yet he knew not why.

Northwood was looking lovely, and Northwood was one more scene where Chrysta surprised them more and more. As if quite naturally, she knew her way around, inside and out. The colonel and Marie-Ann had long since accepted the fact that she was none other than Joanna, yet even they were amazed.

'If I didn't believe in miracles it would seem uncanny,' the colonel said to Phil.

But it was for the staff that one had to feel half sorry, for most of them had watched Joanna grow from a baby. They knew all her ways, knew what she did and how; knew the songs she sang and hummed as she went about the house; and knew the friendly cheery way she had always greeted them. It was one thing for the replica of their young mistress to be a perfect match in looks and voice, but it was much more disturbing when that replica was exactly the same in all other things. No wonder at times they stared blankly at her; no wonder they often forgot the duties they were about.

Jamie, like the rest of the family, was having a wonderful time. The other half of his little world was always close at hand now, then there was the park and the fields for running and walking, and the woods for all sorts of things. Climbing and hide and seek were two of his favourites, so by the end of each day he had almost run himself to a standstill.

But it wasn't until the last morning that the colonel and Phil were able to have an hour to themselves without anyone wondering why. Out of the blue, the daughter of one of their old friends called with her two children; Jamie was well occupied for the time being, and most of the conversation the females were having hardly included them. Perhaps the men were both looking for this opportunity to excuse themselves and glide quietly out of the room, and then make their way to the study.

Once there, Phil told the colonel all about the golden star, the words that his wife had spoke in that unworldly tone, and the blue birds in the morning.

'She is our Joanna, Phil – your wife, my daughter; nothing will convince me of any other explanation and as each day goes by the more sure I am of it.'

'It's certainly getting harder to think any other,' Phil replied.

'Come upstairs, that is if we can get there without anyone seeing us,' suggested the colonel.

Up they went into one of the front bedrooms.

'Look at that lawn and tell me what you see, Phil.'

After studying it for a few moments, he turned to the colonel and said, 'Well, it's perfect all over except for those marks and that large blob at the end, which are all in a much richer green grass.'

'What do you think those marks are?' asked the colonel.

Phil shook his head. 'No idea,' he answered.

'Don't they look like footprints?' asked the colonel.

Phil studied them more closely, then gave a firm, 'Yes.'

'Well, they are Joanna's, and the blob at the end is where she fell, I'd stake my life on it, for I have gone over that tragic day a hundred times in my mind, and those footprints tally perfectly with Joanna racing to rescue Jamie, and I know that is where I saw her fall at the end. You say they are in a much richer green grass, but they are pale now, Phil, compared to what they were before you brought Joanna here on Friday; it seems that her presence here is about to wipe out all that reminds us of the awful sorrow of the past. Three more days, and I'm sure those marks will be gone forever.'

He then went on, 'You know, Phil, we've just got to accept this. A man can lose a watch, but get another one exactly the same, as near as the human eye and hand can make it; yet in no time he finds there are different characteristics between the two watches. But we're not dealing with watches, we're dealing with what you and I both know is the sweetest and loveliest girl in the world; and, above all, we are in a unique position, for we are witnesses to the wonders of our Creator going on under our very eyes. Only God could make two people alike in everything, for there is no different characteristic or anything else between the Joanna we knew and the one we have now.'

He paused for a moment, then continued, 'When Joanna was born, and I lost her mother at the same time, what I couldn't have done to the wretch who brought that curse upon us was unthinkable, and inside me all these years, I'm sorry to say now, my feelings have never been any more forgiving. Only since I met the Joanna we have now has that part of me become human again, and the queer part about it is, I don't know why. All I can think of is that the difference in my feelings now is just one small part of an overall master plan; but there is one thing I do know, the curse is over and finished with forever. That was the end, when we lost Joanna – she was the last of a long line of females who met their untimely end still in the bloom of youth or early womanhood.'

'And there's another thing, Phil, really I should have told you before. I searched for it just after I lost Mary, and I never found it, but all these years I have had the feeling that the answer to that curse is somewhere in this house; and yet all the time I had a stronger feeling that I would be treading on forbidden ground if I resumed my search again. But now I know the time is safe for me to try again. Will you help me, Phil?'

'Of course I will,' Phil replied, as the colonel took him by the arm and led him along the corridor to a room which hadn't been occupied in all those years.

While the colonel was unlocking the wall safe and placing the cases on the bed, Phil was looking round the room. Everything inside was spotlessly clean and spick and span, and he could guess that it was all in the exact same spot as it had been almost thirty years before; it was a shrine, a shrine which had been tended with loving hands.

'Here we are,' said the colonel, 'perhaps we shall be luckier than I was the last time.' He placed some bundles of letters on the bed in front of them as he spoke.

Minute after minute rolled by, and letter after letter was discarded; the keen look of expectancy had somewhat diminished on the colonel's face as the letters that were left could be counted on both hands. Just as he felt almost sure that he had failed, like the first time, Phil gave a gasp and said, 'This must be it, we've got it at last! Shall I read it out to you?'

'Yes, please do, Phil,' replied the colonel anxiously.

DATED THE YEAR OF OUR LORD 1791

For the wrath of all heaven shall be upon thee,
If thou dare to smite me, and take from my fatherless offspring
Their places of shelter and this meagre warmth.
For the sorrow that shall be mine, shall have no measure akin to thine,
Thy doom can I already see, in the hatred which surrounds thee,
Only up to one and a half score years, shall thy life span, and of thy womenfolk after thee,
For two thousand moons the chain of death shall break not,
Not until the Lord in all His tender mercies shall show His wondrous ways,
Not until the mould of two in one, fashioned by His right hand, shall come to pass,
Then, and only then, shall He perform almost likewise
As He did, when He commanded His own Son to rise on the third day.

'The answer to all those years of sorrow, foreboding, and all that has mystified us during the last one, is in those last three lines,' said Phil, as he read them out again, only this time more slowly.

'Not until the mould of two in one, fashioned by His right hand, shall come to pass,' repeated the colonel, very deep in thought.

Phil answered him with these words. 'The Bible says, "On the third day He rose again." In a situation like this, does it mean to die and be born again in someone else, or to be transferred while actually living?'

'That is beyond us, Phil. All we do know – and it must be enough for us – is the fact that it is Joanna who is here with us now. My daughter has returned to me, and you have led the same bride down the aisle twice.'

As they walked back along the corridor, Phil couldn't help noticing that ten years seemed to have slipped from the colonel already. He was his old buoyant self once more, while Phil himself could swear that even more had left him; he felt he was on surer ground now, but deep inside was still that one little bit that wouldn't give way.

For several hours, unbounded happiness held sway at Northwood towards the end of their visit and even as they said farewell, the colonel's spirits were higher than Phil could remember in years. He was in top form as he exclaimed, 'Can't wait until Jamie's Whitsun holidays to see you, so if we can spare the petrol, we'll be down for a night soon.'

'No good using all that precious petrol on one night,' replied Phil.

'Two weeks or nothing, Daddy,' his wife answered, 'besides, Mummy is going to help Penny and me choose the new curtains for the drawing room, aren't you Mummy?'

'Yes, dear,' answered Marie-Ann, and from her face one would have thought she had been let into the secret already. It was a new Marie-Ann these days.

The hectic time which Jamie had been having in those forgotten surroundings, plus the movement of the car, soon took its toll; what had been his normal amount of talk at the start of the journey diminished to nothing before ten minutes were up.

'Come, darling, let Mummy cuddle you,' she said, as Phil stopped the car so that Jamie could get out of the back seat onto her lap in the front. In five minutes flat he as fast asleep. Less than five minutes in those loving arms, and being swept over with eyes that burned of mother love and tender care, were all that was needed for him to know that his little world was as it should be.

So they carried on talking, as he pointed out other places of interest to her, and he had just announced that they were about halfway home when suddenly she said, 'Oh, darling, I rang Penny again this afternoon. I said I expected we would be home about

6.30 p.m., and I asked her if she had planned anything hot for dinner tonight. Luckily she hadn't, except for the soup. Then I explained to her that when we arrived home and got Jamie to bed, not to worry about our dinner, because I want you to take me to the top of High Ridge for the first time.'

'Anything for your happiness, my darling,' he answered, catching hold of her hand and squeezing it tenderly.

Penny wouldn't hear of them delaying their walk just to put Jamie to bed.

'Get yourselves ready, there's nothing to be done here which I can't manage, and besides, it's just the right sort of evening for two lovebirds like you to be strolling over the Ridge.'

'We won't be late, and if you are not too tired, come in while we are having dinner, have a drink with us then and we'll have a few more after we've done the washing-up,' came the reply.

After giving Jamie his goodnight love and kisses, they started out towards the Ridge.

Her beautiful golden hair had been combed out a little more loosely than ever before, and the litheness of her perfect form danced and rippled with a joy that defied all sorrow. She looked the perfect picture of health and happiness as he took note of her, but it was the beauty of her face which took most of his attention. 'Angelic' was the only word for the purity of heaven written all over it – just like his first love in all things, that one per cent told him.

Any one of her heavenly charms was always too much for him, but all of them at once, and all at the peak of their perfection, compelled him to take her in his arms even before they reached the sanctuary of the old chestnut tree. So defenceless was he to all that she was, that the kiss and the flood of passion which followed went far deeper than he had intended, and the one per cent wavered, as it had never done before.

From then on, they were walking on air; they were in a world that only true lovers could enter, a world where each one is completely a part of the other. *What a wonderful evening she had chosen for her first visit to the top of High Ridge*, he thought. For all around was one glorious panorama of the wonders of nature, from the wren scuttering about in the hedgerows, to the lark high overhead, all seemed to be serenading them, as with arms entwined they strolled along in a heaven of their own making.

Up under the bower he led her, and how fascinated she was at this wonder... or could it be just one of nature's freaks, for the benefit of man and beast? They reached the crest of High Ridge and there she stood, turning slowly round in a full circle in silent rapture. It was a fantastic sight that was spread out all around them, and even though he had been there many times before, each time he had felt he was on a higher plane, where the troubles and sorrow of the world below just didn't exist.

But her first words took him instantly back to the past and into that world below.

'Darling,' she said, 'do you know what comes to my mind up here?'

She never gave him time to answer.

'It's the hymn,' she went on, '"Could we but climb where Moses stood, and view the Promised Land" what else does it look like but that?'

That was exactly what his first love had said on her first visit and facing the same direction, so he answered her in the same words that he had used to reply to his first love.

'It's going to be *our* Promised Land, yours and mine, my love.' And once again he tightened his arms around her.

'How lovely!' she exclaimed, as he pointed out the distant places to her, then as much of his own farms as it was possible to see.

'You're in the right job, my darling,' she went on, 'for only someone like you, who loves God's good earth, could make as wonderful a job of all this land. Everything is so neat, clean and tidy, and its richness is there in abundance for all to see.'

For a minute or two she stood alone, looking in the direction of Spring Farm, the sun behind her, and her beautiful golden hair reflecting its rays like tiny shafts of sunlight. She was to him as his first love had been, completely out of this world, nothing short of a goddess; sun or moon made no difference, for that was the only way to describe her.

She still stood motionless those few yards in front of him. Whatever was going through her mind during this silence he was at a loss to know, or even contemplate; was she gazing at some spot of beauty greater than all, in among that which stretched out below and before them? Or was she saying a silent prayer for the past, the present, and the heavenly future to come?

Slowly she turned towards him, and in a few hurried steps she covered the few yards which separated them. Then, without a word being spoken, arms and lips sought out the maximum joy that each could give to the other, and once again that one per cent of his wavered precariously. Out there, before the eyes of heaven and earth, she clung to him as desperately as though they were in the privacy of their own room. How she loved him... a love which she would gladly shout to the whole world, if that was possible.

So, hand in hand, or arm in arm, down the side of High Ridge they went, then along the path towards the Ridge itself, and at each kissing gate they kissed, and made a wish for the future; then on to the Ridge where the old chestnut awaited them in all is majestic splendour. By the time they reached the shadow of its leafy canopy, the longing for each other's arms had become almost unbearable. Time after time that wonderful feeling of ecstasy threatened to overcome them, and time after time that ninety-nine per cent of him almost became a hundred permanently.

'My love, my wonderful love,' he whispered, as once more she nestled closer into his arms in silent rapture. Then he went on, 'What special thing have I done for heaven to bless me with you for the second time?'

Once more that angelic look came over her face as she answered, 'All things are known, and nothing is impossible up there, my darling.'

With her face tilted upwards, her eyes searched for the tiniest gap in that leafy umbrella. For a few moments there was silence as he too looked up, trying to find the slightest glint of the heavens above. Then suddenly he said, 'Limitless... but I've often wondered if perhaps in a thousand years' time, when man travels that blue-black void, I wonder if he will ever find the place which we call heaven?'

The same look was even more pronounced upon her face as

she shook her head, saying, 'No, my love, man in his earthly form can never set foot on the sphere of peace eternal, for it is guarded by the whitest of burning lights, and it is far away; far beyond the corners where the four winds blow; far beyond where the lightning is seen and the thunder rolls; far beyond the placid moon, which stirs the heart of those in love; far beyond the fiery sun, and the place where its light is just a speck.'

'That is where the Word abides my love, the Word that made me yours, from the moment His gentle hand caressed my tiny heart, to start its journey into life; the Word that guided my footsteps against all worldly ills, so that I could hold your hand before His shrine, only this time, in our little church by the ruins of the castle.'

She paused and gently drew his head down until their lips met in one more wonderful kiss. Then she continued, 'My darling, you are my sun rising at each new dawn, giving me light and the comfort of a warmth that is ever glowing; you are every flower that blooms, making the whole of my scene like a garden, where the fragrance lulls, and the colours are like the rainbow; you are every bird that sings, bringing to my day one long and happy song. You are every beat of my heart, my love, you are my very life.'

What else did he need to convince him that she was his first and only love? Three things had happened, and still he doubted. Not only was there the fact that he knew who had returned the golden star to him, but there was also that night, when in her sleep and under some unknown influence, she had said in that unworldly tone, 'I have come back to you, my love.' And even those words of endearment had left no mark upon him. And lastly, and just as important, the answer to that age-old curse had been found, and there once again were those words, 'Not until the mould of two in one, fashioned by His right hand, shall come to pass' – words which he would never forget, but words which seemed to have sunk no further than the surface of his mind.

Any one of those interventions from heaven should have been enough for him, but had not availed so far. Yet little did he dream that there was no more time to doubt or ponder, no more time for that one per cent to hang on to the tiny speck of loyalty which should never have been split in the first place. For now that moment which heaven had decreed was at hand; for as his arms tenderly caressed her, and his lips prepared for one more spell of ecstasy, out of the past, the deep, deep past, two words struggled to the surface and spilled from his lips with all the love and tenderness in the world.

'My angel,' he whispered, only for her to reply without the slightest hesitation, 'My own true love.'

These had been the ultimate words of surrender, tenderly exchanged between him and his first love. At last something clicked in his mind. There was no doubt at all now; and that one per cent flowed over to the other side, making him sure, doubly sure. To his unexpected challenge, she had given her password, a password where all of him, heart, mind and body, awaited to hold and cherish her; she was his first love, his angel, the one he had lost, the someone only God could give back to him, and He had done so. He held nothing back in his love for her, and in this new-found gush of heavenly joy, she found an ecstasy of a long time ago; how she loved him, how they loved each other.

For a full five minutes they enjoyed one deep heavenly kiss after another, urged on to a new intensity by desperate arms that wouldn't give up, while two beating hearts sent out their message of joy, to mingle and to glorify each other as one.

'Darling,' he whispered breathlessly.

'Yes, my love,' she answered, just about as breathless as he was.

'It is so hard to explain what I want to say to you, but I know I must, for the time has just arrived.' He paused as if deep in thought before resuming.

'For a whole year I was under the impression that I had been blessed with two jewels. Not the hard, brash, cold and loveless glitter of the diamond or the sapphire, but the deep, rich, pure, loving lustre of the pearl. But these last few days another dilemma has been before me, and I have asked myself a thousand times, Have I been blessed with two pearls identical or one? How was I to know, how was I to feel sure, when a question mark hung over that vital answer?'

'But now my darling, I do know; it was not two pearls

identical that I had been blessed with, but one, only one. The question mark has gone for ever, and you, my love, my angel, you are to me one more than all those wonderful things that I am to you, for you are not only my angel, but most important of all you are my one and only Joanna.'

Once more the heady wine of ecstasy drove from their conscious minds the world outside, and the gates of heaven could be seen in the distance.

So, with the last golden red rays of the setting sun gradually beating a slow retreat from the upper half of the old chestnut, and with their arms still entwined around each other, on along and down they went, down the last fifty yards of the Ridge... to home, to their son, and to eternal love.

Printed in the United Kingdom
by Lightning Source UK Ltd.
1849

9 781844 260393